CRY UNCLE,
Sumbody

a novel by
Thomas Ray Crowel

$ $uccess
Press

Success Press, Highland, IN 46322
Copyright © 2011 by Thomas Ray Crowel

Published in the United States by Success Press, Highland, IN 46322

FIRST EDITION

Library of Congress Catalog Card Number: 2010941482

ISBN-13: 978-0-9669917-8-9

Printed on recycled paper.

And if a house be divided against itself,
that house cannot stand.

Mark 3:25

For whom duty calls

PREFACE

David Longenecker's diary of 1864-65 has been in my possession for almost a half-century. Previous to that, it lay in an old train caboose jammed with whatnots and thig-a-ma-jigs, sitting on a farm in Indiana. I transcribed it over thirty years ago, but all my notes were either misplaced or lost. Nearly a year ago, I decided to transcribe David's diary once again. I felt compelled to tell his story.

David Longenecker was born on April 16, 1837 in Juniata County, Pennsylvania. He enlisted in the Union Army at Camp Piqua, Ohio and was assigned to Company G of the 110th Ohio Volunteer Infantry as a Private on August 19, 1862.

David was wounded twice—first in the Battle of the Wilderness in Virginia and again at the Battle of Monocacy

Junction in Maryland where he was captured and eventually marched to and incarcerated in a southern prison, a converted tobacco house, located in Danville, Virginia.

David writes of his day-by-day struggle to survive. He even took time to pen some of his views of the politicians, as well as the politics that influenced the Civil War, of the Generals who planned and implemented it, and of the soldiers, both Union and Confederate, who gave their lives because of it.

David cites the horrific battles he fought in, the vile conditions of the prisons he was confined to, and the everyday lonesomeness, sickness, starvation, and fear that was a constant in the minds and on the bodies of the men and boys—young and old alike; the foot soldiers who died by the thousands upon thousands.

I believe that nearly a hundred and fifty years ago, David had something of consequence to say—a story waiting to be told. After all, he didn't only jot down weather conditions, dates, and times in his diary; he also recorded personal activities, reflections, and emotions of both himself and his comrades. The common foot soldier fighting in the Civil War was under the most extreme hardship and suffering imaginable. David was part of its ever-tramping infantry.

THE STORY

Part I

1

In the spring, the fertile Ohio River Valley takes on the colors of a rainbow—each crop and grove making its own contribution, the entirety of the valley, starting with the disappearance of the last snow and ripening over the weeks from green to yellow like golden apples or corn. In this particular corner of the Ohio Valley, David's, a rambling brook on its way from the hills cuts through this smaller valley, twisting and turning until its fresh blue waters pool beneath a covered bridge, tarries there to look around, and then rolls down into the river and the life beyond. The bridge was built in 1836—the year David Longacher was born. The bridge is part of the clay road that passes the edge of a quarter section, the 160 acres of the Longacher farm.

A weathered two-story brick farmhouse situated upon one of the gentle slopes of the hills overlooks the valley. A full second story was a distinct rarity in the country when the house was built; and brick was hard to come by. The builder, David's father, had lived on the property as the house was constructed. Apparently, he didn't want prosperity to make him forget where his people had started, so he'd left the original log cabin intact a few yards away, not dismantled or burned. It was built sturdy, as the house was—it was the family's way—and remained still usable after it was no longer needed. In fact, for one willing to live without the amenities, it remained a comfortable cabin. Now, the farmhouse, itself, though impressive, is in need of minor repair. Missing roof shingles, runs of absent brick mortar, and a cracked window here and there await replacement or repair.

David Longacher, Sr. wasn't just missed in the hearts of his family with his passing. The effect of his hard work was lost and that loss was apparent throughout the Longacher land. When the elder Longacher died in the first Battle of Bull Run, one of the first of the Civil War, David, the faithful son, did what was required: he stepped away from his job—a well paying one—as a carpenter and brought his new wife with him from the city to the family farm. The farm was more than a place to him, more than a reminder of his family past. It embodied the values and virtues his father and grandfather had lived by and taught. David managed to bring in the first harvest after he arrived, though he had only a youthful experience with farming. A local man, Billy Perkins, whose family farm had been lost by his father after a string of unwise investments, had helped out both as a worker and instructor for David. Everything about the farm—the animals, the equipment, the hummocks and gullies reminded David of his father. And part of his struggle with the land was to let it know—to let himself know—that he was the new master, carrying on family traditions, but with a few of his own new ways of doing things.

December 1861

It was midday as David wiped off his feet upon entering the house. He'd shaken snow off of his coat outside and tucked it under his arm. He was tired and chilled to the bone and the thing that would cheer him and warm him, he knew, was the company of his sisters and his wife.

As he came in, Hannah startled. She wadded something up in her hands and tucked it behind herself, trying to look as though nothing had happened.

"What are you hiding there, Hannah?" David asked. His father had been a quiet, undemonstrative man and so David, now the man of the house, liked to play the tease, in contrast, for fun.

"Nothing," Hannah said, rolling her eyes in mock innocence. She stretched, straightening her back, reaching behind herself to check that the mysterious object was well hidden.

David laid his coat across the back of a chair near

the fire. He was going out again soon but he thought he might steam away a little of the moisture. This drying of coats was a science. Too near the fire and the cloth would get hot, perhaps even singe; too far away and it would still be wet the next day.

"Doesn't look like no nothing to me," he said to Hannah. "To me it looks more like what you might call a ..." He stopped and squinted at the ceiling as if searching for the word. "It looks more to me like a ... something."

Hannah let lose an explosive little giggle, the giggle she'd had since childhood; she was afraid David would guess.

"Let me see," he said.

"I don't know what you're talking about," Hannah said, straightening herself in the chair.

"You better show me, or you're in for a good old-fashioned tickling."

"It's a surprise," Nel interrupted. She knew that this was one of the Longacher's teasing routines, but it made her nervous. It was an unfamiliar kind of game for her.

David turned to Nel, hoping to draw her in. "A surprise for who?"

"For you." Nel was always the innocent bystander—and occasional referee—in these games between her husband and his sister. They'd been going at each other since Hannah was a child. When Nel had moved to the farm, it had amazed her that these two could carry on sometimes for as long as a day without anyone paying attention. Ma Longacher and Beth could sleep right through one of these battles, as Beth was doing right now.

David turned back to Hannah. "A surprise, is it?" He made as if to dislodge his sister from her chair. She shouldered him away.

"It's a Christmas present," she said.

"For who?" he asked again.

"It's for you. You want to ruin your surprise?"

David paused. Hannah smiled. She had the advantage. David loved surprises.

"Well you must not love me very much," David sighed.

"How did you guess?" she snickered.

Hannah always made him laugh. She was so dramatic, David thought, so changeable. Hannah herself didn't know half the time whether she was kidding or not. It was what made her such a great partner in their teasing games.

"If you loved me, you'd be planning a big surprise for me. On the other hand, if you can hide something behind that skinny little butt of yours, it can't be very big."

"Maybe I'm not finished," she responded. "Maybe this is only a tiny part of the Christmas surprise ..." She paused to work up a monstrous exaggeration. "Per-haps the whole present is *so* big we can only bring it indoors part by part."

"Such as a new wagon?"

"Such as."

David looked her up and down, then walked over to the chair near the fireplace. He reached down to brush the dew from his coat. "You better not poke yourself in the butt with that knitting needle," he said.

She gasped in mock outrage. "I can't believe you'd say something about your own sister's butt ... twice, I might add." She couldn't believe he had spotted the needle. "Tell him, Nel. He's your husband. Tell him to mind his manners."

Falling into the game, Nel scolded him. "It is rude, David, to mention the bottom of your own family member ..."

"In polite conversation," Hannah continued.

There was a meaningful silence amongst the three as David fetched himself a cup of water.

"Christmas you say," he said as he came back into the room.

"You better get busy. It's only a week away," Hannah said.

"Christmas. Seems like it's come early this year," he said.

It was true. There was so much to be done. That lull in the work of the farm David remembered when he was a young boy—when school started, the years he went to school, had vanished when he took on the full responsibility of the farm.

"It's the seventeenth of December today," Nel said.

"Well, then, darn it. Come on girls, bundle up. It's tree chopping time," he said. "Christmas is around the corner and nobody reminded me?"

"Beth has been reminding you about it for a month," Nel said.

"That's our Beth. She'd like to have Christmas about once a week." David pulled his coat back on. The snow had melted from his boots. A small pool of water gathered by the hearth. "You want to come?"

"We were ready a half hour ago," Hannah said. "... that is Nel and me."

"Beth don't want to go?"

"David, she'll never forgive you if you leave her behind," Nel said. And it was true.

"She's still asleep," Hannah said.

"I'll wake her up," Nel said, getting to her feet.

"No, no, no ..." David whispered as he motioned them to follow him upstairs. "Hannah, you and Nel pick up the end of Beth's footboard. I'll get the headboard. We're going to take Sissy outside."

Much as he loved teasing Hannah, it was a much greater pleasure to give his youngest sister a hard time. She, as a young girl, had taken her father's death the hardest. Ma and friends and relatives had worried that she'd never get over it. One of David Sr.'s cousins—a woman who could find a cloud to cover even a happy event—said she believed that girls who lost their fathers early could never get over the loss, and that they never married happily. Ma dismissed the thought but she worried anyway.

Nel shivered. "It's freezing out."

"And snowing," Hannah added, delighted. She had already thrown on her coat and boots.

"I didn't say we were going to leave her outside,"

David said as he pushed open the door to Beth's room. He turned and put his finger to his lips.

"Oh my gosh, David, how childish. What kind of a patriarch are you going to be?" Hannah said.

"The best kind," Nel said.

Hannah tiptoed to the double doors of the balcony and pulled them open. She turned to help Nel pick up the foot of the bed. David grabbed the headboard and gave the girls a nod. They took great pains not to shift the bed as the three carried the whole piece of furniture out the wide doors.

As the wet snowflakes fell onto sleeping Beth's face, her eyelids fluttered open. "My land, have you all lost your wits?" Beth blurted out, wiping her eyes and pulling the quilt over her head. "Get me off this freezing porch, you, you ..."

David leaned back, hands on his waist, laughing.

"It's not funny, David," Beth mumbled from beneath the quilt.

"I'm going to get our gear together, my little darlings. Help our Beth get dressed and make sure she doesn't dilly-dally," David said. "Meet me at the old cabin."

"You are crazy," Beth said from beneath the quilt.

"Crazy maybe. But I'm going to get us a tree. If you prefer you can stay inside, Sissy, and keep warm."

Beth threw back the quilt and jumped out of bed. "You wait right here," she said as she stamped her foot.

"You girls wait for her," David said. "I'll swing 'round and get you." He started down the stairs.

"David, put on your scarf," Nel shouted after him.

"I can't find it!"

"I told you so," Hannah said to Nel, pleased that she'd thought to knit him a new one for Christmas.

The wait wasn't necessary. On this day, Beth was ready in record time.

Even the old barn was solid. In a perfect world—in the winter in any case—it would have been a shorter walk from the house. But mindful of the smell and flies that were drawn to the animals, David Sr. had built the barn as far from the house as was practical.

David opened one of the barn doors wide, letting in some light. The animals lay on the straw, their sides pressed against one another, as far away as possible from the cold stable walls. The presence of these big beasts comforted David. He spoke out a couple of names, clicked his tongue in a language only he and they understood, and slapped his thigh. The younger mule Browny, eager to move about, got up right away; the older one, Andrew, who, from experience knew what was coming, brayed and took his time getting up.

Hannah and Nel, too excited to wait, followed behind Beth trying to stay in her footprints as she plodded ahead toward the barn through the deep snow.

David was finishing harnessing up the mules to the sleigh when the girls pushed through the other door. Beth came up behind David, reached up, and gave his hair a hard tug. "It wasn't funny," she said, eyeing David as he turned around.

"Sure it was ... at least for me."

"No, pretending you'd go without me."

"Oh, be a good sport, my pet, and I'll let you be in charge of putting the angel on top of the Christmas tree," David said.

"That's my job," Hannah exclaimed.

"Since when?" Nel asked, giving Hannah a nudge.

Beth smiled as she turned to them and stuck out her tongue.

"It's always been my job," Hannah pouted.

"Traditionally, the job of putting the angel on the top of the tree goes to the one who is purest of heart," Nel said.

David looked over at Nel. "Is that true?"

"It's traditional," Nel said.

"And to think that for all these years we let Hannah, with her little black heart, put the angel up there. And now Beth."

"I do not have a black heart," Beth frowned.

"Of course you don't," David said, hugging her. "Yours is a heart of gold." David winked at Hannah. She smiled as she shook her head.

Since the death of their father, David had taken over as head of the Longacher dynasty, such as it was. Of course, David placed himself in charge of the usual practical family business—the management of the farm, provisioning the household, prioritizing repairs, and assisting and supporting Ma who was delegated the responsibility of making major financial decisions and overseeing the girls' education. He also assumed his father's tendency to indulge the baby of the family. Even more playful than his father, David had stepped into his father's role. He never stopped kidding around with Beth, as his way of reminding her how much she was loved. Beth expected that same attention from the entire household.

Climbing down from the sleigh, David, his wife— barely more than a child herself—and his kid sisters scampered down to a small stand of evergreen trees at the far end of their property. David had been eyeing one for the last several months. It was at the edge and was taller than he was—more tree than the house could handle. Perfect to cut off the bottom for their Yule log. But Beth insisted on choosing the tree herself and Hannah and Nel recommended one bad choice after another—one too short, one too bent or too scrawny. In the end, they all settled on the very tree David had planned to cut in the first place. Then it was several hearty swings of the ax and the tree was down on the ground. They loaded it onto the sleigh and headed the mules back toward the house.

They left the tree on the porch and David sent the girls back inside before returning the mules to the barn. Both animals brayed at being put back. They'd gone to the trouble of rousing themselves only to make one short haul and then were retired again. Andrew fought David as he removed the halter. Browny backed away, kicking. *Mules,* David thought. *What's more stubborn?*

"I guess that's why they call you two mulish," he said. "You're so doggone hard-headed." David pulled a carrot from his pocket and divided it. He watched the animals toss their heads as they devoured it.

Ma Longacher had already replenished the fire blazing in the fireplace by the time David returned to the house. Beth and Hannah, tired from their adventure and the cold, huddled near the hearth. Nel was busy helping Ma in the kitchen.

"Hmm, what's that I smell?" David said as he walked into the kitchen and wrapped his arms around his mother's waist.

"Pumpkin pies," Ma Longacher said. "And don't you be poking your finger in them."

"But Ma, they're my favorite."

"They won't be fit to eat until they've set," Ma said.

"But what if … what if …" David searched for the argument. "What if a … if *something* should fall on my head and I'd died without pie?"

Ma wondered for the hundredth time what she'd ever done to give birth to such a silly boy.

"I don't like you to talk that way, David," Nel said.

All the laughter went out of his eyes. Nel could get touchy. She'd lost her mother when she was only a few years old. David and Ma and the girls were the first complete family she'd had in her entire life. She needed to count on them. She was an only child and David had begun to understand that it took motherless children a long time to get over their fears of disaster.

"I'm just pulling Ma's leg," he said. "I'm sorry."

"I bet you're thinking about the other smell," Ma said, eager to change the subject. "... Besides the pie."

"You tell me," David said.

"I'm not sure I should," Ma said. "I should run the likes of you out of the kitchen for taking away all my help."

"Smells like bacon and fresh coffee," David said.

Hearing the voices, the smell of food overcame the need of warmth. Beth pulled herself away from the fire and rushed into the kitchen. "You know what David did?"

Ma Longacher looked at Beth, then over at David, and shook her head.

David gave his kid sister a pat on her rump. "Tattle tail." He had no idea which of his tomfoolery Beth might be planning to report him for.

"I'll help you, Mother," Hannah said, grabbing some glassware from the cupboard.

"I'll spread the table cloth," Nel said.

"I'll keep an eye on those pies for you, Mother," Beth said as she lay the lace napkins on the table and looked over at David. "Don't you come near, until Ma tells you you can."

"Okay, all you children gather around before these blueberry pancakes get cold," Ma said.

Nel grabbed a big platter, with pretty blue edges only

a little chipped, and piled sausage and thick strips of bacon onto it. She carried it to the table. Beth grabbed the chair next to David's.

"Pass me the sausage, Nel," David said, reaching across the table.

Beth smacked his hand. "Before saying Grace?"

David sighed, and whispered just loud enough to be heard by all, "What kind of a savage would I be without all my good women to tame me." Then he bowed his head. "Thank you, Lord ..." he began.

2

April 1862

Beth sat in the parlor stitching together a rag doll. "David, there's a robin on the windowsill," she called out.

"April fool's is past and you're the biggest fool at last," David laughed from the other room.

"No, really. Come and see," Beth repeated. "Hannah, Nel, hurry it's the first robin," she squealed.

David stuck his head in the doorway. He spotted the bird at the window. "I'll be ... and there's still frost on the ground," he said. "You making yourself a rag doll, Beth?"

"No. It's for that little girl from church," Beth said. "She's been up and down all winter long. They say she's got growing pains."

"Having a doll like that might just cheer her up," David said.

"We hope so," Ma said as she came up behind David,

patting him on the shoulder. "Planting is right around the corner. I hope you're ready."

David glanced at the book he had been reading. "Tonight I have a nice surprise for my girls," he announced.

Beth laid down her rag doll, got up, and sashayed over to him. "Tell me, David."

"If I tell you, it won't be a surprise, now will it, Sissy?" David said as he pinched her cheek.

The night was chilly. The temperature dropped once the sun had set.

Nel panted as she laid the firewood beside the hearth and dusted off her hands. "Is that enough?" she asked.

"You want a cozy fire, don't you?" David said, using the bellows to stoke the blaze.

Hannah and Beth set down their last armfuls of wood and hung up their hooded cloaks.

David got to his feet. Ma noted that he sighed as he did so. She worried. The most demanding time of the year was upon them and David was already tired. Maybe he'd taken on too much, she thought. His father had learned how to parcel out his energy with efficiency. David always did things his own way—usually taking on too much. He'd gotten more efficient, but it would take him years to match his father's uncanny way of predicting weather, as well as his understanding of crops and soil.

"Everyone gather around the hearth," David said. He pulled the cane rocker over, handed Ma her shawl, and smacked its needlepoint cushion.

"I'm sitting next to David," Beth said as she plopped on a cushion lying on the floor. "Pull up your pillows, girls." Beth patted the floor next to her.

David sat in his father's worn leather chair. It was where he always sat since his father died. He held up a book.

"*Uncle Tom's Cabin*?" Beth said.

"That's a book about slavery," Ma Longacher said.

"It's a novel by Harriet Beecher Stowe. They say she had a meeting with our president, Uncle Abe, sitting before a cozy fire just like ours when Uncle Abe told her, 'Why Mrs. Stowe, right glad to see you!' Then with a humorous twinkle in his eye, he said, 'So you're the little woman who wrote the book that made this Great War!'"

"Did that really happen?" Beth asked in excitement. "How do you know?"

"It's commonly known," David said.

"David, you know how I hate to hear about the war," Nel said.

"This book isn't about the war, my dear Nel," David said. "It was written almost a decade before this war even started."

"Where'd you get it?" Beth asked. "You didn't waste the egg money on it did you?"

"Billy made me the loan of it. Billy Perkins, down at the feed store. He's awful big on the Union, Miss Busy-Body."

"If it's not about the war, then what's it about?" Beth asked.

"It's about the *whys* of the war," David said. "Or something Miss Beecher Stowe calls Life Among the Lowly."

Beth stopped talking. For an instant, it seemed as though the firewood even burned in silence as the flames danced up the flue. This was America, they thought. A place where people were supposed to be equal. The idea that there *were* lowly—even though they knew it was true, troubled them.

"Do you think Father ever read this book?" Beth asked. It was an unwritten rule that David's father, his beliefs, his death, were not table talk amongst the family. Though the girls and David, even Ma, who after Beth, had suffered most, admired him and were proud of his choices and his sacrifice, they still could not entirely understand how principles could have taken away from them a man they loved so much.

"You'll see," David said as he began reading. "Late in the afternoon of a chilly day in February ..."

After about an hour, the fire's flames were reduced to glowing embers. David inserted the bookmark.

"Read more," Beth said. "Pleaseeeee ..."

"David will read to us later, girls," Ma said. "Right now I'd like you to help me bring in the gingersnaps and apple slices."

David started to get up from the chair, rubbing his belly.

"No, David, you sit. You'll just be in the way," Ma said.

A short while later, all that was left of the goodies

was an empty plate sitting on the hearth.

"I'll gather up the remains in the morning," Ma whispered.

Beth's eyes blinked, then closed as the rag doll she'd been working on fell to the floor. She sat upright as she heard a pounding at the front door. Buck started barking.

"Who's at the door at this late hour?" Ma asked. She took down a lantern and lit it with a straw pulled from the broom.

David had already taken down the rifle from over the mantel and was checking to see if it was loaded. Since the war had started, one couldn't be too careful about strangers arriving.

"Shush, Buck," Beth said as the dog's ears laid back.

Hannah pulled the curtain aside. "It's a young man."

"Who?" Nel asked.

"His hat's pulled down over his eyes, I can't tell," Hannah whispered.

Ma moved to stand in the door but David motioned her to one side and shooed the girls into the corner nearest the door. He walked to the front door and unlatched it, then opened it a crack, holding his boot against the bottom.

As the light hit the porch, the man removed his hat.

"Charles Allen Carmichael," David exclaimed as he grabbed his cousin's hand and began pumping it.

"Girls, my oh my, it's your cousin, Charles Allen," Ma Longacher said. "Whatever brings you up to our neck of the woods?" She stepped back from the front door, clutching her shawl up around her neck as a gust of wind blew some of last summer's leaves inside.

David stepped aside, picking up the leaves. "Yes, Charles Allen, what does bring you to us all the way from New Albany?"

"Set down your traps, Charles Allen," Hannah said, "then give me your coat and hat." She wrapped her arms around his waist and gave him a peck on the cheek.

Charles Allen returned her kiss with a squeeze.

"You remember David's wife, Nel?" Hannah asked.

Charles Allen let one of his arms slide off Hannah's waist as he pulled Nel next to him. "It's hard to believe three years have gone by. And you're just as pretty as the day you married Cousin David," Charles Allen smiled.

"Except that I just turned sixteen back then," Nel blushed. "I'm older now."

"Me too," Hannah said.

"Three years ago I was ..." Charles Allen hesitated. "I'm twenty-two now. So ..."

"So, you were nineteen back then," Beth chirped.

"Beth?" Charles Allen said. "Come over here and let me take a good look at you. My how you've grown."

"I'm fifteen now," Beth beamed.

"Really?" Charles Allen held out his arms. "You look at least seventeen, maybe eighteen."

Beth blushed, then straightened up on her tiptoes and gave him a smooch on the lips.

"Get your cousin some leftovers from supper while they're still warm, Beth. You must be starved," Ma

Longacher said. "If I recollect, as a young boy you ate so much it made you poor to carry it around," she laughed. "By the way, honey, how is my dear sister?"

"Thanks for askin', Aint Eve. She's fine, just fine. Ma sent some things for you and the girls. Cousin Beth, hand me that," Charles Allen said, pointing to a worn sack.

Beth picked up the bag and gave it to Charles Allen. He reached inside and handed Ma Longacher something wrapped in tissue.

Ma unfolded the wrapping, careful not to crinkle it, and set it aside. "Oh, just look at these pretty doilies."

"Here David, this is for you." Charles Allen handed David a gray foulard.

David wrapped it around his neck and walked over to the wall mirror. He studied his reflection for a moment, and then took a step back. "Gray ... shouldn't it be Federal blue?"

Charles Allen shrugged. "Depends."

David turned and caught Charles Allen's eye. They let the matter drop.

"Sorry about Uncle John," David said.

Charles Allen adjusted David's scarf. "You lost your Pa in this war, Cousin David, and I lost mine. Different sides, same war."

"Boys, let's don't talk of the war," Ma Longacher said.

"We won't, Aint Eve," Charles Allen said.

"So what are you doing up here? How'd you get here? How long are you staying?" Ma Longacher asked.

"Ma sent me to help David with the planting. I come

by riverboat ... And what was the last question?" Charles Allen smiled at his Aunt Eve.

"Your pa wasn't much of a farmer," Ma Longacher said. "Your Ma used to say that as a farmer he'd be a pretty good sailor. But I always blamed the land he farmed. You know the poorer dirt of Southern Indiana is no match for the fertile soil of the Ohio Valley."

"Down home it seems like everyone knows how to farm, even if you don't live on one. I did some work farmin' around New Albany. There didn't seem to be enough boys to go around," Charles Allen said. "No offense meant, girls," he smiled. "I was gonna come up sooner only ..."

"Only you almost broke your arm," David interrupted.

"How was it that that happened?" Ma asked.

"I fell off the buckboard after I let the reins drop and my horse decided he wanted to race a friend of mine's horse. I can't take the blame for a horse," Charles Allen said.

"Have you learned how to manage animals, Charles Allen? Driving horses is a big part of farm life," Ma said.

"I know that, Aint Eve. I'm aware." Charles Allen's face clouded over. He had more to say, David thought. But he never would.

"David, why don't you put some more wood on the fire," Ma said. "Charles Allen can sleep on a nice feather bed pallet next to the fireplace tonight, then tomorrow me and the girls will clean up the old log cabin for you. It's warm enough that you could bunk out there. Give you some privacy."

"Now don't you go to any extra trouble for me, Aint Eve," Charles Allen said.

"It's getting late. We'll have plenty of time to talk tomorrow," Ma said as she turned to go upstairs.

"I'll get Cousin Charles a quilt, Mother," Beth said.

"Let's leave the men visit, girls. Your Cousin Charles has all his bedding right here." Ma pointed to a wooden chest beneath the window. "David, there's a bottle of your father's brandy in that chest. Maybe Charles Allen would enjoy a glass."

The girls trailed behind Ma up the stairs. Each, one after the other, turned as they passed the newel post to scrutinize the newcomer.

"Every single one of them as cute as buttons," Charles Allen said. "You're a lucky man, David."

"All off limits," David smiled as he uncorked the brandy. He found a crystal brandy glass for Charles Allen in a sideboard and refilled his own teacup.

Charles Allen placed a pinch of snuff against his gums and twirled the brandy in his glass. He gave it a sniff, then took a sip. "Hmm ..."

David leaned back in his chair.

"David, I believe the Union is all wrong in their position on this war," Charles Allen said. It was as if his whole trip here had been to campaign for the South. "I believe the true Americans, the true upholders of the Constitution, are the leaders of the Confederacy."

"Tell me your thoughts, Cousin," David said.

It was a peace offering. David knew his own beliefs

would not and could not be changed. But as much as David was a committed man, Charles Allen was a stubborn one. So they stayed up until the fire had burned itself out, and a half bottle of brandy had been consumed. In that very room, both David and Charles Allen's fathers had sat debating those same points a little more than a year earlier. Both died, as fate would have it, in the same battle. Whether either expected that they'd end up facing one another in battle was never known. And no one ever wanted to ask. Their sons' beliefs were determined not by conviction, but by the sense that each was honoring his own father by taking up his father's cause. It was ironic, Ma knew, because if those two good men could be brought back from the grave, they'd have urged their sons to embrace and learn to live in peace with one another. They had both breathed their last at Bull Run, understanding finally the true nature of tragedy.

David woke almost an hour past dawn the next morning. Coffee had been brewed and Ma was pulling a pan of biscuits from the oven. Charles Allen, who'd slept on the floor by the fireplace, was gone, his blanket rolled and stored in the corner with the rest of his belongings.

"You boys stayed up late," Ma said. There was something guarded in her voice. "Talking politics?"

"Just small talk, Ma. Nothing of consequence."

She set the biscuits down in front of David along with a lump of butter. She poured him a cup of coffee, which he downed as fast as its temperature would let him.

"It's different now," Ma said. She was a pretty woman still, not old, really, in her mid-forties. But she'd witnessed and experienced the kinds of things that could wear a person down—miscarriages and deaths, bad harvests, and brutal winters. And now this war, the worst calamity of all. It had taken its toll—might well have worn her down even had her husband survived. "I guess that boy hasn't changed his opinions," she said.

"He might be even more fiery since his father was killed ..." David paused.

Ma sat down next to him and took a biscuit. She split it, then lay it down on the table.

"He tell you why he came here with all that talking you two did?"

"He didn't," David said. "Not really. We didn't get to that."

"He did say he came to be of service."

"Well, that's what he said to all of us last night ... But why would he do that, believing as he does that we're on the wrong side of the war?" David asked.

"Blood's thicker than politics, David."

"It's hard to believe it," David said. "Not when good and evil are laid out so clear."

"You sound just like your father."

"Father was right."

"Charles Allen knows we need him," Ma said.

"Why would he stay though? He'd be helping out the enemy."

"I already told you, David."

"What if I was to decide to go, Ma? You think he'd stay and help out then? He'd be freeing up one more soldier to fight for the Union."

"Let's cross that bridge when we come to it. May we never." Ma's voice was soft now. David was afraid she might burst into tears.

"You want me to go and talk to him? You want me to tell him it's better for him not to stay?" David asked.

Ma shook her head.

David got up, went to the stove, came back to the table, and emptied the remaining coffee into his cup—grounds and all.

"I won't say anything," David said. "At least not right now."

"He's planning to be here awhile," Ma said.

"Where'd he go off to?" David asked.

"He was moving about when I woke up. And then he said he was going down to the cabin," Ma said.

David took a sip of his coffee. It was now lukewarm. He gulped it down anyway.

The two of them walked to the cabin. David went on, as was his habit, to check things out in the barn. Ma Longacher went on to the cabin and peeked in the doorway. She stepped over a dead possum that Charles Allen must have tossed out the door. He'd borrowed a broom from the stable and had given the floor a first sweeping. He'd also picked up a gunnysack, rolled it, then stuffed it into a crack between the frame of one of the windows and the log wall.

"Oh my," Ma said. "You've got it halfway homey already."

Charles Allen cracked a smile, pleased to be complimented on his housekeeping skills.

"You've even got a fire going. You sure there aren't any squirrels or birds in the chimney?" Ma asked.

"It's just a little fire. I figured if there was anything livin' up there I'd smoke 'em out," Charles Allen said.

"Well, after you do—and you will is my guess—you remember to keep that flue shut once the fire's died out. If you don't, it'll get cold and damp inside, plus more critters might get in," Ma said.

"Is the roof solid?"

"Well, I never been on it, but I expect David's father would have told me if it wasn't."

"I'll borrow a ladder from David and take a look ... poke around in the chimney a little. Looks like there's a little leak over there in the corner, but I can patch that up easy enough," Charles Allen said.

"I'll send Hannah and Beth down to help you. They'll make it more comfortable."

"Thank you, ma'am. I appreciate your hospitality. I wasn't sure, such as things are nowadays, that you'd want to see me."

"Make yourself at home and stay as long as you like. I'm delighted to have you."

"My younger brother, Frank Lee, wanted to come, but Ma wouldn't let him until she heard from you," Charles

Allen said.

"Is it unsafe where your people are?" Ma asked.

"People are leavin'. It's awful close to the action. We got troops in town all the time now. I'll tell you, the saloon is doin' a good business. Blue and Gray customers both."

"What'll the farmers do?" Ma asked.

"They'll stay for right now. But we're lucky, folks like us. We can board up our business and take ourselves elsewhere. Unless ..."

"Unless you decide to enlist?"

There was a long pause.

"That's right, ma'am."

"Frank Lee's more than welcome. Let's see, he must be around fifteen by now," Ma Longacher said.

"Maybe Frank Lee can come before harvest time," Charles Allen said. "Help get in the crop."

"There will be plenty to do then," Ma Longacher said.

"Frank Lee wanted to enlist in the Confederate Army," Charles Allen said. "He went to Kentucky, but Ma made me go after him. He was stayin' with his girlfriend's family on the Kentucky side of the Ohio River, almost directly across from us."

"Frank Lee's got a girlfriend?"

"I guess if you figure you're ready to join the army, you figure you got a right to have a girl, too. Who knows what's gonna happen?"

"I'll write my sister and tell her to send him to me. He's too young to go to war," Ma Longacher said. "And you are too, Charles Allen." She should have stopped there. But standing in this cabin, where she began her married life, she couldn't keep her thoughts to herself. "And when you do go," she said, "and I fear that you will ... because the ambitious and those answering the call to duty are always the ones who do, they leave the lazy and the frail behind ... When you do go to fight, you better be darned sure you know what you're fighting for and that it's the right cause."

"Yes'm," he said as he poked at the hot embers.

She decided she wouldn't pursue it, then hesitated for a moment. "You boys don't fool me, Charles Allen."

"Who, Aint Eve?"

"You and my David," she said.

Charles Allen looked away.

"Just the same, Nephew, a mother knows."

"I'm going into town to pick up a few things. Can I get anything for you, Aint Eve?" Charles Allen asked.

"Don't be spending your money," she said. "We got enough goods lying around here to turn this old cabin into a general store."

"Just some personal items, Aint Eve."

"Well don't be getting any household contraptions, me and my girls still like to use a fork to whip the batter," Ma said. "As for put up food, just take what you want, the fruit cellar door is always unlocked."

"You reckon you have any chaw in that cellar, Aint Eve?"

"Oh, go on." Ma waved him off. Chewing tobacco and more brandy, she figured, after what he'd put away last night.

3

July 1862

The valley was filled with corn now. Its green stalks blended with the yellow wheat against the blue sky, as if brushed into place by an artist.

At the end of the day, just before the late summer supper, David and Charles Allen had walked up to the top of the small hill behind the house. They stood silent, taking in the beautiful scene the Longacher valley produced.

"Well Cousin Charles, it's off to a good start," David said.

"So it is." Charles Allen shook David's hand. "And the corn's taller than knee high in July." Charles Allen looked back down the hill at the cabin. "I want to re-plaster that spot under the eave. Then that's the end of my list for the cabin."

"There'll be something, there always is," David said. "But at least not for a while, I hope."

Charles Allen stuck his hands deep in his pockets. "So what's next, Cousin?"

David's mouth formed a broad smile. "We'll just have to wait and see."

Caw, caw ...

"What the hell ..." Charles Allen said, looking back toward the house.

David shaded his eyes. Ma Longacher stood in the middle of her garden patch, swinging her broom at a flock of crows.

"Come on, Cousin Charles, Mother looks as though she needs reinforcements."

The two jogged back down the hill.

"Stop Mother," David called out.

"Not until I teach these vultures a lesson," she said. "I can't do much about the crops, but this here garden is off limits to any and all critters."

David took the broom from her hand. The crows stopped their cawing and flew off. The men started laughing.

"I'm glad you two think it's funny." Ma stood with her hands on her hips.

"Ma, Cousin Charles and me are going to make a scarecrow for your garden. Right, Cousin?"

Charles Allen nodded through his laughter.

"I hope it works, son," Ma said.

"Oh, it'll work. They might still fly over, but I can assure you, their pecking in your garden is done with."

The porch swing squeaked as it swung back and forth. David brushed the dust off his shirt, then wiped the sweat from his brow as he sat down next to Nel on the swing. He'd driven the rig into town to pick up some clapboard that morning. He'd decided, since Charles Allen had gotten him almost caught up, to take care of some long-postponed work that the barn needed. But the clapboard wasn't ready, and half the things that Ma asked him for— including some salt pork—weren't available. The whole morning adventure had been a complete waste of time.

"How about a dip under the covered bridge?" David asked. He liked to picnic on the banks near the bridge, sometimes even celebrating his birthday there. Celebrating the bridge's establishment, too. Though David liked to imagine he was showing less wear and tear—at least on the surface—than the covered structure.

Nel moved her hand fan back and forth in quick motions. "I hear your stomach growling. I'll pack us a picnic basket," she said.

David licked his lips. "Just you and me?"

"I think Beth went out to the north field with Charles Allen. She seems to take to farming better than the rest of us girls," Nel said.

"She's always been a tomboy," David said.

Beth cupped her ear closer to the half-open door.

"Hannah thought about following along but she's shy," Nel said. "I imagine she's got somewhat of a crush on Charles Allen."

"He's our cousin," David said.

"She knows that. But she looks up to him. How else is she going to learn what grown men are like?"

David shrugged. "Watching her brother, maybe?"

Nel laughed. "David, my dear, there are no grown men like you anywhere on God's green earth."

Nel touched her big toe to the water. She stepped back from the water's edge. They had set their basket up a few yards away from the bridge where the sun was brightest. She'd brought along corn bread, pickles, and plenty of fried chicken. Fortified, they decided to wait awhile before going in the water.

"You said you were going to go in. Why else would you put on that swimming outfit? You look like a Turk in that skirt and pants."

"It's too cold," Nel replied. "I'll just sit and watch you."

"You big baby, let me help you." Nel put up her hands to defend herself, knowing that it was a lost cause. David grabbed her by the wrists and started backing her down toward the water. She screamed and laughed so hard that she lost her footing. David bent down as if to help her up, then scooped her off her feet and tossed her into a swirl of dark water.

"I'm going to tell your sisters, you bully," Nel shrieked.

"You don't have to, I saw what happened," Beth said, swimming out from behind one of the bridge pilings.

"What are you doing here?" David stood with his arms folded in front of him.

Nel's eyes widened. Pointing at Beth, she stuttered, "Forget what she's doing, just look at her."

"Beth, get out of the water," David said. "I'll be ... no don't."

"I'm practicing naturism. It's not like nobody never swam naked down here." Beth stared at Nel.

"That was our secret, Beth," Nel said. "Your mother's going to hear about this."

Beth swam away, disappearing around a crook in the streambed. A moment later they heard barking, followed by a splash and Beth's voice shouting orders.

"What the ..." David said. "Beth, have you got Charles Allen over there?"

"I can't see anybody, David," Nel said, scrambling up out of the water.

"If he's practicing naturism with her I'll have to shoot him."

"You mean Cousin Charles or Buck?" Nel said. She wondered what David would shoot him with—a chicken leg? She wrapped her hair in a towel. "It's Buck doing all of that splashing. Buck is definitely practicing naturism."

"Where?" David asked.

"I just saw ..." Nel said.

Buck bounded out of the water. Beth grabbed her bathing suit from wherever she'd stashed it and put it on as she treaded water. Straightening her suit, she came up out of the water, in pursuit of Buck.

"Git, Buck," Nel hollered, as the dog shook water all over the picnic basket. "Isn't there any privacy in this family? First Beth, now Buck. And Beth again?"

Buck tucked his tail between his hind legs and headed back home, occasionally turning his head to look back. David prayed the dog didn't get into the house wet as he was. Ma would have a conniption.

"You got a picnic?" Beth asked. "Splendid! I'm famished."

"Nel and I were about to have a conversation, Beth," David said.

Beth shrugged and shook some water from her hair.

"You're too old to be swimming in your birthday suit," David said.

"Why don't you tell that to your lovely wife? I believe she was only sixteen when you and her got caught," Beth spouted.

"We didn't get caught, we got married," Nel said.

"*Pardon moi,*" Beth said, rolling her eyes.

"You're getting a little too big for your britches, Sissy. Maybe I'll have to take you down a notch or two." David started toward Beth. "I don't believe you've finished your swimming." Knowing what he had in mind, Beth turned and ran.

"Look at her go," Nel laughed. "Like a scared rabbit."

David sat down, picked up a chicken leg, and began gnawing on it. He licked the grease off his fingers. "Let's see ... who's left to interrupt us now? Charles Allen? Hannah maybe?"

"Charles Allen's wherever he goes in the afternoon. Back to the cabin to read, I suppose. And Hannah's with Ma. You know she won't come out in the sun. Doesn't want to get sunspots."

"You worry about your complexion too, Nel."

"I don't mind coming out in the sun. If I can come out with you," Nel said.

Nel sat and watched as David wiped off his hands before picking up a deviled egg.

"You have something to say to me, David?"

"I do. Something important ..."

"By your expression, it must be serious," Nel said.

"Your bathing suit still wet?"

"It's damp but I don't mind."

"You want to walk a little? How about down to that blackberry patch?" he asked.

"Them berries won't be ready yet," Nel said.

"Let's go see if we can guess how much longer before they ripen then," David said.

"I'll get the picnic basket ..."

"Leave it, we're coming back by this way," David said. He looked around, then took Nel's hand and gave it a quick kiss.

"Nobody's around, David." Nel kissed his nose.

They walked on until David finally spoke. "I'm going to volunteer."

"We all knew you would, David."

"How?"

"That's for me to know and you to find out," Nel said as she wiped at her eyes with the back of her hand. "Can we go for another walk tomorrow?"

"Not tomorrow, I have an appointment to see the Probate Judge," David said.

"About what?" Nel asked.

"That's for me to know and you to find out," he laughed.

"It isn't funny, David," she whispered. "... All right, I knew because I found some of those recruitment broadsides in your pockets when you came back from town last."

"Doggone it, I thought I hid those."

"You didn't hide them good enough."

"Where'd you put them?" David asked.

"I burned them. Then I hid that book ... *Uncle Tom's Cabin.*"

"I've got to return that to Billy," he said.

"I'll give it to you before you see old judge what's-his-name," Nel said.

They climbed up on the trunk of a cottonwood that had fallen at the edge of the water and sat down beside each other. David wanted to talk about what the family knew. What did Ma think? What did his sisters say? The big issue was left on the table untouched. So Nel meant to get David to tell her direct.

"Why, David? Why do you have to go?"

"It's just got to be done. If you believe in something in your heart you got to do more than just talk about it."

"How about your family?" she said. "Who's going to take care of things?"

"Charles Allen is here, he ..."

Nel interrupted him. "He wants to join the Confederates."

"That's just talk," David said.

"What if it's not? You two go on about it all the time. You think he's going to ignore his principles? You won't. You men ..."

"It's just different."

"How, David?"

"The family will be all right."

"Well, then what about me? I don't have family, David, what am I supposed to do if something happens?"

"Ma and the girls are your family."

"They're not blood. Yes, they'll keep me, and they'll be kind to me, but you think they'll really want me around when all I'd do is remind them of you being dead some place far away because you were off fighting for some cause that nobody will be able to explain as time passes on."

"They'll take care of you, Nel."

"But it goes both ways. I don't want to be here always reminded of you, of what we lost."

"What kind of country would it be, Nel, what kind of world would it be if slavery continues? When you take away one man's freedom, everybody else's freedom is a little less too. And if every time some part of the United States has some problem and wants to go off its own way, what then? Then there's a group of little kingdoms squabbling like the ones overseas and there's constant war and no guaranteed liberties and no democracy. We got to stop this madness now. We got to live out the dream of our forefathers."

There was a long silence. David could have gone on and on but it would have been cruel to do so, he knew. His mind was made up. And Nel knew it. She was right; she had probably known his mind before he did.

It had been a wet spring. The berry patch was bigger than when they'd last seen it the summer before. It was covered with buds and green berries. They wouldn't be ripe for at least a month, was a good guess. Nel wondered if David would still be around when they were ready for picking.

"We had another dream you and me," Nel said. "We were going to come out here and have a family. Boys you were hoping for, but I was hoping for both. Maybe we'd build on to the house. Remember? That was my dream, David. That was my *kind of* dream before I met you." She picked at the bark of the cottonwood. "I know you're not God, David. I know you can't make things happen. But just tell me how you can give up so much that's right here before your eyes? Tell me how you do it because I couldn't. I love and trust you and I even think I believe in what you'd be fighting for. Only I wish I could believe in it without the fighting part. I couldn't sacrifice my family for that."

He took her by the hand and raised her to her feet. She remembered—what a funny thought to have here in a field in Ohio, by a cottonwood trunk across a stream— she remembered a picture she once saw of some great lord and his lady. Both of them wearing white wigs and fancy clothing. But he, the picture of elegance, had taken her hand and was raising her out of her chair. They were going to dance, Nel had imagined when she saw it. They were at a ball and about to go dancing. So now, it was as if David, here in the middle of Ohio, were asking her to step out onto the dance floor with him.

Nel stood up and put her hands on both sides of his face. David looked straight at her, all the passion welling up in her now. "You just promise me, David. That I don't have to give up *my* dream, *our* dream, so that you can live yours. I still want that family, I still want children."

He wasn't used to that kind of force from her, but he respected it. "Nel, I swear, I want to go fight for this cause only because I want that dream to come true too. I want to be able to look at my son and tell him he should fight for his principles. The way I am."

She let her arms slide around his waist and put her head on his chest.

"I want them to grow up in a great country, Nel. A free country. That's what brought us here, a few generations ago. I want it to keep going."

Nel grasped his hand and led him on. She looked up toward the road. "Here comes that mollycoddled baby sister of yours."

"She just can't leave us alone can she?" David said.

"I just want you to know, David, that whatever you have to do, I'm behind you."

He pulled Nel close to his body and kissed her lips.

Beth walked up in her bathing suit, put one hand behind her neck and the other on her hip. "Coming up for air, love birds?"

Nel jumped back, blushing. "You're dressed," she said. "What a pleasant change."

"Guess what I have in my hand, David," Beth said.

David squinted his eyes at Beth.

"I'm sorry," Beth said, handing a custard pudding to David.

"Just you remember, David, that's how she made Buck so roly-poly," Nel grinned. "You better not try to make my handsome husband fat."

Beth gave her a closer look. "Have you been crying?"

Nel smiled and took Beth by her hand. "You and I will be picking berries soon."

Beth squeezed Nel's hand. "Mmm ..." She smacked her lips.

4

David sat waiting for the Probate Judge. He sniffed the smell of old leather as he scanned the law books that were wedged into the bookcases. Stacks of books were piled high in every corner. He smiled to himself as he realized the scent in the air was the same as the old lending library in town. David stood as he heard the inner office door squeak open.

"I'm glad you could make it, David," the Judge said as he held out his hand. "When do you leave for Camp Piqua?"

"News sure does travel fast," David said.

"Nothing could change your mind I suppose?"

"No, sir."

"You're sure this is the right place and time?"

"Sure as sure can be."

The judge fixed a hard stare at him and tugged at his earlobe. "You sound like your father."

"Thanks."

The Judge forced a smile as he rolled a chair to the front of his desk for David. Already laid out on his desk was David's father's last will and testament. The Judge pulled his spectacles down from his forehead to his nose and turned the pages of the document that needed signing toward David.

"Everything is in order, David," the Judge said. "It ought to be, I prepared and witnessed these papers myself. Bottom line is the entire estate was left to you, with provisions that you will see to it that your mother and sisters, and your wife, of course, are cared for. I trust you've talked this all over with them already."

"I mostly talked to Nel about it. My Ma and my sisters ... I think they figured it was a foregone conclusion."

"Brave women. They've lost a lot already. As have you, David."

"That's one of the reasons for going. I mean to try to balance things out."

"They agree?" the Judge asked.

"I believe so. Or if they don't, they will now."

The Judge picked up his pen and then realized that his inkwell was dry. He turned his attention to rummaging through the drawers of his desk to find ink. "As a purely personal matter, just out of curiosity, how will they run the farm when you leave? That puts—what?— three young women and your mother in charge of a whole section. Can you hire help? Able-bodied men are scarce in this neck of the woods since the war."

"I know that, sir."

"There will be people around town who will tell you that it's … shortsighted to enlist when there's so much to be done at home. Your crops, young man, are provisioning our armies."

"But we do have help. My cousin, Charles Allen. He came up a few months ago. He'll help with the crops until I get home, which, God willing, will be fairly soon."

The judge was intent on his inkwell now. David noticed that the man had a slight tremor in his hand and reached out to hold the well steady. The judge let him finish the pouring.

"Charles Allen …" the Judge said. "Your father mentioned him. That's that part of your family from downstate Indiana. I remember him talking about them. Aren't they Southern …?"

"… Sympathizers?" David grinned. "You know, they're from river bottom country. They got a couple of funny ideas."

"How old is your Cousin Charles?" the Judge asked.

"Couple of years younger than me," David said.

"He ever talk to you about joining the Confederacy?"

"Heck, every time he gets me alone that's all he talks about."

"And you're going to leave him alone with your family and your farm?"

"Well, he promised he'd help out."

"You trust him?"

"Of course I do. He's my cousin."

"How do you know he's not a spy?"

David laughed. The idea of Charles Allen, who was so outspoken, being a spy? He continued laughing. "We can trust Charles Allen," he said.

The judge shrugged and nodded. "All right, here's the paperwork, son. Do you have any questions for me?"

David stared at the document. "This takes care of what happens to the property if I don't come back?"

"Covers every eventuality I could think of."

"When does all this transferring of property take place?" David asked.

"There's the usual waiting period, as all legalities have," the Judge said. "However, everything should be finalized and set to go within a few months."

"Well, sir, you've already been officially enlightened as to my desire to volunteer for service to the Union," David said.

"Yes, my boy. And I guess you can tell that I have some doubts and concerns. But I admire your patriotism and I thank you as well as congratulate you." The words sounded like thousands of other testimonials, but the judge was thinking his way through them; they came from his heart. The Judge extended his hand once again. "I only wish I were going, but ..." He patted his oversized belly, then rubbed his thinning gray hair. "Plus I've got this damned little jiggle in my hand. But I try to do my part from here at home."

"That goes without question," David said. "You've been real helpful to me and my family."

"I've also prepared a last will and testament for you,

David. No need to get into any of the details, is there?"

"No sir," David said, pulling the papers closer. "Where do I sign?"

There was a bounce in David's step as he exited the judge's office and started down the street. He first headed in the direction of the local tavern, figuring he'd run into a few of his friends, maybe even someone home on furlough. But by the time he got to the end of the street, the weight of what he'd just done, what had been set into motion, what was planned, began to press down on him. He walked right past the tavern and on to the general store, pulling out of his pocket the list of groceries Ma wanted. He was in a hurry now. He shopped as quick as he could, adding to the list only a few bags of candies for the girls. It wasn't much, but it was all he could think of. He reached inside one of the candy bags and popped a horehound in his mouth.

Charles Allen accompanied David and his family to church on Sunday. The bell stopped ringing as they entered. David nudged Charles Allen. "Look around, Cousin, I told you it would be this way, we're the only men in church."

"I don't see any boys over fifteen," Charles Allen whispered.

David's mouth dropped as their preacher emerged from behind the baptismal curtain and walked up to the pulpit. Charles Allen fidgeted in the pew. Reverend Booker sported a Union officer's uniform with the rank of captain embroidered on the epaulets. The congregation began whispering.

The Reverend grabbed his sash and spoke. "Brothers and sisters, as you can see, I'm going to be preoccupied for awhile. I've contacted the church hierarchy, and a retired minister will be sent to you in a few days. I realize this is short notice, but duty has called. And when it's Our Lord's will that we're doing, we don't ask Him to come back at a more convenient time." There were murmurs of assent from some of the parishioners. "Our boys need spiritual support now more than ever." He paused to open his Bible.

David caught a glance at Mrs. Booker looking around, primping her hair. Then he realized that she actually winked at Charles Allen, who sat grinning like a Cheshire cat.

"Today, the sermon will be from Psalm 23, those eternal words of the Psalmist, 'Yea though I walk through the valley of the shadow of death' ..." the Reverend began.

Nel wiped the perspiration off her hand and folded it into David's. David leaned over, looking at his mother who sat next to Charles Allen, patting his hand. David had his moments of wondering if it was in God's power to make things all right. But he had a pretty good idea that if anybody could make the country run the way it ought to, it was folks like Ma Longacher. She was, far and away, the truest Christian he would ever know.

It was late in the evening of that same day that Ma

Longacher finished her task. She had sat in a corner by the fire at her work since they got back from church. She took off the glasses she used to do close work and held up the Union coat she'd tailored herself for David.

"Mother, wasn't it hard to get that jacket the proper size for David?" Hannah asked.

"Why no, Honey, Captain Ullery's grandmother gave me a jacket she made for him. They're about the same size. In fact, she let me take the Captain's jacket apart so I had a perfect pattern," Ma said.

"It's beautiful," Nel said. "I wish I could sew like you, Ma."

"Fancy," Hannah said. "It's even grander than Reverend Booker's. Just look at the red braiding."

"You don't think it's too much, do you girls?" Ma asked.

"No, no," they chimed.

"When I get finished with David's coat then I'm going to help Nel with David's kepi. It's a little tricky attaching the leather bill and strap," Ma said.

"It sure shows up what I have to give him," Beth scowled.

"Don't be a silly goose, Beth, David will need those warm socks," Nel said.

Beth took the blue hat from Nel's hands and cocked it on her head. Beth lowered her voice. "Attention boys ... Straighten that cap, Soldier."

Hannah held up a pair of blue trousers with extra padding in the knees and seat. She picked at one of the seams.

"Mother will help you with those, Hannah," Nel said.

"Let's hope no other girl ever has those in her hands," Beth said.

Nel's face flushed as she snatched the hat off Beth's head.

"Beth! What kind of talk is that for a young lady?" Ma said.

"I was just teasing," Beth said.

"David said she needed to be taken down a notch or two," Nel said.

"Beth, you apologize to Nel," Ma said.

Beth moved closer to Nel and put her arms around Nel's shoulders. "Oh Nel, I wouldn't do anything in the world to hurt you." She kissed Nel on her forehead. "You're my favorite sister-in-law."

"I'm your only sister-in-law," Nel laughed as she reached over and tugged Beth's braid.

Once things had started, they moved with astonishing speed. The sewing of the uniform had been finished only the night before and in the morning David had taken it upstairs to try it on.

Running through the still damp grass, Beth came up from the barn carrying a small, wrapped package that she'd hidden in the hayloft.

"David, David," Beth called out as she came through the door.

"I'm upstairs, Beth," David yelled down.

Beth pitched herself headlong up the stairs with Nel right behind her.

The bedroom door was cracked open.

"Are you decent?" Nel asked.

"Come in," David said.

He stood near the mirror in his woolies with shaving cream smeared on his face.

Beth pointed at him. "You're in your underwear."

"Good guess, Sissy," David said.

"Can I give it to him now, Nel?" Beth asked.

"Yes, Sissy," Nel said.

Beth handed David the fancy wrapped gift. "Well open it, my dear brother," she said.

David had been feeling transformed by the uniform. He was anxious about what he had undertaken and excited at the same time. But old habits die hard and it was impossible for him not to try to get a rise out of his sister. He wiped off his face, checking his reflection in the mirror. Then he put on the jacket and adjusted his cuffs before picking up the package and turning it over in his hands.

"David, for goodness' sake," Beth burst out. "Don't take all day!"

"Open it, David," Nel said.

He peeled back the paper careful, as Ma always was with the wrapping, to keep the paper nice. Inside was a small, sturdy, leather-bound book.

"A diary," David exclaimed. "Almost like the one you bought me, Nel."

"I know. Beth asked me if I would mind," Nel said.

"Look," he said, slipping the diary inside the pocket of his jacket. "It's a perfect fit. Now I am completely prepared."

"Except dear," Nel said, "you don't have any pants on."

Beth reached over and clasped Nel's hand, then lowered her head.

David reached under Beth's chin. Her tears fell on his hand. "It's a grand gift. Don't cry, Sissy."

"I'm sorry, David, I can't help it," Beth said. "When you write us, make sure you refer to me as Beth, not Sissy."

David kissed her and gave her a hug.

When he looked away, he spotted Hannah standing in the doorway. The scene was altogether too sentimental for Hannah's taste. "I don't want to slow you down, David. But I have to let you know that your personal appearance could be improved now that you're a man in uniform." She came into the room, picked up his shaving brush from out of its mug and pasted a dollop of shaving cream on his nose. "There," she laughed.

Beth and Nel giggled.

It rained for a good part of the morning, though the sun came out in the early afternoon. Hannah and Nel went out to work in the garden. Beth, who hadn't slept the night before, dozed off after lunch in the parlor. When she awoke, the house was quiet, except for soft voices coming from upstairs. She tiptoed to the door of her mother's bedroom. It was ajar and inside she could hear David explaining something to Ma.

"... been talking to him about the farm since the moment he arrived at the door. I've been showing him things, Ma ..."

"I'm not complaining, David," Ma said. "I'm just trying to think everything through."

"All right, let's say something were to happen to Charles Allen ..."

David's voice became too low for Beth to hear, though she could still pick up on the tone. She sensed what the feelings were inside that room. Ma was quiet in that way she got when she was sad. And David was being David, the man of the house. Laying things out step by step. Beth caught on to a few scraps of the conversation.

"Billy Perkins can help Charles Allen with that ... I talked to the old man two farms over, he'll trade day labor of two of his grandsons if Charles Allen will ..."

Then Beth turned away. She could accept the idea of David riding off glorious into battle. And she would learn to live with the loneliness of the family, waiting at home for his return, spending evenings and rainy days knitting socks for him, putting up preserves for him in the fall, writing him. But the business being discussed in that room right now—the arrangements made for running the farm, the reassurances, the backup planning—troubled her. It all made David seem less a hero and more like an ordinary farmer, caught in the middle.

5

August 1862

Ma Longacher and her girls stood outside the house wiping away their tears as they waved their goodbyes with their handkerchiefs. David held his cap high as he waved it back and forth. He turned around on the buckboard, taking one last look.

"Y'all look mighty pretty, Cuz," Charles Allen said cracking the horse's reins, sending the grays into a trot.

David sat quiet, bouncing his leg. His inner thoughts were mixed. Were pride, honor, and glory the reasons why he was leaving, or was it the principle of it all? Then he remembered Nel and Hannah's parting remarks of how brave and handsome he was.

"Y'all look pretty, Soldier Boy," Charles Allen repeated, nudging David in the ribs. "Button up that there good-lookin' jacket."

"Why don't you do yourself a favor and muster in when we meet the 110th in town," David said.

Charles Allen spit a well-aimed stream of tobacco juice, hitting one of the cracks in the wallboards of the covered bridge as the wagon passed through it. "With Yankees?" he snapped.

David turned and took one last look at the farm, noticing the white smoke rising from the chimney and drifting into the cloudless blue sky. The old place wasn't just a house to David. It had become his home again. His only home.

Ma Longacher and the girls stood and watched the wagon disappear as the wind kicked up a trail of dust behind.

Ma wouldn't stand in the way; she knew her son was passionate about his beliefs. But when he was departed, really gone, she could finally speak her mind.

"It just isn't right," Ma Longacher said. "I already gave them my husband, a brother-in-law, and two nephews."

One of her nephews was killed fighting alongside her husband by the Rebs in the first Battle of Bull Run. Another nephew and her brother-in-law were both mortally wounded by Union soldiers in the same battle, but fighting for the Confederacy.

"Oh, what's to become of me now that my David is marching off to some godforsaken place in the Deep South," Ma said.

The girls stood close to each other.

"Oh Lord, please look over our David," Ma said.

Hannah wrapped her arm around her mother's shoulder.

Beth looked out across the fields. "It's almost harvest time," she said.

"Charles Allen is going to help bring in the harvest, right?" Hannah asked. "That's what David said."

"That's what you two talked about yesterday afternoon, wasn't it?" Beth asked.

Ma Longacher reached up to re-pin her graying bun. "David's got things worked out. We'll be just fine. I wouldn't count on your cousin too much, though," she said. "But let's not concern ourselves with him for the time being. I promised my sister we'd make him welcome."

"Where is New Albany anyway?" Beth asked.

"Way down at the foot of Indiana, on the Ohio River," Hannah said.

"David says they're mostly Copperheads down there," Nel said.

"You know how David is when those two get going," Ma said. "David gets as silly with Charles Allen as he does with you girls, then he talks a lot of nonsense."

"Yes, ma'am," Nel said, afraid of having said the wrong thing.

"When Mr. Longacher died, and before you two moved down this way, my sister came to help out. We'd both just lost our husbands. We could help each other out in ways no others could. "

"And you went there when ..." Hannah started.

"Yes, I did go down that winter when she got so sick. And I can tell you that in those hard times nobody ever said a thing about Copperheads or Yankees. Wars happen, then they're over. But families ... They continue. On and on."

It was a longer drive than either of the cousins had anticipated, but through the entire journey, the two young men were silent. There had never been such a time before. The two had spent their whole lives when they were together the way they spent the night of Charles Allen's arrival—talking till they fell asleep and at it again the next morning.

Now they could find nothing to say to each other. Only once did they break silence. Charles Allen noticed David was holding a small piece of quartz—an old arrowhead, it looked like. He was polishing it with his thumb, and the bit of stone shone as though David had been polishing it for a long time.

"What's that you got?" Charles Allen asked. "An arrowhead?"

David tucked it back into his pocket. "Yea."

"A charm or somethin'?"

David almost laughed. "I found it the same day that I proposed to Nel. Brought me luck then, so I kept it."

They fell back into silence. Charles Allen wondered whether, if he had a pretty little wife like Nel, he would go off and fight, risking all that.

They didn't exchange words again for the rest of their journey. Charles Allen wondered what had possessed him to offer to drive his cousin to the camp. David asked himself over and over what had made him accept.

Charles Allen pulled into camp and pointed to the company of recruits. "Looks like you're gonna have to grow a beard, David. They're all tryin' to look like Old Abe. You'd think that one would be enough."

David shook his head and reached for his haversack before jumping down off the wagon.

A sergeant approached. "Name?"

"Yes, sir. David. David Longacher."

"Go over by that table, Longacher, and sign in," the sergeant spoke out. "You think you're a Long-acher now, well you're gonna be achin' a whole lot longer." The sergeant slapped David on the back.

David spent a moment adjusting the straps on his haversack. "I'm grateful, Charles Allen, for all you've done. And for all you're going to do for Ma and the girls."

"I gave you my word, Cousin."

"Thanks," David said and the two men shook hands.

David turned to walk away.

"David!" Charles Allen called out. "However this war works out, I sure hope you come back safe."

David stared at him a moment then gave a tug of his cap and turned away.

The sergeant was busy organizing the other enlistees. Lining them up in a row, he strutted back and forth down the line. "As for the rest of you greenhorns, get acquainted with your feet." The sergeant walked over to one of the recruits and stepped on his left boot. "Hay foot," he said. The sergeant then kicked the recruit's right boot. "Straw foot."

"Hey, Mister ... you in the wagon," the sergeant yelled. "What's your name?"

"Charles Allen Carmichael. But I ain't volunteerin'." Charles Allen turned the grays back toward the Longacher place. "Git," he said, snapping the reins. "No I ain't," Charles Allen said to himself as he drove away. "Not till Hell freezes over."

Late that night in the barracks as David lay in his new rope bunk, he pulled the diary Beth had given him from his haversack and made an entry: August 19, 1862. As he wrote, he realized that he'd been gone for less than twenty-four hours.

6

Reveille sounded at about sunrise. For the coming weeks, David and his fellow volunteers, many of them his boyhood friends and acquaintances, got familiar with Army life while stationed at Camp Piqua, Ohio. Though the camp was only six miles from David's home, it felt like hundreds. There was no time to dwell on these feelings but it seemed to David that it wasn't a physical distance that separated him from home, rather a mental, maybe even a spiritual distance. For one thing, there were the changes in routine. For another, the food was terrible, the accommodations smelled like fly paper and in their quarters there was barely room for a man to turn around. A great deal of time was occupied with trying to finish some duty that didn't make sense to him in the first place. And when one wasn't working up a lather doing something new, there was always card playing, mumblety-peg, or thumb twiddling.

Camp seemed to bring out the worst in people. There were recruits and enlistees who were good enough fellows back on the farm, or in town, but who started acting out the minute they got to camp. There was none of the civilizing influence of women. David knew a lot of the new soldiers were homesick. The war seemed to change these young men into beings that didn't think for themselves, but rather into ones who learned to take orders and regulations. Although David knew that this was necessary, to him it felt strange, sometimes even contrary to nature. He fixed on home as a place where things were serene and changeless. He held his images of the Longacher farm, the valley, his sisters, mother, and wife to keep himself going.

Within weeks, the 110th Ohio Volunteer Infantry unit would be transported by train to a camp near Washington, D.C. And by then, everything David had left—which was also everything that he was fighting for—had become, for him, fixed in the military way. There was a rule or regulation for almost everything.

Surely David thought, this standstill in camp, opening the door to his terrible longing for home, was only temporary. Soon, he thought, he would be fighting traitors, proving what he was made of. Soon, home would be not something he felt incomplete without, but something he was proud to protect.

What he didn't understand was that these preparations for battle were not only transforming men at arms, but they were also having the same effect on the country as a whole. That little world by the covered bridge was not a sealed, safe place anymore.

Late that afternoon Charles Allen returned from taking David to camp. Ma Longacher sensed there might be trouble. For all of his apparent outspokenness, Charles

Allen had always held something inside. He could get into arguments with David, and with his own brother, Frank Lee, but with Ma and with the other adults, even his own mother, Charles Allen was very private, almost reserved. He had a hard time showing feelings, but those who loved him and lived with him believed they could always tell what those feelings were.

Charles Allen spent the two days after David had left checking out equipment and tack, sharpening tools. He spent another two or three driving back and forth into town to pick up supplies and talking to Billy Perkins. A full week after David had been gone, Charles Allen announced that he had lined up two more hands who'd help at harvest: one of the neighbor boys and a friend of his, another of the Pennsylvania Dutch—Charles Allen couldn't remember either of the young boys' names.

"You're going to help them with their harvest as a swap?" Ma asked, by way of clarification.

"Somethin' like that," Charles Allen said.

"'Something' sounds a little vague."

"I got it worked out, Aint Eve."

Ma had a keen eye. She'd seen Charles Allen writing in his big loopy script on a piece of stationery. She also saw him bring a letter back from town a couple of days later. The letter fell out of his pocket at supper. The return address on the back was from Frank Lee.

Charles Allen's scheme came clear sooner, months sooner, than even Ma Longacher, for all her cautiousness, could have dreamed.

62

7

September 1862

Through the window that looked out of the kitchen, Ma watched as Charles Allen strode up from the cabin. It was mid-morning and on most days he'd be in the fields. Today he was headed toward the house and he was dressed for town.

He'd just come in the door, his hat not yet off his head, when he spoke out. "Aint Eve, I'm fixin' on leavin' in a few days."

"Where are you going?" she asked, as if she didn't know.

"When I took Cousin David up to Camp Piqua, I just knew that I should be joinin' up myself. David knew, too," Charles Allen said.

He was, at least in his own eyes, a grown man, but he was still a boy to her. And he was accountable. "You've made some promises, Charles Allen. No one compelled you to, nobody even believed that you owed us your promises. But you made them. And because you did, my David enlisted."

"I promised David I'd make sure you could get the harvest in, Aint Eve, that you wouldn't be abandoned here."

"Then what do you call going off this time of year? You made a deal with a man to help at harvest whose name you don't even know. And if you aren't here to pay him back ... Charles Allen, it'll be the ruin of us."

"I got it all figured out, Aint Eve. I have a solution maybe even better than we had before."

"Honey," she began as she kept fussing with her apron strings. "I wasn't sure that David could handle the farm, particularly the harvest, after his father was killed. David's learning it but he was trained as a boy to farm. Then David and you persuaded me that you could fill his shoes, though in fact, you don't know near as much about farming as he did when he was a young boy. But you being family, I thought that we could make things work. As it stands now, David's not a seasoned farmer. And now you're asking me to take, in place of you, some young hired boys whose names I don't even know?"

It was amazing to everyone in the family, Charles Allen remembered, that Ma Longacher had never become a schoolmarm. She seemed to be one of the few people he'd ever known who talked in complete sentences and had complete thoughts. She was a hard woman to argue with.

"Aint Eve, you're not givin' me a chance," he said.

"This isn't how you treat family, Charles Allen. You wouldn't treat your friends this way either."

"I won't let you down, Aint Eve. I promise. I promised my ma. No harm is going to come. You're family."

All of a sudden, she realized she'd been standing in the middle of the kitchen talking aloud. She hadn't urged Charles Allen to have a seat, hadn't offered him a glass of water. Had she been shouting at him? She thought the girls might have overheard, had they been around.

"I'll make us some coffee. You sit down. We'll have a piece of pound cake," Ma said.

Charles Allen pulled up a chair. "But it ain't how you think, Aint Eve ..."

She paused for a moment, not looking at Charles Allen but out the window where she could see the covered bridge. "I guess you must do what you must do. You're stubborn. All you boys are stubborn, just like your fathers. I don't know what I could say to make you stay." She sighed and went back to the stove. "We'll both have some coffee and then we can talk about your plans, make some lists." She pushed back a lock of hair that had fallen over her eyes. She started to pin it, but the loose hairpin fell to the floor. "Things around here are changing awful fast."

"Yes ma'am, but not the way you're sayin'. Everything's gonna turn out for the better."

As Ma thought, Charles Allen had been in touch with his brother Frank Lee. Frank Lee had returned home from Kentucky months earlier. Charles Allen wasn't sure if his little brother was homesick, disenchanted with the Rebel cause, or just plain tired of his girlfriend and her pa.

"They aren't quality people," he'd confided to David.

"Then that girlfriend ought to be well suited to him," David told him. "He's like you, Charles Allen, he's just got a strong attraction to lost causes."

But Charles Allen knew that though most of the boy left in him when their father was killed, Frank Lee had so many more qualities. Charles Allen spelled them out for his aunt. For one thing, Frank Lee was handy. There wasn't any tool or machine he couldn't repair or improve. He also had a way with animals. He could talk to them the way David could. Sometimes it seemed he knew what they were thinking. And though Frank Lee had a reputation for restlessness, Charles Allen knew that he was a hard worker when he wanted to be. He told Ma Longacher he had asked Frank Lee to come to the farm in his place. He'd written to his mother as well, and waited for the return letter that said she'd talked to Frank Lee, that he had promised to come and do what was expected of him.

"I got Frank Lee's word, Aint Eve. I got Ma's, too. They won't let you down."

"How will Frank Lee know what to do? Harvest is only a few weeks away."

"Billy Perkins is going to come up here the first two days. He's the one who helped you out a couple years back. He won't work himself, he's got a game leg. But he can organize. He'll give Frank Lee good advice. You take my word for it, you'll be a heck of a lot better off with Frank Lee replacin' David than with me."

"Frank Lee's Beth's age, Charles Allen," Ma sighed.

"He's just like our Beth, if you don't mind me sayin' so," Charles Allen said. "Frank Lee can be pretty convincin' when he takes a mind to. And anyway, no one's goin' to take advantage of you, Aint Eve. Heck, everybody in town and for miles around knew Uncle David and they know that our David's comin' back. They're gonna be real careful not to do anything slipshod."

"And the reason for doing this ... playing musical chairs with our lives, breaking hearts, breaking promises ... all that is happening so that you two boys can go out and put your lives at risk? It makes no sense," Ma said.

"It's got to be done," Charles Allen said.

"And you serving in opposing armies, the way your father and my husband did? Has there ever in the world been such madness? Don't any of us ever learn?"

"It'll all be back to normal in a few months, Aint Eve. Everybody knows that."

Ma wasn't crying now. At least not so that Charles Allen could see. "I have to ask you, Charles Allen, because they ask me, folks who know us at church and in town. They ask me and I ask myself, what happens when you're out there on a battlefield and you come up against a troop of enemy soldiers? What happens when kin come face to face? Then what?"

"The mathematical odds of that happenin' ..."

"I don't believe in chance, Charles Allen."

"We don't talk about it, Aint Eve. We just don't."

Ma picked up the coffee cups along with the empty cake plates and carried them to the sink. "If you were women you would."

"I wouldn't shoot him, if that's what you're askin'. He's my cousin."

"You know the girls and me are going to miss you, Charles Allen."

"I know, but ..."

"Will you at least wait for Frank Lee to get here?" Ma asked.

"I can't," Charles Allen said. "The longer I wait, the harder it will be for me to get down south."

"Honey, how could you get into Kentucky at all?" she asked.

"I've got a thought or two," Charles Allen said.

Ma Longacher hugged him. Charles Allen felt her wet cheeks press against his unshaven face.

"Don't you set out without telling me, Charles Allen," Ma said. "I know how you men are. Tomorrow, you go into town and wire your mother. Tell her we talked things over and that I welcome Frank Lee's arrival here."

Charles Allen nodded. "You explain everything to the girls for me ... and to David when he writes," he said. "Tell them I love them all dearly."

8

Charles Allen left the farm two days later, catching a ride with a businessman who was traveling down to Cincinnati. He had timed his departure perfectly. The *Masonic Gem* was in port at Cincinnati when he arrived. He took a room at a boarding house. But he couldn't sleep well and he walked the riverfront. He was back at the dock at dawn. He recognized the steamboat as he had seen her docked at his hometown of New Albany many times.

At first light, Charles Allen stood at the loading plank and cupped his hand to his mouth. "Helloo, Helloo," he called out.

He glanced at his pappy's gold pocket watch. Several minutes had passed. He tossed the carpetbag his Aunt Eve made him over his shoulder and started to board the vessel when a large hand grabbed him from behind.

"Where thar dickens y'all think yer goin'," a gruff voice said.

"I'd like to talk to the Captain, sir," Charles Allen said.

The boatswain lifted the wooden whistle that dangled from his neck, cupped his hand and moved his fingers over the whistle holes. Charles Allen watched the big man pucker his lips and puff his cheeks as a clear, shrill sound came out.

A stout man in a captain's cap and double-breasted navy blue coat came before Charles Allen with his hands behind his back. He eyed Charles Allen as he rubbed his salt and pepper beard.

"May I have a private word with y'all, sir?" Charles Allen asked. "I've been waitin' on the dock for some time." He checked the time, making sure he stood close enough that the Captain got a good look at his watch—an elegant timepiece with a gold back and gold chain from which hung a small charm.

The Captain sized up Charles Allen, turned, and gave the boatswain a wink, then put his arm around the young man's shoulder. "Follow me, son, I'll show you the sternwheeler."

The men walked to the stern of the riverboat.

"She's a dandy, ain't she, son?" the Captain said, straightening up his stance.

"She is, sir. You must be very proud of her. But I didn't come to see your steamboat, though I do appreciate y'all showin' me."

"Then state your business, boy."

"I'd like to be able to work my way to Louisville on the *Masonic Gem*, sir."

"The *Masonic Gem* has all the hands she needs." The Captain paused. "I wonder if I might see that watch again?"

Charles Allen unhooked the chain and handed it to the Captain. "It's not for sale, sir. Nor barter either."

"Of course not. I've an excellent watch myself. And the value of such things has plunged. There's a glut of watches, rings, jewelry of all kinds. People selling everything they have because of the cost of this war." The Captain glanced at the watch only long enough to verify his impression of the gold insignia that dangled from the chain.

"I guess I won't try to sell my ring then either, if it would bring such a low price." Charles Allen dug into his pocket and produced a Masonic ring, slipping it on his finger and displaying its square and compass.

"I come from the East," the Captain said. "I'm telling you this on the square." He stared at Charles Allen. Charles Allen figured that this was a Masonic Code, but he didn't know the answer.

"So, you're not a Mason?" the Captain asked.

Charles Allen remained silent.

"I thought not," the Captain said. "What are you doing with that ring?"

"My pappy *was* a Mason," Charles Allen blurted.

The Captain put his finger to his lips. "Shh ... Might be some unfriendly ears around, son."

The Captain walked Charles Allen over to the brass rail of the boat.

"Now, you say your pappy was a Mason?"

"Yes, sir," Charles Allen said. "He lived and died one, killed in the first Battle of Bull Run."

"North?" the Captain asked.

"South," Charles Allen answered.

The Captain stroked his beard. "I could work you as a deckhand for your passage and then drop you off at Mauckport," he said. "You *are* joining up, right?"

"Yes, sir," Charles Allen said. "But can't you let me off at Louisville?"

"Too risky," the Captain said. "Don't you worry, I'll give you the name of a good man, one that can be trusted."

The Captain grinned, then patted Charles Allen on his back.

"I can't thank y'all enough, sir," Charles Allen said.

"You report to the boatswain and tell him your Captain wants you to have some bellbottoms. We wouldn't want you falling overboard now would we, mate?"

Charles Allen swaggered toward the boat's fore as the boatswain blew his whistle three times. Several deck-hands scurried about, releasing the dock lines. So far so good, Charles Allen thought. To be on this boat, captained by a son of the South, made Charles Allen feel he was right where he belonged.

9

The livery boy guided his horse and wagon through the covered bridge. "There's the Longacher place," he pointed.

Frank Lee remained silent as he gave the rich valley a look-see. All the varieties of trees had just begun to flash their fall colors. Harvest time was just around the corner.

"Whoa." The livery boy pulled on the horse's reins. "Here we are."

Frank Lee reached into his pocket.

"No, no," the boy said. "Your brother already took good care of me."

"Did he now?" Frank Lee said, looking over at him.

"Yes, sir."

"He didn't explain to you why I was comin'?" Frank Lee asked.

"He paid me and told me not to charge you anything."

"Strange ..." Frank Lee said.

"People do stranger."

Frank Lee jumped down.

"Don't forget your traps," the livery boy said.

Frank Lee took his bandana and wiped the dust from his boots.

Frank Lee was the youngest child. And growing up with a powerful father and an older brother he'd had to become his own man. He ran away to Kentucky when the opportunity arose. And now opportunity brought him back. He walked up the hill, sizing up the Longacher place. There would be nothing to it, Frank Lee thought, taking charge of this farm.

He brushed the rest of the dust off his suit and combed his fingers through his hair. Setting down his gear under a tree in the front yard, he hoped that someone from the house might come to greet him. He looked over the fields, paying attention to the contours of the land and to the edges of the fields, which were where, of course, most trouble with varmints occurred. The edges were the place where profits could be most easily enhanced or, literally, eaten into. Beyond, he watched the livery boy emerge from the far side of the bridge, heading off to continue his route.

He heard a screen door slam. Frank Lee turned to see Ma Longacher coming down from the house.

"Francis Lee ... Frank Lee, let me take a look at you," Ma Longacher said as she hugged her sister's youngest boy. "My oh my, you're the spitting image of your pa. Oh Frank Lee, I'm so sorry for your loss."

"Thank you, ma'am, for sayin' so."

"Aunt Eve, call me Aunt Eve, honey," Ma Longacher said.

"Thank you, Aint Eve," Frank Lee said.

"How was your trip here?" she asked.

"Without incident," he smiled.

"I'm going to set you up in our house, Nephew."

A frown formed on Frank Lee's face. "Shucks, Ma and Charles Allen both told me I'd get to stay in that old log cabin," he pointed.

"You're like your brother, you like your privacy."

"I got nothin' to hide, Aint Eve. But I do like bein' on my own."

Ma Longacher laughed. "Then the log cabin it is, child. I'm so glad to have you with us. But I have to warn you, there's no time to get real comfortable. I hear they're ready to start harvesting at a neighbor's just a mile up the road. That means it's only a matter of days before we're ready."

"I know how to farm," Frank Lee said. "My girl's pa taught me."

"Billy Perkins is coming up tomorrow, I believe. Your brother had some conversations with him. You'll fill Billy in on some of your thoughts. Then you'll have to tell my girls and me everything," Ma said. "You'll be taking your meals with us in our home, won't you?"

"Yes, Aint Eve," Frank Lee said. "Ma said that next to her, you're the best cook in the world."

"You sweet boy, your ma's right. After all, her and your granny taught me all I know," Ma said. "Can I fix something special for you?"

"I sure do like custard pies," Frank Lee grinned.

"Bless your heart, then custard pie it'll be," Ma said. "Now come along with me and I'll show you how to work the fireplace flue in the log cabin."

A loud howl came from behind them. Frank Lee jumped back.

"Shush, Buck," Ma Longacher said. "Poor thing misses David."

The hound approached, the hair along his back raised. Frank Lee held out his hand. The dog sniffed it. Buck's tail began to wag. Frank Lee reached down and scratched the dog behind the ears. Buck twisted his head around and started licking the back of Frank Lee's hand.

"Everything's going to be all right, isn't it Frank Lee?" Ma asked.

"Don't give it a thought, ma'am. I'll take care of the harvest and you take care of those pies."

Part II

1

January 1864

By the beginning of 1864, nearly a year and a half after his enlistment, David had become one of the veterans.

The first day of the New Year was a Friday. The drinkers had depleted the entire store of spirits ringing in the New Year as though it were their last. And for many it would be.

David was one of the few without a headache. He laid on his bunk, staring at the rafters, then turned to look over at Jerry Dixon, one of his boyhood friends, who bunked next to him.

"When do you think we'll move out?" David asked.

David reached over and gave Jerry's bunk a shake.

Jerry rolled over and stopped snoring.

"May God grant that peace will be restored to our lands and we soldiers will soon be back home with our loved ones," David murmured.

David pulled out his most recent letter from Nel. No one he knew received such wonderful letters—beautiful to look at with their clear cursive handwriting, full of news about Ma and the girls; descriptions of nature, the successful harvest followed by the coming on of fall—yellowing leaves, pumpkins, and then the first frost. He turned his head and looked out the barracks window, then yawned. A thick snow was beginning to stick to the windowpane. He reread Nel's letter and dozed off. The letter dropped out of his hand onto his chest.

David bolted upright as he felt his bunk move. Private John Hart's brogan rested on the bunk's wooden frame. "Mornin' glory," Hart said.

The camp bugler blew, "Time to get up, time to get up in the mornin' ..." The early morning sun began to peek through the windows. David covered his ears, then his eyes, wondering if he'd ever get used to this routine.

Several new recruits had come in the previous afternoon. David noticed many of them looking around, trying to remember what the First Sergeant had told them.

"Where's the box of eatables you were going to bring back from furlough, John?" David asked as he rushed to get dressed.

"Lost them on the train ride back," John shrugged.

"You probably dropped them down your throat on

accident," someone mumbled.

Jerry was already dressed. He ran his hands through his long hair and beard. "Welcome back, John. What's new back home?" Jerry asked as they made their way out of the barracks.

Outside, the company began to fall into formation.

Sergeant Ullery read the roll call. David, Jerry, and several others heard their names called out for painting detail. Jerry was the only one who knew the ropes, so David decided just to follow his lead since one of the officers put Jerry in charge of the painting detail. It was easy duty. You got to remain indoors for long stretches of time.

"Fall out," Sergeant Ullery yelled.

"Come on, boys, let's paint these damn wagons," Jerry said. They moseyed in the direction of the barn where the wagons were kept.

"Hold on you two," Sergeant Shull called as he nodded over to David and Jerry. "The Lieutenant said he wants you two to go out on picket with me."

Shull had just returned from Camp Parole a few days earlier. Camp Parole accepted Union prisoners of war from the South to be exchanged for Confederate prisoners similarly confined in the North with the understanding they would be returned to their respective units and await reassignment to active duty, rather than desert.

"Can you believe this, boys? We're on picket near Poney Mountain where some Union deserters are buried," David said.

No one spoke up.

"You boys remember Poney Mountain, don't you?" David continued.

"How could we forget? It's only been a year at most," Jerry said. "Those poor sons-of-bitches shot down just like dogs, standing in front of their own pine boxes, hands and feet chained, ready to meet their Maker."

"They were deserters," Shull popped off.

"Just the same," David said as he remembered seeing tears running down their faces as the men begged for their lives. "They all had loved ones back home ... family and sweethearts." David shivered, rubbing his hands together. He slapped his cheeks as he reminisced, What a strange sight, or rather what a simple thing it is to see men sitting or standing out in the cold winter's wind witnessing a fellow soldier lose his life. "By a firing squad," David whispered under his breath.

"It sure cut down on the boys lightin' out," Jerry said.

"I heard rumor from the tattle line that the Generals wish they would have made an example of deserters from the get-go back in '61," Private Hart said.

"I wish I were never ordered to watch that firing squad detail," David said as he scanned the area where the graves were now grown over.

It seemed that while Generals and politicians planned the battles, the negotiations of treaties, and the trades or paroles of prisoners over cigars and brandy, the foot soldiers waited for mail from home, wrote letters to their loved ones, and stayed on alert, awaiting orders from the top brass.

The squad leader yelled out, "Mail call." The unit gathered around as he flipped letters to the men. "Longacher, Longacher, Longacher ... "

David smiled as he claimed his mail.

"Your folks sure do like to write," Jerry muttered.

"If you expect to get mail, you have to send mail," David said as he tucked the envelopes into his pocket. "How many people do you owe a letter to, Jerry?"

Jerry held up his thumb and forefinger, forming a zero.

"And how many owe you one?" David asked.

"Half dozen women," Jerry said.

"You should keep writing them anyway. It helps keep your sanity, whether you get one back or not," David said.

Jerry shook his head as he sulked away.

David decided he'd read the letters later when there was privacy. Nothing was as aggravating as having others stick their noses in your letters, snatch them away, read them aloud in silly voices, and then complain like Jerry.

David strolled toward the barn where the wagons were kept. He figured he'd have to cover for Jerry until he got over his hurt feelings. He was sure he could pull in at least another fellow soldier or two.

"Come on, Sam, we got some wagons to paint," David said.

"Where the hell is all them wagons coming from? We been painting them all week," Sam said.

"Don't fret," David said. "Old Abe takes care of his boys."

Sam was a regular down at the barn. He worked hard and was careful and fast. Not a great talker, but a good man to have join in on a detail.

David looked around in the maintenance shed. "I'll get the paint and brushes. You get the can of grease, Sam."

In warmer, dryer weather, the wagons would have been rolled out of the barn and several could have been painted at once. But in the cold, the paint dried slow, pitting the surface, and the damp could make the drying take days. So by way of compromise, the men opened the doors wide and left the wagons half in and half out, where they could be rolled under cover quickly or out of the structure if the sun shone. At night they rolled them back inside. This meant that only one or two wagons could be done at once so the others assigned to paint detail handled a lot of other chores such as shining hardware, mending straps, and greasing axles—or more than likely, making themselves scarce.

"I hear that tomorrow we start painting the new ballroom for General Carr," David said as they were finishing up. "Remember boys, if it stands still, paint it. If it moves, salute it."

The men laughed as they began wiping the paint off their hands. David pulled one of the letters from home out of his pocket.

"What's the news at home, David?" Sam asked.

David started to put the letter back in his pocket. Sam never made fun of his letters before, David thought. He smiled, handing Sam one of the envelopes from Ma Longacher. Sam took the letter from the envelope and glanced at it, then held it out toward David.

"I can't read, David."

"I'll read it for you," David said as he took the letter back. He unfolded it and began: "Dear David, It seems entirely inappropriate to be building and painting General Joseph Bradford Carr a ballroom to make so much merry while such a gloom is spread over our land."

Sam thought about this for a moment and then realized David was pulling his leg. "She didn't say that, for real, did she?"

David looked over at Sam and winked, "Well, no she didn't ... but she would have if she knew what was going on around here."

Sam elbowed David's shoulder and laughed. "I get it."

Then the two ducked into a corner of the barn and David read his mother's letter aloud.

2

The rumor about the ballroom turned out to be true. It was scheduled for sprucing up sometime in January. The news from the upper echelon was conveyed by Jerry who, in the always mysterious manner of military assignments, had secured a plum assignment as a butler in the

General's quarters. This was not a permanent position. Jerry was only called upon to appear for parties and special events. If he succeeded in his ambition to become the General's boy, then he might avoid field duty altogether. In the meantime, however, he got to hobnob with officers, sneak a bit of decent food, and pick up whatever gossip he could.

Jerry stepped inside and looked around the great ballroom. He straightened the fancy dress coat David lent him—the red braid Ma Longacher had sewn on was still clean and bright. He arrived for his assignment an hour early and at first stood at attention, attempting to look as though he belonged. Guests began arriving. Jerry observed another enlisted man, whom he did not know, enter the room with a tray of crystal filled with dark amber liquor and pass through the crowd. Still uncertain of what was expected of him, he nudged a man next to him whose own job seemed to be only to stand and look soldierly. "Where's the kitchen?" Jerry asked him.

The soldier pointed to the rear of the hall.

Jerry eased his way through the swinging doors. "You boys cooking up anything special?" he asked.

"Steak, ham, and chicken hors d'oeuvres, Jerry," one of the cooks said, standing over a skillet of caramelized onions. He hooked one with his spatula and held it out. Jerry tossed it around in his mouth and blew. It was the best thing he'd had to eat in weeks.

"Give me a tray with some glasses and brandy," Jerry

said. "I'm going to serve the brass hats."

"How'd you get out of cooking?" the cook asked.

Jerry tapped the side of his head with his finger.

"Usually they start you off in here before they send you out into the hall," another cook said.

"Now remember, they don't want you droolin' all over the guests when you serve them their vittles," another said, clicking his teeth.

Jerry winked at him and gulped down a glass of brandy, then clenched his teeth. He took a deep breath, put a shoulder to the swinging door, and reentered the ballroom. He approached a small gathering of officers. "Libations, sirs?"

The officers took the brandy-filled glasses off Jerry's tray without so much as looking away from their conversations.

A young girl tapped his shoulder. "*M'excuser, le garçon. Le champagne s'il vous plaît.*"

Jerry had never heard a girl talk French before, though he understood the word champagne. Was the rest a compliment or an insult? "How old are you?" he asked.

"Maybe you'd like to ask my father, the General," she said.

"You wait right here," Jerry said. "All I have is brandy. I'll be back with a chilled champagne for you."

Jerry ducked back into the kitchen.

"You again?" the cook said.

"There's a girl out there, looks like she's maybe fifteen, wants some champagne," Jerry said.

"Don't they all?"

"Can I give it to her?" Jerry asked.

"You recognize her?"

"She says she's the General's daughter," Jerry said.

"Oh *that* one," the cook laughed.

By now, the conversation caught the attention of several of the cooks. All had advice.

"Does that mean I give her champagne?" Jerry asked.

"You doggone well do whatever she wants."

"What if her daddy gets mad at me?" Jerry said.

"Is she the pretty one, or the one with the squint?"

Jerry shrugged. "I didn't notice no squint."

"That girl's pappy, to answer your question, ain't never said no to her as long as she's lived," the cook said.

"Well then, give me a *couple* bottles of champagne for the officer's ladies," Jerry said.

3

The next day, David walked into the barracks. Jerry sat on his bunk, sewing a button on his blouse. He'd washed it and hung it to dry after the previous night's party. He was hoping to get the same detail again.

"Where'd you get the 'housewife' from?" David asked, gesturing at the small sewing kit laid out on Jerry's bed.

"It's yours," Jerry said.

"Don't you ever ask?" David snapped.

Jerry handed the sewing kit back to David.

"Next time you need anything sewed, you can count

on ol' Jer."

David looked over his kit. "Thanks a lot, ol' Jer. You managed to get everything botched up." David dumped the contents out onto his own bunk and began rearranging it.

"You enjoy General Carr's ball last night?" David asked.

"If you call opening the door for all the brass hats and their ladies fun," Jerry said.

"Any of the boys get in?" David asked.

"Yep, a few boys were inside doing toady jobs, hanging ladies capes, and serving officers drinks ... that is when the brass weren't dancing or trading war stories with each other," Jerry said.

"You hear anything interesting?"

"A few tidbits," Jerry said. "Did you know that General Carr had so much trouble with the politicians, that there were a lot of times he was subordinate to his own brigade commanders? He also commanded an entire division of Darkies."

"That so?" David said. He wouldn't share this thought, but his impression was that the General was more of a bureaucrat than a military commander. "Talk is the Negroes are fierce fighters, so I guess that means Carr can be a good leader into battle, too." He looked over at Jerry. "Come on, that's *all* you got out of that shindig?"

Jerry pulled out a bottle of champagne and flashed it.

"Someday you'll get busted, buddy," David said.

Jerry shrugged.

"I'll tell you what, I wish that you would've brought back an explanation as to why the heck we're encamped," David said as he put the last of the needles back into the housewife. "When are we going to engage those Rebs? Because I feel pretty useless here."

"I don't think that the politicians see the war the same way us soldiers do," Jerry said. "They think war's like a horse race, or an election. Some kind of change of pace ... you know, some kind of distraction."

David stowed the sewing kit, stood up and stretched. They'd quit painting early that day on account of a sleet storm. It was a pleasure to have a few unexpected hours off duty, though David knew they'd be tacked onto tomorrow's workday.

"Private David Shoe has the smallpox," David said. "That pox sure don't pick and choose. I heard that Old Abe caught it himself."

"Abe got better though," Jerry said. "Let's you and I go on sick call and get vaccinated."

"I don't think I want to go inside any hospital," David said. "The boys there are dying two and three a day."

"Don't have to," Jerry said. "The sawbones are setting up a dispensary for shots, and quinine and sorts."

"Then count me in," David nodded.

A week later, Private Shoe died. David sent a memorial to Shoe's parents and, at the same time, mailed his 1863 diary back home. Another chapter of his military service had come and gone. When the weather improved, the fighting would pick up and David expected to be in the thick of it.

4

February 1864

The first deployment came a month sooner than anyone expected. David and the rest of the boys of Company G were given three days rations and ordered to be ready to march at nighttime on the 6th of February. Company G did not move, however the balance of the Corps did. David and a squad went on a reconnaissance on the Rapidan River.

Ohio isn't tornado country like some of the heartland. But as a boy, David had seen one pass just north of their farm. David recalled the strange feeling in the air, and how the stillness settled over the earth. The birds got quiet, listening for what, he didn't know. To David, reconnaissance duty felt much the same way. The war was but a few miles away, doing its damage. But here, it was only an oppressive rumor, and everything stood still for it.

The cannonading hung thick in the air just south of camp at Morton's Ford. The pungent smell of gunpowder carried for miles.

On the second day, the sounds of the battle came closer. Nathan Albright, a soldier who had fought in the Battle of Antietam nearly a year and a half earlier, had made it his job to teach David how to identify the different sounds of war from a distance. Albright knew them the way skilled hunters recognized the songs of different birds, or the scat of animals they were tracking.

While David crouched down over the campfire, Albright identified the caliber and size of various cannon explosions. Then there was a noticeable buzzing noise. David looked up from the fire to Albright. "Musket?" he asked.

"'At's right, a minié ball."

"Keep down, some musketry is coming our way," David called out to a small platoon nearby. He checked and rechecked his rifle to make sure that it was loaded. The others followed suit. He pressed the point of his bayonet into the ground, wiggling it, making sure it was secure. He fingered the arrowhead in his pocket. It broke in half. He tossed it down, then knocked on the wooden stock of his rifle.

Later that evening, the battle surged to the east. Then Lieutenant General Ewell's Confederate Army sent the Union Army west. It was David's good fortune that his company was one of the first to withdraw. The heat and pressure of war, the heaviness of the air continued. He noticed how the officers lined up their men and moved them out by the numbers. David paced up and down the breastworks. He knew that there weren't enough of them and not enough heavy artillery to stay and fight. But if that was so, why shouldn't they be moving out, why this delay? Looking around at the other men standing ready to march, David realized that they all had a scared look and remained quiet. If they hadn't been reigned in, kept in order, they'd have lit out.

They marched back to camp within a few days. Just long enough to unpack, collect mail and ammunition, both shot and shell. The troops were on edge, worried about what would happen next.

Shorty, a boy who David knew from back home, came back into camp a half day later. He'd had to cross skirt a battlefield just after the Rebels had turned east. At first he wouldn't talk to anybody. After mess, he came and sat near David.

"You can't imagine it," Shorty said.

"The battlefield?" David replied.

"Nothin' you ever heard or seen is like what it really is." Shorty hung his head.

"You see corpses and the like?" David asked.

"Corpses is the easy part. There's loads of wounded out there, some of 'em screamin', some just breathin' shallow, staring off at somethin' invisible," Shorty whispered.

"Rebs, huh?"

"Rebs, patriots ... all mixed together like there weren't no difference." Shorty's eyes widened.

"You mean they're our boys, too?" David asked.

Shorty leaned forward. "Lots of 'em. It ain't so clear to me that we're winnin' this war."

"How'd you get them out?" David asked.

"Ours? We didn't, David. That's the whole thing. The wounded were callin' out for their loved ones and we couldn't do nothin'. There was too many of 'em and dead weight is hard to carry. We'd have busted 'em up worse." Shorty stared at the ground.

"So you left them?"

"They said there were medics comin', David, but I never saw any."

"A lot of them just staring into space? Must be terrible to have to wait like that for help to come," David said.

"I think a lot of 'em don't expect help. I think if I was one of those boys, I'd be thinkin' that my death had already come and gone and I'd been cast straight into oblivion without even a goodbye."

David tossed and turned, waking when he heard Shorty sobbing. But for all of the horrible pictures his mind conjured, everyday life, as it always does, had a way of washing them away.

5

It was unseasonably warm the next day. David sat outside back at camp, eating a pie.

Jerry, who had become the person who made it his business to know everyone else's business, came up as though he knew what he was going to find. "Hey, where'd you get the pie?" He licked his chops.

"Hayworth and Jones from Miami County came here on a visit and brought me a letter from Nel," David said.

"They still on furlough? Where was I?" Jerry asked.

"Sacked out back at the barracks while I was painting

wagons," David said. "The good sergeant sent them over to see me ... that is, after they gave him a pie."

Jerry held out his hand. David ate the last piece of one of the two pies that were left and was about to start on the remaining pie. "Here, take it," David said.

David wiped his hands and opened the Valentine from Nel. Jerry glanced over David's shoulder, dropping pie crumbs on him. David stood up, closed the card, and tucked it in his haversack next to his diary. He looked at the dry paint on his hands. It seemed as though the wagonettes, buckboards, and railroad cars in need of painting were endless. David held up his hands.

"They look like palettes," Jerry said.

"That's why I don't get any soft jobs pouring champagne for the General's daughter," David said.

"They sent 'em all back to boarding school," Jerry said.

"I'll see if I can get you back on artist detail if you want," David said.

Jerry's mouth opened wide into a full yawn as he tossed the empty pie box aside. "Is there enough work?"

"They think so. The brass won't be happy until we've painted every car on the railroad," David said.

"When did you start painting railroad cars?" Jerry asked.

"Day before yesterday. You been hibernating or something, Jerry? Pretty soon they won't even be able to move those cars though. They say there's Rebs blowing up tracks everywhere."

"If I was you, David, I'd start up at the tender car, then I'd start painting my way backward towards the caboose and not stop until I got all the way home."

6

The line of battle receded. For the next two weeks, David painted in double-time. The men worked rain or snow. The days dragged. David's moods swung from lonesome to very lonesome. He wrote letters regularly to family and friends back home. Some of the boys joshed him that he got more mail than the total of boys in Company G. Keeping in touch kept David's mind busy.

In the evenings, David and his buddies played checkers for hours upon hours. David even taught some how to play chess, a game he'd learned from his father. He imagined David Sr., in those earliest days of the war, teaching other soldiers to play, as he was now doing himself. New recruits began reporting to camp, bringing with them the latest stories and fresh conversation from home.

After that brief approach of war, things returned to the humdrum. It took Shorty a couple of weeks to get a decent night's sleep, but in time he was like his old self. What he'd made so vivid, the carnage and chaos of battle, had made them feel close to what they had come here to do—defend their country, prove their skills as riflemen and, well, their manliness. What David had proven to himself thus far was that he could paint wagons and railroad cars.

What became memorable were not the acts of bravery, but the accidents, the embarrassments, the little pranks. One morning, David headed over to the railroad station for painting detail. He spotted a canteen on the ground. It was one of the officer's and it was fancy like their uniforms. David opened it and gave it a whiff—bourbon. He pulled an empty quinine bottle from his haversack and filled it to the brim with the liquor.

That evening after taps, he passed the canteen over to Jerry.

"You and some of the boys who imbibe share this," David whispered.

Jerry sniffed the contents and took a long pull, then nudged the boy next to him. Jerry put his fingers to his lips, whispering, "When it's empty, give it back to me. I'll ditch it before roll call." Jerry's wide grin displayed his broken front tooth.

The next day, General French and his staff reviewed the 3rd Division. Some of the local ladies were present. The men stood tall in a stately formation. Every once in a while, one of the women would smile, batting her eyes at one or another of the soldiers.

Afterwards, David was bent over a campfire cooking up some stew when Jerry approached him.

"General French ain't long for losing his command," Jerry said.

David continued to stir the stew.

"Rumor has it he fights battles too slow," Jerry said.

Another man, who'd set a small pan on a stone next to the fire, heard the story. "Havin' all those ladies with you would slow up anybody," he added.

"You got a wife, soldier?" Jerry asked.

"Hell no, I outrun 'em all."

"I hear we're going on a reconnaissance early tomorrow," David said.

"Where to?" Jerry asked.

"Toward Madison Court House," David said.

"Who told you that?" Jerry asked.

"Scuttlebutt," David said.

7

Reconnaissance was over after a few days. It seemed clear from rumors circulating in camp, from the occasional newspaper somebody got in the mail, and from letters, that the battle line was moving away from them. Certainly they would pursue the enemy in order to engage them.

Company G received orders to hold themselves in readiness to march at a moment's notice. On Sunday, David took a stroll toward the town of Culpepper and spent part of the day reading his Bible. Since that last time he'd gone to church with Charles Allen he'd decided to read through the whole Book of Psalms. He'd gotten buried now in the long 119th: "Let, I pray thee, thy merciful kindness be for my comfort, according to thy word unto thy servant. / Let thy tender mercies come unto me, that I may live: for thy law is my delight." David thought about dying and not being, then decided to turn over his thoughts on ever lasting life to the Lord.

The orders from headquarters seemed to change day by day.

Jerry covered the camp news like a reporter. "Captain Moore of Company E and Private Reiber died last night at the hospital," he told David.

"Smallpox?" David asked.

"Don't know about the Captain, but the pox got Reiber," Jerry said. "I'm sick and tired of picket. All it ever does is rain or snow. It'll be the death of me, probably pneumonia."

"I'll relay your complaints to the General when I have cocktails with him," David said.

"Smart aleck," Jerry said, kicking at David's bunk. "I heard the smallpox got Furnas's wife back home, too."

"You have any pleasantries?" David asked.

"I'm still alive."

"The pay master came last night," David said.

"Everybody knows that. You get a decent payout?" Jerry asked.

"What I had coming," David said.

"Maybe you'd like to buy your old buddy a shot or two?"

"I'm sending the money home."

"So that's why you mentioned about going over to the railroad depot," Jerry said.

"How'd you know about Isaac Furnas's wife?"

"I keep up," Jerry said.

"You're not alone," David said.

"Who else is there?" Jerry challenged.

"I got other sources."

"Like?"

"Well, there's a couple of guys working on the railroad cars, they got access to telegraph. Then there's Shorty, who's got a job in the mail room ..."

"He steams open letters?" Jerry asked.

"Shorty wouldn't do that. But he does know who's getting packages," David said.

"If your *sources* are part of the tattler's line, why don't they tell us when we break camp and join this war?" Jerry said.

"I asked an officer. He says they don't use the telegraph. Too easy for us enlisted men to find out stuff we're not to know. Instead, the brass sends couriers."

"Their couriers are enlisted men, fool," Jerry said. "I bet those generals have a hard time getting used to the telegraph. Probably too old to catch on to such a revolutionary thing."

"Old ways die hard, you know," David said. "Take battle plans, we'll still be the last to hear."

"Maybe not. I got a friend, one of the General's head toadies, he collects all of the General's papers. He's supposed to toss 'em, but he saves them for me," Jerry boasted.

"Waste paper is old news," David laughed.

"Not always," Jerry said. "Now, what about that drink?"

"Got to express some money home for Nel. I've been

married five years today. Oh what a change in five years." David laid down the Bible and made an entry in his diary: March 8, 1864.

"So, you buying Nel some sort of doodad?" Jerry asked.

"Nope, a one year's subscription to *Harper's Weekly*," David said.

"How thoughtful, maybe she'll send them back to you once she's finished with them," Jerry said.

David grinned. "When are you going to get hitched, buddy?"

"Can't think that far ahead," Jerry said, rubbing his scraggly beard. "I'll probably end up a casualty ... if not in battle, then probably by some deadly disease."

"Like pneumonia, curmudgeon?" David said as he got up off his bunk and moved over to Jerry's.

Jerry scratched his head as David placed his arm around his comrade's shoulder.

"Why don't you come with me and join the Christian Union?" David asked.

Jerry frowned and gave a thumbs-down. David patted Jerry on the back and stood up.

"We better get cracking, Colonel Keifer is reviewing the brigade in an hour," David said.

"He's never on time," Jerry said.

"It's a present arms inspection," David said.

"That means you're going to show off your Spencer repeater, right?" Jerry said.

"Bull's-eye," David laughed.

It was David, though, who scored the scoop of the week. One of the painters up at the railroad station had heard a message come in by telegraph.

"Grant was at Meade's headquarters. Grant's now the General-in-command. The rumor was he's passing by," he told David. There was also something reported about a photographer being on the scene, the eavesdropper said. It must be a big to do.

March 1864

David began to notice that every time Jerry found him reading the Bible, he made some kind of wise remark. He'd ask David if he was bucking for promotion to heaven. Or had he committed some major sin. Or was he studying how to walk on water—all silly little quips. David took it to mean that Jerry had begun to take an interest in religion. And David had been brought up to believe that a little evangelizing never hurt anybody.

"So why don't you join me Sunday? Our new Chaplain, Reverend Booker, is preaching and then speaking about the U.S. Christian Commission," David said.

"Ain't Booker your minister from back home?" Jerry asked.

"The Reverend Captain Booker to you," David said.

"Rumors are flying around 'bout us marching off to battle," Jerry said. "That's probably why the Chapel is getting crowded at prayer meetings."

"You could do worse things with your time," David said.

"I read Uncle Abe ordered another draft of 200,000 men," Jerry said. "I wish he'd send my replacement here."

"Bully for old Abe," David said. "I heard that Jones of the 1st Ohio Cavalry married Lib Jay and Hart of the 13th hitched a Miss Moore."

"Bully for them," Jerry said.

"You ought get a move on, Jerry, before all the best girls are taken."

8

As the crocus began to spring from the ground, the sounds of battle grew closer. The cannonading picked up south of camp. Every so often musket balls crossed the river. Painting detail was often interrupted. Troops were put on alert. Sometimes they were confined to quarters before sunset.

"Those Rebs ever sleep?" Jerry asked as he paced back and forth.

David was busy with his pen, filling out a form. Jerry shook his bunk. "You deaf?"

David's pen slipped. "Can't you see I'm busy?"

"Busy doing nothing," Jerry said.

"I'm putting in for a furlough, Mister Buttinski," David said.

"Good luck with that," Jerry said. "Come to think of it, it is almost April Fool's Day." Jerry never considered putting in for a furlough. "Besides, they won't let you go now," he continued. "We're practically surrounded by Rebs."

"I think it might be the right time. They're not going to deploy us for at least a month. They're saving us for a big offensive," David said.

"Says who?"

"I told you, Jerry, I made friends with the guy who can hear the telegraph key."

"He's probably lyin'," Jerry said.

"They're more likely to give furloughs now, so that men'll go home and get their affairs in order and be battle ready upon their return to camp ..."

"To get killed," Jerry muttered.

"You've sure got a funny way of thinking," David said. "Anyway, I got stuff at home that has to be taken care of."

With no prospect for immediate action, there was less to do. It was bad for morale. To David and the boys, there was nothing worse than idle time. Painting and cleaning detail at least kept the boys busy grumbling. Everything in the Army was hurry-scurry. In the end, any kind of change was better than waiting to be killed.

Later on, David found Jerry, walked up and waved his furlough papers in his face.

"Hope you don't miss the battle," Jerry scowled.

David began doing handsprings around Jerry, then grabbed three paintbrushes and juggled them. White paint splattered. Several droplets hit Jerry in the face.

"What the hell ..." Jerry felt his nose.

David pointed at him. "You should see yourself," he laughed. "You look just like a clown, buddy."

Jerry flipped his paintbrush at David. "Now you do, too," Jerry said.

9

On Sunday, David left camp early. He boarded a train to Alexandria, then a boat to Washington. Homeward bound. To be away from the rattle of drums, the blasting of cannons, the constant braying of mules, and the smell of paint was a welcome relief. Even if it was only temporary.

His mind and spirit seemed unable to keep up with his body. The trip home was a whirlwind during which David needed to undo all the old habits of camp life—the constant alertness, the jockeying for position in line, the smart-aleck remarks about death and disaster made to keep fear at bay. When he jumped off the wagon that had carried him the last leg of his journey he wasn't yet prepared to be in his hometown. This return to normalcy hadn't sunk in. So he didn't visit the stores and offices he knew so well. And he didn't arrange to get a lift out to the family property. Instead, he walked, taking in all the sounds and smells, rediscovering the curves and byways of this part of Ohio he knew so well and loved so much. Rounding a curve in the road and coming upon a field that belonged to his family, David experienced a moment of giddiness being back home again, a moment in which he could now rediscover all of this beauty.

David strode through the old covered bridge that crossed the creek leading to his home. He stopped to climb up one of the braces, rubbing his finger over the carved heart, high up in the rafters: *Davy + Nel*. Then he heard the barking. Stepping out of the bridge, he turned toward the house and from that direction a storm of sheer commotion hurtled down the road toward him. Buck knocked him down. He'd barely gotten to his feet when he came up against the second front—the Longacher women. He put his arms around Ma and Nel as Beth and Hannah jumped up and down.

"Now stop that crying, girls, it just might be contagious," David said.

"They're happy tears, son," Ma smiled.

For the time being, David was no longer lonesome. The women pampered him and he stuffed his belly with chicken pies, usually polishing off his meals with custard pies and ginger snaps. He overslept, making up for months of early pickets. And when he woke, Nel was next to him. Really there, as she had been only in dreams those long months away.

April 1864

David awoke as the scent of fresh coffee drifted into his room. He tossed on his robe, splashed water on his face from the washbasin, and walked into the smells of the kitchen.

"Hungry, David?" Ma Longacher asked.

David smacked his lips and gave his Ma a peck on her cheek. She slid a chair out at the head of the table. The aroma and sound of bacon frying was one of the many things David missed.

"Where is everyone?" David asked.

Ma looked at him.

"Still asleep?"

"No," Ma said. "Nel is out gathering eggs, Hannah's milking the cows, and Beth is ..."

"And Beth is right here, big brother," she said, throwing her arms around David's neck, smothering him with kisses. "I was wondering when you'd get up. I want you to show me how to shoe them stubborn mules."

"Let him have his breakfast first," Ma said, patting Beth's backside.

"Okay, I'll be outside," Beth said as she sat down to pull on her brogans.

"What does Auntie tell you about Charles Allen?" David asked.

"She says he enjoys soldiering," Ma said, setting a cup of coffee in front of David.

David looked up at his Ma. "Funny we joined up at the same time."

"Except he joined the wrong side," Beth said as the screen door slammed behind her and she clomped across the porch. Same Beth, David thought.

David raised his head up only once as he wiped his plate with his last piece of toast. "We got to talk, Ma."

"I know, David."

"I put on my furlough application that I had pressing family business to take care of," he said as he reached for his coffee cup. "What did Frank Lee tell you when he left?"

"That he promised to come back."

"Did he say when?"

"In time for sowing."

"Did he say he'd be in touch? Or where he was going?"

"No," Ma said.

"Strange ..."

"He's like that, David. He keeps to himself."

"So he's been gone now for ...?" David began.

"Almost five months," she said.

"I wrote asking all four of you what happened with Frank Lee. No one answered."

"We didn't want you to worry. He'll show up," Ma said.

"What about the crops?"

"Frank Lee told me not to worry about the crops. Your aunt reminded him again that he's to help us until you're home for good."

"How can you be so trusting, Ma?"

"Intuition, David. Frank Lee won't let us down."

"So what do you know about Charles Allen?" David asked.

"Frank Lee hardly ever heard from him while he was here. I know my sister does," Ma said.

David sighed and shook his head. "Why *would* Frank Lee come back? He's independent. He wants to be a Rebel like his brother. Why wouldn't he just stay away? He might just drift south, the way Charles Allen did, not bothering to write."

"David, I hope you won't ever talk to Frank Lee about his affairs the way you're talking now."

"Ma, I'd have to find Frank Lee first before I could do that. But you're right. I'm sorry. I shouldn't be jumping to conclusions about Cousin Frank. I guess I just don't get it," David said. "His ma must know something."

"No, David, she's always had her worries with that boy. He's always been an independent rascal and they are too much alike. Frank Lee was closer to his pa. But now ..."

David sighed again. There was too much mystery to cope with here. Too many problems to be solved. And not nearly enough time. Why was it that the people in your own family, the people you'd expect to be most attuned to, were so often the ones you couldn't make any sense of at all? Going over this and that with Ma, David didn't make it out of the house the whole day.

The next morning Beth was standing in the entrance of the barn, tapping her foot. "Just what do you think you're doing?" she bawled out.

"I'm re-shoeing the mules, if it's any of your business," Frank Lee said. His bag set by the door. He hadn't even gone to the cabin, let alone the main house. He hadn't announced himself. He'd just walked up the road, gone to the barn, and started working.

"Well go find something else to do," Beth said. "Slop the pigs, or better yet, clean their pen."

"Why, you little brat!"

Beth stuck her tongue out at him. Frank Lee leaped to tackle her. Beth stepped aside, then swung and missed him with a roundhouse. She kicked him in his shin. He grabbed her by her hair and slung her over his knee and began paddling her. Beth bit his leg.

"Ow, ow," Frank Lee yelled, pushing her off.

David ran into the barn. "What's going on?" he demanded.

"Nothing," Beth said, smoothing her hair back.

"Who's this?" David pointed.

"This is our long lost cousin, Frank Lee," Beth said.

David squinted in the dim light. "Frank Lee? Good Lord, you've grown."

Frank Lee extended his hand. Instead, David caught him in a bear hug. Frank's body stiffened.

"I recollect the last time I saw you, I picked you up with one hand and tossed you in the creek," David said.

"I remember," Frank Lee replied.

"Looks like you put some meat on your bones."

"Aint Eve saw to that."

"Well, I'm glad you're back." Remembering something, David turned to Beth. "And by the way, you never wrote me a darned thing about Frank Lee's comings and goings."

"He came up from New Albany to replace Charles Allen, but he's a crappy replacement if you ask me."

"What kind of talk is that, Beth?" David said.

"Everyday talk for her," Frank Lee said, glaring her down.

Beth walked over to David and lowered her head. She took a hold of David's hand. "Are you going to tell on me?" she said.

"I ought to," David said.

"I'm sorry, Cousin Frank," Beth said.

Frank Lee gave her a squeeze on her neck.

David ruffled Frank Lee's hair. "We're glad to have you here, Cousin Frank. Real glad."

Beth nodded.

"Have you heard from Charles Allen?" David asked.

"Not a word," Frank Lee said, kicking up some dirt.

"Charles Allen told me that you were considering joining the Army," David said.

"Not anymore."

"Good, because we have a lot to do on the farm. Right, Beth?" David said. "I'll say one thing, Cousin Charles was a good worker and I'd be lying if I said we didn't become good pals, too."

. Frank Lee shrugged his shoulders while he continued kicking at a clump of dirt.

"Come on, Frank Lee, I'll help you with your chores." Beth put her thumb and forefinger in her mouth and whistled. "Here Buck," she called. Buck scampered inside the barn.

David turned, seeing Nel out on the porch waving at him. "Nel wants me back up at the house," David said as he walked away with Buck tagging behind him.

Ma came out the door as David approached. "Hey Ma, talk about a coincidence ..."

"I saw," she said.

10

David had precious little time left. He left Frank Lee and Beth to continue the chores as he sat down on the edge of the porch in the sun. From behind him came footsteps. Nel crouched down beside him. "What a beautiful spring day," David said. "Look at all the buds on the trees. You can even see some new sprouts of green breaking through the ground."

"We haven't had much time to be alone since you've been home," Nel said.

"I guess I just worry about too much," David said.

Nel embraced his arm. "And I'm just being selfish. Take me for a walk, David. I packed us a picnic."

The two set out toward a field beyond the covered bridge.

"Look, there's a mother bluebird feeding her babies," David said.

"And there comes papa bird," Nel said.

"Someone once told me they take turns at building their nest," David said.

They walked arm in arm taking in the fresh air.

"David, I'd like to have a baby," Nel blurted out.

"Now's not the time to start a family, Nel."

"You don't want to talk about the war, and now you don't want to talk about having a baby," Nel said. "Just what do you want to talk about, David?"

"Okay Nel, you win. When I get back to camp, our company will be marching into enemy territory. Right now I have enough to worry about ... you, Ma, the girls, the harvest ..." David paused. "... And then there's always something that needs attended to."

"Frank Lee is here now," Nel said.

"So was Charles Allen," David said. "Now he's gone to God knows where. What if I get killed or maimed? There's lots of boys without limbs, and plenty more crippled up."

Tears swelled in Nel's eyes. David wrapped his arm around her waist and gave her a squeeze.

"Oh sweetheart, this war's not going to last forever," he said.

"Ain't it? It's been going on for three years now. And when it started, everyone said it would only last until harvest time. Only a hundred days the big-wigs in the White House bragged." Nel raised her handkerchief to her eyes.

"You act as if I don't want a child, Nel."

"It's not that, dear. But if I did lose you, at least I would have your baby," Nel said.

"Okay, now you did it. Knock on wood." David took her hand and they stopped in front of a big oak tree. "Knock," he said. "That'll undo the hoodoo you just put on me."

"Oh silly, you're just like the rest of your family," Nel said. "Superstitious." She tapped on the tree.

"There's a meadow," David pointed. "The sun's overhead. I'd say it's almost dinnertime. Can't you hear my stomach growling?"

"No," Nel said. "And don't you try to sidestep our conversation."

Nel took the picnic basket from David as he spread the blanket out at the base of a tree. She picked him out a chicken leg.

"This is just the way I like my chicken," David said. "Not too hot, and not too cold. Just right."

"You sound like one of *The Three Bears*," she laughed.

After they'd eaten, David lay back and watched a flock of geese fly over. His eyelids became heavy. He began to snore.

He had no idea how long he'd been asleep when he felt Nel nudge him. "Ma's going to think we got lost," she said.

David rubbed his eyes.

"Come on, David, everything's packed and ready to go."

"Not yet, honey." David pulled her down beside him and pressed next to her. He took her in his arms and kissed her. He paused for a moment, looking into her eyes. "You're so beautiful, Nel."

She closed her eyes and parted her lips. David kissed her again. With a sultry glance, she reached back and untied her hair.

"This war is making an old man out of me, dear, but you still look like the girl I made love to down by the old covered bridge."

The shadows began to lengthen. Nel sat up. "David, it's getting dark out."

David got to his feet and grabbed Nel by her hands. "Upsy-daisy, dear," he said. "I wonder what Ma has for supper."

"David, you just ate," Nel said as she lowered her head to retie her hair. She stood upright and smoothed out her dress. "Is food all you can think of?"

David kissed her head. "Have you thought of a name for our baby?" he asked.

The fifteen-day furlough flew by. Tears flowed and the hugs lingered as David packed. Had there been a photographer present, he could have shown that this departure was much like the first.

As his family stood waving, David looked back. Their images faded. He held up his hand as if to make a final wave. The difference, this time, was that they knew David *could* leave and still come back. *Would* he return again once he'd actually entered battle? None of them allowed the question to enter their minds.

David walked to the train station, thinking about Nel and their being alone. His daydream was cut short by the blast of the train's whistle. He took in a deep breath. "May God grant I may live to return," he whispered as he exhaled. Oh, he knew there'd be at least another trip. What he couldn't know was whether that last journey would be made sitting up, looking out the window, or horizontal, in a pine box.

11

David arrived back at dark, awakening from his nap with a jolt. He jumped down to the platform. From the next car up came another soldier, blinking and yawning. David didn't think he'd ever seen the man. One of the trainmen stood on a step, holding a kerosene lantern in his hand. He looked first up, then down the track to make sure there was nobody too near the train. When he saw that all was clear, he raised and lowered his lantern twice, a highball to the engineer for the train to proceed at full speed. Then there was a burst of steam and with that the great metal wheels began to clack along the rails.

His haversack slung over his shoulder, David headed down the path toward the barracks. He didn't exchange a word with the other soldier, who'd split off to the left halfway to the camp. David never saw him again. David thought about him later and wondered if the other soldier had lived. Or had the soldier been a ghost? Did ghosts ride trains? David made his way inside the barracks and plopped down, still dressed in his civvies, so as not to wake the others. He began reminiscing.

It was daylight when David got up, took his uniform from his knapsack, put it on, and headed outside. He came upon a few of the boys on picket. One spoke up. "The Colonel's been looking for you ... Good luck."

A little surprised, David headed for the C.O.'s building. A sentry was posted outside. Once cleared, David walked up to the Colonel's desk. He popped a salute.

"Longacher, David. Reporting for duty, sir."

"Weren't you due back yesterday, soldier?"

"No, sir," David said. "I was given fifteen days. There was trouble, sir. My family's ..."

"Return to your company, Corporal Longacher. There'll be a review tomorrow morning." The Colonel half-saluted. "You're dismissed, Corporal."

The next morning, a heavy downpour postponed the company's review. David lay on his bunk reading his Bible when the boys came in from picket.

"You sleep tight, buddy?" Jerry asked.

"I got back to the barracks and sacked out when you were out on picket," David said. Someone had also told him that Jerry had drawn duty for another of the General's frequent parties. "I should've known you was the fool that loosened my bunk ropes."

Jerry grabbed David's hand and gave it an extra hard grip. "Good trick, huh? Me and the boys missed you. Right, boys?"

"Bully for David," they all yelled as they grabbed David out of his bed and began tossing him around.

"At ease, boys," David blurted out, smoothing his hair back. Kind of childish, David thought. A bunch of grown men, fighting men at that, roughhousing like boys. Maybe it was because they missed family so much that they tried to recreate family here, of all places, in a barracks not ready for inspection. Much as they tried to transform themselves, and each other, into something familiar here at the edge of a horrible war, it was more likely they all doubted that they could ever go home again and be the same.

The sun rose like a balloon that had just floated free of the horizon. It was going to be a beautiful day. Few were awake to see it. Some were pulling on pants over underwear but they were like sleepwalkers, their eyes barely open.

So Jerry's cheerful wake-up voice was particularly grating. "Attention," Jerry shouted. "Sergeant Deeter promoted to first Lieutenant, Sergeant Martin and Private Locke promoted to second Lieutenants and Corporal Longacher promoted to Sergeant, along with yours truly." Jerry took a bow. "We're all proud of you soldier boys," he continued.

"Oh for God's sake, Jerry. Put a cork in it."

"You wouldn't be such a wailer, Duff," said a voice from across the room, "If you'd put a cork in that jug you were makin' love to last night."

"Man's gotta drink, if he's as sensitive as I am," Duff said. "Can't tolerate ignorant farm boys like you without a little snort."

"Liquid spiritual nourishment," another added.

"Shut your yaps," someone else called out.

"Where the hell you gettin' all this current information from, Jerry?" one of the boys asked.

"I'll tell you," another answered. "When Jerry goes on cleaning detail at headquarters, he not only sweeps the floors, he also makes sure he dusts *inside* the file cabinet."

Jerry was getting better all the time at gathering information, David thought. For all the guff he got from disbelievers, more often than not, Jerry got most of the story right.

David hoped he was right this time. The sound of the phrase, "Sergeant Longacher" had a nice ring to it, not to mention the pay raise. He knew it would make Nel and the rest proud.

The next day, Sergeant Deeter of Company G went to the hospital with another of Company G's boys returning from the hospital. Though being admitted was almost a daily occurrence for one or another of the soldiers, being released intact was rare.

General Grant was to review the 6th Corps near Brandy Station, Culpepper County, Virginia. This was to be an important event; Grant had been appointed head of all Union forces a month earlier. David and his company marched four miles to the place of review—a tiresome tramp. Could Grant's visit mean they were about to enter combat? The general was a battle seasoned commander. He'd been in charge of the Army of the West for a few years. By contrast, the Army of the Potomac had had a different old man often—David had memorized them: General McClellan; General Burnside with his unusual whiskers and shaved chin. Then there was Hooker and Meade. When Grant was appointed Commander in Chief,

Sherman had succeeded him. Both Grant and Sherman were Ohioans originally, David liked that. There were a lot of stories that might have made many people doubt Grant's character, how he couldn't take care of a farm or run a business, about his drinking, and yet he persisted. He won battles. And that tenacity, David thought, that's maybe what Old Abe liked best about him.

Old Abe was pretty tenacious himself. He was fighting hard to keep the Union together, giving speeches that read well. David saw copies of them in the newspapers. He was determined to set things right, policies that had been wrong for a long time. He invited Negroes to conversations in the White House and issued the proclamation making them free. David was proud to be a part of the whole enterprise. And he thought he was a lucky man to be sporting his new sergeant's stripes when Grant reviewed the troops.

Jerry was looking exhausted when they returned. "I'm going to have to rest, buddy," Jerry said. "I got the flux pretty bad."

"Don't be too long," David said. "Fifteen or twenty minutes at the most is all I'll be able to cover you for."

When Jerry returned to the ranks, talk was that one of the Regiment's Lieutenants resigned his commission and was heading home. Many of the regulars felt the Lieutenant got the willies from too much hand-to-hand combat and sniping. The boys knew a big battle was near. Generals Meade, Sedgwick, Tyler, and a number of their staff officers had gathered at Brandy Station.

With all the events that began taking place, such as the knapsack drill, target practice, and new recruits arriving, mostly Hundred Days men, Jerry wasn't missed. He arrived back an hour late, but as usual, David covered for him. David made an entry in his diary:

> All is quiet now but it only is the calm before the storm. Mails from here North reported to be suspended, hope it is not so. The boys throughout the camp have the willies.

New recruits always dreaded the march into battle. The veterans knew all too well the sights and sounds of the wounded and the dying. Everyone hoped and prayed they wouldn't be among the unlucky ones.

David and Jerry attended a preaching in the afternoon.

After the Sunday sermon, David took a walk and sat down beneath a tree and began reading his Bible. He'd nodded off and the Bible dropped down on his lap. He headed back to the barracks.

The following Wednesday, David helped with payroll, wrote Nel a letter, and later in the evening went to a prayer meeting. The next day, the company Chaplain, Captain Booker, resigned.

"Why'd the preacher resign?" Jerry asked. He'd attended a few prayer meetings and found the Chaplain pleasant and a stand-up preacher, but now Jerry was curious.

"I don't know," David said. "I figured you'd know. At

last night's meeting he asked us to pray for his wife. He says she's sick."

"You believe that?" Jerry asked. "Maybe he's having problems back home."

"You always look for the worst," David said. "I wouldn't want to accuse the good reverend of a falsehood. But it kind of seemed like he was covering something up. I bet he figured it might worry us if we knew what was really happening."

"Maybe they asked him to go to the front," Jerry said. "But why would he want to keep that secret?"

"Let me ask you something, Jerry. How much of what goes on around here do *you* really understand?"

Jerry thought about calculating a high number and then, realizing that David knew him all too well, revised downward towards the truth. "I'd say I got a pretty good handle on maybe thirty, thirty-five percent of operations at this here camp."

"Exactly," David said. "And you, Jerry, are Mister Information. In fact, you're kind of like our very own 'rag.'"

"Thank you ... I think," Jerry said. "But it is just pitiful how much they keep us in the dark, isn't it?"

David agreed.

"Did you hear that Stanfield fell and sprained his ankle on drill?" Jerry said.

"Yes, he was sent to the rear with some of the others on sick list," David said.

"Seems like all the bummers will be finding themselves a gopher hole," Jerry said.

David raised his brow. "Not all the sick are bummers, Jerry."

"The officer of the day told the boys on picket to leave the line and get back to camp," Jerry said. "Then he told them to be ready to move out tomorrow at 4 am with three days rations."

"It's going to be a big one," David said. "Don't you think?"

"They say that back in '63 when we gave them Rebs their comeuppance, a Reb yelled out, 'There's those damn Yankees from 6th Corps again.'"

"They know us," David said. "And they know that if they mess with us, they best be ready for a good licking."

12

May 1864

When reveille was sounded the next morning, the boys jumped up, washed down their hardtack with some swill that someone tried to pass off as coffee, shouldered their gear, and began their march south. The road surface was damp though not slippery and the drizzle had kept down the dust. They crossed the Rapidan at Germanier Ford. The men were ordered to march out of unison on the bridge. Marching in lockstep could hammer and break any weakened support beams. Out of the corner of his eye, David caught sight of the water. It flowed rapidly, as its name suggested. This river means business, David thought. Not like that stream at home beneath his dear covered bridge, which seemed to exist only to celebrate itself.

On the far side, no enemy was in sight. David glanced at Jerry, who looked anxious, as if expecting some unfortunate surprise.

"Look." David pointed to a once stately mansion that had been badly damaged.

"Where's all the livestock?" Jerry asked.

"Confiscated by bummers," David said.

"No crops, no chickens, no nothing," Jerry said.

"That mansion was once filled with wealthy Southern gentlemen and their ladies," David said. "Now they're all beggars. What a waste."

"No one to pick their cotton," Jerry said.

"The contraband either escaped or joined up," David said. "And there ain't no cotton to be picked."

They pitched camp in one of the deserted cotton fields. A decent night's sleep in spite of little water and no latrines. The ground was cold but lying down was not uncomfortable. It made David realize again that army life back at camp was actually pretty civilized compared with being out in the field.

Packing up in the morning was always frenzied. But after a good night's rest, the Union troops' march toward the Rebel lines continued pleasantly enough, though the unit did not get far. They were ordered to bivouac beside the road until dusk. They had just set down their packs and were unloading their equipment when the crack of musket fire silenced the sounds of camp.

"Oh my God, here they come!" Jerry yelled.

The main body of Rebels swarmed up the road and another group of unknown number came from their left. The Union soldiers were in better position for the attackers on their flank, because the roadbed was a little elevated here, running along a ridge, and Northern soldiers could drop beside and below it and have protection. But the Rebel troops coming at them directly were a different matter; they held the higher ground, making it possible for them to shoot down at the Sixth Corps. The Union cannons were wheeled into position to fire at vanguard troops coming down the road, giving the Northerners a little time to spread out and find more security in better shelter. The air clouded with artillery smoke. The horses began to buck and strain and whinny. A Rebel sharpshooter fired from a stand of brush on their right and then quit, having either moved back to his base or having been picked off.

David sensed an ambush. Looking to the rear, there were flashes of musket fire as far as one could see. Attacking Rebels seemed to be closing in from all sides. David and a few others headed back down the road with Jerry right behind them until they found a tiny stream running toward the river, where the bank gave them a little protection.

"Why didn't the pickets see this coming? Did anybody read their reports?" David asked.

"No warning, none at all," Jerry shouted.

"Heck, Jerry, they should have talked to you. You must have known something you could've told them," one of the men yelled back.

All the divisions up and down the road and to the west into the fields were now in a severe engagement. David fired his Spencer at random. Men fell to the left and right but the smoke obscured them and oftentimes the men found themselves firing at silhouettes or vague moving shapes. It was as if there was a lesson in the smoke itself: They were all alike, all frightened human beings.

The Rebels, careless about losses, moved up fast. Jerry and David and the others hurried to fix their bayonets and unsheathe their knives. From above, the battleground would have looked like a sea of blood, filled with viscera of men and animals.

An officer yelled out, "Follow me." As he charged forward, his horse was shot out from underneath him. He stumbled away from his mount, lucky he'd not had a leg pinned beneath the dying animal. And then he plunged forward on foot, a man who could not be stopped.

David felt a sharp pain in his leg from a minié ball. "Jerry," David cried out as he fell to the ground. "I'm hit." He determined he was not bleeding heavily but there was no time to examine the wound. All at once, as if he had dropped from the sky, a young Reb was running straight toward him. David rolled to his left. Hugging his rifle he sat up, leveraging his upper body with his one good leg, and grabbed hard onto the stock of the gun. The Rebel soldier, a bowie knife in his hand, stooped to make the kill when David rose and plunged his bayonet into the boy's throat. He tried to avert his glance as the young boy's eyes rolled back into his head. But he would never forget the face—the smooth, square, baby face of a boy who would never return home. David lay back as the Reb's blood ran from his mouth, spilling into David's face. David pulled himself free. He ripped the dead Reb's tattered sleeve off and wiped his own face. He cleaned the blood off his bayonet, all the while staring at the boy's open eyes. When he'd finished cleaning himself as best he could, David bent down and closed the Reb's eyelids.

As the afternoon wore on, the Rebels began to fall back. The gunfire diminished. Then, from the sounds of musket and cannon both, it was clear that the troops had moved some distance away. The Union boys stayed in their places, awaiting orders, waiting to see what was happening. Up and down the line, some of the self-proclaimed experts developed theories about how far back the enemy had retreated. And what were their motives? Were they preparing to attack again?

Jerry had pulled David back to a safe place and sat with him. "Damn," Jerry said to David. "We don't know ourselves why we do what we do. How are we supposed to read the minds of them Reb officers?"

In the mid-afternoon, they heard battle cries and the Union troops began to move forward. Jerry unwrapped David's wounded leg, and determined that the bleeding had stopped. "You stay here. Keep an eye on things, all right?" Jerry said. "I'm going hunting. And for supper I'd like a big piece of ham, with some yams, and pie. Got it, buddy?"

David took off his cap and tried to swat Jerry, then grabbed his throbbing leg and lay back.

Jerry and the others picked up their gear and moved forward. With similar groups emerging from their own bulwarks and hiding places, the troops formed a ragged line. David stayed put. He was not in as much pain as he might have expected but he was dizzy and he couldn't think straight. Fevered, he blacked out while the Union Army drove the Rebs back into their own breastworks.

"We got 'em on the run," a loud voice came out of nowhere. The crier, a young soldier, ran back toward the commanders. David came to and sat up. He managed to pull himself erect holding onto a sapling. A few moments later, a second lieutenant on horseback turned off the road in David's direction. He rode along the line of a small stand of trees—the edge of a piece of forest that must have been cleared many years earlier. He stopped at each thicket to find soldiers who had not advanced for one reason or another and ordered them back to camp. One with a shattered shoulder made his way to the road. A couple more set off in the opposite direction of the action. At another stop, the officer talked for a while to a young boy and then turned away. The young boy bent down and tore a strip of white shirt cloth from a fallen man out of sight in the tall grass. He tied the white ribbon around a sapling and then paused for a moment with his eyes shut. The boy crossed himself, then ran away toward some cover. The officer would tell one of the wagoneers to pick up the bodies of the dead; they would be marked by white ribbons.

David stood as the second lieutenant appeared, putting all his weight on his good leg.

"Wounded, soldier?" the officer asked.

David pointed at his leg. "Yes, sir."

The officer leaned forward to look at the tattered hole in David's pant leg and the bruised and bloody flesh beneath.

"I can see that you're not a malingerer," the officer said. "Can you make it to the road? One of those branches could make a good crutch."

"Yes, sir," David said.

"There will be wagons coming back in an hour or so. Hitch a ride."

"What's it like up there, sir?"

The officer pulled his horse's reins to turn away. "It looks like a slaughterhouse," he yelled out as he galloped off.

David had some time. Afraid of the possibility of gangrene, David decided that the minié ball should not remain in his leg. He broke off a tree branch and shortened it, then put it in his mouth. Opening his knife, he bit down hard on the branch, then cut into the muscle of his leg. He pried the spent ball out with his fingers. Tears of pain flooded his eyes. He poured whiskey from his quinine bottle into the open wound and wrapped it with a blouse sleeve he'd cut off the dead Reb who'd nearly killed him. He took a long sip from the bottle. Then he examined the ball—a deformed little piece of metal, slippery with blood. The minié ball had had some distance to go before it hit David, so it wasn't embedded deep. David tucked it away in the pocket of his torn pants. Another lucky charm, he thought; he was still alive.

Afterwards David could hardly remember the rest of the day. He knew he'd been helped onto the bed of a wagon along with some other wounded boys—a baker's dozen in all. It was clear one of them was dying. A few more were in a state of panic. David's body shook with chills and he was only half conscious by the time they unloaded him. A medic cleaned his wound, which was becoming inflamed at the edges, and sutured it up. He then had David carried back to his unit. More should have been done, but this was a field hospital where any treatment at all was a luxury.

13

When David woke, it was well after dark. Jerry was sitting beside him and it was apparent he had been talking for a long time. "Hey, you finally awake?" Jerry asked.

"I was awake the whole time," David said. He sat up rather quick and grabbed his head as he let out a moan, then fell back. "What happened?"

"We ran 'em off," Jerry said. "I think we could have chased them all the way back to Richmond but we left outposts and a few of us came back. Generals are cautious, you ever noticed? I'm telling you, we could have driven them Rebs into the sea but 'Oh no, we got to have supper on time.' That's how Generals think."

"I won't be able to fight for a little while. I feel kind of weak," David said.

"You lost a lot of blood, David."

"I wasn't bleeding that bad."

"That was before you decided to practice field surgery on yourself," Jerry said. "You ever hear that old saying, 'Physician heal thyself'?"

David grimaced.

"Well, it don't apply to farm boys, David."

"How are the others?" David asked.

"We lost a few of our buddies, David. And your friend, Sergeant Ullery's missing."

David shut his eyes, remembering a scene from back home ... Ullery's home.

"It's your call, Sergeant," David said.

Sergeant Ullery and he were the only ones left in the poker game.

"You calling me?" David repeated.

Sergeant Ullery scratched his thick, uncombed hair, looked at his cards, then pushed four kernels of faded yellow corn toward the pot.

"I'll call your two, and raise you two," Ullery said with a straight face.

"I'll fold," David said.

Sergeant Ullery cupped his hands and began scooting the pot his way. David flipped Ullery's cards over.

"Why, you were bluffing," David said.

"Hey, you ain't supposed to look at my cards," Ullery grinned.

David fainted back to sleep.

He was awakened by Jerry pushing on his shoulder. "Wake up," Jerry said. "You keep falling back to sleep on me. Can you walk yet?"

"My leg doesn't feel half as bad as my head," David said.

"They say your leg's not in such bad shape. Stitched it up, nice lookin' bandage and all."

David had gotten to his feet, though he felt a little unsteady. The throbbing in his leg was bearable. He shook his head and followed Jerry to where the rest of the boys were camped.

"Talk is we're going to be marching up to the Spotsylvania Court House," Jerry said.

"I don't know if I can tramp another mile. We already come twenty, maybe thirty miles," David said.

"Rumor has it there's over 60,000 Rebs laying for us," Jerry said.

"More like 100,000, I bet," David said.

"Based on what evidence?"

"Based on nothing," David said. "Doesn't matter."

"Well, it does matter," Jerry said.

"I killed a man yesterday," David said.

"Only one?"

"I killed one up close. You see this blood on my jacket? That didn't come from my leg. I bayoneted him after he shot me."

"I didn't know," Jerry said. "Must have been hard."

"I'll tell you, Jerry, when there's one right on top of you, doesn't matter if it's sixty thousand, or a hundred thousand, or only two. One is all you need to kill you."

After mess, the men assembled and marched on through the night. David stayed to the rear. At every halt, David dropped down and dozed off.

In the early hours, the unit reached a field that the scouts said was easily defendable.

Jerry walked over to where David slept. Jerry sat down beside him and heard David snoring, then soon joined him. In the field, there were no pup tents to sleep in. The troops made beds on the ground as well as they could, covering up with whatever was handy—brush or weeds. A tree was always a welcome sight in rain or snow.

The weather the next morning was clear and warm. The boys built a long line of breastworks as the birds chirped away in the woods. The songbirds had the same songs as the birds back home, David noticed. Same kinds of birds, same nesting, same mating drill, same chicks being hatched. For birds it was business as usual, business the way it had been since creation. David struggled to remember on which day it said in Genesis that the birds were created; he could never get the order of creation straight. But for men, business was not as usual. For the men on the ground, everything was different. Same grass and ferns and weeds popping up through the ground. But the smells were all wrong—gunpowder, overflowing latrines, and death. And so were the dreams and the plans all wrong. For the soldiers, these battlefields were the opposite of Eden. The men lay fidgeting with their muskets, checking bullets and bayonets up until sunset.

And then, just as nature was supposed to get quiet, the Rebs began firing cannon shells their way.

David poked Jerry. "Wake up." He shook Jerry. Jerry rolled over.

"Keep down," David said. "There's sharpshooters in the trees."

There was a voice coming from beyond, in the dark. A voice with an accent, all too close to the Union boys.

"Y'all come out and git yer good rations. Y'all Yanks must be hungry," the Southern drawl needled. It was a high voice that carried well, one hard to get a fix on where it was coming from, or how far away.

"It's twilight!" Jerry clamored. "Looks like we're gonna fight until somebody cries uncle."

Union General Sedgwick, who had been walking through the camp, talking to various troops, meandered into a clearing at the edge of the woods with his hands on his hips. "What? Men dodging this way for single bullets? What will you do when they open fire along the whole line? I am ashamed of you," he called out to his men. Sedgwick was actually a favorite of the troops. He liked jokes, practical jokes. He had a jaunty air about him and seemed to like to take risks. He was being playful, his men guessed, warning them they might shame themselves. The question of shame wasn't an issue for them. Their interest, as the General knew, was survival, whatever it took. Honor was a concept for other people—officers maybe, or politicians who weren't on the front lines—to talk about.

"I believe the skirmish is about to begin, buddy," David replied, glancing over to see Jerry standing, looking around.

Jerry moved forward to get a better look.

"Get down," David whispered, his finger resting on the trigger guard of his Spencer.

The men checked once again that their rifles were loaded and waited for an order or for an attack, whichever came first. They waited in silence. A few watched Black Dan of Company G fortify a tree stump with knapsacks. He crouched down and set up a tin pan, then got back behind his cover. "Now hit that, Reb. Come on, sharpshooters, take your best shot," Black Dan yelled.

There was a distinct crack. The pan flew up in the air as Black Dan lit out before it landed. Now they knew. These Reb snipers were good.

"They couldn't hit an elephant at this distance," Sedgwick shouted. Someone guffawed.

The minié ball sounded like a bumblebee flying through the air. Then it struck. General Sedgwick fell. Blood spurted from his left cheek just below the eye.

The soldier nearest to the General knelt and, using the General's bandana, applied pressure to the wound. The bleeding wouldn't stop. The soldier propped the mortally wounded General against a tree, now with a gaping hole below his left eye.

"Our General's dead ... look," Jerry said, pointing a shaking finger toward Sedgwick.

David turned the other way. The face of the young Reb with the bayonet in his throat flashed through his head. A chill ran down his spine. He pulled the brim of his cap over his eyes.

14

The ground was puddled from the rainfall throughout the night. The Rebs opened fire on the Union troops with all the artillery and cannons they had. Their musket fire did little damage. Moving forward would be risky. The roads were rutted, and now, in the rain, the footing was bad for men and horses alike, making both advance and retreat difficult. Wet muskets were unreliable in the rain—as both armies would soon discover. The Rebel soldiers dug in and waited. There was a foreboding quiet. Gunfire was exchanged from time to time when one or another soldier thought he saw or heard something, or had a clean shot at a tree sniper.

And then the air exploded. Heavy fighting began left of the line early in the morning. By afternoon, the Union troops made a rapid advance through a field that lay about a quarter mile west of the road. When all the reports were in, late in the night, eight thousand or so Rebs had been captured along with seventeen pieces of artillery. Losses were heavy in killed and wounded on both sides.

David's division, the 110th Ohio, also had their share of fatalities. But they had returned as good as they got. David saw a few men from Company G get hit. Moving the wounded to the rear was perilous, nevertheless it had to be done. David and the others knew that if there were no support for brave men, no honoring their courage, or attending to their injuries, the armies would fight halfhearted.

Forces were redeployed. The 3rd Division moved to the left a half-mile and relieved the 2nd Division. The 126th Ohio was detached from the brigade and put in with the 1st Division at a place called the "Slaughter Pen."

General Grant's assault on the Mule Shoe was initially a complete success, in part because many of the Rebs had to try to use damp powder in their muskets.

The next day, David's division advanced to the left of the captured Rebel works and lay there until 3 pm before moving back to where they'd been the previous night.

There was an old farm trail that ran along the edge of one field and intersected the road on the far side. David had seen an outbuilding he was curious about. It sat behind a grove of trees where new growth partly obscured it. That's odd, David thought. The building would seem to be, for the most part, useless even in peacetime. It was too far from the road, the ground leading up to it was crisscrossed by many wheel ruts. If there'd been a dock over there, or a train station, a place that commerce flowed through, all these wheel tracks would have made sense. But why would there be so much traffic into an out-of-the way barn?

David took a couple of men with him to scout out the building. Jerry didn't see him again until suppertime. He was sitting by a fire, finishing his beans, when he caught sight of David approaching. David had reported to his commanding officer and now was coming back to his unit. He was pale. The two men he took with him followed in his wake and they too had a grayness, a somberness about them.

David sat down amongst a group of his comrades who were resting on their knapsacks.

"You sick, David?" Jerry asked.

"Not the way you mean," David said.

The other two were no more forthcoming.

"Boys," David said finally, "I seen the most sickening sight at the Rebels works ever." David hesitated. "That farmhouse off in the field, the one that the road loops around. It's a kind of a ... I don't know what you'd call it. I beheld Rebel dead laying in the mud, stacked three and four deep."

Few of the men really wanted to hear what David described. And once he'd started, David wanted to stop. But he couldn't stop, nor could the men tear themselves away from the story. Many of the dead, David said, were barefoot and it was clear they had been for some months. Their feet were calloused. Others' feet were white but bootless. Many were missing all their clothes. The survivors apparently had collected what they could off the dead soldiers.

Gray-haired men and peach-fuzz-faced boys lay amongst the piles. The stench of gangrened flesh hung in the air surrounding the field of battle.

"And to think, they were once Americans just like us," David said.

"You probably killed some of them yourself yesterday," Jerry said.

"Today I prayed for them," David said.

15

David's strength returned in no time. The pace of the action increased, as did the intensity.

Near dusk on Saturday, David led his squad when the 110th made a big charge through the Po River. The men pushed their way up the hill through pines and brush, then built their breastworks.

The next day, the 6th Corps was on picket. Most of the men grumbled that their uniforms were still damp from wading the Po the night before.

Monday there was Reb cannonading heard left of the Union line.

At sundown on Tuesday, David and the boys began a march that would last through the night.

They bivouacked at noon on Wednesday, frying up some hardtack and wormy beans.

Jerry kept spitting into the fire. "I'm sick of hardtack."

"Maybe we can bake up some chicken pie for you, Sergeant," one of the boys said.

"Who said that?" Jerry snapped.

"At ease, Jerry," David said. The men lay down on the grass and dozed. It was the only rest they had experienced for days.

At daylight on Thursday, the Union men advanced their line about a mile and a half. They'd just built a new line of rifle pits when the Rebels made an attack. The Rebs were repulsed but lost three hundred prisoners. And many of their boys lay either dead or dying—it was hard to tell the difference, for all in all, now this battlefield had an eerie quiet to it.

By Saturday, the whole Union Army began its move at 6 pm toward Guinea Station on the Fredericksburg and Richmond Railroad. The Rebs made a feint toward the Union's front line about sundown, then shelled a Union train.

"Why are we always the last to leave the battle?" Jerry kicked at a gray kepi lying beside a dead body.

"You'd rather stay?" David chided.

"I'd rather lead us out of battle," Jerry said.

"In that case," David answered, "You'll be wanting to become a General."

"That'll be the day," Jerry snapped.

Marching toward Noel's Station near the North Anna River, the men passed through some good country.

The hand-to-hand fighting continued to sour Jerry.

"Look at those fine farms and residences," David pointed. Somehow, the sight of normal human habitation comforted him.

Jerry slapped his knee. "How'd someone miss burning them down?"

The column bivouacked about 8 am the next day, drew rations, ate, then moved on. They reached the North Anna River, where the 5th Corps had a severe engagement about sunset. The fighting was bloody and the Rebs were defeated with heavy losses.

A few dozen of the captured Rebs, surrounded by Union soldiers, many of them on horseback, had been herded into a circle just off the road.

David eyed some of them. Most were barefoot and hatless. The jackets of those few that had them were battle torn and faded from wear.

"Where we sending them?" one of the squad asked.

"Looks like the entire caboodle's going to Port Royal, according to the Lieutenant," David said.

"All four hundred of them?" Jerry said.

"Who said we have four hundred?" David asked.

"Count them," Jerry answered.

David shrugged.

The Union Army recrossed the North Anna. All was quiet except for a little cannonading to the south.

"This is the third time our brigade's the last to leave the front," Jerry muttered.

The men marched several miles and halted for breakfast before moving on. Once they had reached Ruther Glen, the squad drew two day's rations then bivouacked at dark in a prairie.

"This has been another hard march, boys," David said, dropping his haversack. He plopped down beside it, pulled off his boots and began rubbing his blistered feet. His leg wound remained sore, but it seemed to be on the mend.

At 6 am the next day, the men crossed the Pamunkey River on pontoons at Nelson's Ferry. They halted on the north bank. The rumor up and down the lines was that the Generals expected an encounter.

"Anyone have something we can make coffee in?" David asked.

One of the men found a pot and brought it over to the fire.

David waited for the dark liquid to boil, when they heard their Lieutenant.

"Fall in, fall in," he ordered.

David jumped up and grabbed his rifle.

"You heard the word. Move out, boys," David said.

"There goes the last of breakfast," Jerry said as he doused the campfire with the coffee.

David's squad lay entrenched near Nelson's Ferry. The 6th

Corps moved at daylight toward the Hanover Courthouse. The soldiers were out of rations and they'd heard there was no prospect of a supply train arriving. They formed a line of battle in front of the enemy's rifle pits, close enough to hear the Reb musicians playing.

David put his fingers to his lips. "Is that a locomotive whistle, boys?"

Jerry shaded his eyes from the noon sun. "I hope it is," he said.

"How's hardtack sound now?" David asked as he poked Jerry.

Jerry cocked his ear toward the train whistle, cupping his hand over it to get a better listen. "I'm so hungry I could eat the ass end out of a skunk," he said.

One of the men sauntered down to the railroad track and put his ear against one of the rails. He listened for a long time and then got up, his body a little stooped from fatigue.

"Hear anything?" David called out to him.

"Nothing," the man's voice cracked. "Unless maybe it's a different line, or one of the Rebs' trains stopped waiting for who knows what."

The boys began to throw up earthworks at sunset, working hard until midnight. The 10th Corps joined the 6th and entrenched. They rested the next day, barely fortified by the arrival of several wagons of hardtack and beans. Out of their works they charged the Rebs the next night. Childers of Company G was wounded in the skirmish. Shorty was killed. After the carnage he'd seen on the battlefield, some said he expected it.

"Look at them Rebs skedaddle," David shouted.

In disarray the officers had trouble controlling, the Union boys jumped into the Rebs' trenches. Some of them had been issued new repeating carbines, which were proving to be a significant change for the better.

"Them Rebs left their muskets, blankets, and knapsacks," someone yelled out.

"Bully for them," Jerry said as he picked some cornbread and tobacco out of a dead Reb's tattered haversack.

June 1864

Flummer was the next casualty of Company G. He lay wounded in the thigh for the better half of a day before he could be carried off the battlefield. The Battle of Cold Harbor, as it came to be called, had been successful so far, but at a cost; it was one of the bloodiest battles in the war thus far. The Rebs, it was clear later, had been less well prepared and more desperate than the scouts and generals had believed. They had been reduced to digging in using cups, bayonets, and their bare hands. They eventually stacked the corpses of their fallen comrades as part of their earthworks. In essence, they appeared to be essentially defenseless.

The 110th went to the rear along with six hundred Reb prisoners.

The next day, the Union's entire line had advanced to within two hundred yards of the Rebs' entrenchments.

Fierce fighting took place all day along the battle line.

Amongst the galling fire, the boys heard a commotion from one end of the entrenchment.

"I'll be damned," one of the men called out, pointing at Captain Snodgrass. The Captain was running toward the Rebs with his sword drawn.

"Follow me, boys," the Captain yelled, waving the sword high.

"He's drunk," David shouted.

The Captain stumbled and fell. Jerry ran after him, grabbing his legs. He ducked down and dragged the Captain back toward the rest of the line. Pearson was killed helping him. Jerry took a hit in his right arm and fell before he could make it back to the entrenchment.

David rushed over, grasping both Jerry and the Captain by their collars. He dragged them both back of the line.

"Thanks, buddy," Jerry said. "Easy, easy," he added.

"You trying to get everyone killed?" David said as he looked at Jerry's arm. "It's just a flesh wound. There's no ball lodged." He took a corked whiskey bottle from the Captain's haversack and poured some on Jerry's wound. "See, it's already stopped bleeding."

Jerry grabbed the bottle and took a pull. He smacked his lips. "How 'bout him?" Jerry said, pointing over to their Captain. Snodgrass was passed out on the ground. Vomit dribbled out the corner of his mouth.

"Seems to me he's already sanitized inside and out," David said. "We'll carry him to the rear."

On the evening of Monday, June 6th, a truce was called for
an hour. The Union Captain met the Reb officers half way
on the battlefield and exchanged papers from headquarters. Skirmishing resumed until a few hours later when
another truce was called and all firing in the front ceased,
though heavy cannonading continued off in the distance.
Then the Rebs sent some shells over the 110th.

David spotted a tobacco vendor driving his wagon
too near the front of the skirmish line, more ignorant or
greedy than brave, David suspected. In an instant, the
vendor was shot dead. His horses ambled on as if nothing
had happened. Union boys scrambled across the battlefield and helped themselves to his stock of tobacco. David
was all at once reminded of Charles Allen, and how his
cousin enjoyed a piece of chaw every now and then. Where
was Charles Allen today? Did he have his chaw?

David watched the company colors fall. Ordering his
men back from the wagon, David noted several soldiers
lying dead on the ground with body parts missing, their
eyes staring as if looking for help. It was appalling—but
probably necessary—that they leave these fallen men
unburied, if only for a short time. It was a travesty that
the honored dead should remain unattended. But David
had come to expect this from both sides. Many times they
seemed to have had no system for taking care of the casu-
alties. They were short on many things; it was apparent field ambulances were among those things. Was it
because they didn't expect losses? Maybe they were too

weak and desperate to do what was right. What would happen to men's spirits, David wondered, thinking of the Confederate bodies used as earthworks, or stacked like logs in a woodpile as he'd seen at the farm he'd reconnoitered a few weeks ago? Perhaps both armies had too few living to be able to dispatch the dead.

Then, in one pile of Union dead, David noticed an arm move. David ran back out onto the battlefield. He picked up the flag along with the wounded Yank. The boy had been knocked cold. Blood trickled from his nose and mouth. David noticed blood seeping through the boy's blouse. He started to rip off the sleeve, but instead unbuttoned the boy's shirt.

"Ouch," the boy blurted out.

"Take it easy, son," David said. "You've been hit by a minié ball. It's lodged in your upper arm."

"Am I going to the hospital?" the boy asked.

"No, I'll take care of it for you," David said, snapping off a piece of the flagpole.

"You a doctor?" the boy moaned.

"You might say that," David said. "Here, bite down hard on this."

As the boy bit down, David took his jack knife from his knapsack and sliced the flesh of the boy's arm. The ball came loose easily. David figured it was almost spent when it hit. He poured some whiskey on the wound, then ripped the banner from the company flag to wrap it. The boy passed out. David poured some of the whiskey into the boy's mouth and patted his face. The boy's eyes fluttered.

"Here, keep a hold of this," David said.

The boy took the minié ball. He grimaced at David.

"Someday you can show it to your grandchildren," David said.

"Where the hell you been?" Jerry said to Private Gill. "You've been missing all week." Jerry had become the unofficial company scold. Even so, he made it his business to know the physical and psychological condition, not to mention the whereabouts, of every one of his squad.

"Feel the back of my head. One of them Confederate Butternuts must have hit me with a log," Private Gill said. "... Or a fry pan ... Hell, the lump is bigger than my thumb, it's bleeding ..."

"Go over to Sergeant Longacher, he'll pour some antiseptic in that knot, son," Jerry said as he ruffled the boy's hair. Was there more "antiseptic"? Jerry wondered. He was in powerful need of a libation.

"Damn," the private yelped, abhorring the pain of the injury but fearing the cure even more.

Jerry was happy to note the fact when Privates Walker and Stanfield returned to Company G. Both had been wounded, though neither showed signs of weakness. Jerry was happiest when all of his squad was back, in reasonable health, and ready to continue the fight rather than desert.

16

For all of the apparent success of the Union boys, or

Nationals, as General Grant called them, the evidence was that the tide had turned and that the battle was going the Rebs' way. It was an unstated assessment, though everyone up and down the line seemed to feel that change was in the wind.

One afternoon, David's division was relieved to go to the left of the line when most of the gunfire had ceased for some time.

"Keep them caissons and limber chests under bomb proofs," a staff officer ordered.

"The musicians and bummers, too," someone quipped.

"Don't worry about them, they have their gopher holes," someone answered.

"Knock it off, boys," the staff officer shouted.

The staff officer tried hurrying up the unit, but it was slow going.

The weariness, the muck underfoot, the filthy clothes, the near absence of food, the constant shifting of positions for no particular reason might otherwise have seemed comical. But by now there was too much weariness and frustration for there to be any humor in the situation.

"I'll never forget these days the rest of my life," David said.

"Then you better start a scrapbook," Jerry said. "There's more to come."

David patted his diary tucked away in his jacket.

Exhausted and underfed troops started dropping out of

ranks a few hours after the march began. As Company G moved on, many of the boys stopped to catch a second wind and then couldn't continue. The column scattered about.

"Come on, boys, quickstep," a staff officer yelled out. "Come on now, we're going to the rear, so if one of your buddies drops, pick him up."

Every so often a vet reached out for a straggler, though pride kept most of them on their feet.

David looked over at the young boy marching beside him, holding up on sheer determination as the column tramped on.

"Look son, see those good farms?" David pointed. "The corn looks promising, doesn't it, Private ...?"

The boy nodded and then spoke. "Krouse, my name's Krouse."

"What a relief it is to be out of heavy cannonading, Krouse," David continued.

The boy braced up.

Just as well Jerry was out of earshot, David thought. He'd manage to find something disheartening or grim about these healthy-looking farms.

17

The Army advanced toward the James River. For the next two weeks, the 110th was on the move. They fell back from the Rebs' front and headed toward the Jones Bridge on the Chickahominy River where they bivouacked before beginning what would be a hard march toward the Charles City Courthouse.

"We'll be here for a while," the first sergeant announced.

David sat down beneath a tree. The young boy joined him. It was hard for David to believe how much had changed in such a short amount of time. He'd returned to the army April 15, not two full months ago. Since then he had been shot at, wounded, starved; he'd seen more devastation and misery than he imagined existed anywhere. Could it really be only two months? He pulled the diary from his jacket pocket and flipped through it.

"What's that?" Krouse asked.

"I keep a record of what happens," David said. "Helps me remember things."

"Seems like a strange thing to do to me," Krouse said, twisting his back against the tree, trying to get comfortable. "I'd just as soon forget."

"Let me take another look at that arm, Private Krouse," David said, pulling a bottle from his haversack.

Krouse held out his arm. David rolled up the boy's sleeve and poured the rest of the whiskey on the wound.

"How's it look, Sergeant?"

"David ... call me David, son."

"How's it look, David?" Krouse repeated.

"Not bad, but we need to get some clean dressings on it."

"How you figure on doing that?"

David pointed over to a clearing amidst the trees. In

the clearing sat a gaudy painted sutler's wagon. "A few of the boys tell me there's a wagon over there with some fancy girls in it, you know, camp followers."

Krouse strained to get a better view.

"Here's what you do ..." David whispered.

"Aren't you going with me?"

"I'm a married man, son." David prodded him.

"So?" Krouse said as he got up, brushing off his uniform.

"Go on, git," David said.

Jerry walked over and dropped down next to David. "Where's that Krouse from?" Jerry asked.

"He's a Hoosier," David said. "Got detached from his unit."

"Is he regular Army?" Jerry asked.

"No, he's a Hundred Days man," David said. "And he heard that the Rebs are heading for Washington. He's been with General Lew Wallace of the 8th Corps who's on his way to Monocacy."

"Great, another greenhorn," Jerry said. "With a cockamamie story to boot. Why do you coddle him?"

"He's been shot and I carried him off the battlefield ... just like I did you, soldier," David barked out. "But if you have to know, he's from New Albany, Indiana."

"Ain't that Copperhead territory?" Jerry asked.

"Yes, and Krouse is a little younger than my cousin, Charles Allen," David said.

"Charles Allen Carmichael?" Jerry said.

"That's him," David said.

"He's at your mom's place, ain't he?" Jerry said.

"Was," David said. "Krouse tells me Charles Allen's fighting here in the Wilderness with the Rebs."

"What a coincidence," Jerry said. "Another Copperhead from Southern Indiana."

David got up. "Enough of the chin music."

As David walked away, he heard Jerry mutter, "Your new friend could be a spy."

The 3rd Division of the 6th Corps marched south and then east that week to reinforce the 10th Corps at Bermuda Hundred. There was some skirmishing with the Rebs along the way. Heavy cannonading was heard at Petersburg but there was no direct encounter. The 3rd Division then moved to the right, near the James River and lay in breastworks.

There was no appearance of Confederate armies and Jerry, who'd been called away by one of the Generals, believed that the brass was receiving conflicting scouting reports.

Pressing forward, David's unit crossed the Appomattox on pontoons and bivouacked beyond the opposite bank. The next day, seventy-five Hundred Days men came to the regiment. Eleven of them reported to Company G.

Jerry usually finagled ways to be assigned one light duty after another. Most of the officers knew him by his first name. He walked up to find David sitting on his haversack, with his diary out.

"Private Ketchman was wounded on the skirmish line," David said as he tucked his diary away.

"You patch him up?" Jerry asked. He'd come to think of David as an unofficial medic. As long as he could continue to get "antiseptic," Jerry thought it was a responsibility he would have liked to have had himself.

David shook his head and circled his temple with his index finger as he got up to walk away. Jerry assumed David meant that he was crazy. He gave David the finger.

"It was Ketchman," David said, circling his temple again. "I think Ketchman has lost it," he said, looking back at Jerry. "I didn't have time to do first aid, hadn't had time to take him to a real doctor, then Ketchman grabbed his rifle and tried to cross the lines to pay back the Rebs. Now I wonder about you, Jerry."

H.Q.'s orders of the day came down: No advance for the present. If ever there were glad boys, it was the boys of the 6th Corps. Then another order came from headquarters to set up the camp and dig latrines and wells. Looked like they were sticking around—for a while. It was a pleasant enough spot, a string of hay fields, though the house was on the other side of the lines, a disappointment for the Union Generals who would liked to have set up headquarters somewhere comfortable. Heavy cannonading at Petersburg continued through the night and into the next day. The men dug, cleaned, washed, and polished in their own good time, sharing the illogical belief that if they made something that felt permanent they could stay and get no closer to those cannons and the Rebel soldiers who were firing them.

David was in one of the officers' tents, at work on payroll, when Private Krouse returned to camp with a clean gauze bandage on his arm. David pointed toward an empty chair.

"Take a seat, Wolf," David said. "I've been meaning to ask you, how'd you get the first name Wolf ... from your amatory adventures with the ladies?"

Private Krouse leaned back and laughed. "No, my proper name is Wolfgang Krouse."

"Since we're on the subject of girls, tell me about your dealings with them fancy girls," David said.

"You mean ones you *ordered* me to call on."

"The very same."

"I'd have told you sooner, but I figured your buddy, Sergeant Jerry, filled you in." Wolf hesitated.

Well, David thought, Jerry's been doing some probing around himself. This was excellent ammunition the next time Jerry started to give him a hard time about something.

David expected Wolf to light up with delight at being asked to recount the visit to the Madam and her daughter. Instead, he looked almost rueful.

"Why beautiful girls would become whores is beyond me," Wolf said.

"War seems to bring out the worst in us," David said.

"But a mother and daughter?"

David shrugged. "Did you get what you set out for?" he asked.

Wolf reached into his haversack and pulled out a bottle of iodine, a jar of salve, a roll of gauze, and finally a spool of catgut with a large needle stuck into the spool. He set it all on David's payroll ledger.

"This is what they gave you?" David said. "I figured they would clean your wound. And if they gave you a little private attention, take your mind off things, so much the better."

"I guess that's so," Wolf said. "But I didn't ask for that. Didn't feel right. They were kind, though."

David looked at the young man. He seemed the thoughtful type. One of those rare individuals who was trying to keep his integrity intact, even in wartime—a difficult thing to do. David held up the spool. "What's this for?"

"The mother said, 'Tell your friend he can do some *real* suturing now,'" Wolf said. "That is, if the need ever arises."

"Bless her soul," David said.

18

Frank Lee continued loading fieldstones into the wagon. Each passing day had gotten a little warmer. He took his bandana and wiped the sweat running down his neck and arms. This was a job he wanted out of the way. Beth watched the fresh dirt turn over as she kept a firm grip on the plow handles, occasionally yelling "Gee" or "Haw" at the mules.

"It's almost dinnertime, Frank Lee," she called out to him.

"You want to quit for the day?" Frank Lee asked as he walked across the newly plowed section. "It's going to be awful hot for such work by afternoon."

"We'll decide after we have lunch down by the covered bridge," Beth said. "I have something to ask you."

"What?" Frank Lee asked.

Beth smiled at him. "First, I'm going up to the house to get the picnic basket I fixed for us. I'll meet you down there."

Beth watched Frank Lee shove half of his sandwich, a deviled egg, and a bite of cold potato pancakes into his mouth all at once. She wrinkled her nose at him.

"What?" Frank Lee mumbled as he grabbed a soda pop. "Ain't you hungry, Cousin Beth?"

She took a sip of her soda pop. "Not really," she said, savoring the flavor. It was supposed to be good for you. She drank it, truth told, because she liked the tickle of the bubbles in her mouth. "If I tell you a secret, can you keep it to yourself?" she asked her cousin.

"Sure," Frank Lee said.

"Cross your heart," she said.

Frank Lee crossed his heart, thinking it was a bit childish but still effective.

"Do you know someone by the name of Wolf?" she

asked.

"You gotta be kiddin', I'll bet everyone around New Albany knows Wolf. Why, he was one of the star athletes in the county. How'd you ever hear about Wolf?"

"David met him in the army. He introduced us, sort of. By mail. Wolf started writing me, and I him. He seems very nice," she said.

"You're sweet on Wolf, ain't ya?"

Beth blushed.

"Doggone if you ain't," he laughed.

"You needn't make fun of me, Frank Lee."

"I'm sorry, Cousin Beth," he said with a straight face. "What do you want to know?"

"David tells me he's quite handsome." Beth leaned forward. "Well is he?"

"All the girls back home seemed to think so. Why, he's almost as good lookin' as me."

"You're a boy," Beth said.

"And you're how old?"

Beth looked as if she were about to cry. Frank Lee put his arm around her.

"Cousin Beth, Wolf is one of the best men I know. Charles Allen is real close to him," Frank Lee said. "I'll tell you one thing for sure, if Wolf tells you he's going to do something, he'll do it."

"Oh, Cousin Frank, I'm in love with him."

"Well, if he marries you, he's going to have one of the prettiest girls I know as a wife."

"I'm glad you came to help us, Frank Lee. And I'm

doggone glad you're my cousin."

"Likewise," Frank Lee said. "By the way, this food is tasty. Doggone delicious."

Beth stood up. "Come on, I'll race you to the house," she said.

"But I'm not finished eating yet," Frank Lee said.

"Then don't forget to bring the basket," Beth scurried away, laughing.

19

Just after dawn, the boys got up, struck their new tents, and checked their ammunition. After chow, they fell into formation. This camp they'd put so much work into was about to be abandoned, sooner than they had hoped. So all the work they did came to naught.

"Company attention," the top sergeant ordered.

Generals Horatio Wright and James Ricketts passed along the line in review. Afterwards, the officers returned to their headquarters.

"Parade rest. As you were," the top sergeant shouted. "Prepare to move out."

"Where we goin'?" a voice murmured from the ranks.

"Knock it off," the top sergeant barked.

David looked up at the sun. "It must be around three o'clock," he said.

"Where we heading?" Wolf asked.

"Rumor has it, Petersburg," Jerry said.

By 10 pm, the column reached Ream's Station on the Weldon Railroad and bivouacked. Early the next morning, the unit, working in shifts with crowbars and mules, tore up the Rebs' railroad tracks, bent them into bowties, then continued its march to Plank Road. They arrived at sunset and bivouacked. Some of the slackers and wounded lagged behind, not joining up with the rest of the company until later in the evening. The cannonading blasted away at Petersburg through the night. Word was the guns at Petersburg had not stopped firing for days. The boys sniffed the gun-powdered air.

"We're getting real close," the top sergeant said.

July 1864

The next day, the first of the month, the troops moved forward, closing the gap between the armies. "I know it's hot, boys," the top sergeant said as he began unbuttoning his sweaty blouse. "Fall out," he added. It seemed likely that they would encounter opposition today, though the rumors had been wrong before. But the sergeant, who believed that encounter was inevitable, thought that the advantage would be theirs and the engagement would be at a time selected by the Union Generals. "Fall in men, we're going to make an advance soon," the top sergeant's voice cracked.

The troops began loosening their jackets on the march. They nodded at the top sergeant as he proceeded up the column. When too many men in the column fell back, the soldiers bivouacked where they dropped out.

But there was no encounter and so the troops marched in a semi-circle around the opposing line, then marched east.

Later in the week, the unexpected happened. The company embarked on boats for Baltimore.

"Wasn't this a delightful surprise?" David said as he stared down into the dark waters of the James River.

"Here were General Grant's options ... Send us to Petersburg ... or Baltimore ... let me see ... Then General Grant thinks about it for a moment. And Baltimore wins hands down," Jerry beamed. "Smart General."

"One thing's for sure, boys, you can't depend on the tattle line," David said. "When one rumor goes away, another one pops up."

"I heard from a railroader back at Ream's Station that the Rebs are heading for Monocacy," Wolf said. "Do you think General Lew Wallace got there yet?"

"I sure hope so," David said.

"Maybe those fancy girls are there, too," Jerry said. "And your buddy, Wolf, can reconsider their offer to him."

"I doubt it," Wolf said as he leaned over and eyed Jerry.

"What offer?" David asked.

"Ask Wolf," Jerry said.

David shook his head. "You're corresponding with my sister, Wolf."

"I'm mindful of that, Sergeant. And I would never, ever, betray her or embarrass either of you," Wolf said. "Things that happen in a place like that could be misunderstood."

David gave Wolf a pat on his back. Jerry raised his eyebrows.

Two days later, David and the 110th landed at Baltimore and immediately boarded railroad cars for Monocacy. The stars and stripes floated from nearly every house along their route. Many of the ladies threw kisses and cheered the boys on.

"Welcome home, boys," they yelled out their doors and windows.

Wolf nudged Jerry. "Look at all those darlings," Wolf said. "Where are we anyway?"

Jerry grabbed a rose tossed by one of the ladies.

"Just outside of Frederick, Maryland," David said.

Wolf looked over at the railroad station: MONOCACY JUNCTION. "I hope that railroader was wrong about the Rebs advancing," he said. "This is too close to the White House."

During the night, the 1st Brigade returned from Frederick. With them came reports that the Rebs were indeed advancing from Frederick and marching into Monocacy Junction.

"And Jerry, you were whole-hog that we missed the Petersburg battle," Wolf said.

David polished off his morning coffee, then checked his rifle and cartridge bag. "I want you right beside me, Wolf. And don't be running toward the Rebs for any reason," he said.

Wolf nodded.

"How 'bout me, your old buddy?" Jerry asked.

"You're a veteran, buddy. So if you see any of them Hundred Days boys in any trouble, give them a hand," David said.

"How am I supposed to recognize one?" Jerry asked.

David spotted several greenhorns. They stood with their eyes wide open. Their uniforms were new issue. David pointed over at them as they puttered with their muskets, many of them with the heavy, older models. "See for yourself," David scowled.

There wasn't much point in trying to turn one of these greenhorns into a sharpshooter overnight.

The murmur amongst the Union troops, which had ebbed during the dark hours, had risen to a chatter with the first light and then stopped at sunrise, as did the singing of the songbirds. Men and nature waited.

"How many Rebs are coming?" Wolf whispered.

"Over twenty thousand according to headquarters," David said. "Your General Lew Wallace has about four thousand of you Hundred Days boys ... tenderfoots."

"That's scary," Wolf said.

"Not for you. You've seen battle and been shot," David said. "Think of the rest of them Hoosiers, they're all greenhorns. Just stick by me." Playing big brother was a kind of pose. Wolf wasn't foolish or naïve. If he had been, David wouldn't have given him permission to write Beth.

David wiped at the sweat trickling down his neck. It had the makings of another hot day, but it was more than temperature that caused David to sweat. He looked up at the new day's sun appearing above the horizon.

The cannons began pounding.

Within minutes, clouds of gray began to roll towards them. David thought of those thick black plumes that rose above cornfields at burn off time in the fall. They sometimes made him melancholy—marking the end of a season, the onset of winter. But there was promise in them too, the soil nourished by the charcoal for planting in the spring. There was no promise of growth or renewal in these clouds.

The sky turned gray, filled with bursts of black and red artillery fire. The sweet smell of the grassy battlefield was overlaid and then obliterated by the scent of gunpowder. Wolf peeked over the breastworks. David grabbed his collar and pulled him down.

The Rebel yells began as the first skirmish commenced. Heavy fire from the cannons continued pounding. Independence Day celebration popped into David's mind. It was only five days ago. David shook his head and began pulling the trigger of his Spencer automatic rifle continuously, stopping only to reload. He couldn't see who he hit or missed. But he was having an effect. Men fell and bodies began piling up all around him like sandbags on a levee.

Through the smoke, David heard a god-awful scream nearby and turned. Wolf had run his bayonet clear through a Reb and, though it seemed impossible, had hoisted him off the ground, holding him in mid-air like a pitchforked bale of hay. Blood splattered their faces. The impaled man struggled in spasms.

"Push him off," David yelled.

Wolf let his bayonet drop. He kicked his foot against the Reb's ribcage, pushing him away. David took aim, finishing him off. Wolf pulled his bayonet free. He started to wipe off the blood with his sleeve.

"Forget it," David said. "Keep shooting."

The Rebs withdrew as their bugler sounded retreat over and over. The Union bugler raised his horn to sound the charge, but fell dead across the pommel of his saddle—the battle cry unsounded. The minié ball shattered the bugler's head, the horn locked in his mouth, its bright brass spattered with blood and brains. Their Captain drew his sword. "Charge boys! Charge these devils!" he yelled, waving his sabre, leading the Union Cavalry forward.

The Union's rifle troops held their battle line until late afternoon when one Rebel advance after another surged forward in swells. Soldiers passed amongst their own wounded and dying, first with muskets and handguns, then, in closer combat with pikes and bowie knives, attacking half-crazed, as if they had no concern for their own survival. They advanced not toward something, it seemed, but rather driven by something from behind. David thought it was as if these Rebs were pursued by something, or maybe piloted by something from within, that made them throw themselves forward as they did, intent on nothing but killing. He shook his head to clear the ugly, unwanted thought that maybe he and his comrades were exactly the same as their enemies.

In fierce battle, death seemed like nature, a tornado. Horses and mules were blown apart, their riders' limbs, organs, intestines, strewn about, along with decapitated heads of warriors that had either been chopped or blasted free. The battlefield filled with death.

David, hunkered in a stand of weeds and brush, suddenly realized he was alone. The men who had been at his side a few minutes earlier had moved to the right, crossing a little island of quiet, a tiny no man's land, to a small stand of timber, a fragment of shelter. One of them called his name and David started to run towards them across a patch of field cut up by horses' hooves and rutted by wagons and cannon. Halfway across, his foot slipped on something. It felt odd. In the dirt beneath his boot was the head of a man. His neck was broken at a sharp angle and most of his lower body, his legs and pelvis, were crushed flat into the dirt. David guessed he'd been lying in that field a day or more, cut up and crushed by horses and cannon trolleys. Somehow no one had seen him. He was already decaying, but his face was upturned and it seemed to David that, through the muck, the man was looking at him, expecting something. His comrade called his name once more. The sound of gunfire and cannon from the opposing army grew louder. The Rebels were moving forward swift and powerful. David ignored it. For no special reason, except for a wish to respect the dead, he bent down and pulled a scrap of lapel out of the slurry of dust and blood. He brushed it off, wondering if the man had worn blue or gray. It was when he stood up again that he felt an incredible hot, sharp pain in his calf.

"Jesus," shouted the man in the thicket. "Hurry up, damnit."

"I'm hit," David yelled back.

He was suddenly dizzy and began seeing double. He turned in the direction the shot came from. A Rebel soldier ran toward him, dropped to one knee and reloaded his rifle ready to fire point-blank. David saw him cock the hammer of his musket. To the left, not twenty yards away, was a cluster of his own comrades—David didn't even know them. For some reason, they had dropped their rifles and knapsacks on the ground. One of them, an officer, began yelling. For an instant, the kneeling Reb took his eye off David and looked over at the Union officer.

The officer had tied a bit of cloth to a tree branch and was waving it back and forth. A white flag. Surrender. The Rebel soldier raised his rifle and pointed it at David's head. David managed to throw his arms high in the air. "Surrender," David choked out, pointing at the white flag. His leg gave way and he fell down hard on the ground. The Reb lowered his musket. He could have finished David off, adding one more to his personal body count, but the prospect of being on the scene as a whole squadron of Yankees surrendered was an even greater thrill. David sensed a kind of shame. He was alive because of a coincidence, an accident, a fluke, a lamentable surrender.

"We whooped you Yanks," the Reb began shouting at the top of his lungs.

David rolled over and puked. He reached down his leg, sticking his finger in the open wound to stop his blood from squirting.

"Lord, help me," he moaned, his lips quivering. And then his eyes closed. So far as he knew, all was over.

Part III

1

It would later seem to David that he must have lain on the ground for so long and in such a state of suspended breath and soul that it felt like death. But it was not. As if from deepest water, David rose into consciousness. The long dark slumber had done him precious little good. He was only barely conscious when he felt a kick in his side. He staggered to his feet, thinking he could use his rifle to support himself; his wounded leg was weak and painful. He felt around for his Spencer. David lost a minute or so wondering where he could have dropped it before realizing that he'd been relieved of the rifle and other implements by his captors. He stood unsteady on the field, with various other walking wounded, Union men like scarecrows, surrounded by Reb guards. All the pieces were now falling into place: the smoke, the blaring cannons, the sharp vicious crack of rifles, the stench, the sudden searing pain, the fall into unconscious, and now the reemergence: He was captured. And the pain in his leg reminded him it wasn't just a state of mind.

His fellow prisoners looked downtrodden. All had surrendered their weapons. David spotted his own Spencer now in the hands of one of the guards. He gave David a push. "Ya'll follow me, Lil' Coot," the guard said.

David shaded his eyes from the sun as he followed the Reb guard, stumbling as he went, toward a mill. It was still morning. His leg throbbed with every step, then progressed into a sharp pain that pulsed with every heartbeat. David was marched forward with a half dozen others into a little hollow, split by a brook, which served as a sort of natural corral. There were about four hundred Union prisoners, meandering, shuffling back and forth, hungry, weak, afraid. The Rebel guards stood in a circle looking down at them, watching every move their captives made, ready to take action. David spotted Jerry first, standing a full head or so above the others. And then Wolf.

Wolf walked up to David and whispered, "Thanks for shooting that Reb off me."

Marching south meant marching ever deeper into shame. With every step they took, the prisoners became a little less human. And that, in a way, was the point of the exercise.

The prisoners had been marched down the main street of Urbana. It was a Rebel town, though David thought it scarcely mattered. The lesson was the same, the Rebs were the winners of this particular battle, they must have killed many and the rest—these prisoners—were being put on parade for all to see. Some shuffled along and hung their heads, while others stared straight ahead. Another prisoner, nondescript, seemed to be muttering to himself—one of a number of those discovering a personal reality more agreeable than the one they now found themselves in.

But David knew that this might be the last chance he would have to contact Nel. He looked over the guards who walked on either side. One was young, loose limbed, with a wall eye. On the other side was an old veteran with a limp and a constant scowl.

A few yards behind them both was a third confederate, a burly man with an unkempt beard. "Grizzly" they called him. David recognized him as the one who'd taken his rifle. They'd stopped for fifteen minutes at roadside. A number of the men were wounded, gaunt, and exhausted. Some passed out. Grizzly got down on his knees next to one of them and poured a little water from a canteen into his mouth. The man's eyes fluttered open as Grizzly slapped him on both cheeks. A kind man, David had thought, in his own way.

And now David needed something too. He drifted toward Grizzly. He'd have to act quick or they'd be out of town.

"Can I leave a letter here to be mailed?" David asked.

"A letter? Let's see it."

David pulled the letter from an inside pocket and handed it over. Grizzly squinted at the address.

"What's in it?" he asked. "Information on troop movements? You a spy?"

David shook his head. "It's to my wife."

"What's her name?"

"Nel," David said. "It's right there on the envelope."

Grizzly nodded and stepped aside from the moving mass of men. David watched him approach a small, bald man—a shopkeeper he looked like, give him an instruction and hand over the letter. David thought then that he made a movement to his pocket, as if he were giving the man something else. What it was, he couldn't tell. Grizzly seemed to be a man in charge.

The funny part was, as David later discovered, that Grizzly couldn't read at all. The letter could have been full of military secrets, for all Grizzly knew. He was a shrewd judge of character, which was at least as valuable as being literate.

They marched on for a day and then another. Beyond the pain and fear and confusion he felt as a prisoner, David was overwhelmed by a sense not only of powerlessness but of uselessness. His whole life there'd always been something that needed tending to—painted, planted, pruned, there were human demands. Not here. Not now.

Of the four hundred taken prisoner, there were four

others from Company G and at least thirty-four more of the 110th. After Urbana, they passed through Frostburg, Hyattstown, and finally halted after dark, twenty-three miles from Washington.

They stopped for an hour in the heat of the day. David leaned against a withered tree and wiped the beads of sweat from his forehead. Grizzly came up to him.

"You trying to march us to death?" David asked.

"Not at all, Yank. But me and y'all's even now," Grizzly said. "You gave me yer Spencer, and I let you leave a note for yer sweetheart at Urbana."

"It was my wife," David reminded him.

"That's right. A wife. They say, 'If'n ya got a warm woman and a long rifle, y'all got nothin' more to worry 'bout.' 'Course, as me and y'all know, rifles do change hands."

"I wish I was with my regiment again," David said.

Grizzly poked him with the butt of the Spencer and spit. "I bet ya do, Yank. How many of our boys ya figure y'all killed with this here repeater?"

David looked down. The gob of chaw had just missed his boot. He didn't answer.

The man who talked to himself moved into the conversation, keen eyed, alert. He was still talking to himself softly but he seemed to be paying close attention. David turned his back on him, feeling he'd lost his privacy—a feeling he would become all too familiar with in the months to come.

"Well now, before it's all over, I'll just try an' even up

the score," Grizzly said. "What ya think 'bout that, Lil' Coot?" Grizzly wiped the tobacco dribble off his chin.

David buttoned up his blouse and dusted the dirt off his jacket. He smoothed out his hair before pulling his cap down over his eyes. "May God grant that soon we may all be at liberty again," he said.

"Amen," Grizzly mumbled.

2

Nel sat with Beth on the bank near the covered bridge tossing small stones at a lone cattail. It had been blistering hot for days and the air was damp. It was that curious lull in midsummer when the crops grew fast and the harvest, the future, was all in God's hands.

"I'm winning, Nel," Beth said.

"Winning what?" Nel said. "Neither one of us hit it yet."

"I came the closest," Beth said.

"Ah how impossible to trace the track of the stone in water. It is like the life of man himself ..." Nel said.

"Did you memorize that or something?" Beth asked.

"No, I said it. It came to my lips as if I'd been touched by an angel's wing."

"Oh, poppycock." Beth leaned back and stared at the sky. "I want to hear that letter from David again."

"It's personal, Beth."

"I read it once before. It wasn't *that* personal."

"You weren't supposed to," Nel said.

"No, but I did. And I bet you got it with you."

Nel reached into her pocket and pulled out David's note. The one he'd mailed from Urbana.

"Wolf and I have been captured. The Rebs are marching us to Danville Prison. I'll write when I can. I miss you and the family. Love, David."

Nel looked over at Beth. Her smart-alecky disposition had disappeared as tears began to gather in the corners of her eyes. Beth sat up, wiping them away.

Nel put her arm around Beth. "They'll both be okay, dear."

"You want me to read one of my Wolf's letters?" Beth asked.

"Yes, please. I'll bet you've got one of those in your pocket, too," Nel said.

"Nope, I put it somewhere safe in the house. I'll fetch it," Beth said.

"It can wait," Nel said as tears began to well in her eyes. "Now see what you started?"

Beth hugged Nel and handed her a pebble. "Okay, if one of us hits the cattail, everything will be all right," Beth said.

Nel smiled. "You Longachers are all alike," she laughed.

"Are not."

"Are so," Nel said. "And I can see you've got your fingers crossed, silly."

"That's because I'm hoping that they'll be home soon."

3

The prisoners moved at sunrise from their bivouac, passing through Rockville. They arrived near Tennallytown, D.C. just before sundown. Skirmishing continued all around them. Several large shells thrown from the Rebs' own forts passed over them. They bivouacked in an orchard.

Early apples lay rotting on the ground. And the wild grass beyond, where it had not been cut down by hooves and wagons and grapeshot, was tall and green. But the smell of the place was nigh unbearable. There were men, or what had once been men, beyond, lying in graves not much more than a foot deep. Some were on top of the ground with a few spadefulls of dirt and lime tossed over them. The crows were everywhere in flocks, strutting in their proud way with bits of flesh in their beaks, black as death.

It was commonly known, as Jerry said, that the Rebels, for whatever reason—brutishness or, more likely, fear, disorganization, poverty, shorthandedness—could not take time to bury their dead. Indeed, they often left or had to leave their wounded behind. And it was a point of pride, it was said, that when Union soldiers cleared the field, they also brought in wounded Rebs along with their own men. The veterans suspected that one's odds of being saved once wounded and abandoned were about the same whatever the color of the uniform. That is, close to naught.

At the crack of dawn, a pair of Reb guards picked their way across the battlefield. From time to time they'd stop and turn something over with a boot, or prod it with a bayonet. One bent down to retrieve something that he pocketed. This field, at least it appeared, mostly had been cleared of Southern dead. The field beyond was full of Union dead.

When the Union prisoners awoke, they found that the Rebs had taken the boots off some of their feet while they slept.

Called to attention, they stood shivering and boot-less, expecting the worst. They were a pathetic lot, David thought. There were a number he didn't know. Their clothes, often as not were tattered. A few had wounds to their arms and chests, or arms in slings, but one or two looked mentally confused. A pale blonde kid with a gash in his forehead kept moaning. David took a longer look at the man who talked to himself. He was of no particular age or type. He moved about the men, sometimes intro-ducing himself, sometimes looking as though his mouth was moving, saying things too soft to hear. He chattered almost non-stop. "Cork" was his name, David was told. No one seemed to know his real name.

After a half hour of standing surrounded by unsmil-ing, stolid Rebel soldiers, a pair of guards instructed the prisoners to remove from their pockets any valuables and to hand them over. The young guard with the wall eye passed up and down the line, hat in hand, and collected a few coins but mostly watches, of various kinds. One soldier stared straight at the guard and dropped his watch in the mud. The Reb guard stepped forward into the soldier's body, never dropping his hat, and kneed him hard in the groin. The Union soldier collapsed on the ground.

"While y'all's down there, Yank," the Reb guard said, "would y'all mind pickin' up that there watch that's lyin' by your nose? Seems I done dropped it."

They had no breakfast. In groups of five, the prisoners were sent into the field to relieve themselves. Even the crows paid them no mind.

"Them Rebs are pretty keen on our goods, aren't they?" Wolf said to David as they started down the road again.

"They're pretty broke is my guess," David said. "The Reb Provost Marshal wants to exchange Confed money for our greenbacks."

"Why exchange?" Wolf said. "The Rebs just stole some of our belongings."

"First of all, Wolf, you must understand the officer's code. Always be an officer and a gentleman," David said. "And you ought to know about supply and demand."

"What's that?" Jerry asked.

"There's only so many of us with greenbacks and only so many Rebs that have money to trade, so the market price for currency is set between the buyer and seller," David said. "Because the Rebs with money don't want to fight each other over our greenbacks, trading is the only civil answer."

"Same as horse swapping," Wolf said.

David reached for Wolf's hand. "Yes, Wolf, and a friendly handshake seals the deal. Better get used to it, boys, it's going to come in handy in the Confederate prison."

"I'm with you," Wolf said.

"Me too," Jerry nodded.

"I'm so worn out, I could drop," Wolf said as he shifted his knapsack to his other shoulder.

Beyond, the man named Cork prattled on to a young Union boy who clearly couldn't hear a word he said.

"He's a straggler, that one," Jerry said, pointing over at Cork.

"What do you mean?" Wolf asked.

"He's unattached from his unit."

"Like me," Wolf said.

"In many ways," Jerry agreed. "Couple of the boys say he don't remember what unit he used to be with at all. Some of these guys even bounce from one army to the next. There's no figuring them out."

"Why would they do that?" Wolf asked.

Jerry shrugged. "Just love army life, I suppose. Or maybe they forgot themselves."

They almost never stopped but, weak and wounded, with no incentive to cooperate, they made slow time.

"We've only marched twenty miles," Jerry sneered.

"You looking forward to your arrival?" David asked.

"The Rebs are probably rolling out the bandwagon right now."

The column halted at noon and each man drew rations of a pint of flour. They waited out the heat of the day. And then at dusk, the Reb Army with its Yankee captives began their move toward the Potomac.

The men marched all night, passing through Poolesville and reaching the Potomac at sunrise.

A command came down telling the guards where the prisoners were to be taken. Those issuing the orders apparently had not supplied the details. To cross a damaged bridge would have required an extra few hours of repair work, if not more, and the prisoners were exhausted. A few had already been left behind along the road to die. The decision was made to ford the river. The pontoons were small and could carry no more than a dozen men at a time so guards were posted on either side as the men conveyed across in small groups. There was not much likelihood of attempted escape, for there was no place for these bootless, dispirited men to go to, and no way to get there.

David watched Cork with fascination. He had become more animated. He wandered from group to group, as though he knew everyone, and attempted to engage them in conversation. It looked as though his madness was taking him over. The men mostly ignored him. A couple of the younger ones turned aside. One shoved him away and Cork moved to another group, unfazed.

When he finally approached David, he said quite loudly, "You killed one didn't you. That's what they say."

David pulled the brim of his cap down.

"I got my eyes on you, sir. You're a hero." Cork skipped away, whistling.

After the men had forded the river, they moved south to a big spring near Leesburg, Virginia. Another squad of Union prisoners was brought in. Some cannonading could be heard to the east. In all, the Reb guards had marched their prisoners twenty-four hard miles.

When they had finally stopped for the day, each man was given food.

David held the pint of flour and the half-pound of beef in one hand. "This is our rations for today?" he asked.

"Same as us, Yank," Grizzly muttered.

The next day, the Rebs and Yanks were busy trading. Many of the Rebs' feet were leather hard and most were dressed in tattered civvies. It was beginning to sink in that David and the boys would remain prisoners with no parole or exchange in sight for some time to come.

Around noon that same day, a messenger moseyed in on a swayback horse and handed one of the older Confederate officers an envelope. David watched as the officer read the note and then conferred with several others. A half hour later, they were told to prepare to stay put for the rest of the day.

"What do you suppose that's about?" Wolf asked. "You think they might be ready to swap us already?"

"You're a man of faith," Jerry said to him, raising his eyebrows. "I think they're readying rooms for our arrival."

For the remainder of the day, the prisoners meandered about, holding out personal goods they wanted to trade and exchanging scuttlebutt with each other.

"I hear that besides our unit, the 122nd and the 126th Ohio, the 138th Pennsylvania, the 87th Pennsylvania, the 9th New York Heavy Artillery, the 106th and 151st New York, the 10th Vermont, and the 14th New Jersey were engaged in that fight at Monocacy," Jerry said.

"Don't forget the Maryland Home guards and the Hundred Days men," Wolf said.

"Excuse me." Jerry touched his forehead as if to tip his hat.

"The odds were overwhelming," David said.

"General Lew Wallace with about four thousand Yanks against thirty thousand of General Jubal Early's Rebs." Wolf raised his voice, "Can't call that a fair fight."

"Y'all don't beef when the odds are on y'all's side," a Reb meddled in. "Let's face it, we won. Y'all lost."

"Those numbers sound right to you?" David asked Jerry.

"Numbers can't be verified," Jerry said.

"They never add up," David said. "In fact, even back at camp those numbers coming by telegraph to the railroad clerks ..."

Jerry cut him off. "That place we bivouacked last night. You know, where the crows were? How many men you think died there? You want to be the one who does the count? Guess you'd have to ask the crows, now wouldn't you?"

"Still, sounds like our boys must have done all right, against those odds they must have acquitted themselves ..."

Wolf had been listening to the two men. "We had to hold Washington," he said.

"That's what the newspaper said, the last time I saw one," David answered. "They were moving on Washington to try to divert forces who might intercept Lee's army."

"Here's what I think about the numbers," Jerry said. "I think that if we can only muster four thousand against thirty thousand, then we're in trouble. And meaning no disrespect," he said, glancing at Wolf. "I believe that most of the boys our General Grant could send were Hundred Days men."

"That's a sad fact," David agreed.

4

By Saturday, the pace of the journey more than doubled. The prisoners marched twenty-eight miles with no rations. On Sunday, after marching another ten miles, David paid eight dollars in greenbacks for a small shoulder of meat and everyone drew a pint of cornmeal for rations.

"What's this we're eating?" Jerry asked.

"Who knows," Wolf said.

"Who cares as long as it fills our bellies," David said.

"Look over yonder," a Reb guard pointed.

One of the prisoners was taking a piece of bread out of a scruffy dog's mouth and eating it. The Union prisoners were more than ever feeling the effect of short rations. One might have thought that the Rebel guards were starving them on purpose, to break them down. Except that it was indeed true, most of the guards were eating not much better.

They continued marching through the early morning. The Confederate Provost Marshal blew his whistle. "Halt," he called out, then pointed toward an orchard. "Y'all go over and pick yourselves some green apples so y'all have something to gnaw on."

The men scattered amongst the trees, grabbing as much fruit as they could carry. Some fought over even the gnarled, wormy apples.

"I sold my gold fountain pen holder for five dollars Confed to buy bread with," David said as he stuffed apples into his haversack.

Everyone's attention was drawn by a ruckus. Cork, his arms up as if to defend himself, began howling, running backwards, ducking and dodging around trees as the blonde soldier with the gashed forehead hurled apples at him.

"Don't you hear them? Don't you hear the whistling? Bumblebees. Shells. God have mercy," Cork yelled. "The ghouls are coming. We'll all be dead men before sunrise."

"Can't we help him?" Wolf asked.

"I wouldn't know how to," David replied.

"He sees things, sometimes," a soldier nearby said.

"I was with him before you boys joined us. He has bad dreams with his eyes open."

"Where did he fight?" Wolf asked.

"Nobody knows," the soldier said. "It's all the same, ain't it?"

Wolf called out to Cork, "We're not going to die. We're prisoners."

"You think the Bluecoats won't kill us anyway?" Cork shouted. "We're shields for the Rebs. They'll hide behind us. Our own boys got their cannons all around us. We're goners, I tell you."

Wolf pressed on. "Cork, listen. There's no way our boys could ever get us back." Wolf held out his empty arms. "No weapons, no nothing. Look here," Wolf said, stepping a few feet into the open. He pointed out the places up the road and on the ridge behind them where Union fire was coming from. There were a couple of cannon on carriages. A nest of sharpshooters too far away to do much damage. Cork calmed himself down. He put his hands over his ears, let out a wail, and plopped down on the ground.

Wolf walked back to David. "That poor fellow's got more battles in his head than any ten of us seen since the start of this."

As the area around them quieted, the more mundane—and more immediately important activities of life began to take over.

"I paid two and a half in greenbacks for a stale loaf of bread," a fellow prisoner said.

"Where's the bread?" Jerry asked.

The prisoner pointed to his belly.

"We're going to have to learn to share," Jerry said, shoving more apples into his over-stuffed pockets.

"You start then," the prisoner said.

"With what?" Jerry asked.

The prisoner pointed at Jerry's pockets. "Seems like you're getting to know the Rebs who dole out the rations. I bet you got more stashed somewhere."

"Well then, bet all you want and believe what you will." Jerry spit an apple seed toward the meddler.

The Reb guards halted at Fisher's Hill. They sent their own wounded up the valley to a Confederate hospital, though the odds of them getting decent medical care were against them.

"There's the Hazel River, boys," Grizzly said. "If'n y'all are hankerin' for a bath, go on and jump right in."

"Any soap?" Jerry asked.

The Reb guards laughed. "I believe we got some damsels 'round here who'll wash y'all's back for ya. Grizzly, where'd them damsels go?"

"Damsel if'n I know," Grizzly quipped. No laughter, a few groans. "However, I'd be more'n happy to step into the river and wash y'all's backs." Grizzly held up his bowie knife. "Who's first?"

While some of the boys took up the offer of the river, many of the prisoners keeled over and slept. Eighty-five more Union prisoners were brought in, some wearing only their woolies after the Rebs stripped them of their uniforms. Word was the Rebel trains were moving south and that the Union forces were at Middletown. Some of the Reb guards went out and foraged flour from the local farmhouses—most of which, along the way, had broken windows and caved in doors. It was a safe bet that everything of value had already been confiscated.

"Any y'all Yanks want baked cakes, they're one greenback each," a Reb guard announced.

"I'm too tired to eat," a Union private said. "Not to mention too broke."

"Why don't we try to escape, David?" Wolf whispered.

Jerry laughed. "You do keep my spirits up, Wolf. You truly do."

"Why not, David?" Wolf persisted.

"Can't," David said. "I'm all tuckered out."

"I don't feel so good myself," Wolf said. "That wouldn't stop me though."

"What's wrong?" David asked.

"It's my wound, it itches," Wolf said.

"That's a good thing," David said. "Now don't you be grieving about that wound to any Rebs. I overheard one of the guards saying that their hospitals are packed and the Reb boys are dying like flies in there."

Wolf motioned as if to button his lips.

David pulled back Wolf's sleeve. "Let me take a look at that scratch of yours," he said.

As the prisoners continued marching south, they passed a number of Dunkards. They seemed to be overdressed for the heat, the women hidden in their bonnets, wearing layers of clothing.

"Must be Sunday," David said.

"How'd you know," Jerry said.

"Them Dunkards are heading for a Church of the Brethren. Oh how I wish I could join them," David said.

"What's a Dunkard?" Wolf asked.

"They believe that when a Christian is baptized, they should be immersed in water, not just sprinkled," David said. "My late father-in-law was a Dunkard preacher."

"Golly, you believe that?" Wolf asked.

"No, I'm a Methodist," David said.

"I'm a Baptist. I think we believe in dunking," Wolf said.

"Theologically speaking, that would be something you should make it your business to find out," Jerry smirked. "I wonder if they keep on dunking up in heaven?"

"He's right, Wolf," David said. "You should find out being in close proximity with death as we all are." It was not like David to be sarcastic, but the heat, the hunger, and the sheer fatigue had made him flippant. And things that once would have troubled him now seemed immaterial.

"Who cares about religion," Jerry said. "I'm starved. My belly thinks my throat's cut."

By 9 am, the men reached Staunton. They passed through town and halted in a field to wait for transportation. David pulled out his diary and made an entry.

"What are you writing now, buddy? That ol' Jerry's

starving?" Jerry said.

"In a roundabout way," David said. "I heard one of the Rebs tell that in Charlottesville apples are one dollar a dozen, ginger cakes three dollars a dozen, and ice cream five dollars a dish in Yankee money ... which we don't have. The Rebs sure are keen on our greenbacks. I guess Dixie money is deflating."

"That's warfare for you," Jerry said. "Them poor Rebs. They saddle 'em with slavery, send those young boys to go defend a lost cause, subject them to gunfire and hand-to-hand combat, starve them, wound them, force them to mistreat and steal from men like us, who, in my opinion, are clearly brighter than them. And what do they get in return?"

Wolf hadn't quite figured out Jerry's sense of humor. "What? What do they get?" he asked.

"They get," Jerry said, "a dish of ice cream and charge their fellow Rebs five Yankee dollars."

"That's right," Wolf said. "And then the only thing worse is being a Southern ice cream vendor. No customers because they charge too much, therefore no money."

"And before you know it," David continued, "No dog-gone ice."

At daylight, the prisoners were put on cars bound for Lynchburg. When they arrived, they were paraded down yet another town's main street. A surprising number of townspeople had come out on the sidewalks to jeer the prisoners. A couple of them threw things. A rotten head of cabbage landed near Jerry, followed by a mangled pole-cat. Jerry kicked it back toward a Southern belle standing on the walk.

"There's the Southern prison," David said. "Ugh ..."

There was an open area in the center of this town—a sort of shabby, half-hearted commons. There was a statue of a public figure there, a municipal building, and a couple of churches. David's group of soldiers, who had been growing in numbers, were lined up four and five deep in the center of the square and told to stand at attention. Behind them, out of nowhere, came a group of maybe thirty prisoners, all Negroes. David had thought his own comrades looked pathetic but he'd never seen such battered, spiritless men in his life. Many of them had fresh wounds; some bore old scars on their heads, shoulders, and calves. They'd been beaten long before the war ever started, being reduced about as far, he thought, as the human animal might go. Been reduced to animal level and then called, "animal." And that was before they'd been sent into battle. David remembered once again, reading *Uncle Tom's Cabin* by the light of the fireplace back home a hundred years ago. The Negro prisoners again supported what he already knew—that this cause was just and that these battles, even his father's death, made sense if only to keep such an abomination as these abused men from the sight of their Maker. David didn't want to think about where these men were being taken.

From way over to his left he heard someone shouting.

The words were incoherent at first. As the voice came closer, David understood. "Do you see them niggers? See them? Look where they're going. Oh my, look at their heads and their legs." It was Cork again. And even if the words themselves made sense, what he meant to accomplish with them wasn't clear at all. "Let's stop 'em, boys. Let's emancipate our African brethren." He made as if to force his way forward, before a guard pushed him down. "How many of you with me? Ain't these slaves Christian souls like us?" Cork pointed up at the sky.

The Reb's rifle butt made a thud as it struck Cork's head. "Pick y'all's nigger-lovin' buddy up, Bluecoat," the Reb guard ordered.

A big, red headed Union prisoner threw Cork over his shoulder. "Like carrying a short sack of spuds," he said.

From the time they were captured, the Rebs either took, or attempted to take, the Union prisoners' blankets, tents, and knapsacks. There were few left in any condition to be useful. For many, they were little more than mementos of better days. Many of the boys either cut or tore up their traps when they saw what the Rebs were doing.

David stopped Wolf from doing away with his goods.

"Don't you remember our conversation about bartering?" David said, showing Wolf the money he'd gotten off the Rebs by trading some of his things.

The going rate was $1.00 in greenbacks for $3.50 in Confederate money. While in prison, there was to be a constant trade of money, clothes, and food.

5

The train arrived in Danville at 4 am on a Friday. The men were then marched to an old warehouse known as Prison No. 1.

"Looks like an old tobacco house," Wolf said.

Jerry stared.

"That's what my nose is telling me," David agreed.

"I sure could use a good segar right now," said a soldier nearby.

"We'll have to set the place on fire to afford you that experience," said another.

"Ya'll Yanks pick a spot, here's y'all's home for now," Grizzly said.

Seven hundred and thirty men were crowded onto three floors, where they were quartered and given one pound of corn bread, two ounces of salt pork, and a pint of rice soup for their day's rations. David gobbled up his rations and fell into a deep sleep.

The prison was like many in the South, a converted tobacco house, as Wolf had guessed. Prison No. 1 was a three-story structure. All of the upper level doors were sealed off, making it almost impossible to exit, or to enter from the outside. Most of the windows were boarded up. The building had no heat, no beds, no tables.

Because of security, there were very few outside latrine privileges. And with the numerous cases of dysentery, the prisoners were forced to relieve themselves on the floors. Rules were set up by various groups in various sectors. But no one agreed. In time, the sectors dedicated as toilet areas began to overlap and merge and be overrun. Under close supervision, one group got their hands on some broken picks and shovels and began to dig trenches around the edges of the main area that were meant to contain the waste. "I always knew that all that digging earthworks on the battlefield would come in handy," said one of the men. "Canal building," said another. And the only half-joking question debated by the laborers was, "Which would you rather barricade against—Rebs or shit?" The stock response was that there was no difference.

The prison was so overcrowded there was no floor space in between where the Union soldiers slept. Dying was an every day event. Dysentery, typhoid, pneumonia, and malaria became far more deadly than the battlefield itself. Still others, more than likely, would die in a makeshift hospital. While waiting for death, they were mortified, humiliated, and denied many basic human rights, but not because of rules and regulations. Wartime imposes its own constraints, makes its own demands, bigger than governments, more like the laws of nature.

And when the men of Danville Prison thought that they had reached the absolute lowest possible level of human suffering and degradation, a half-dozen men arrived on a wagon for reassignment. None of the prisoners had ever seen such men. They had so little fat or even muscle that you could see not only every rib but even the outline of kneecaps, the whole crown of the pelvis.

"They brought 'em in from Andersonville," Jerry said. He'd overheard Grizzly and had inside information. "It's in Georgia, someplace. Grizzly says it's hellish there. They're all kept in one area that's nothing but a huge overflowing latrine; in fact, the river they get their water from parallels it. They feed 'em every other day."

"Why'd they bring these here?" David asked.

"They were looking ragtag and they needed transferred someplace where they could get their health back," Jerry said.

They could also have served as a reminder to any who might resist, or disobey, or try escape. But as examples, the six from Andersonville were of no use at all. Two died within twenty-four hours of their arrival. The rest were gone by the end of the week. They buried them all in two common graves.

The next day, David wrote a letter. It was as remarkable for what it left out as for what it contained.

> *My dearest Nel,*
>
> *It's Saturday. Well here I am in Danville Prison crowded together with hundreds of Yankee soldiers. We hardly have enough room to turn over on the filthy floor we sleep on. Tomorrow I will begin to read the Testament with the intention of reading it through. Four hundred*

more prisoners from Petersburg arrived – among them sixty niggers, Brigadier General Bartly, and forty Union officers. The officers say they were marched through Petersburg in the same ranks with the enlisted Negroes. The officers will be sent to a special prison here. More than likely its much better than ours. Rumor is the Negroes will be paroled and sent back to their slave owners.

He hardly needed any further proof, but to David it was another indication of the true nature of slavery that at least some of these Negroes would have preferred remaining in prison to going back to bondage.

A Reb guard shot a Yank for getting too close to a window. I almost had the blues today. My darling Nel, I can't tell you how much I feel grateful to God for his goodness to me in giving me my health. May He grant you and I soon meet again.

Your loving husband,
David

August 1864

David sat propped on his haversack as Grizzly made his rounds.

"When the 3rd Division Union officers arrived in Lynchburg, they and the captured officers from Petersburg left for better quarters in South Carolina," David said.

"Ya don't say, Lil' Coot," Grizzly said. "Ya don't reckon

them brass hats were gonna hob-nob with y'all foot soldiers, did ya?"

"Where you from, Grizzly?" David asked.

"The hills of Tennessee," Grizzly said.

"I see you got yourself one of those old Harper's Ferry
muskets now. What happened to that Spencer I gave you?"
David asked.

"Gave me? An officer confiscated it from me," Grizzly
said.

"Well, easy come, easy go, Grizzly," David said. "I
reckon taking is one thing Union and Reb officers have in
common."

"Y'all hear our cavalry burnt down Chambersburg,
Pennsylvania?" Grizzly asked.

David walked over by the window next to Grizzly.

"What's the chance of me and some of my unit going
down to the river for a wash?" David asked.

"Y'all want me to risk my neck, not to mention my
stripes, by lettin' y'all go take a bath?"

"We'd smell better. That has to be good for everyone."

"Go on, but remember, if'n y'all attempt to escape,
I'll be usin' this here musket on ya," Grizzly said. "I guess
y'all heard that a Yank was shot in prison number two
yesterday."

"For what?" David asked.

"Washin' up. 'Course, he was on the wrong side of
the river," Grizzly said, patting his musket.

To save Grizzly from a reprimand, they planned their bath

in the river with all the care and secrecy of a true escape. David talked to Jerry and Wolf. Jerry, in turn, talked to the rest of the group. Two more were chosen who'd been there longer than the rest. One by one they congregated near the door where Grizzly stood. They took off their shoes for security purposes before Grizzly let them out.

David dunked his head beneath the murky waters of the Dan River.

"Wish we had some soap," Jerry said.

"At six dollars a bar, I'd bet the Rebs wish they had some, too," David said.

"What do you make of all this increase in horse trading?" Jerry asked.

"Sounds like the Rebs are losing the war as well as the value of their money," David said as he continued splashing water on his face.

Grizzly had enlisted another guard to stand watch over the men by the bank. He was a talkative young Tennessean full of misinformation. He'd heard about a dispatch that all prisoners were to be paroled immediately and sent to their respective states until exchanged.

None of this came true.

When they returned to Prison No. 1, Wolf brought along a discarded newspaper that had belonged to one of the Reb officers. It read that Fort Powell was blown up by the Rebs themselves and Fort Gaines surrendered on either the eighth or the ninth at Mobile.

Jerry doubted that the paper was real. The paper stock seemed too heavy and the editing atrocious. It looked to him like a piece of propaganda. The war had made him doubt that there was any such thing as truth.

"Maybe we could find out if we had more observers," Jerry said. "But that would require a telegraph key in every building. Maybe one in every haversack."

David laughed.

"That'll be the day," Wolf said.

"Who'd want that?" David asked. "You'd never have privacy and you'd never be free."

"That's kind of where we're at right now, buddy," Jerry pointed out.

"Well, I don't believe any of this crap. You wouldn't see any Union boys blowing up their own forts," Wolf said.

"How 'bout some of them boys from Southern Indiana?" one of the other prisoners added. "They're nothin' but a bunch of rednecks themselves."

"Who you referring to?" Wolf said.

"If the shoe fits, wear it, son," a big Irishman said.

Thus, the first prison fight began when a prisoner from one of the New York units punched Wolf in the jaw. Wolf sat on the floor rubbing his face when the New Yorker strode over to finish him off. Wolf jumped to his feet and threw a roundhouse right hook that landed in the New Yorker's solar plexus. He finished with a left uppercut to the New Yorker's chin.

"Copperhead, eh? You popinjay," Wolf said as the big man collapsed. "I'll have you know I'm originally from

Northern Indiana, imbecile."

"I don't think he can hear you," Jerry said.

Wolf kicked at something lying next to the New Yorker. He bent down to pick it up. "It's his tooth," Wolf laughed as he laid it in the New Yorker's outstretched hand.

That afternoon, one hundred more prisoners from the Army of the Potomac arrived along with five Union officers. The additional prisoners were crowded into Prison No. 1, while the officers were sent to their own building. Eggeman, one of the men on David's floor, was taken to the hospital.

David sat down next to Wolf and set his plate of beans aside. "Remember, any Army hospital is somewhere you never want to go, Wolf."

Wolf nodded.

"The papers say almost five hundred sick and wounded were sent for exchange," David continued.

"Where'd you get a paper?" Wolf asked.

"Jerry finds 'em. But he's a fanatic. He's the only person I know who's in favor of a shallow latrine," David said.

Wolf shook his head and retched.

"Well, he's got other sources," David said. "Working in the kitchen he sees parcels come in wrapped in newspaper. I'm not sure it's in a whole lot better shape than what's in the trench."

Wolf put his hands over his ears.

"You feel better now that you gave that guy a licking?" David asked.

"I couldn't let that son of a ..." Wolf began.

David nudged him. "Now don't work yourself up again."

Wolf took in a deep breath.

"By the way, though, where'd you sign up at, Wolf?"

"Indianapolis."

"Where would my Cousin Charles have enlisted?" David asked.

"Anyone fighting on the Rebs' side would more than likely go to Kentucky," Wolf said. "Now, if Charles Allen were here, that New York dandy would be correct in calling *him* a Copperhead."

"I'm sure he signed up with the Rebs. He's always been a stickler for state rights," David said. "Charles Allen wouldn't be here, though. And if he was, he'd only be here guarding us. That was my Ma's biggest fear."

6

The fact was, Charles Allen had been in Rebel territory from the moment he arrived at Cincinnati. Having used his father's connection to the Masons to get a job from the riverboat captain, a Dixie sympathizer, he headed downstream. Charles Allen stepped off the *Masonic Gem* at Mauckport and crossed the Ohio River to join up with John Hunt Morgan of the 2nd Kentucky Cavalry Regiment. It was the second time Charles Allen flashed his father's Masonic ring.

General Morgan was a Mason, as was his father before him. Morgan took a liking to Charles Allen immediately, promoting him to sergeant as well as his aide-de-camp. It was a much more attractive situation than his cousin's. At least for now.

7

Though it seemed impossible, the food declined in quality every day. One evening, David reached for his plate. He spotted something in the beans. "Rat dung," he said. "Oh shame on the Confederacy."

"Grizzly says they're eating ... or not eating ... the same food we are," Wolf said.

"He's been saying that from the get-go," David said. "Though I haven't noticed him getting thinner."

David rubbed his throat and swallowed hard, polishing off the last of the beans. The irregular rations the prisoners received were beans, peas, and rice—most of the time with rat droppings, bugs, or worms in them. The infrequent, stingy portions of meat were usually spoiled or rancid, and came from the worst part of the animal such as the head, throat, or guts.

The prisoners made their coffee out of wood chips or chicory roots, whenever they were available. The men battled smallpox, scurvy, and frequent cases of flux, which was worsened by either being deprived of, or given limited latrine privileges. On top of all this, the boys had almost no clothing, few blankets, and insufficient heat. The mortality rate was high. Even boys who hadn't been wounded were dying daily. Symptoms of what seemed to be a cold or the flu would transform into some deadly illness within a day or two. Maybe it was they died from fear or despair itself; it sometimes seemed so.

The wartime destruction of railroads, at times, brought the shipping of supplies into non-existence. The prisoners were often fighting the same odds as the losing army.

David came in from the river, a bucket in each hand, carrying water for his squad.

"There was another shooting today," Wolf said. "One of the guards mistook a towel for a Yank trying to escape out of a window."

"The Rebs recruiting the blind now?" David said as he started coughing. He sat the buckets down and cupped a handful of water to his mouth. "It's my lungs. Bad days or good ones are a toss of a coin."

David walked over to Jerry who was at the checkerboard.

"Your malaria acting up again?" Wolf asked.

"Malaria, wounds, lungs ... but I'm still better off than some," David said as he sat down across from Jerry. "It's this loathsome prison."

Wolf shook his fist. "Like you always say, 'Hold on, this war's coming to an end.' I heard that General Grant now holds the Weldon Railroad two miles from Richmond.

Look out, General Lee."

"Who told you that?" Jerry asked.

"Grizzly."

"He's *my* source, damn it all," Jerry said. "You're poaching, Wolf."

"I couldn't do that, Jerry. You're the best."

"It's your move, Jerry," David said.

"Then take your fingers off your checker," Jerry said. "I know that trick."

"Everything's a trick according to you, Jerry," David said.

Jerry let out a loud belch.

"I suppose it was a trick when I pulled you from harm's way out on the battlefield," David said. "Or did you forget?"

"How can I?" Jerry said. "You won't let me."

Wolf intervened. "Hey, did I tell you that one of the boys bit another one's ear off in a fracas on the third floor today?"

"Did I tell you that I picked quite a number of rat berries out of my soup today?" David snapped.

Jerry glanced over at Wolf. "I stopped picking mine out. I heard from a *confidential* source that they have protein," Jerry said.

"Protein?" Wolf said.

"Food stuff," David said.

"That's to say that *my* source believes that rat shit is good for you," Jerry muttered.

David snatched one of Jerry's checkers off the board.

"Sorry buddy, you forgot to jump me."

"Back to that ear biting ..." Jerry said. "I believe I heard your story about two boys from Indiana who were wrestling when one bit the other's ear off, then a third person picked it up and declared, '*Whose* ear?'"

David and Wolf shook their heads.

"Don't you boys get it? Whose ear? *Hoo-sier?*" Jerry slapped his knee, laughing.

"Your move, Jerry," David said.

"That's a stupid remark, Jerry," Wolf said. "Don't make me have to teach you a lesson, too. In fact, maybe sometime I'll give you a lesson or two about wrestling."

"How 'bout a fisticuffs?" Jerry said as he eyed Wolf.

David pushed the checkerboard toward Jerry. "Still your move."

"I'm game for any kind of free-for-all, old man," Wolf said.

"Maybe if you boys would've taken your blows out on them Rebs back at Monocacy, we all wouldn't be here," David said.

Jerry looked back down at the checkerboard and made his move. "King me," he said.

It had started to seem to David that there was a lot of hostility in this horsing around. On several occasions, he thought Jerry and Wolf might actually come to blows. The living conditions put everybody on edge. After the checkers game, David found a quiet spot and sat down to read his Bible again. He had worked his way down to the end of the Psalms, Number 150. "Praise the Lord in his sanctuary." No sanctuary here, David thought. He closed his Bible and walked over to the checker game.

"Who's winning?" David asked.

Jerry smiled.

"We have two games apiece," Wolf said as he leaned back and cracked his knuckles. "This is the rubber game."

"You're next, buddy," Jerry said, pointing at David.

"I saw one of the cooks steal a ham from the cook's house," David said.

Jerry looked up at David. "Why didn't you tell me?"

"Thought I'd give it a day or so. Didn't want you to go seeking justice."

"You can't trust them Rebs," Wolf said as he made his move.

"I'm talking about our degenerate Yankee cooks. They steal, then trade ... or give it away," David said. "I've seen ham plenty of times at the cook's house, but none of that kind of food ever touches our mouths. You know those boys, Jerry. You must have seen 'em do it a hundred times."

Jerry pushed all the checkers together. "I hope you're not pointing your finger at me. It's my duty to see that food is distributed equally amongst our troops."

"Yes, but how far down in the line are you, Jerry?" David asked. "How many hands pick over those rations before they get to you? Heck, it's even been cooked before you get your hands on it."

"That doesn't mean I don't know what's happening,"

Jerry spouted.

"You're kind of like a waiter in one of those fancy res-taurants," Wolf added.

"I take issue with that. If I wasn't working with the cooks ..."

"Oh, don't be such a cry baby," Wolf said, cutting him off.

"Some fellow told me the Richmond papers say that their government is ready to exchange prisoners man for man," David said. "I hope soon we'll be out of this despi-cable hole."

"I'm tired of hearing the same old rumors over and over with nothing to them," Jerry barked.

David pointed over at two other prisoners who sat looking at each other with blank stares. "Those two used to be the best of buddies before they lost all hope," David said, nudging Jerry's shoulder. "Be careful, nay saying is catchy."

Knowing Jerry did have its advantages. He'd started a little campaign in the cook's house. It was his insistence that fish could be pulled from the Dan River. There were hoots from the cooks. Even if there were fish in that river, they'd be polluted. Jerry pointed out the obvious—that eating fish from the Dan River couldn't be much worse than swallowing rat dung. This time, one of the Reb cooks went to Grizzly and asked him to oversee an expedition to the Dan. Nothing much resembling a fishing pole could be found so it was agreed that Jerry would be allowed to have a look, to see if such local fish were a reality. The guards agreed to let the water detail take a few extra minutes to poke around.

Jerry and David and a private named Fletcher set out one late afternoon, when the fish would have been near the surface, snapping up mosquitoes. None were really sure what they were doing. Grizzly stood by the bank, keeping an eye on them. Jerry pointed at a broken tree trunk that had washed up near a sand bar.

"I'm warning you, Jerry, you ought to leave that log be," David said.

"You're always complaining about food," Jerry said. "Well, I happen to know that turtles have six or seven different kinds of meat and turtle soup is delicious."

"I'd listen to David if I were you, Jerry," Fletcher said.

"You're not me," Jerry said as he waded out into the water amongst the cattails where the log lay.

David and Fletcher went about their business and carried the squad's water buckets up the bank. Then they heard Grizzly fire a round. David turned to see Jerry out near the sand bar.

"Help," Jerry yelled.

"What's going on, Grizzly?" David shouted.

"Yer buddy's tryin' to escape." Grizzly rested the butt of his rifle back against his shoulder to take aim. He wetted his thumb and wiped the rifle's crosshairs before firing another shot. "Got 'em," Grizzly blurted.

"He was just going after turtles," David said. "He can't even swim."

Jerry flailed in the water, going under a second time. David ran back down to the river and jumped in. He swam toward the sand bar.

Fletcher turned to Grizzly. "Can I help David? Please, Sarge ..."

Grizzly lowered his rifle. "Git," he motioned.

David and Fletcher pulled Jerry back to shore. David pushed on Jerry's chest. He started choking as water expelled out of his mouth.

"Stupid shit," Grizzly said, hitting Jerry in his ribcage with the butt of his rifle.

"I think you shot me, Griz," Jerry moaned.

"I could've killed y'all if'n I wanted." Grizzly rolled him over.

The seat of Jerry's pants had a small tear.

"See David?" Grizzly grinned. "I only grazed his ass." He slung his rifle back over his shoulder. "Now, where's them turtles, boy?"

A fellow Reb guard walked up. "That were a hell of a shot, Griz ... just skinnin' his pants."

"I was aimin' at the turtle." Grizzly leaned back and horse laughed.

When they came back inside, Cork was waiting for them by the door. "You find any fishies men? Any trout, say. I think I heard the word 'turtles.' You bring back any of our finny friends for supper?"

"How did you know?" Jerry asked.

"Oh my," Cork exclaimed. "When you're speaking of fishies, news travels fast."

Later on, the news in Prison No. 1 was that McCallum, Griffith, and Wages of the 110th were exchanged. As the men lay talking about the exchange, a guard came upon them.

"You boys stand up," the Reb guard said.

"Another shakedown," Wolf mumbled.

"Shut up, Yank," the guard said as he rummaged through several of the prisoner's pockets. "Y'all best not be holdin' out on me."

The guard held up a greenback as he walked away.

"One dollar, a big thing," David said. "Vile business for the Southern chivalry to go around feeling men's pockets."

Jerry spit on the floor. "Damn Rebs."

A newspaper left by a Reb guard read that General McClellan and George Pendleton had been nominated for President and Vice President at the Democrat Convention in Chicago.

"McClellan, eh? He was a terrible General," one of the boys nearby said. "Makes sense they'd kick him upstairs. Ain't that always the way?"

"I read an article that General Fremont withdrew his name as a presidential candidate," David said as he handed the paper along to another man.

"Some tell Gentleman George has close ties to them Copperheads," said the man with the paper as he scanned the pages.

Jerry turned and looked at Wolf.

"I read in another paper that General Sherman captured Atlanta," David said. "It also said General Morgan and some of his raiders were killed while attempting an escape during a Union raid on Greeneville, Tennessee."

8

September 1864

Charles Allen's war was equally desperate. And after he heard the details, David was glad he hadn't known, couldn't know, what had befallen his cousin while he languished in prison.

General Morgan and his Raiders were ambushed by the Union Army during their raid on Greeneville, Tennessee on September 4, 1864. Morgan was shot dead off his mount and Charles Allen's left arm was sliced to the bone by a Union cavalryman's sword on the battlefield. He somehow ended up in a Union hospital. On that early September day, as Charles Allen lay bleeding and near death in the hospital, David sat in filth in a Confederate prison. Both were a long way from the Longacher farm where they belonged, where, nearly two and a half years earlier, they debated the war without knowing a thing about it.

9

"Danged if I know why they let these newspapers get here. Gotta be bad for these Rebs to know ... How bad it is for them, I mean," Jerry said. "They must have some

Copperheads sneaking them in."

"I'm hearing that term 'Copperhead' too often, Jerry," Wolf said, kicking the side of Jerry's boot.

"I didn't say anything," Jerry said.

"Don't be looking my way every time you use the word Copperhead, either," Wolf spouted.

Grizzly walked up with another guard.

David laid the newspaper aside. "Hey Grizzly, want to hear my new soup recipe?" he asked.

"I'm a-waitin'," Grizzly said.

"Take muddy sand and filthy water from the Dan River—put in wormy beans and rat berries, boil 'til half done, then throw in a little straw and ashes—no salt, and it's ready for Yankee prisoners."

"I thought y'all was lookin' for fish," Grizzly said. He turned his attention toward Jerry. "Then y'all decides ya want turtle soup. Now y'all's got nothin'."

"We could have found them if you'd given us half a chance," Jerry said as he walked away.

"Y'all knock off your bitchin'. We got the same grub as y'all," Grizzly said.

"Matter of fact, we must eat even what the niggers won't," the other guard said.

"Did I hear some talk 'bout Sherman?" Grizzly asked.

"Matter of fact, you did, Griz. The war seems to be coming to an end," David said. "Benjamin Butler wrote a letter that details all the articles of incarcerated prisoner exchange and your Major posted the letter in every building here at Danville. Butler's your typical politician."

"I hear Butler has the nickname 'Spoons,'" Grizzly laughed. "Whenever he's an intruder on one of our plantations, the confab is to keep an eye on yer' silverware."

The second Reb guard tapped Grizzly's shoulder.

"Officers entering the prison, boys. Get upstairs where y'all belong," Grizzly shouted, then he mumbled under his breath, "I don't give a damn whether y'all go or not. Personally, I'm goin' upstairs."

"How about a game of chess, Wolf?" David asked.

"Why not checkers?" Wolf said.

"Jerry wanted to play a game of checkers, he don't know how to play chess," David said as he set up the chessboard.

Jerry shuffled back to them from the cook house. He had lost his eagerness and seemed to get tired more easily. His face was gaunt and he was pallid. While other kitchen workers usually maintained their weight, Jerry got thinner.

"Deeter, Shertzer, and Furnas of Company G were all killed in the Battle of Winchester," Jerry said.

"Didn't know them," Wolf said.

"Furnas and I had a mutual friend. He sent me a message. They said Isaac was pretty broke up when his wife died. Maybe he stopped caring."

"I know that name Deeter," David said. "But I can't call up his face."

David and Wolf looked up. Standing over them was a Confederate Major General. David started to stand.

"At ease, son," the General motioned. "My officers

tell me that there've been complaints about the food, so I wanted to inform y'all myself that our own boys must eat their cornbread without meat. Y'all's General Sheridan has been orderin' his men to destroy foodstuffs to try an' starve us out. Therefore, y'all can thank your own general for the meager provisions."

Someone in the back shouted, "You look like you been getting some grub." The Major General was, in fact, a portly man, with a ruddy, bulbous nose—a sign of too many toasts.

"In all campaigns, true, it is the officers who are fed first. If we didn't keep up our strength, our judgment would be impaired and anarchy would ensue." There was a resounding silence. "Second, I'd like y'all to disregard any rumors 'bout the niggers bein' in the way of the prisoner exchange. More lies from the White House to shed a bad light on the slave owner—that is, niggers gettin' exchanged before white Yankee soldiers. And finally, tell your buddies that the Confederate Army is goin' to give everyone a chance to enlist in our service, including niggers."

David opened his mouth.

"Y'all have something to say, son?" the General asked.

"No sir," David said.

"Then pass it on," the General continued.

David started to stand again.

"As you were, boys," the General ordered as he swaggered out of the room.

"What was that all about?" Wolf said.

"I'll tell you, Wolf, it's about lying to and insulting every Union soldier in this miserable death trap," David said. "First, we were rationed an ounce of meat today. I can personally testify to seeing the Rebs eating better. And as far as the Negro boys, the General has no say whatsoever. Mainly because the Southern politicians consider them all contraband, fugitive slaves seeking protection behind Northern lines. The politicians are being pressured to return the slaves back to their owners. And what Union soldier would bring dishonor to himself by joining up with the Rebs? Especially since they're about to be defeated. It's all nothing but blow from the brass."

David pointed to the floor. "And the silver-tongued General attempts to deliver his message as we sleep in our own and everybody else's swill and defecation." David's lips quivered as he spoke.

"Maybe now's not the best time to tell you this, but Beth said in one of her letters that your Cousin Charles is in a campaign in Tennessee," Wolf said.

"My family told me a little, not much about Charles Allen," David said. "They said his brother, Frank Lee, is working out. I'm grateful for that."

"You know Frank Lee farmed in Kentucky for his girl's father," Wolf said.

"I don't remember hearing that," David said.

"You told me that yourself," Jerry said quietly. "You told me months ago you were worried over Frank Lee. He was thinking about going to the Rebel side with some

Kentucky girl and you were afraid he wouldn't stay with your family."

"I told you that?" David asked. "I don't remember. Sometimes it's hard to remember anything but being here."

"Frank Lee for Charles Allen seems a pretty fair exchange," Wolf said. "Both are good farmers for boys raised in town, but word is Frank Lee is more dependable. And anyway, he's no Charles Allen. Charles Allen would die for the South's cause."

10

Charles Allen blinked his eyes. The chloroform was wearing off. His arm throbbed. He took a deep breath and stared at his mangled arm. He swallowed back his vomit. The sabre had cut deep—to the bone—it hung on only by his swollen and discolored flesh. Turning his head back, he saw, in a corner, what appeared to be pieces of arms and legs piled on the floor. He trembled. He now knew this was no nightmare. He turned his head again. Everything on the operating table next to him became a blur, except for a bloody saw. He slipped back into the darkness.

A doctor stopped at the bloody table and looked at the young man. There was a nurse with him, a pretty blonde girl who must have seen far more than her share of amputations.

"You have a name for this one?" the doctor asked.

"He told one of the men who brought him in that his

name was Charles Allen," she replied.

The doctor scratched his head. "Another Son of the South, eh?"

"You think he deserved this?"

"If you want my opinion, they all deserved this. Damned fool war. Men flocking to battle like sheep. Doesn't give me much hope for the human race ... Hand me some more of that chloroform, Nurse," the doctor said. He was a man in his sixties, a man who remembered the days when he operated without it.

The nurse poured the liquid onto some gauze and handed it to the doctor. She pushed her blonde curls back as she wiped her forehead on her bloodstained sleeve.

"Poor boy," the nurse said, stroking Charles Allen's head. She allowed herself a long look at the arm. She gagged. Gangrene had set in but there was no hope anyway of saving the soldier without him giving up his arm.

The doctor had numerous battlefield experiences and he knew his job. Once Charles Allen was under, he began sawing to even out the jagged bone. He thought of how he disliked being called a "sawbones."

The doctor held Charles Allen's amputated arm in his hand, then glanced over at the pile of amputated body parts.

"No, don't." The nurse grabbed the arm from him and pointed at the Masonic ring on one of the fingers. She worked the ring free and placed it in her pocket.

"What do you intend on doing with that?" the doctor asked.

"Who knows," the nurse said as she held onto the boy's arm. "I know his name," she whispered.

To the doctor, it seemed to be an extraordinary sentiment on her part, when he was the one confronted every day with saving the lives of ignorant boys who had thought life was cheap—as if it were something that could be tossed away. He picked up a scalpel, wiped it clean and went back to work on the arm, cutting away the remaining shreds of gangrenous flesh, pulling down muscle and skin so as to cushion the bone when the stump healed, and suturing the wound tight.

11

Late the next night, David lay on the floor next to Wolf. David gave Wolf a slight nudge on his shoulder. Wolf rolled over on his side to face David.

"There's around eighty or so Hundred Days men like yourself in our building, right?" David whispered.

Wolf nodded.

"And you say they've been grumbling about not getting discharged and sent back home when their service time is over ..." David paused. "Ain't your hitch up?"

"It is," Wolf said. "But it looks like we're going to be in prison until the war's over, Hundred Days men or not." Wolf stopped talking as he thought he'd heard footsteps. After a moment, he continued, "I talked to our top sergeant and he told me a plan."

"You and them boys going to escape?" David asked.

"Not me, I'm sticking with you," Wolf said.

"I'd hoped you say that, because I feel the exchange is near," David said.

"Shh ..." Wolf turned and lay quiet as the moonlight shone on a Reb guard passing through the hall. Then he went on, "The Southern politicians don't see it that way. They know they have to exchange the niggers and officers first, or they lose the support of slave owners and the military. And if they exchange slaves and Reb officers, sooner or later they better exchange Reb enlisted men, or there'll be all hell to pay at election time. Voters don't forget," Wolf added.

David tossed and turned. There was a ruckus at the far side of the room. David saw it was Cork, on one of his midnight walks. He had attached himself to one and then another group away from David, Wolf, and Jerry, but lately he'd begun sitting with them and soon, David knew, he'd be sleeping nearby as well. Cork was a hanger-on.

The floor was crowded with sleeping soldiers. Cork tiptoed using the moonlight to maneuver about. Having picked his way through the bodies, he sat down next to where Wolf lay and then pointed at David. "You're the one with the relative in the Rebel army, ain't ya?"

"You could say that about a lot of us," David answered.

"That's what makes this war so ..."

David placed his finger on his lips. "Shh ..."

Cork nudged closer, squeezing through a couple more lying nearby. "You have to tread carefully," he now spoke in an undertone.

"That's right," David said, "Don't want to disturb the sleepers."

"Sleepers, yes, I like that. I was going to say 'honored dead.'"

"Not yet," David replied. But Cork gave him the willies. David took a closer look at him, as if to challenge his own fear. Up close, even by moonlight, he saw that Cork had lines radiating out from the corners of his eyes and around his mouth. He was an older man than David had thought at first. And he wasn't sure he'd ever seen a human looking so worn out.

"I served on a battlefield not long ago. So many dead ... the young, the old, even the niggers from both sides. They was so close to each other end to end, side by side, some two and three deep, that you could've walked across that whole field and never touched ground; just walking on the backs of the fallen."

"Where?" David whispered. He knew Cork was telling the truth this time. He'd seen places like those himself.

"What battleground? They're all the same, once you've seen a few, don't you think? Men just lying there dead as can be. Like lily pads. You could be a frog crossing over them." Cork took a deep breath and curled up on the floor. "It was a shame about them fishies—not finding them. I had a taste for fish." He rolled over and began whistling *Camptown Races*.

David pressed his finger to his lips once again. "Shh, Cork, them Rebs will hear your doo-dahs ..."

Surviving on chop bread and muddy water continued to take its toll. Most prisoners were weak and some housed on the second and third floors were hardly able to crawl up the stairs. The cravings of a hungry stomach were close to unendurable—worse than some of the other sicknesses the soldiers had. Good moments were rare.

"One of the boys discovered we can make coffee out of the crust of the stale cornbread," Wolf said.

"Where's Jerry?" David asked.

"I believe he's over at the cook's house," Wolf said.

David pulled out the chess pieces.

"Let's play checkers," Wolf said.

David continued to set up the chess pieces. "Did you read that handbill some Reb put up?"

Wolf shook his head. "No, but I had some corn crust coffee."

"I seen it," said one of the men nearby. They'd taken to sitting in larger clusters—a dozen or more—exchanging information, ideas. Making plans. They sensed that the end of the war was near and they wanted to talk about the good times ahead once they were free.

"The Rebs want us to work on their defenses. The guards already ordered Dunning, Reese, Green, Fletcher, Nyswonger of the 110th, and Fullwiler of the 6th Cavalry to work," David said. "Work on Reb fortifications? God save us from such a disgrace."

"They know we're good at building fortifications because we have the best engineers teaching us. We know the difference between a spade and a pitchfork, y'all," a New York boy said.

Jerry came back just in time to barge in. "General Grant thought we were too good at it," he said. "That's why he wanted us to learn drill and discipline."

"Damn waste of time, drill," the man said.

"They wouldn't be pressing us into service now if we weren't so good," another commented.

The group broke up, several men going off to get some shut-eye, a few more to talk about what they would do when they got back home.

"How the heck do you know what General Grant's thinking?" David asked Jerry.

Wolf decided to sit this one out and leave things in David's hands.

"I got it from the wire back when," Jerry said. "... from those friends of yours at the depot."

"You were talking to them, too?"

"Long after you were."

"They told you things?"

"Sometimes," Jerry said. "And sometimes I just over-heard."

"I thought that everything was in code," David said.

"So it was; but I knew the cipher."

"How?"

"David, with all due respect, I'm a lot smarter than you give me credit for."

David pondered Jerry's remark. He had always thought Jerry was clever. But not book learned. "You're smart ..."

"Got to be. That's how you survive. That's why Grant is as good as he is."

"The General's smart?"

"He's cunning. That time he reviewed us in Culpepper County, what did you think of him?"

"He was pretty far away ... I thought he'd be bigger. And older. He didn't look that much older than us," David said.

"That saved him from trouble. Maybe even danger. People always expected him to be bigger and older. When they met for the first time, people would gather around one of his assistants—a couple are men in their sixties—imposing, white haired. Kind of like Lee. They would swarm the one who looked like a commander and Grant could slip right past them."

"So much for seeing and believing," David said.

"Trickery got us where we are today," Jerry said.

Wolf held his tongue. Sometimes it seemed as if the war had turned Jerry into a Copperhead himself.

David turned his focus back to the chessboard. "I hope to God they can get us out before it's too late."

"Two of the 2nd Massachusetts Cavalry had a fisticuff last night," Wolf said. "The Reb guard had to call for help in order to break them up."

"That's why the Hundred Days men's escape will be in broad daylight," David said.

"That's crazy," Wolf said.

"You know it's not. You've heard the same rumors, that the guards have no discipline. Some of their companies are just a bunch of ragtag bummers," David said. "It'll be your job to divert the inside guard's attention."

Wolf scratched his head. "How?"

"You'll figure something out," David said. "If you see one of them not trying to stop the fight, get him in a conversation."

"Hell, David, the Reb guard on duty with Griz is trigger happy," Wolf said. "None of the boys dare go by a window much less a door."

"I'll take care of Grizzly," David said.

"How?" Wolf asked.

"You'll see," David said.

October 1864

"A new handbill was put up asking us to enlist in the Confederate Army again," Wolf said.

David walked over to the bulletin board and when the guard's back was turned, he tore the handbill down.

"Two of our boys already did enlist," David said. "That's two too many. There'll be more if we don't get some of them out of here. Most of the Hundred Days boys aren't in for the long haul like you, Wolf."

"You still believe they could make a clean getaway in plain daylight?" Wolf asked.

"With a plan," David whispered. "Some of the prisoners tried to cut out last night but were discovered before ever setting foot out the front door. I'll tell you what

General Grant would have done and your boys can chew it over."

There was a loud crash from the other side of the room and then a quarrel over in the corner. Cork sat not far away, muttering more feverishly than usual. He'd been agitated for several days. And now there were others like him. Mutterers, cursers, and weepers—all living most of the time inside their own nightmares. David and Wolf paused, afraid the commotion would wake up an eavesdropper nearby.

"We might have a stool pigeon amongst us," Wolf said.

Both having the same thought, they laid back down.

"Stow it," David whispered.

A Reb guard approached. David rolled over on his back, pulled out his diary and began reading an entry to Wolf:

> "In my imagination I this evening am at home among or with loved ones though I cannot speak with them – I see them seated in their pleasant rooms chatting. I can't help thinking of the happy scenes now transpiring in the free and happy North. There the families are gathered around the fireside or are at church and know little how we are suffering in Southern prisons. I am thankful to God for His goodness to me in giving me good health in this lonesome prison. How I would love to spend the evening at home."

The guard tilted his head toward their conversation. David put the diary away.

The escape plan was agreed to and set into motion. The next day, in early afternoon, when things were quietest, one and then another prisoner somehow got through one of the several doors. The first two ducked into the shade of a large willow tree by the river. At a signal from the third, a fight erupted in one corner of the compound. And then another. Some with foreknowledge of the plan joined in the melee. They threw anything handy at one another—clothes, blankets, until the entire prison house was in a state of anarchy. The guards had been warned to expect it. They immediately went to their posts and aimed their guns into the ruckus of men. They'd been ordered not to shoot unless they got a clear look at the leaders, but there was too much of a free-for-all to single anyone out.

Outside, eight more prisoners—eleven in all—lined up. Many wore ragged jackets and hats they'd accepted from Reb soldiers in exchange for their better quality Union uniforms. Forming up, the eleven marched down the road as if they were a small detail of troops. They'd have aroused more attention had they been armed. But in the Confederate army's state of disarray, a small detail of any kind drew little attention.

David never knew what became of the eleven. He had never known any of them by name.

But for the prisoners inside—even for those who didn't know the plotters—the escape changed the climate.

Most felt easier, not because they planned getaways of their own, but because they'd been reminded that the world they'd left behind so many months ago, might remain, God willing, more or less the way they remembered it. And therefore it could be returned to. But for the crazed ones and the ones over whom a deep cloud of depression had settled, the escape was cause for even greater anxiousness. They jabbered more loudly. A few actually found each other and sat in a little knot, sharing their cathartic visions. Only Cork seemed calmer, almost serene. David watched him joking with one of the prisoners and then with the guards.

"Jefferson Davis was in Danville last night making a political speech that promised the people peace in thirty days," Wolf said.

"Who told you that?" David asked.

"A Yankee prisoner who'd escaped from a train car passed it along to a deserting Reb on the run," Wolf said. "Hey, why don't you read me another one of your letters from home?"

"It's been over three months since I heard from home," David said as he turned toward a pounding sound. It was Grizzly boarding up one of the window frames.

"More wooden glass." Wolf shook his head. "Keep men in, keep light out."

It did not keep the men in. The eleven who got away had emboldened the prisoners even more so. Seventy-five

Union prisoners—Hundred Days men and some Army regulars—escaped before noontime several days later. Some had been working on the Rebs' fortifications and some were from inside the prison having been rounding up for mess. David made a small contribution by egging Grizzly into a drinking contest with another guard. Wolf had also been one of the plotters. Nothing would have persuaded Wolf to leave David so he provoked a couple of the guards into an argument to distract them. The two had ultimately come to blows, which was exactly what Wolf was hoping for. And then things got out of hand. In the heat of the fight, the one guard turned away to pick up the Colt Navy he'd dropped and Wolf caught him from behind. A prisoner got to the revolver first. Wolf held the guard's arms as the prisoner stepped to the side and fired the pistol point-blank behind the guard's ear. The guard's lifeless body slumped out of Wolf's grip.

The shot was like a signal. First, everything stopped, then everything went awry. The prisoner threw the gun at the glass window, shattering it. Several more angry prisoners rushed forward, pushing Wolf aside, and picked up the guard's body. Using it like a battering ram to clear the rest of the pane from the frame, they threw the guard's body out into the open air. Quiet filled the room. Then more guards rushed in, a couple of them firing their muskets into the air. The prisoners sat down.

There was great concern in town as consequence of the escape. The Reb soldiers collected in groups discussing the bold Yankee trick. David did not understand how so many got away when they had nowhere to hide and, of course, were weak and unarmed. He tossed it around in his mind, who was braver, who was more desperate?—the eleven or the seventy-five? David rubbed his chin, mumbling to himself.

Late that same night David and Wolf lay talking about the escape.

"No news about the escapees, but I hear a lynch mob from the town of Danville are after them with bloodhounds," David said. "Rumor has it six Reb guards were killed in the affray. You said that you boys would get the head guard in a conversation, not kill him."

"He had nothing to say," Wolf said.

"Was it necessary to toss him out the window?" David asked.

"I wasn't part of that, but I'll say one thing. His potshotting days are over."

There was a kind of swagger in what Wolf said. It was as if from beneath his Hundred Days soldier exterior, a veteran trooper had emerged. The boyish Wolf was transforming into manhood before David's eyes and he longed for the day when this was over, the day when, hopefully, they could all recover themselves.

Not a man in the prison house slept well that night. Cork was noisy. He mumbled and was up and down. Toward morning, he started screaming about horses. In his mind, they were dying. They were raring and kicking, and then dead. A few had wings and flew off into the sky. When Cork awoke, he wondered if the nightmare was some kind of metaphor.

Indian summer was upon them. "You hear about the sick from the hospital that were taken to Richmond for exchange?" David asked. "One of them died at the depot before he got on the car."

"Yes, and they brought his corpse back to prison number one," Wolf said.

"Just think, far away from his home, he has breathed his last. Perhaps his folks, or even his sisters and brothers will never know his fate ... Such is life," David said. "Go to sleep, Wolf."

Two days later David and Wolf sat on the floor playing checkers.

"Where did Grizzly disappear to?" Wolf asked.

"Haven't heard," David said.

"Will he tell that you caused him to get drunk?" Wolf asked.

"Only if he remembers."

They heard footsteps. David looked up. It was two Rebs from the Provost Marshal's office. David and Wolf stood.

"What y'all been up to, Yanks?" the Reb first sergeant asked.

"Oh, playing board games and waiting to come back to the fight after our exchange," David said.

"Where were y'all when one of our guards on this

floor was killed?" the Provost Marshal asked.

"I believe we were eating, if that's what you call it," Wolf said.

"Were there any other officers or guards around when it happened?" the first sergeant asked.

"Officers?" David said. "I reckon the Reb officers were all at headquarters sitting down at a fine table spread."

The first sergeant guffawed. The Provost Marshal shot the sergeant a look.

"Don't y'all get smart-alecky, Yank," the first sergeant said.

"I heard a noise like glass breaking, then I heard more noise. Men were yelling and others were cheering," David said.

"Y'all know Grizzly, don't ya?" the Provost Marshal asked.

David knew Grizzly had been injured during the scuffle. He'd seen him lose his balance, stumble into a wall, and bang his head on a door jam, too drunk to get up.

"We're old buddies," David said. "Even used the same Spencer rifle off and on."

"We've already captured twelve of them escaped Yanks," the first sergeant said. "Y'all go on and be sure to spread that news 'round."

"Bully for you," Wolf said.

The butt of the first sergeant's musket landed in Wolf's stomach. Wolf doubled-up on the floor.

"If you Rebs caught twelve escaped Yankees, why

not ask them? Maybe one of them might know what happened to Grizzly," David said as he grabbed Wolf's hand, pulling him up. He eyed the Rebs. "Truth is, I saw him trying to break it up."

"You damn Yanks won't be workin' on our defenses anymore. And y'all can count on gettin' your food rations cut," the first sergeant said as they walked away.

Wolf rubbed and then pressed on his midsection.

Two new prisoners walked up to David and Wolf.

"Mind if we play the winner?" the short man asked. "Where did you get the board?"

"It belonged to one of our friends," David said. "I'm holding it in trust."

"Where you boys coming from?" Wolf asked.

"Number six," the tall man said.

"You two the ones who informed on the escape in number six?" Wolf asked.

The taller one handed David a large piece of cornbread and looked over at Wolf. "You shouldn't be spreading rumors like that, son. Innocent parties could suffer in consequence," he said.

"The price of bribery has sure went down since Judas was handed the thirty pieces of silver," David said as he accepted the cornbread and broke it in two, handing half to Wolf.

"Here boys, take the board," David continued. "Don't forget to return it, or a ghost just might come looking for you."

If the newspapers and rumors were true, if all the signs shown by rations and shipments and movement of troops, the demeanor of guards and the occasional officers coming through meant anything, then the war had to be winding down. The Rebels seemed to be losing, in disarray, out of supplies, out of weapons. But the officers carried on as if things would go their way, in time.

Only a few weeks after the leaves had started turning, the temperature dropped. The prisoners began to fret about an early winter. One day, two Confederate officers walked into the room with a couple of Reb infantrymen and ordered them to install a woodburning stove on each floor of Prison No. 1.

"Looks as if the Rebs aren't going to let us freeze all at once," Wolf said. "I expect they're planning to hold us through the winter."

"They know they're losing this war," David said. "They just might find themselves in our circumstances soon. I think they're planning ahead for themselves." David pointed to the two prisoners from No. 6. "What do you think, Wolf, should we leave our comrades with the board? When we're exchanged, they might still be staying for a while. Rebs do like stool pigeons."

"I'd watch my back if I was you two," Wolf called over to the tattlers.

Some time had passed when Grizzly returned on guard duty in Prison No. 1 again.

"Hey L'il Coot, y'all got a moment?" Grizzly asked. "Not you, Wolf."

Wolf walked away.

"I've been in the Reb guard house," Grizzly said.

"What for?"

"Y'all know the what fors," Grizzly said. "But don't y'all worry, I had it better than the brass that's tryin' to explain how all them Yanks escaped."

"They must have gotten away then," David said. "Probably home by now."

Grizzly looked uncomfortable. "I don't know nothin' 'bout that, L'il Coot. The higher ups don't care if'n they made it, they just don't like it that they had the chance."

"Does anyone in the guard house know how the presidential election is going?" David asked.

"I'll fill ya in, Lil' Coot. Gossipin' is the only thing the boys have to do in lockup. Pennsylvania's gone Democratic."

"So?"

"Y'all don't think that'll help bring the war to an end?"

"This war won't end until one side or the other gives up. Sometimes when I look back upon the scenes of the past five months, I shudder to think of the awful slaughter of humans. And why? Because a few hot headed leaders could no longer rule, they began this war and now the blood be upon their hands and not ours," David said. "Old Abe will win."

"We lost to y'all at Cedar Creek in Virginia," Grizzly

said.

"I found out two of my good buddies, Holsinger and Simes were wounded," David said. "Did you hear anything about them?"

"Are they ..."

Just as Grizzly was about to speak, a fistfight broke out between two New Yorkers from the 106th.

"Stop that, ya lil' coots," Grizzly yelled out, pulling the men apart. "I said knock it off."

Grizzly took a bandana from his pocket and ripped it in half. "Now wipe y'all's bloody noses."

It was near sunset. David had been walking for so long that it reminded him of one of the battle marches in the Wilderness. He climbed the porch steps of his home, walked over to the front window, then exhaled, wiping the evening mist off the glass. There they were: Ma, Nel, Hannah, and Beth, all gathered around the hearth.

An oil lamp sparkled as the wick burned brighter. David squinted his eyes to get a better look. Everyone held a book in their hands. David smiled as he saw his mother's head nod and her book fall from her hands onto the hearth.

Minutes later, he watched the good women go into the kitchen, then return to the parlor— Hannah with a large waiter well filled with pies and cakes, Beth with a basket full of apples. Nel walked over to the front door, pulled back the latch, and opened it.

And now David was inside, with Beth beside him and

231

someone, he was sure it was Nel, at his side. He stepped forward to get a better look. The door opened once again to a view of the entire valley. In the distance stood the old covered bridge.

He looked down toward the barn. No livestock. He realized that there was no sign of life outside, except for a crow standing at the edge of the porch. It looked at David, hopped down from the porch and once or twice along the ground, then took flight. The bird opened its mouth wide, wide enough to see its tongue, but there was no sound. The crow worried David. Where had everybody gone?

David cried out and bolted upright. He rubbed his eyes.

"Go back to sleep," Wolf said. "It's just a nightmare."

"No, it was almost provoking. I dreamt I was at home and had chicken pie and plenty of custards," David said. He wiped the tears from his eyes and scanned the dark walls that surrounded him. "Then the crow came."

"Now you know it's a nightmare, we would have cooked up that vulture," Wolf said. "The war will be over soon, buddy."

"That's creepy," Jerry said. "So, David, since your family's got more than one horse in this contest, who do you figure will win?"

David lay back down. He didn't like thinking about what the war might have done to Charles Allen, but it was better than reminiscing about a nightmare. He had no idea where his cousin had gone, what he'd done, what he'd seen, just small tidbits of information from Ma's letters. He dare not think about what the affect would be on Charles Allen of the South's defeat.

"I'll tell you who'll win, Jerry," a man nearby piped up. "The ones who made it. The living!"

"Like us," another agreed.

"I was thinking," a reedy voice added, "The victors are the ladies. They've had all the weaklings and the cowards weeded out and now have only the strong and the fearless from whom to pick their husbands."

"'From whom'?" someone said. "Who taught you to say *whooommmm*? You some kind of foreigner?"

"Hey," another shouted, annoyed, "Nobody never learned you arithmetic. The ladies gotta outnumber suitors by a few hundred thousand. There'll even be pretty widows who can't find a mate."

"It will be necessary," said a deep voice nearby, "for patriotic men to take unto themselves more than one wife. Like the old kings and prophets of the Bible."

"Those people out west got the right idea. They take themselves wives by the numbers."

"Who?" asked the reedy voice, clearly interested.

"The Mormons," said a new voice. "They're required to."

"Do you get to choose, or would you have to take an ugly one?"

"As to Mormon courtship practices ..." said the deep voice, "you'd have to ask a Mormon."

David was wide awake as the morning sun's rays filtered

through the cracks in the walls. The Reb bugler blew reveille. David got up and went to the half-opened door. A single sentry stood there. It was understood that there would be no escapes today since it was likely that the repatriation would begin in a matter of days.

David took in a deep breath of the cool morning air. He walked back over to Wolf and poked him. "Come on, Wolf, help me carry water for our squad," David said.

"You call that mud from the Dan water?" Wolf said. "What's for chow?"

"Stale cornbread," David said.

They passed Green and Kane who were wrestling by the riverbank.

"I'm sick and tired of the cooks stealing all the meat," David said. "I hear sweet taters sell at three dollars ... greenbacks ... per dozen."

"I wish you'd stop talking about food," Wolf said.

"Okay then, how's this for you ... I heard the elections in Indiana and Ohio have gone Republican," David said. "I also heard for the third or fourth time that General Jubal Early was completely wiped out at Cedar Creek."

"He's the geezer who put us in here," Wolf said.

"Well, I hope it's not for much longer," David said. "Have you noticed that we don't get much news by the tattler's line now? I don't know if it's because our boys have been deceived so often, or because the Rebs have been getting their comeuppances lately."

"Did you notice that a lot of our boys look like Rebs?" Wolf asked.

"That was part of the escape plan, getting our men to trade uniforms, hats, and their boots with some of the Rebs before they busted out. That way they could walk through the town of Danville looking like the rest of the local yokels and they'd have some Confed money in their pockets," David said. "Trading my boy, that's what it's all about."

"So where'd you get the whiskey to get Grizzly drunk?" Wolf asked.

David's access to liquor to be used as disinfectant had vanished. Even moonshine had become scarce.

"Traded my Testament to a Reb sergeant," David said. "Once I gave Griz and his comrade the bottle, they couldn't help themselves."

"Good trick," Wolf said. "But you're pretty serious about religion, David. What will you do for spiritual guidance?"

"I memorized a lot of it," David said. "And what I don't know, I'm going to have to leave in God's hands."

"Did you see the fisticuffs this afternoon?" Wolf asked.

"There's so many affrays, I believe fighting is what keeps some of the boys at peace," David muttered. "How ironic."

Good conversation had become as scarce as decent food. There was rarely enough information about the election to keep an intelligent political discussion going. There was nothing to be said about the food. A few men still persisted in talking about their future plans—their farms and businesses, their wives and families, their proposed adventures. In time, even these grew tiresome. And so the prisoners talked about insults, fights, and barter.

"Larue from Company D called Reese a liar and received several hard knocks on his blinkers for it, so hard that he measured his length on the floor twice," Wolf laughed. "It was better than the knockdown in the 2nd Massachusetts. Then there was that brawl between a couple of Reb guards at the river side."

"I traded another one of the Reb guards in the fight a pair of my suspenders for a pint of Irish whiskey. I got my Good Book back. I was thinking that trading it might have brought bad luck," David said. "Besides, the Reb said the General wanted something to hold up his pants. He probably had enough whiskey to float a warship. And all the officers already have the Good Book."

"For not being a drinking man, you sure used to get a hold of quite a bit of liquor," Wolf said.

"Medicine, Wolf, medicine," David said. "How about the Reb sergeant trying to butter up our boys to join the Reb Army? The boys laughed him to shame. The sergeant says they pay sixteen dollars a month. With the exchange rate, that would be about two dollars in our greenbacks."

"A man with a family couldn't live on that," Wolf said. "Heck, a man *without* a family couldn't either."

"The Reb sergeant said that they cared nothing about the families. It's soldiers they're after. It shows how hard up them Rebs are," David said. "Old Collins of our regulars enlisted in Old Jeff's service."

"What did the Rebs give him?" Wolf asked.

"Collins got all he could stuff his belly with," David said. Collins had always been a greedy and opportunistic man. David hoped he'd choked on the Reb vittles.

Jerry walked up. "How about a game of checkers, David?"

Wolf looked at Jerry, then got up to walk away as David set up the checkerboard.

"What's wrong with Wolf?" Jerry asked.

David turned up his hands. "Where you been, Jerry?"

"Rebs' isolation stockade," Jerry said. "Somebody said that I'd been stealing food for myself."

"Well it's the truth, ain't it?" a voice called from the corner.

"It's not," Jerry said. "But now I know who bore false witness."

"Say no more," David said. "Are we playing checkers for fun or profit here?"

"For tomorrow's breakfast rations," Jerry said.

"And if we don't get any cornbread tomorrow?" David asked.

"Then the loser pays up when we do," Jerry said.

"I'm supposed to trust you?" David asked as a sharp pain ran up his legs. He rubbed them before sitting down on the dank prison floor.

Jerry moved a red checker out. David turned the board around. "I'm red, you went first last time," David said as he moved his man.

Jerry leaned over the board, pondering his next move.

"Scuttlebutt is Miller of the 34th Ohio Volunteers replaced you as chief cook," David said.

"Then it's a miracle we ain't been poisoned already," Jerry sneered. "Who told you about Miller?"

"Grizzly told me he was right there in the cook's house when you got your stripes ripped off," David said.

"That's right, and his ass rode the rails up and down because he left his guard post to come nose around the cook's house, mooching grub," Jerry said.

Wolf returned, still standoffish toward Jerry. "You get another paper today, David?" he asked.

"Yesterday's *Examiner* says Lincoln carried all the states except Delaware, New Jersey, and Kentucky," David said.

"So what, everybody knew that all the prisoners here were for Lincoln," Jerry said.

"Not all of the prisoners," David said. "Our officers went for McClellan."

"That figures, General McClellan was one of them," Jerry said, moving one of his checkers. "Someone raided my haversack again last night. You wouldn't happen to know who's responsible, since you seem to know everything else?"

"Beats me," David said. "But I do know that one of the new kitchen workers, a fellow named Rummel, sent me a pound loaf of cornbread to share with some of the boys."

"What are you trying to say?" Jerry asked.

David had heard all the rumors about Jerry and defended him. But he had doubts himself about Jerry's honesty. He didn't feel like mincing words. "What I'm telling you," David said, keeping his voice down, "is that stealing *is* possible."

"I stole half a chicken once to feed an old vet when he was dying," Jerry said. "And that was all."

"I heard that it was more," said a voice David couldn't place. There were a number of assenting grunts.

"Food gets shipped here and it gets passed to you," Jerry said.

"And on the way to us, it's stolen by the cooks. That's what the boys all say," David shrugged.

"I'm telling you that precious little gets to us in the first place. The brass, the two or three head cooks, they sell it to civilians, to commanders," Jerry said. "A plantation owner came by last week looking for salt pork. Don't think he left empty handed."

The man in the corner who'd accused Jerry first shouted again, "Anyway you was chief cook, wasn't you?"

"I was chief cook for all of four days before they put me in the stockade. Look at me, do I look like I'm fattening up?" Jerry asked as he lifted his shirt to reveal the outline of his ribcage. His eyes had darkened during his time locked up.

"That stealin' happened on your watch. You should be penalized," the man in the corner added.

Jerry's nerves were shot and, in fact, he'd been

caught in a lie. He'd seen some transactions—a few bags of flour and a side of beef being diverted to one of the general's aides. Jerry had no choice but to agree. He'd have been relieved of duty if he objected. But he'd taken payment. He'd have been cashiered if he hadn't played the game.

His back to the wall, Jerry lost even the pretense of composure. He pushed aside a couple of men to get at his accuser. The man was not yet on his feet when Jerry jumped him. The man fell backwards with Jerry kicking at his head.

David grabbed Jerry from behind, putting a forearm over his eyes. Jerry elbowed David hard below the rib cage, and winded him. Jerry spun around toward David, his fist cocked.

Jerry and David had known each other since childhood. They'd been best friends almost from the time they first enlisted and arrived in camp. But Jerry had changed and personal history seemed to count for little with him.

"You gonna hit me, Jerry?" David asked.

"Get out of my way, Longacher. I got no time for the likes of you."

Wolf had worked his way through the crowd that had gathered and he caught Jerry from behind. Another man, a checker-playing friend of Wolf's, grasped Jerry's right arm.

David faced him down. "You owe me, Jerry."

"For what, you pious bastard ..."

"You sure do have a short memory," David said.

"Does drowning ring a bell, imbecile?"

"Pulling me out the Dan River? Whoopee for you," Jerry said.

"That Reb guard could have shot you dead," David said. "Fletcher and me had our rations cut because of you, and you repay us by acting niggardly and uncharitable."

Jerry pulled free from Wolf but stood his ground. The checkerboard that he and David had talked across for so many months lay between them, waiting for Jerry's move.

Jerry kicked the checkerboard across the room and went for David's throat. Wolf pushed Jerry from the side, turned him and gave Jerry an uppercut square on his chin, knocking Jerry to the floor.

A Reb guard came running and tossed a bucket of river water in Jerry's face. The guard motioned two prisoners to hold him.

"You miss solitary confinement, Yank?" the guard shouted. "I reckon you like no grub at all. How 'bout your dirt bed over at the hole?"

A couple more guards pushed their way through to the fight. Elbowing the prisoners aside, they handcuffed Jerry, and marched him down the stairs that led outside.

"How ironic ... Dan River water. The same water he was drowning in," David said.

Wolf began picking up the scattered checkers.

Jerry was only gone a week this time. When he came back, he didn't announce himself. A whole day had passed before David even realized that he'd returned. He'd gotten a kitchen job back again. Perhaps Jerry was a better cook than David realized.

Though this time, Jerry seemed to have changed even a little more. He kept his distance, spending most of his time to himself. He refused to play checkers. When he wasn't working, he stayed out of sight.

12

November 1864

The last bugle call of the night was blown as Wolf lay snoring. David rolled over to face Wolf and poked him in the ribs.

"You know, Wolf, we had no supper so I go hungry to bed and hungry rise, which will certainly diminish my body in size," David said.

Wolf blinked himself awake and looked over at David. "That's your idea of poetry ain't it? You woke me up to recite some of your childhood poetry and remind me that I'm hungry?"

"You're right," David said. "Things are better when you're asleep."

Wolf rolled back over and within a few minutes he was snoring again.

David began shivering as he watched the snowflakes fall just outside the window. He closed his eyes, only to be awakened when he heard sobbing.

"I served my time in this Army faithfully and now when I should be at home with my loved ones, I lay here freezing and starving. Please help me, God," a man cried out.

All of a sudden, the walls rattled. One of the Reb sentinels shot at a prisoner standing next to a window. The minié ball missed. The sentinel ran up, striking the prisoner with the butt of his gun. A loud shriek rang out through the hall as his musket fell to the floor. The sentinel ran down the hall, calling, "Turn out the guards, turn out the guards, vote for Old Abe in all prisons stands, one majority for Lincoln."

David placed his hands over his ears and shut his eyes. "Craziness is all around us," he said in an undertone.

A few days later, a report came in from Reb headquarters that David's unit was being sent to Savannah for exchange. If the Ohio boys had had any strength left, it would have been a night of celebration. They took the news quietly. But not for the first time, this report turned out to be yet another bogus one. A day later, the counter order was handed to Grizzly and, because he didn't have the heart to tell the men, he passed the note to David. David crumpled it up and tossed it aside. He made no announcement—which might have sparked some action—but instead whispered the news to one soldier and told him to pass it on.

Things were stirring in town. The number of false reports, some of them intended to be discouraging, was on the increase, as though there were larger political forces rousing.

Cork had reappeared. He vanished from time to time,

always coming back a little calmer than when he had left. It was believed that when he got agitated, they would lock him up alone somewhere. Who knew what else they did? Now, as the gossip increased throughout the prison, Cork was everywhere again, bouncing from group to group, spreading hearsay and nonsense to those who would still indulge him.

"Lincoln's been re-elected and rumor says General John Hood's marchin' into Tennessee with General Beauregard movin' toward Memphis," a Reb guard announced.

"Must be retreating," David said.

"Smart aleck," the Reb guard replied.

A batch of mail had finally arrived at Danville. It had been months since David heard from anyone back home. Some of the prisoners got letters, but David hadn't any, so he and Wolf headed down to the river for water.

"You brought only one bucket?" David said.

"How many you want me to bring?" Wolf asked.

"You got two hands, don't you," David said as they stepped down the bank to the river's edge.

They carried the water back to their floor in Prison No. 1. Wolf looked over at David's haversack where the guards, at times, laid his mail.

"No mail for you today," Wolf said.

"He's got mail," said one of the guards as he passed by. He handed David four letters he'd gotten late from the Reb mail sergeant.

David sorted through them. "Two from Nel, one from Hannah, and one from Beth," he said, handing Beth's letter to Wolf. Wolf's brow raised.

"It's addressed to you," David said, sticking the rest of his letters into his pocket. "Let's get more water, buddy."

Once they'd finished, they sat down. Wolf's eyes shifted back and forth as he read Beth's letter. He smelled the inside of the envelope several times.

"How's my baby sister, Wolf?" David asked.

"Hunky-dory," Wolf said. "Just hunky-dory."

"She say anything about the farm?" David wrinkled his forehead, thinking about the harvest. The women wrote little about the farm, in general, maybe because they had so much trust in Frank Lee, or even, David feared, because they were hiding things from him.

"She says Frank Lee brought in a bigger crop than you had last year," Wolf said.

Frank Lee was another cause for concern. David worried at one time that Beth might fall for her cousin. But her letters to Wolf were so full of life, so full of Beth's own essence, David didn't think that Wolf had any serious competition.

And then there was the fact that Charles Allen had joined Rebel forces and Frank Lee had nearly done so. Beth was too loyal to her father and her brother to be drawn to any man with any trace of Reb in him.

"Oh how I would like to drop in unannounced at home this evening. It would be the greatest pleasure I could ask for," David said.

Wolf nodded as he continued reading.

One late November day Jerry came back from the cook-house, sweaty and dirty. He looked preoccupied. To no one in particular he announced: "It's Thanksgiving in the North and the Army of the Potomac is going to have fifty-thousand turkeys and fifty-thousand barrels of apples today."

"I wish we could all be there," David said. "Peace rumors are afloat again and yet thirty prisoners died in the hospital yesterday."

"Who gave you that figure?" Jerry asked.

"Wolf heard it."

"And you trust Wolf?"

"He's got some friends amongst the guards. Thirty is too many, then?"

"Too few," said Jerry. "It was a lot more."

"They need better food," David said. "We all do, of course; but they're sick. Sometimes it seems that even our own are meaner than the Rebs."

"Any new rumors about the prisoner exchange?" Wolf asked.

"Those thirty that died at the hospital, they are permanently exchanged," David said.

"I believe I found a trace of meat in the soup today," Wolf said to Jerry. "My respects to the chef."

"You call beef heads boiled all together with teeth, eyes, and dirt, in sandy river water, meat?" David said, squinting his eyes at Jerry.

"The boys don't care ... And what do you expect me to do, David?" Jerry asked. There was something pleading in the question. Jerry knew he was in debt to David for many things. He wished he could earn back his trust.

"I don't know what I want of you," David snapped. "I just wish I could be sure that you were still my friend and comrade."

"That same guard who accompanied the officer who stripped me of my stripe is trying to put me in solitary again," Jerry said.

"What for?"

"The bootlick just doesn't like me."

"That figures," David said.

"What do you call a person who gets pleasure out of another's pain?" Jerry asked.

"A green-eyed monster, or a sawbones," David replied.

Wolf interrupted them. "Kane of Company K is back from the hospital," he said. "He looks like he's not going to make it."

"If I were missing an arm and a leg, I'd just as soon die," Jerry said, pausing to look over at David.

Wolf interrupted again. "While you're talking about bad news, your friend Grizzly was standing on a barrel with a ball and chain wrapped around his leg for getting drunk again while on duty."

All news was getting easier to come by. The Rebs were talking openly about the battles and daily events.

"One of the Reb colonels gave a blouse, a pair of his old boots, and a blanket to one of the prisoners over in number two," Jerry said.

"How'd you know?" Wolf asked.

"I know the prisoner he gave the gift to," Jerry said. "He's a Union corporal."

"Gift? Sounds more like a shenanigan to me," Wolf said. "The corporal must be his snitch or something."

"Who cares," David said. "I dreamt I was at home and had plenty to eat. I could smell the mincemeat and pumpkin pies baking in the oven."

Wolf smacked his lips.

December 1864

Mail arrived late again. The timing of these deliveries was erratic, building up anticipation that no letter could ever live up to. David got nothing this time, though Wolf did.

"Beth said in her letter that Josh Deeter and Henry Shetters are both dead," Wolf said.

David started shaking.

"Take your quinine, buddy," Wolf said.

"I'll be okay," David said. "With the new Reb guards coming into the prison, some of the old guard are going to the front. I hope a few get their heads cracked."

"Grizzly too. He's on the Rebs' shit list," Jerry said. "I hear Private Bangle of the 106th New York died of diphtheria last night along with Corporal Parker of the 2nd Massachusetts Cavalry."

"I got a look-see at the Danville newspaper a while ago," Wolf said.

"Any big news?"

"It wasn't the headline, but here's a tidbit ... Old Abe says the debt of the United States is $1,800,000,000.00 as of December of '64," Wolf said.

Jerry pulled his trouser pockets inside out. "I'm debt free."

"Grizzly will be okay," David said. "He's up for discharge soon, so he'll probably be home before us." But it wasn't a certainty. Like other flawed but honorable and reasonable men, Grizzly was at risk from allies and enemies alike.

13

The top of the fir tree nearly touched the living room ceiling. The wide and evenly spaced branches were perfect for hanging the candleholders and Christmas decorations. A closer look and one could see which girl made what ornament. The carved whistle that hung below the tree top angel dressed in her yellowing robe had a tag with David's name on it.

Across the room, around the fireplace sat Ma Longacher and the girls, stringing popcorn to drape around the tree. Frank Lee snored off and on while sitting in David's chair.

Christmas at the Longacher home had always been a gay event. There beneath the tree laid various gifts that the family made for each other. They would remain wrapped this Christmas of 1864 until their David returned home.

14

David wasn't about to become sentimental over Jerry. He'd seen his weaknesses as well as his bitterness and he was wary. Jerry continued to look gray and wan. And when he disappeared once more, David struggled with himself and then went looking. He asked a man who worked in the cook's house if he had information, but Jerry hadn't worked there for weeks. Grizzly said Jerry was known to root out light duty. He said he'd ask around. Later in the day, he found David and gave him the news. Jerry had been taken to the hospital several days ago.

"What's he got?" Wolf asked—he was the first man David told.

"Some kind of wasting illness," David said.

"You think he'll pull through?" Wolf asked.

David shrugged his shoulders. "How would I know? I don't even know what his symptoms are. Stupid war," he said. "Even those of us that stay alive get corroded one way or another. I hope it's all worth it." He pulled a book out of his haversack: *Uncle Tom's Cabin*.

"What's that book about?" Wolf asked. He recognized the title and had heard it was a favorite book amongst abolitionists.

"It's a novel written by Harriet Beecher Stowe back in 1852," David said. "Many say this is the book that started this war."

"How so?" Wolf asked.

"Over slavery," David said.

"Read it out loud," Wolf said.

Some of the other prisoners began gathering around.

David pointed at Wolf. "See what you've done."

"Hell son, you read parts of your mail to us. Why not a book?" a gray-haired soldier asked.

"Read it, Yank," a Reb guard said.

"You'll put me in solitary if I do," David said.

"I'll put y'all in solitary if'n ya don't! If'n I had to choose between hearin' you read a story, or draggin' yer sorry self, kickin' and screamin' off to solitary, which would I choose?"

"I suspect you'd choose wisely," David said.

"Just don't read too loud. We don't need any of the brass nosin' around," the guard said.

David looked into the eyes of the Reb guards and the other prisoners. "Don't say I didn't warn you Southern boys," he said as he opened the cover. "Boys, the scenes in this story are as its title indicates. It's about black men, or niggers, living in shacks or cabins on plantations. They're a race that has been abused and ignored by the white race. The Negro was taken from a land of extreme heat and wild jungle, Africa, where their customs and lifestyle are entirely different from that of the white race, causing only distrust, contempt, and brutality by many whites. Now we have before us one of the bloodiest wars in our history." David turned to the first page, "Chapter one, page one *Uncle Tom's Cabin*, or *Life Among the Lowly* ..."

It was a curious scene, Christmas approaching, as

251

the terrible war continued—these American adversaries gathered to hear a story read aloud. It was as close to peace as any of these men had experienced during the war.

At the hour, there was a changing of the guard. David got a high sign, finished a paragraph, marked his page, and closed the book.

"Read more," the men begged.

"In time, boys, in time," David smiled.

It rained hard through the night. The next day was cloudy and unpleasant.

A Reb guard David barely knew came looking for him. David heard his name called and walked over to the guard.

"You Longacher?"

"Yes, sir."

"Grizzly told me to come and find you. Your buddy, Dixon, died last night."

"What happened?" David asked. Sure Jerry was sick and troubled. But sick enough to die?

"How would I know what happened? He's dead, that's all. And lucky to get away from this shit hole," the guard said. "It really wasn't that big of surprise to me. He handed me a letter addressed to his folks back home a couple of days after he was taken to the hospital."

The news about Jerry traveled fast. Like him or not, Jerry was known.

From across the room came a booming voice David

recognized as one of Jerry's accusers. "Killed by his own cooking."

They won't remember Jerry, Wolf thought. But they'll remember the lousy, stupid joke.

"So gather the rich and poor," David said as he lowered his head.

"And Craig of Company F and several others of the 110th escaped last night through the roof of the telegraph office," the Reb guard continued.

David shook his head and cut his eyes toward the Reb guard as Wolf was about to speak.

"I saw that," the Reb guard mumbled as he walked away. "A fella just can't be nice to some folks."

The approaching holiday had no effect on the war effort. Prisoners kept arriving—though most now were being transferred in from other prisons. Only a few came straight from battle. Maybe, David thought, they weren't being taken. Maybe they were just being left there to die.

There was a regular rotation of the guards. Grizzly, who spent so much time in the brig for drinking, managed to stay through several cycles but was finally shipped out to a battle station. With each arriving prisoner or each new guard, there was an influx of new information. Undoubtedly, some of the information was true and some false, but it was difficult to separate one from the other.

Wolf came back with news, delighted with himself. "Well, buddy, we were right about that Union corporal being a tattletale for that Reb colonel. Grizzly told me all about it before he was sent to the front."

"Before he left, Grizzly invited me to his home in Tennessee," David said, pausing for a moment before he continued. "I knew Craig, just like I do plenty of others from the 110th. I hope he makes it home. My boyhood friends are either dying off in battle, or in the hospital with disease. I remember when we were around nine years old, a bunch of us were building a couple of tree houses and we chose up sides to play Robin Hood. Jerry decided to shoot flaming arrows at our tree house to burn us out. Lucky for us the tree fort wasn't too high, or we all would've ended up with broken bones from jumping out."

"So Jerry was always a problem," Wolf said.

"No, not really," David said. "It was all in fun, like the time our raft sank."

"But I thought Jerry couldn't swim," Wolf said.

"He didn't have to," David laughed. "We were in a crick, so he just stood up." He continued, "By the time we were ten, me and my friends either worked by our fathers' side farming or doing some other sort of labor. I do remember one boy going off to sea. I can't even remember his name now." David frowned.

"You want to play chess, buddy?" Wolf blurted out.

"Maybe after supper," David said. "I'm going to get a letter off to Jerry's ma and pa."

David moved his pawn. "You hear that hammering? The Reb officers are having a platform built for their big Christmas dance. They're after some of our boys to fiddle for them at the officer's ball tonight. Oh what a horrible Christmas for us prisoners," David said.

"Poppycock," Wolf said. "I heard General Sherman captured Savannah and the Rebs are evacuating Richmond. The Rebs' shindigs are coming to an end."

It didn't prevent their dance from coming off. Who did the fiddling? The prisoners had no idea. But the fact that their captors were free to celebrate filled them with both envy and sorrow.

15

January 1865

"Oh this horrible prison life, when will it end," David said as he captured one of Wolf's pawns. "It is almost a living death. Men are freezing and starving. What a great blessing good health is."

"The Dan River is over its banks. I saw some of our boys carrying water barefoot through the cold mud, then using the thick, muddy water for cooking and drinking," Wolf said. "What a way to start the New Year."

"Every day there's new escapes," David said.

"How'd Private Ben Blackburn die? I heard he froze to death," Wolf said.

David shrugged. Death was becoming bigger than life. How strange David thought.

"The mess cook saved me two sheep heads. Bully for him. We'll have a mess of mutton brains for breakfast," David said as he countered Wolf's move. "Check."

"Do I ever get to win?" Wolf asked.

"Maybe this war, but not at chess," David smiled.

"I'll go first," Wolf said, setting up the board for another game.

David nodded. A loud crack came from his leg as he stretched it out.

The warehouse was warm. The prisoners from the North, as well as the soldiers from the South sat wherever they could. The building was filled to capacity with officers and enlisted men.

A lanky man dressed in a long black tailcoat with a preacher's collar stood behind a makeshift pulpit, holding a worn leather Bible in his oversized hands. His eyes were deep set with heavy arched brows, his black and white hair pulled back into a pigtail. He smiled as he spoke with a drawl.

"Brethren, the question that many times crosses our minds is whose side is God on?" His smile widened as his voice filled the hall.

"Then why do we pray to Him?" a one-legged Union prisoner yelled out.

"Son, our Lord loves all his children, Reb and Yank alike. Y'all pray to Him in good times or bad, that way He knows you believe in Him, that you have faith." The preacher held up his Bible and shook it. "It's all in the New Testament, Brethren," he declared as he thumped the Good Book.

"Does God have any idea who's gonna win this here

war?" a freckle-faced Reb private hollered.

"He does, son. He knows all," the preacher said. "Jesus died on the cross for all of us. Look around. Do any of y'all see happiness in your fellow man's eye? Do you?

"Our Lord God is interested not in our bodies, but in our souls. Bow your heads and let us pray together. Our Father who art in Heaven ... Amen."

The preacher then sang out, "Shall we gather at the river ..."

"Not the Dan," someone shouted out.

A fellow worshiper turned and slapped the joker on his shoulder. "This is a prayer meetin', don't mock the Lord."

A small melee followed which the preacher paused for and held up his hands. "Bless you, son. Jesus loves a sense of humor." The preacher continued singing as he motioned the congregation to join in.

The warehouse filled with song.

The weather was frigid but the door was left cracked for ventilation. From the pulpit, the preacher was barely audible as Wolf walked over to a doorway. The preacher's voice grew louder as he shouted out for converts. He seemed only to take a breath whenever he yelled out, "Praise the Lord."

There was a small group of prisoners gathered near the back of the room, as far away as possible from the preacher. "We're Catholics," one explained. "We can't listen to such balderdash."

"We're all Christians in this room," Wolf said. "Just different doctrines."

"There's only one true Church," another said, "and the Holy Father in the Vatican is the Vicar of Christ."

"So you would be Roman Catholics?" Wolf asked.

"We would indeed."

"Heck, I grew up with Catholics. New Albany's got its fair share of cathedrals. I believe there's other Catholics in there listening to the pastor," Wolf said.

"It's on their souls," said a sandy haired one. "We know what's right and what's not."

Wolf noticed that Cork was among them. "You a Catholic, Cork?"

"I am," Cork said, "a believer in the One True Church. And it has come to me, gentlemen, that we need have no fear of death."

"Is that so?" Wolf said.

"What do you see here, soldiers? We were taken prisoner in a no man's land. We were brought to this place, filled with foul disease and anguish. We are in the South, but we are not *of* the South. We are on the side *of* the North, but situated in the South. My friends, we are still in no man's land, so it must be we have already died. And this is Purgatory." Cork rambled, then the small group became silent.

Wolf told Beth later that he had never heard a silence so profound. The overzealous evangelist at the end of the room, those giving witness, the moaning of the crazed ones, the off-key songs of the congregation, none of them could penetrate this silence.

"Would any one like to say a prayer?" Wolf asked, hoping to break the quiet. "If you'll have me, I'll join you."

Furtive glances were exchanged and everyone in the circle, save for Wolf, crossed himself. Finally, one began to pray.

Wolf smiled to himself. It made him feel good to know that a handful of Catholics were standing up for their catechisms amongst a shipload of Southern Baptists and other evangelicals.

After the prayer meeting, the prisoners meandered back to their respective prison buildings.

"With all the talk about peace, God grant that it may soon come," David said.

"I thought that Reb minister preached a rather interesting sermon," one of the others added. "But I don't know about gathering at the river ..."

David glanced over at Wolf who had rejoined them.

"The Dan is almost frozen," Wolf laughed.

February 1865

David made an entry in his diary—February 2nd, 1865:

The sun shone enough for the ground hog to see his shadow, so according to old wondrous saying, we will have cold for six weeks yet.

"I wish I had those six weeks at home. Men here are dying by inches," David said to himself.

"Secretary of State Seward is reported to be in

Richmond on a peace mission," Wolf said.

"How ironic," David said. "A peace mission in a war-torn city."

"Today is Uncle Abe's birthday. What are we going to do this sunny day?" Wolf asked.

"I volunteered you and me to work in the warehouse," David said. "Clothing for the prisoners came, along with boxes of other goods and letters."

"You expect to find anything interesting?" Wolf knew David was as honest a man as he'd ever met. He was also one of the most curious.

"They said there were some old Northern newspapers that arrived also."

"You'll want to be giving those a careful going over," Wolf winked.

16

The battlefield gods kept their heads down for the most part during the winter, but economic and political forces continued to be bent and twisted by the war. And the echoes of their battles could be felt as far away as Europe where the manufacturing and commercial interests aligned themselves with one or the other of the warring parties.

Bits of information from the front, and from Washington and Richmond and Atlanta, began to point in one direction. It was beginning to seem clear who was winning and who was not. Even at the most ordinary level, in the smallest details, signals were that the Southern cause was collapsing. It could be seen, for example, in the bartering that had continued—with ever smaller and less valuable articles being offered—between Rebel guards and Union prisoners. At first the guards' eagerness to trade seemed tied to the sinking value of the CSA dollar. But now there was a note of desperation to it. Guards were trading for blankets and boots because they weren't receiving them from their own military suppliers. And if what Jerry had said was so, that the food wasn't going to prisoners because there were more powerful persons— civilians in particular—then it had to mean that they, too, were also being starved. Even some of those who had lived in comfortable Main Street homes were trading their heirloom furniture for basic necessities. One could get foodstuffs, all right. But only by competing on the open market.

"The Reb guards are begging us prisoners for our bread and goods," Wolf said. "I'm astonished to see some of our boys sell their traps to the Rebs."

"Why? Blankets sell for thirty dollars, trousers thirty-five, and blouses twenty dollars. Reb officers in the prison buying blankets off the boys, respectable business for Reb officers to be trading our boys out of their traps," David said. "Who cares, at least we can get all the meat we want now ... that is for twelve greenbacks a pound."

One evening in mid-February, the Reb guards heard a

loud "Hurray" coming from the men of Prison No. 1. David and approximately one thousand other Union prisoners were to be exchanged for the same number of Reb prisoners. And this time the rumor had been substantiated by the arrival of a new squadron of guards whose sole intent was to escort the prisoners back north. Some of the Reb prisoners from an earlier exchange ended up at Danville for Army duty. The Ohio volunteers were to be part of a second wave of exchanges.

David listened as two of the Reb guards talked.

"I'm glad the Yanks are goin'. It hasn't been a cinch for them here," the older guard said.

"How 'bout us?" the younger guard asked.

"Yup, but at least we're not locked up," the older guard said. "And we have free use of the latrine."

"By damn, I ain't talkin' 'bout here. I was exchanged out of that Yankee prison they call Camp Chase up in Ohio," the young guard said. "The meat there was rotten, that is whatever scant amount we got. The shed roofs leaked. Our clothes and beddin' was usually wet and we was always cold. I'll tell you, up North is a different kind of cold than our boys are accustom to."

"Okay, son, I get the gist of y'alls argument," the old Reb said. "Point is, war ain't fair for nobody."

"I don't know about that. Our captured officers were allowed to walk freely around Columbus on their honor," the young guard added.

"Officers, Reb or Yank, have the privileges of rank. Everybody knows that, son," the old guard said.

David and the other parolees discarded what few things they didn't require into a large pile. They didn't have much, but they also didn't want to keep anything that would remind them of the time they'd spent locked up. They exited Danville prison at midnight. They were put on a train to Richmond where they arrived at 2 pm. From there, they were marched to Libby Prison where they were quartered, then bedded down without any rations.

Reveille was sounded just as some Rebs arrived back from Mountain Lookout.

"Look how fat and hearty them Rebs look. My guess is they hunt critters," Wolf said, trying to get a better look out the grated window. "At least this prison's cleaner than Danville."

"We won't be here long I pray," David said.

The Union soldiers were paroled at 5 pm. The men were advised not to take up arms again until the orders came transferring them to their own Federal camp.

"We're headed north," Wolf yelled over the jubilation as they filed out of Libby Prison.

Part IV

1

The newly exchanged Union soldiers arrived by boat at Annapolis, Maryland, at 9 am and were marched to College Green Barracks where they washed up and were issued brand new uniforms.

David rubbed his face and smiled. "How do I look?"

"Like a plucked chicken," Wolf said, strutting about. "How 'bout me?"

"You look like a shipwrecked pirate in oversized pantaloons," David chuckled. "All right then," he said as he rubbed his belly. "Let's go muster in for pay and then get some chow, what say ye, Matey?"

"Arrgh," Wolf mimicked as he tightened his belt.

As they lined up before the paymaster, they were

surprised to see Cork, in his new uniform, his hair cut, his face shaved. He might have been unrecognizable except for the furtive air about him, and his squinting glances. In an untypical, chirpy mood, he joined Wolf and David. They hadn't always enjoyed his company—indeed they had a well-founded fear that he might start acting out again. But they weren't about to cold shoulder a fellow warrior.

Cork told them he was hoping to get mustered out somewhere in eastern Ohio, maybe Columbus, where he could get aboard a train back to New York.

"You've seen some war, haven't you," Wolf said, patting Cork on the back.

"I've seen things," Cork said with a fresh hint of madness in his voice.

"Why do they call you Cork?" Wolf asked.

"Must be short for something," David added.

"They call me Cork, because no matter how the tempests blow, or how high the tide, I stay afloat," he said, tipping his hat.

That evening at an inn in Annapolis, David sat across the table from Wolf, as he stuffed his face with a heaping plate of oysters, ham, and eggs. Wolf looked up, reaching to cover a loud belch. "Pardon me," he said.

David flipped his lip and pointed. "I think you missed a piece of egg," David mumbled as he swallowed the last bit of his own food.

"So what are your plans my young friend? Heading

home?" David asked.

Wolf pulled a small packet of letters tied with a fancy ribbon from his haversack, then held them to his nose and sniffed them. "Yes, buddy, matter of fact, to *your* home ... if it's okay with you."

"Who am I to deny puppy love," David laughed.

"Puppy love?" Wolf reached over, lifted David's cap, and mussed up his hair. He handed David his cap back as he cocked his own and smiled.

"You and Beth ought to get along like two peas in a pod," David said, reaching over to knock Wolf's hat back in place. "Okay, let's get back to the barracks. Tomorrow we catch the B&O heading toward Columbus with the rest of the boys."

David watched the beads of rain gather, then stream down the passenger car's window. Wolf breathed heavily, his head resting on David's shoulder. David reached over to shake Wolf's shoulder as he bolted upright, awakened by his own snort.

"I saved the company colors," Wolf muttered, rubbing his eyes.

David nudged him. "Just a dream, buddy."

"It was a nightmare. I heard a bumblebee flying at me," Wolf said.

"Good thing you woke up before the minié ball hit."

"I had this bad dream before," Wolf said as he leaned to look out the window. "Where are we any how?"

"On the way to Martinsburg," David said.

"I don't think I'll ever play checkers, or chess, again," Wolf said.

"Why not? You could use the practice," David said.

"It would remind me of that foul prison," Wolf said sliding back into a slumber.

David continued his gaze out the window. And when he saw Cork approach and sit down across from him, he began to regret that they'd befriended the man.

"You farm?" Cork asked.

"How did you know?" David said.

"I can tell by your manner, your natural dignity."

David nodded.

"You ought to be happy you aren't farming here," Cork said, gesturing toward the window. "There were battles out there."

"I seen rich farmland in the South before it turned to battlefield," David said.

"Rich farmland it was and is," Cork said, resting his head back. "But the Rebel boys kept trying to dig in as they retreated. They had to work fast, so they'd take the dead—Union boys, preferably—but their own if need be—and they'd line them up end-to-end and shovel earth right on top of them. A quick and efficient way to create a trench and a barricade, and a graveyard into the bargain. Come spring all those frozen hummocks are going to thaw out. The farm boys are going to be turning up the honored dead at plowing time for decades to come."

2

The train pulled into its next stop at daybreak.

"Martinsburg," the conductor yelled.

"Martinsburg," David said. "Remember the Confederate General Jubal Early back in July of '64? Here's as far as he got with trying to take the Shenandoah Valley."

Wolf rubbed the pink scar on his arm. "Yep."

"Detrain, gentlemen. We're going to have a layover," the train conductor called down the aisle. "Bridge out."

"How long?" David asked.

"Don't know," the conductor said, looking at his musical pocket watch as it played. "It's Sunday. Everyone's in church."

David and Wolf collected their belongings and stepped out onto the station platform.

"Where are we going to stay?" Wolf asked.

"We'll wait at the train ..." David stumbled, puked, and collapsed.

Wolf bent down beside him. "David, you all right?"

David's body trembled. His forehead broke out in a sweat. Wolf sat down and wiped David's face with his handkerchief.

"Give me a hand, Wolf."

"I'm going to find you a doctor," Wolf said.

"Just get me over to that tree by the depot," David pointed.

"Look at this place," Wolf said, holding onto David.

The depot, like many of the local structures, had

been reduced to a charred frame. Both the North and the South had attacked Martinsburg at one point or another during the war. Of the buildings that remained, some flew the Stars and Bars, while the others displayed the Stars and Stripes.

"Tricky business taking sides in this burg," Wolf said.

David leaned on Wolf's shoulder.

"Maybe there's a doctor nearby," Wolf said as he steadied David on his feet.

"No, no, Wolf, I must get on the train with you. I want to go home."

"But ..." Wolf started.

"No buts about it," David said. "Here's what you do. Neither the Rebs nor the Yanks would burn out a doctor's home. That would be like shooting themselves in the foot. I need quinine, that's all."

Wolf was gone for about an hour. When he returned, David lay semi-conscious beneath a tree. A woman opened the quinine bottle and poured a small amount into David's mouth. David gagged then coughed. His vision was blurred as the woman knelt before him.

"She's a nurse from here in Martinsburg," Wolf told him.

David smiled. He took the quinine from her hand and finished it off.

"You need to rest," the woman said.

"Outside?" Wolf asked.

"Right here is fine," she smiled. "I'll be by later this afternoon to check on you, Sergeant Longacher."

The nurse returned with another woman. "This is a colleague of mine. You two will stay at her Aunt's boarding house until Monday morning," she said.

"What if the train pulls out today?" Wolf asked.

"We're all Dunkards from the Church of the Brethren, so is the conductor, and the rest of the locals who work on the railroad line. No labor on Sunday, not even cooking. The train won't leave until Monday, maybe even Tuesday," the woman assured them.

Nothing was as it seemed. All witnesses at Appomattox reported that General Grant arrived looking scruffy and smoking a cigar to meet General Lee—a gentleman, dignified even in defeat. Grant allowed Lee to keep his sword. They were once again comrades. West Point ran deep in the blood of the cadets.

And there was no logic to the sequence of events at the end of the war; releases and exchanges, as well as the transport of prisoners was erratic. It would take years upon years to heal the emotional and mental wounds of the nation.

3

Charles Allen had been exchanged for a wounded Union soldier at Camp Chase in Columbus, Ohio, and, despite his injury, sent to a prison hospital in Libby, Virginia for assignment to light duty. After being discharged from

Libby, it made no sense to him now to try to go home. His future was in the south. But he promised the Longachers that he would return. Whether or not he could be of help to them with one arm remained to be seen.

When the peace treaty was signed, Charles Allen set out for Ohio, dressed in a Union uniform he'd bought from a soldier while he was still at Libby. By train and by foot, often accepting a lift from passing wagons, Charles Allen headed toward the Longacher farm. Several days after his departure, he woke up in a boarding house in Troy, Ohio where he'd taken a room for the night. It was the middle of the morning and there was a pounding at the door. A woman's voice came from outside: "We come looking for Charles Allen Carmichael."

"What makes you think that person might be here?" he called out.

"We got hold of his discharge and hospital records," the woman's voice answered. "He said the Longacher family were his next of kin."

"We also talked to a friend of his," one of her traveling companions added.

Charles Allen, bleary from sleep, stepped into the doorway to confront his pursuers—a blonde, a brunette, and a younger strawberry blonde.

"My land, if it ain't my favorite patient," the blonde exclaimed.

Charles Allen peered at them, recognizing only his blonde nurse, but not able to place the other two.

The blonde gave Charles Allen a lingering kiss, then

took his hand and placed the square and compass ring on the finger of his right hand.

"Sally ... Sally Blackwell," he said. "I thought I'd never have the chance to see y'all again." Charles Allen looked at his Masonic ring, then polished it on his pinned up sleeve.

"Chance had nothin' to do with it. It's God's will. But at times I did think I'd never find you," she sniffled.

Charles Allen motioned the women inside his room. Everyone pulled up a chair.

"Sally, I need to know what happened to me back on that butcher table, I don't remember a thing," Charles Allen said.

"Oh honey, some things are best let go," Sally said. "By the way, these are two of my best friends."

Both mother and daughter stood and curtseyed.

Charles Allen nodded and continued, "I heard stories, all sorts of stories, from other boys. Some said they should have never lost their limbs. Others told me they saw piles upon piles of arms and legs tossed out for the hogs to slop on," he said, fussing with the safety pin on his sleeve.

"Shh, Charles Allen." Sally wiped her eyes and whispered to him, "First off, y'all's arm was almost completely severed when they laid you up on that operatin' table. There weren't no saving it. When the doctor was about to throw it into a pile outside the hospital tent ..." She stopped herself. "... Well, you have to understand, Charles Allen, the doctor wasn't to blame. There were so many boys that had to be tended to." She reached over to fasten the clasp of the safety pin.

Charles Allen patted her hand. "Thanks ... Please, Sally ..."

"I asked the doctor to hand me your severed arm when I noticed your ring. My daddy was a Mason and I didn't want the ring to be defiled," she said. "But more important, I couldn't stand the sight of a piece of you just bein' tossed away. I took the ring, then wrapped your arm in the lace of my petticoat and buried it later that night under a tree. I'm not sure why, I just did."

Charles Allen squeezed her hand, then leaned over and kissed her.

4

By late Monday, the Sabbath over, the bridge at Martinsburg was repaired. The soldiers boarded at daybreak on Tuesday. David slept through the train's arrival to and departure from Cumberland.

Now it was Wolf's turn to watch over his friend. Up and down the car, men were passing, some sick, some drunk, some arguing, some singing. Again, Cork was amongst them. Wolf acknowledged him and he sat down nearby.

The experience and memory of war was like a wound to the spirit, and even now that it was healing, a number of men couldn't let go. Wolf knew Cork had more stories.

"Horses," Cork spouted, looking out the rain-streaked

window. "God bless the horses."

Wolf remembered that Cork had a particular fondness for horses. "You saw lots of horses get wounded, I guess," he said.

"Aye-aye, sir," Cork answered. And then he was silent for a moment. "You ever seen a dead horse? They puff up just like a balloon. And after a while you get those maggots filling up their big hollow insides."

"I'm not sorry I didn't see that," Wolf confessed.

"Wasn't nothing special," Cork said. "Same thing happened to soldiers. I seen acres of bodies, in the early stages of ... putrefaction."

Wolf took a deep breath. Such a crazy man, Wolf thought. A true casualty of war. What would become of him?

Cork tipped his hat, stood up from his seat, and bowed. "Pleasant to see you again, and exchange reminiscences," he said as he turned to make his way down the aisle.

A half hour later the train began releasing steam.

"Wake up, David." Wolf shook his shoulder. "We're stopping at Oakland's water tank."

Wolf handed David the quinine bottle. David pushed Wolf's hand back. "I'm okay," he said.

"Want to take a walk? We're not leaving 'til noon," Wolf said. "Maybe we can find a tavern so I can wet my whistle. Besides, a sarsaparilla would be good for your innards."

David and Wolf were back on the troop car before

dinner.

Wolf stood in the aisle looking over the seating arrangement. "I could've had one more whiskey," he said.

"I'll bet," David said, sliding next to the window.

March 1865

The train passed Grafton at dark, arriving at Todd Barracks in Columbus, Ohio by morning.

"You Ohio boys muster in for pay immediately," the paymaster barked as the men got off the train.

"But I'm from Indiana," Wolf said.

"Quiet," David whispered. "You don't need any money now. I can cover for both of us. Uncle Sam can square up with you later." David nudged Wolf out of the Ohio unit's pay line.

Wolf waited for David back at the barracks as night set in and all was quiet.

"What took Uncle Sam so long?" Wolf asked.

"He's the 'wait' part of hurry-and-wait, Wolf. We stood in line for the better part of the day and ended up not even receiving our pay," David said. "The only good news is once I signed my name to the register, I stepped back in line and signed your proper name, Wolfgang Krouse. Now let's try to get some shuteye."

"I'll be damned, if it ain't my old buddy, David Longacher," First Sergeant Jacob Holsinger said as he threw his arms around David.

"Jacob, this is my buddy and, though he doesn't

deserve it, soon to be my brother-in-law, Wolfgang Krouse ... or Wolf to his friends," David said.

The men shook hands.

"What are you doing here at Camp Chase?" Jacob asked. "I thought you were in Danville."

"We were, but we got exchanged a week ago. I can't get paid now, so we can't get home," David said.

"I hate to be the bearer of more bad news," Jacob said.

"This entire war has been nothing but bad news," David said.

"One of the Furnas boys, either Joshua or Isaac, I'm not sure, was killed in battle along with Henry Shertzer and Louis Butt. Then I heard Levi Childers died in the hospital of a wound," Jacob said.

"They were all from Company G?" Wolf asked.

"Yes, all friends of ours. Right, David?" Jacob said.

"Right." David lowered his eyes. "Just another misfortune of war." David swallowed hard. "I heard about Furnas. I had to write Jerry's folks. Darn ... who's left?"

David, Wolf, and Jacob lost track of time sharing their tales of battle. They were surprised to hear reveille ring throughout camp. They hadn't slept a wink.

Jacob stood up and embraced David. "Don't you worry yourself about anything else. Your ol' buddy, First Sergeant Holsinger will take care of everything and that goes for you too, Wolf." Jacob nodded, shook their hands, then started walking away. He stopped and turned. "I'll see you both back home ... Soon I hope." Jacob tossed a sloppy salute as he exited the barracks.

Wolf looked at David and tossed up his hands. "What's he talking about?"

"Don't ask me," David smiled.

Not more than thirty minutes later, a private entered the barracks. "Longacher, Krouse," he shouted out.

David raised his hand, catching the private's attention.

"You and Krouse are to report to Captain Yardly over at the orderly's office. It's nine buildings down from this one," the private said. Jacob had pulled a few strings after all.

It was a pleasant walk down the row of buildings, each one a scene of joyful reunions, the wages of victory. At the designated building, David and Wolf saluted the officer on duty outside and entered, a little hesitant.

David spotted the Captain in one of the back offices. "Come on, Wolf, follow me." The two weaved their way through the soldiers who meandered about inside.

David saluted. "Longacher, David, reporting, sir."

"At ease, Sergeant," Captain Yardly said. "You two pull up a chair. I was given your names by my first sergeant." The Captain thumbed through some papers. "You both came from Danville Prison." He paused and looked up at them. "I see you've been there a while."

"Yes sir," they both answered at the same time.

David shot a glance over at Wolf.

"You, Private Krouse, are with the wrong unit. You're a Hundred Days man from Indiana. You should have been discharged a while back, but it looks like you were sent to Danville with Company G of the 110th?"

"I was shot and captured," Wolf said. "And the Rebs wouldn't honor my discharge."

"I telegraphed your commander and he said you and Longacher, especially you, Krouse, are my responsibility now, part of my kettle of fish, so I had to come up with a solution," the Captain said. "Sergeant Longacher, you will receive your back pay before you leave camp. You, Krouse, are the real knot in the string. I'll try to get you your pay rations, but that will take time. I'm going to process the discharge paperwork for both of you immediately, but you, Krouse, will eventually have to report back to your base in Indianapolis, where you'll be officially discharged. It says here you boys were wounded in battle." The Captain paused and shook his head. "More record review, more bookkeeping ..." He sighed.

David and Wolf nodded.

The Captain pushed his chair away from the table and stood up. He handed them their papers. "Good luck, men." The Captain shook both of their hands and saluted them. "I wish you two the best ... Oh yes, I'll process your military decorations."

David and Wolf turned and looked at each other.

"The Army thanks you," the Captain smiled and snapped a salute.

One of the Captain's aides rushed to catch up with them as they started out the door. "Would you like us to notify your families that you're coming home?" he asked.

"I would, thank you," David said.

Wolf put his arm around David, then turned, giving the aide a salute.

Walking back from the meeting with the Captain, making plans for their future—first a visit to the Longacher farm, the anticipated meeting with Beth, Wolf's journey to Indianapolis followed by his return to the farm, the spring planting, wedding, eventually children and on and on, they were stopped, as were many, by a sight not quite like anything any here had seen before. A middle-aged man, elegantly dressed, with polished calfskin boots entirely unsuited to the muck and mire of the camp, stood at a makeshift table surrounded by a circle of soldiers. The man jotted notes in a small book as he spoke with them. A few feet away was a photographer with a camera on a tripod, a stack of photographic plates stacked to one side.

"Who's the dandy?" Wolf asked.

A soldier walking away from the group overheard Wolf. "That's William Swinton," he said. "War reporter for the *New York Times*."

"I heard of him," David said. "He was accused of being a spy. Nearly got executed."

"The same one," the soldier said. "Grant reprieved him."

As they approached the gathering, they discovered that Swinton was now deep in conversation with, of all people, Cork. David and Wolf looked on, wondering what nonsense Cork was giving the New Yorker. While they watched, Swinton directed Cork to the photographer to have his picture taken. But turning, Cork spotted the two and waved them over. "Come talk to Mr. Swinton, boys. You've got some stories to tell, too."

Swinton beckoned them to join the group.

"You work for the *New York Times*?" David asked. "A fine newspaper."

"Thank you, sir," Swinton said. "I've discovered a number of boys here don't read at all. If you don't mind, would you write down your names in this notebook and where you may be reached. Here's a pen."

David obliged, jotting down both of their names with a single address at the Longacher farm.

"Were you talking to Cork?" Wolf asked. "He's a bit ..."

"You two are acquainted? What a remarkable man. I'm hoping to collaborate with him on his memoirs," Swinton exclaimed.

Wolf scratched his head. "With Cork?"

"Thomas J. Corcoran, born in Savannah, raised in Brooklyn by Rebel sympathizers. He worked both sides of the lines. One of the most accomplished Confederate spies throughout the war until, of course, he switched sides."

"Switched sides? When was that?" David asked.

"About the time you boys were released. He was given safe conduct." Swinton leaned in toward them. "He has a lot of information."

"But all he ever did," Wolf said, "was act crazy and tell stories that would scare the daylights out of anybody."

"That's what made him so effective as a spy," Swinton said. "No one took him seriously. I'm sure he never shook the morale of you two. But others?..." He studied the faces of his audience. "Life is complicated, boys. Especially in wartime. I'll tell you what war's really like ... You two ever seen a house of mirrors?"

Both shook their heads. "We never paid him any mind at all," Wolf whispered.

"You come to New York and look me up. I'll show you one."

That was when a gunshot went off. Cork lay dead as two Union officers grabbed a man with a smoking pistol still in his hand.

"I was aiming at Swinton, that Reb spy S.O.B.," the shooter screamed.

"Well, you missed," one of the Union officers said. "You got the spy, but his name ain't Swinton."

"Now you'll probably hang," the other officer said.

"Was the assassin a Northern or a Southern boy?" Wolf asked.

David shrugged. "Who knows."

One of the Union officers turned to them. "Who cares," he said.

They went to a general store near the station and with their new resources bought bread, sausage, cheese, and a bottle of bourbon for the trip. As soon as they got on the train, they began to take steps to make up for their long months of deprivation.

Wolf brushed the breadcrumbs off his blouse and cocked his cap. "Homeward bound."

David continued to stare out the passenger car window. "In a couple of hours, we'll be in Dayton. Then we'll have to transfer to the Dayton and Michigan Railroad line."

"You're the boss, you got all the greenbacks," Wolf said as he pulled the cork out of the bottle of whiskey.

David smiled. "I can already see the sort of brother-in-law you'll be." All of a sudden, he grabbed his left leg.

"That old wound pestering you?" Wolf asked.

"My old wound is on my right leg. It's my left leg that's giving me pain," David said. "It feels like bone spurs or something from the last hit."

"You should see a doctor," Wolf said as he pulled his cap down over his eyes. "Let me know when we get to Dayton, buddy."

David patted Wolf's shoulder and turned back to gaze out the train's window.

"Troy, Troy," the conductor bellowed as he made his way down the aisle.

The train's engine let out steam and the wheels screeched on the rails as the train came to a halt at the station.

"Detrain! Everybody detrain," the conductor shouted out. "We have an overnight layover."

"Why are we getting off here?" Wolf asked.

"Busted track," the conductor said. "Probably a

washout. Shouldn't take more than a day."

"Let's get some more quinine," David said. "Plus we can catch up on some shut-eye at the hotel in Troy, clean up, then head for Camp Piqua early in the morning."

"How far is it?" Wolf asked.

"Seven, maybe eight miles," David said.

"I thought you said the last train stop was Camp Piqua," Wolf said.

"I did, but the walk will do you good," David said.

"Walk?" Wolf said.

"Hey, I'm the one with the game leg," David said.

Wolf pointed at the sign hanging on the hotel door: NO VACANCIES. A half-mile from the station they found a small boarding house that David did some work on when he was a carpenter in Troy. Weary from excitement, food, and whisky, Wolf slept hard. Hearing David moving about, he pulled the quilt from his head and ran his hand through his hair. "What time is it?"

David had already finished shaving and was buttoning his jacket.

Wolf yawned and stretched. "How about another few minutes?"

"We're burning daylight, buddy. Splash some water on that kisser of yours and be ready when I get back," David said as he stepped out into the hallway and shut the door behind him.

David and Wolf set off on the clay road leading to Camp

Piqua before first light. As they reached the town limits, the sun was beginning to break over the treetops along the way.

"How far do we have to go?" Wolf asked.

"Same distance as when you asked me yesterday," David said, pointing over to an oak tree. "Let's sit there and have our dinner."

David handed Wolf something wrapped in wax paper.

"What is it?" Wolf asked.

"Surprise yourself."

Wolf bit off a mouthful of the sandwich and grinned.

"Fresh bacon and eggs right out of a real kitchen," David said. He paused and looked off into the distance, then shut his eyes as yet another sharp pain shot up his left leg.

"I don't know if I even want to go to Camp Piqua, home's only six miles from the camp," David continued.

"Six miles? We already marched ... uh ... walked nearly seven. According to you, we're only a mile or two from the camp," Wolf said.

"This war has finally wore me down," David said as he reached out. "Give an old vet a hand."

Wolf stood and took a hold of David's hand, pulling him up.

"Ow," David yelled out. "Let go, Wolf."

David grabbed his knee and fell back on the ground. So close to home, David wondered now if he would make it.

"You okay?" Wolf asked.

David bit down hard on his lip. "I'm all right."

5

Ma and the girls were finishing lunch when one of the neighbor boys from up the road came to the house on his old grey horse. He looked at a piece of paper he held in his hand but wasn't sure whose it was. The Western Union told him it was for the Longachers. The boy knocked on the door and handed it over to Ma Longacher.

"Why do you have this, son?" she asked.

"Western Union said you folks weren't home," he replied.

Ma Longacher put on her spectacles as the boy hopped on his horse and rode off. "It's from David. He'll be home soon, maybe tomorrow. Thank God," she said.

"Who's with him?" Beth asked.

"You know our David, girls. He can be a man of few words at times." Ma handed the telegram to Nel as she dabbed the corners of her eyes.

"Beth, have Frank Lee carry you to the church and tell the Reverend to bring his family and anyone else he can think of over to our place," Ma Longacher said. "Tell him our David's coming home."

"I'll drive the wagon myself. Frank Lee's out working the field," Beth said.

Nel hugged Ma Longacher, then Hannah, as Beth skedaddled out the door.

"Come on girls, our David will be wanting chicken

pie and custards," Ma Longacher said. "Let's get busy."

"I'll get out the linen table cloth and our best table-ware," Nel said.

"Don't forget to polish it up," Ma Longacher said.

"Oh Ma, I'm so excited I can hardly think," Nel said.

Ma Longacher took her hand. "Let's pray, child. God has been good to us."

"Come and join us, Hannah," Nel said.

The tables they'd placed in the summer kitchen were filled with pans of fried chicken, three large hams, and smoked wurst sausage. They decided to keep the German potato salad in the fruit cellar until everyone arrived.

"What ever are we going to do with all this food, Mother?" Hannah asked.

"There are a lot of guests coming," Ma smiled.

"I hate wringing chicken necks," Nel said.

"Is that why Mother and I did the deed?" Hannah said.

"Well, I *did* pluck their feathers," Nel said.

Beth walked up. "I helped too. I had to wear a bandana over my nose when we scalded them before you plucked them."

Nel began choking. "Stop it, Beth."

"Did you tell Reverend Booker about the shindig, Beth?" Ma asked.

"No, a church elder told me Reverend Booker went off to New York to beg his adulterous wife to come back home. And he wasn't the friendliest," Beth said.

"Oh my," Ma gasped, wringing her hands. "... Well, is he going to put up a bulletin?" she asked.

"I put them up myself," Beth said.

6

Having been through all they had, it would have seemed a tragedy that David could not make it the rest of the way. But he was alive and he had Wolf with him.

After having had his ring restored to him by Sally Blackwell, Charles Allen was persuaded that she and her companions should accompany him to the Longacher farm. Traveling along the same road that led to Camp Piqua, their greatest surprise was to come.

Wolf sat near a campfire boiling coffee. David's knee, which was now swollen so much that a slit had to be cut in his pants, needed to be rested before it carried him home.

Charles Allen and the women spotted David, sitting under a tree, his leg locked in an unbendable position. David was with a young man who looked familiar to Charles Allen. And as the wagon pulled off the road, Charles Allen ducked into the back of it.

The young strawberry blonde yelled out, "Wolf, Wolf. Hello, hello, we're over here."

Wolf turned to see a young girl waving at him from atop a buckboard with two other women. Their wagon was painted up in the colors of a rainbow. As the wagon pulled closer, the girl jumped down.

She held out her hand to help an older woman down, a brunette.

"I'll be darned, if it ain't my favorite ... entertainers. Real angels of mercy." Wolf waved, then walked over to the wagon. "What are you fancy girls doing out on the prairie by your lonesome?"

"Who you calling fancy girl, sassy soldier boy?" the strawberry blonde said, tossing her banana curls over her shoulders.

"Don't pay no mind to Mister Wolf," the brunette told her daughter. "But he is a handsome boy, isn't he, daughter?"

The strawberry blonde batted her eyes and giggled.

David tipped his cap. "I'd stand, ladies, but my leg gave out on me," he grimaced.

Sally walked over and knelt down beside David. "You poor soul. Do y'all mind if I take a look at it?" she asked. "Lord knows it must hurt somethin' god-awful."

David passed out.

"Mister Wolf, you help us girls get him up into our wagon," Sally said.

"Don't you be fixing to butcher on his leg, Missy," Wolf said as he and the two women lay David on some blankets in the back of the wagon.

"Hush," Sally said. "Remove his trousers." She felt around David's knee. "Seems to me he has some grape shot lodged next to his kneecap."

She glanced over at his right leg. "He's been shot in that leg, too," she said.

"That one's fine. He dug the minié ball out himself, same as he did mine." Wolf smiled wide.

Sally took out a knife and made a small incision. She finished with a couple of stitches. "With some rest his leg will be as good as new. That grape shot weren't deep," she said. "Many of the boys want the shrapnel as a keepsake." She put them in a vial and handed it to Wolf.

Several minutes later, David came to. Wolf shook the vial containing the grape shot as David reached down to feel his leg.

"Don't y'all be fussin' with those stitches, Yankee Doodle," Sally said.

David turned toward the other two ladies who sat watching.

"This is the mother and daughter that I got the quinine, whiskey and such from before we were captured," Wolf said. "Remember?"

"The fancy girls?" David said.

"Not anymore," the brunette said.

"They're strictly drummers of medicinal goods now," Wolf said. He looked at David's leg. "I reckon walking home is out now."

"How far you figure we are from Camp Piqua?" David asked.

"Now you're asking me?" Wolf laughed.

Charles Allen pushed some drying pantaloons and petticoats out of his way. "Tell him we're one mile as the crow flies." He smiled as he threw his arm around Wolf's neck. "Miss me, son?"

"If you ain't a sight for sore eyes," Wolf said.

"Give me a hand."

Wolf reached to place his arms beneath Charles Allen's armpits. "You lost part of your ..."

"What's going on?" David called out from the other side of the wagon.

The mother and daughter propped David up.

"Would someone be kind enough to get me out of here," David said.

Charles Allen motioned the others into position. "You ladies get under his legs. Cousin David, put one of your arms around my neck and the other around Wolf's ... on three," he said as they lifted him out. David steadied himself against one of the wagon's wheels. He stared at the pinned sleeve of Charles Allen's jacket.

"Cousin Charles ..." David pointed.

"That sweet gal who just put your leg on the mend is nurse Sally," Charles Allen said. "She also helped the doctor with this." He raised his pinned sleeve.

David looked over at Sally. "Do you have anything for pain, ma'am?"

"I sure do, honey."

"If'n that leg hurts too much, Cousin, she can always take it off," Charles Allen said.

"That ain't a bit funny, Cousin Charles," David said.

Wolf muffled a snort. Charles Allen pointed over at him. "He seems to think so."

7

As the day wore on at the Longacher place, the women sat together on the porch and watched as the sun began to set over the valley.

Ma Longacher got up off of the porch swing for the hundredth time and pulled her shawl tight around her shoulders. The wind began to blow against the treetops.

"You girls each grab a log or two. We'll go inside the house and sit by the fire," she said, holding the door open for the girls.

"I'm worried," Nel said. "David should have been home by now."

"Oh Nel, you and Ma are beginning to make me nervous," Hannah said. "Can't you stay in place for at least five minutes?"

Nel bit at her fingernails.

"Come over here and sit by me, I'll comb your hair out so you'll look extra pretty for your husband," Hannah said.

"Do you think they ran into trouble?" Nel asked.

"Trouble? The war's over," Hannah said.

Beth sat in Ma's rocking chair.

Nel looked over at her. "Beth, are you certain that your Wolf is coming with David?" she asked.

"You talk as if he's some kind of pet," Beth said.

"My eyes must be getting old, I just dropped a stitch," Ma Longacher said.

"Mother, please put your embroidery back in the basket and comb out my hair so I'll look pretty, too," Beth said.

"For your Wolf?" Hannah giggled.

Beth waved her off.

"Bring that footrest over here by my chair, Beth, and give that rocker a rest," Ma Longacher said.

"Forget about my hair, I'm going to make us some tea," Beth said.

"That's a good girl, Beth," Ma said. "It'll calm everyone's nerves."

Hannah cupped her hand to Nel's ear.

"Don't you be talking about me," Beth called out from the kitchen.

Nel turned to Ma Longacher. "The ladies' sewing circle at church says a lot of David's friends were either killed or died of disease."

"I pray every night for all the families," Ma said. "North and South."

"There's still a lot of hate for the South yet," Nel said.

"The deeper the cut, the longer it takes to heal," Ma said.

"Then this is one that's going to take a very long time," Nel said.

Nel peered out the window. "The rooster's crowing," she said.

Beth gazed into the flames as they danced off the burning logs. Her eyes closed until a loud crackle sounded. Several glowing embers landed on the hearth. She straightened up. "What Nel?"

Nel was caught between a yawn as she spoke. "Wake up, Beth, or better yet, go to bed."

"I'm awake." Beth covered her mouth, attempting to conceal her own yawn.

"Come on, Beth, this will be the last time you'll be able to sleep in David's and my room," Nel said.

Beth slid from her chair and dragged up the stairs. "Last one upstairs is a monkey's uncle," she called out.

"Don't be so childish, Beth," Nel said. "Anyway, it's not monkey's uncle. It's a monkey shine."

"Monkey's uncle, monkey's uncle, monkey's uncle," Beth laughed.

"Get some sleep, girls," Ma Longacher called to them. She waited until she heard the upstairs bedroom door slam shut.

"I can't sleep," Hannah said. "Do you want to stay up with me a little longer, Mother?"

Ma reached over and poked the logs. "Okay dear, I couldn't sleep anyway."

"Shall I get us some more tea?" Hannah asked.

"No, dear, I don't want to be running out to the privy," Ma laughed. She looked over at her daughter. "Would you like me to comb out your hair, Hannah?"

"No, Mother."

"So what's on that pretty mind of yours?" Ma asked.

"How do you know something's on my mind?"

"Oh, let's just say mother's instinct."

"Well, with David coming home to Nel ..." Hannah paused.

"To Nel?"

"Oh, you know what I mean, Mother," Hannah said. "And Beth will probably wind up marrying Wolf ... I guess I was just thinking that maybe I might be sort of a fifth wheel."

"Did one of the girls say something?" Ma asked.

"Of course not," Hannah said. There'd been a boy once, from church. After Hannah met him, she started dressing differently. He seemed to take a shine to her. But one Sunday, without warning, he was gone and one of his brothers said, vaguely, that he was headed west. It was almost as if he was running away from something or someone. Hannah never knew any more than that. But once in a while she'd say something that made her family believe she hadn't forgotten him.

Ma got up and walked over behind Hannah. She bent down and kissed the top of her head. "Well, let me put all that business to rest, dear. I wrote to David about the very same thing, and he would have none of it. In fact, he wrote back that if Beth and Wolf ever got married, he wanted them to live right here on this very land with the family."

"Well Mother, I guess you and me think alike then."

"You just realizing that, dear?" Ma said.

"I'm going to get another tea," Hannah said as she made her way toward the kitchen. Hannah smiled when she heard her Mother call out to her, "Get your old mother one, too."

8

The returning soldiers and their pretty attendants rested the next day by the roadside. They ate, swapped yarns, and consoled each other. Early on, David sat propped against one of the wagon's wheels, nodding off. He awakened as Charles Allen approached and stood in front of him. David reached out his hand.

Charles Allen grasped it, but instead David pulled Charles Allen down beside him and put his arm around his cousin's neck. "Now tell me, Cousin Charles, where'd you get that pretty Yankee uniform?"

"You don't notice anything else?" Charles Allen asked.

David leaned back, eyeing Charles Allen for a moment. "I'll be darned … I do. You're still sporting a Reb cap."

They all laughed.

"Well boys, me and my daughter are going to be joining Sally for a spell," the brunette said.

"Y'all's weather's a mite cold for us girls. We'll be makin' our way South with the war bein' over," Sally said. "Now that General Lee has surrendered, I have to get back to Alabama and help out."

Their last task up North was to give the soldier boys a lift into town.

When they arrived, David and Wolf made some small repairs to the girls' wagon and tied down the bundles inside. "We'll miss having you ladies up here," Wolf said.

"Look at yourselves. There's a lot of patchin' up to do

for the Southern boys, too," Sally said. "They need com-fortin' just like y'all. Men are such babies."

"I'll take Wolf with me, Mother, and see that he gets some tender care," the strawberry blonde giggled.

"No you won't, honey. He's already spoken for," her mother said. "Besides, he had his chance with you and me."

"Charles Allen, you better come with me," Sally said. "You're used to warmer climate now. Besides, that Reb kepi belongs down South with you in it." She pursed her lips at him.

"Nothing would be sweeter," Charles Allen said. "But I got some work to finish up at the Longacher's. After the harvest, I believe me and my brother will head back to Indiana." He reached into his pocket. "Here." He handed Sally a piece of paper and then pulled her close to his body, giving her a long kiss.

David palmed some greenbacks into Wolf's hand and gave him a nod. "See that the young one takes this for her and the other girls," he whispered.

"You coming with us, Sally?" the mother called out.

Through the prairie dust they watched the girls waving their colorful bandanas.

"Them's good women," Charles Allen said.

"Listen ..." David said.

In the distance, a melody rang out. "I come from Alabama with a banjo on my knee ... Oh Susanna, don't you cry for me ..."

David pulled his diary out of his knapsack. He made

an entry, then looked over at Charles Allen and Wolf.

The two looked at each other and rolled their eyes.

"What?" David said.

David and the boys snuck into town. There was an air of celebration there and even total strangers were buying each other drinks. A returning hero would have received a welcome that lasted days. They went around back to Billy Perkins' place—who was a substantial welcoming committee all by himself—and borrowed a horse and wagon. David, Charles Allen, and Wolf went out of town by a side street.

David was moved by everything he had seen. "It's an amazing thing Old Abe has done," David said, "with all due respects. He's transformed our country. Now maybe we can look forward to peace and liberty once again."

"I'm not so sure about that, Cousin," Charles Allen said.

It was not to be so simple. Lincoln would be assassinated a week after David, Wolf, and Charles Allen returned home.

9

"Who's that coming to see us?" Ma Longacher pointed at the covered bridge.

"Maybe it's someone who saw the bulletin at the church," Beth said.

Ma and the girls watched as the fancy surrey pulled up.

"Why bless their souls, it's Mister and Missus Dixon," Ma said. "Jerry Dixon's folks, girls. We should have a good get together."

Mister Dixon helped his wife down. They all stood at the foot of the porch.

"Oh dear, I'm so sorry about your boy," Ma said as she hugged Missus Dixon.

"We dropped by to tell you not to count on anyone coming to your social, Missus Longacher."

"But ..." Ma's lips began to quiver as she started to speak. She stepped back, turning out her hands.

Missus Dixon handed her a letter. "It's from our Jerry."

"Your David sent us a note, too," Mister Dixon said, clearing his throat. He rubbed his mouth with his large hand and looked down, taking in a deep breath.

"Most folks around these parts don't understand Charles Allen and his family siding up with the South ..." Missus Dixon started.

Mister Dixon interrupted. "But many of the boys who fought the war do get it. Have David tell you about a Confederate named Grizzly ... and about how your boy saved our son's life. It's all in the letter."

"Knowing David, he probably won't want to," Missus Dixon said. "That's why I'll leave you to read Jerry's last letter to us. We'll be back in a few days to pick it up. We so want to see David."

The Dixons climbed back into their surrey. Mister Dixon wiped his coat sleeve across his eyes and turned the horses. They made their way back toward the covered bridge and the road beyond.

10

The rig bounced along the dirt road.

"How far to go?" Wolf asked.

"I think I see the covered bridge up ahead," Charles Allen said as he shaded his eyes.

There was a wagon approaching. As they passed, David squinted to get a better look. They're dressed awfully well, he thought, for this time of day. Nobody in these parts dressed in their Sunday best, except for ... The man nodded as their wagons passed. And suddenly David recognized them.

"Pull over, Wolf," David said. He turned to call out after the Dixons, but the dust from the road had already consumed the Dixon's buggy and they were out of shouting range.

"Wasn't that David Longacher?" Missus Dixon asked.

"I'm not sure," Mister Dixon said, telling his wife the first lie of their marriage. "And if it was, I wouldn't want to slow him down getting home." And they rode on, acutely aware of the homecoming they wouldn't have, their soldier who would never return.

Missus Dixon sniffed the single rose and pressed it into her Bible.

"Jerry would've liked it that we had his company engraved on his headstone," Mister Dixon said.

Missus Dixon patted him on his knee.

A mile away, Ma had begun to worry in earnest. "What in the world are we going to do with all the food?" she said.

Buck's ears turned up and twitched. He ran lickety-split down the road barking, his tail wagging. Ma and Beth stepped out on the porch. Not sure she could get down the steps without getting dizzy, Ma grabbed Beth's arm.

"Oh David my love, you came home to us," Nel said to herself softly as she let out her breath. "Shhh, baby David ..." Nel picked up a bit of rag, dipped in milk, and put it back in his mouth. She looked over at Hannah who was gently rocking baby David's twin sister, who was sound asleep.

"I believe it's Cousin Charles and Wolf with him," Hannah exclaimed.

Beth took in a deep breath, wiping her sweaty palms on her dress.

Ma Longacher put her arms around the girls and pulled them close. "We'll find out real soon, my loves." She smiled as teardrops ran down her cheeks.

Frank Lee pulled the two gray mares up and held out his hand. "Everybody up on the wagon. We're gonna beat Buck to the covered bridge and David, too."

The soldiers' wagon passed the neighboring farm.

"Hold on tight, folks!" Frank Lee yelled.

"I hear my Buck," David said.

"I see a rig barreling down the road from your place,

Cousin David," Charles Allen said.

"Hold on to your breeches, boys," Wolf said as he snapped the horses' reins.

The sun rolled out from behind several puffy white clouds and shone down on the roof of the covered bridge, casting its rays over the valley, radiating the various eternal colors of the landscape.

Many stories have been told about the Civil War. David's diary told me his. I believe David would be pleased that you now know it as well.

THE DIARY

Inside front cover of diary

118   D Longenecker
85   Co [Company] G 110 O.V. [Ohio Volunteers]
ex   Military Prison
Danville Va [Virginia]
Sept 24/64 [1864]

Friday, January 1, 1864.

Was clear pleasant AM, PM it turned cold, A very lonesome New Years day to me away from home and its loved ones. May God grant that ere another New Years day peace will be restored to our lands & we soldiers at home enjoying ourselves with those we left behind — Recieved [sic] letters from Kate, M D Myers, & Mr VanCleaf.

Saturday, January 2, 1864.

Clear cold, All quiet and nothing to break the monotony of Camp life. Recieved letters from Eof & Amy.

Sunday, January 3, 1864.

Clear until 3 PM then clouded over. Sent letters to Kate Amy & Mr VanCleaf.

Monday, January 4, 1864.

Began to snow 9 A.M. & snowed all day. 3 in. fell

Tuesday, January 5, 1864.

Cloudy — Snow melted — Sent letter to Eof.

Wednesday, January 6, 1864.

Cloudy cold. I was at the Station

Thursday, January 7, 1864.

Very cold last night. Cloudy cold day, Sent letter to Stahl.

Friday, January 8, 1864.

Clear and very cold, John Hart returned from furlough and brought letters, but lost box of eatables, Sent letter to Joel.

SATURDAY, JANUARY 9, 1864.

Clear cold, 110th went on Picket near Poney Mountain. Nothing unusual transpired. Sent letter to Amy.

SUNDAY, JANUARY 10, 1864.

Clear cold, Remained on Picket, What a strange sight or rather what a simple thing it is to see men sitting or standing out in the cold winters wind watching waiting for their fellow man to take his life. What a contrast to what is transpiring at home this fine Sabbath day. David Shull joined Co [Company] from Camp Parole —

MONDAY, JANUARY 11, 1864.

Clear cold, Remained on Picket, All quiet and nothing new to note.

TUESDAY, JANUARY 12, 1864.

Clear and thawing. Came to Camp from Picket. 3rd Corps was under orders to move but did not go.

WEDNESDAY, JANUARY 13, 1864.

Cloudy damp. Sent letter to Amy — Recieved letter from Joel.

THURSDAY, JANUARY 14, 1864.

Partly cloudy — All quiet, Recieved letter from Jennie,

FRIDAY, JANUARY 15, 1864.

Clear and thawing — Recieved letters from Kate and E D Book, Sent letter to Jennie — Drew a new blouse —

SATURDAY, JANUARY 16, 1864.

Clear pleasant, Recd letter from Amy,

Sunday, January 17, 1864.

Partly cloudy & cold, A very lonesome day. Sent letters to E.D. Book, Joel & Amy.

Monday, January 18, 1864.

Rained all day and was very unpleasant, Was detailed to paint Division train. Reported this forenoon to Capt Hart & returned to Camp again

Tuesday, January 19, 1864.

Clear and windy — I went to paint Wagons but paint was not ready so I came back to Camp

Wednesday, January 20, 1864.

Clear and very pleasant Did nothing to day.

Thursday, January 21, 1864.

Was cloudy cold, I painted wagons to day. I was not well,

Friday, January 22, 1864.

Morning cold cloudy, but cleared off & was pleasant, I and My partner Mr. Patterson Co G 10th Vt [Vermont] painted 6 Wagons, Recieved letters from Amy, & G. Shoemaker,

Saturday, January 23, 1864.

Morning cold, Day pleasant, I was painting. Gen Carr is building a ball room where they intend to have a merry time, It seems to be entirely inappropriate to be making so merry while such a gloom is spread over our land, Sent letter to G. Shoemaker —

SUNDAY, JANUARY 24, 1864.

Clear and pleasant, A lonesome day to me. Recieved letters from Joel & J.K.F, Sent letter to Amy —

MONDAY, JANUARY 25, 1864.

Clear and pleasant — I was painting Wagon beds — A great Ball at Carrs Hd. Qurs [Head Quarters] — not a private Soldier was admitted, Soldiers stood guard while the officers were dancing —

TUESDAY, JANUARY 26, 1864.

Clear pleasant — I was painting, David Shoe has the Small pox,

WEDNESDAY, JANUARY 27, 1864.

Very pleasant almost like May, Painting — Recieved letter from M.D. Myers.

THURSDAY, JANUARY 28, 1864.

Very pleasant — Painting — Have nothing to write —

FRIDAY, JANUARY 29, 1864.

Very pleasant, Painted — Recieved letters from Amy & Mr VanCleaf

SATURDAY, JANUARY 30, 1864.

Clouded over last night & was unpleasant day. Did not work. Rumors of marching orders —

SUNDAY, JANUARY 31, 1864.

Was cloudy and drizzled a little. I was quite unwell. Wrote letters to Amy and Mrs VanCleaf, Sent my Diary for 1863 home by mail — Was at preaching in the evening —

Monday, February 1, 1864.

Was cloudy drizzly — Done nothing — Was vaccinnated —

Tuesday, February 2, 1864.

AM Cloudy. PM it cleared off & was pleasant. I painted one Wagon bed —

Wednesday, February 3, 1864.

Thundered & sleeted last night & hailed — Cloudy, stormy & cold — David Shoe died of small pox last night. I was at the Station & got some oysters — Sent letter to M.D.M.

Thursday, February 4, 1864.

Cold stormy. Day was spent in idleness as I was not well

Friday, February 5, 1864.

AM clear, PM it clouded over, I was quite unwell, but worked a little at painting — Reg't [Regiment] went on Picket,

Saturday, February 6, 1864.

Was cloudy drizzly — Ordered at 5 A.M. to be ready to march at 7 with 3 days rations, We did not move, but the balance of the Corps did. Was to the Rapidan on a recconnaisance — Cannonading began at noon South of Camp at Mortons ford and continued till after dark & Musketry was brisk, Capt Ullery, Serg't Simes 23 others of 110th went home after recruit Letters from Amy & W. Hart, Sent letter to Amy.

Sunday, February 7, 1864.

Cloudy cool day, All quiet to day, Hayworth & Jones from Miami Co [County] Ohio came here on a visit and brought me a letter & 3 pies from Joel ~~and 3 pies~~

MONDAY, FEBRUARY 8, 1864.

Troops returned from Recconnaisance to Camp, Recieved letter from Kate, Chopped and hauled wood,

TUESDAY, FEBRUARY 9, 1864.

Cold morning, Day cool, All quiet, Sent letters to W. Hart & Genet,

WEDNESDAY, FEBRUARY 10, 1864.

Cloudy cold. Painted 3 Wagon beds, Recieved letter from Mr VanCleaf,

THURSDAY, FEBRUARY 11, 1864.

Clear and sharp cold wind blowing. Sent letter to Kate, Recieved letter from Lavenia Shellenberger. Our Mess [Messenger] sent 52 Valentines,

FRIDAY, FEBRUARY 12, 1864.

Clear pleasant, Painted five Wagon beds,

SATURDAY, FEBRUARY 13, 1864.

Clear and pleasant, Recieved letters from Amy & Joel,

SUNDAY, FEBRUARY 14, 1864.

Clear and very windy, Hayworth and Jones left for home, Sent letters to Amy & Joel, also one to Lavenia, A very lonesome day, Spent part of this day reading,

MONDAY, FEBRUARY 15, 1864.

Forenoon was cloudy & PM it snowed but all melted as it fell. All continues quiet,

TUESDAY, FEBRUARY 16, 1864.

Forenoon was cloudy and a little snow fell. PM it turned very cold & windy — I was at the Station, Played checkers in the evening.

WEDNESDAY, FEBRUARY 17, 1864.

Clear and very cold the coldest day we yet had this Winter, Remained in quarters all day, I spent evening reading,

THURSDAY, FEBRUARY 18, 1864.

Clear and cold. In quarters all day — Recieved letter from L.H.C.

FRIDAY, FEBRUARY 19, 1864.

Clear and cold — Day spent idly —

SATURDAY, FEBRUARY 20, 1864.

Clear and pleasant, Benjamin Reiber and John Mothers new recruits came to our Co and 8 or 10 to other Co's, Recieved letters from Amy, M.D. Myers & JKF, Sent Memorial to Kate & Hettie,

SUNDAY, FEBRUARY 21, 1864.

~~Recieved~~ Clear but cool, A very lonesome day, Sent letter to Amy,

MONDAY, FEBRUARY 22, 1864.

Cloudy damp, Went to paint but did not paint any on account of rain.

TUESDAY, FEBRUARY 23, 1864.

A very pleasant day — We painted six Wagons, Wrote letter to L.H. Coate,

WEDNESDAY, FEBRUARY 24, 1864.

Morning very pleasant but soon clouded over & was very Windy. Painting part of day. A detail of our Reg't went on Picket, Wrote a letter to Mr VanCleaf — Evening had a lesson in Regulations.

THURSDAY, FEBRUARY 25, 1864.

Forenoon cloudy, PM clear and pleasant, Did not paint Gen French & Staff Reviewed the 3rd Div [Division] — Many ladies present, An Officer lost a Canteen of whiskey & I found it & the boys drank it, Our box of boots & c [et cetera] came, Recieved letter from Amy & sent one to M.D. Myers,

FRIDAY, FEBRUARY 26, 1864.

Clear and very Windy — Day spent idly —

SATURDAY, FEBRUARY 27, 1864.

Clear and quite pleasant, Painted 4 Wagons, 6th Corps went on a Recconnaisance toward Madison C.H. [Court House] Capt Moore of Co E died last night,

SUNDAY, FEBRUARY 28, 1864.

Smoky and miled Wind from S.W. Had orders to hold ourselves in readiness to march at a moments notice, Wrote to Amy and after that took a walk toward Culpepper, Spent part of day reading bible —

MONDAY, FEBRUARY 29, 1864.

Cloudy cool, All quiet, again have orders to be ready to march at a moments warning — Benjamin Reiber died —

TUESDAY, MARCH 1, 1864.

Began to rain last night & rained slowly all day. Snowed in the evening, Another detail of our Reg't went on Picket,

WEDNESDAY, MARCH 2, 1864.

Cleared off last night and day was pleasant. 6th Corps came back, Kilpatrick is near Richmond,

THURSDAY, MARCH 3, 1864.

Clear pleasant, Painted, Recieved new Memorials,

FRIDAY, MARCH 4, 1864.

Was partly Cloudy, Painted 4 Wagons, Recieved letter from Genet,

SATURDAY, MARCH 5, 1864.

AM Cloudy & rained a little, PM it cleared off & was pleasant,

SUNDAY, MARCH 6, 1864.

Partly cloudy cold, A very lonesome day to me, A member of Christian Commission preached for us. Gen Kilpatrick got through to Yorktown, on Friday after doing the Rebs considerable damage, Amelia Furnas died.

MONDAY, MARCH 7, 1864.

Clear and pleasant, All quiet in front, I painted two Wagon beds to day, Pay Master came this evening,

TUESDAY, MARCH 8, 1864.

Clouded over last night and rained this forenoon, Cleared off PM, We were paid for four months this forenoon, This is my 5th Anniversary of my Wedding, O what a change in five years, Wrote a letter to Amy — Sent one years subscription to Harpers Weekly for Amy & Mrs Pearson, Sent letter to Probate Judge,

WEDNESDAY, MARCH 9, 1864.

Clear pleasant, Jerry and I were to the Station and expressed $19.21 of our Co's money home, P.M. I went to paint but no beds being ready I came to Camp. Col Keifer reviewed 2nd Brigade —

THURSDAY, MARCH 10, 1864.

This has been a rainy unpleasant day, and I hardly knew how to spend it, Wrote a letter to Kate in the evening, Recieved letter from Mr VanCleaf & Kate,

FRIDAY, MARCH 11, 1864.

A very wet unpleasant day, I hardly knew how to spend it. Went to preaching in the evening and was pleased that I was there, Eleven of the 110th gave in their names as members of the Christian Union. Recieved letter from J.K.F. Lieut Gen Grant was at Meades Hd Qurs.

SATURDAY, MARCH 12, 1864.

Clear and very pleasant, I went early in the morning to have a negative taken for Photographs, but did not have it taken till near noon, am to have six next Saturday. Paid $1.50 in advance, Our new Chaplain came. Evening I was at our brigade Chapel to hear our new Chaplain preach, Wrote & sent letters to D Strayer G Shellenberger & J.K.F. Recieved letters from Joel & [unclear: Mat] also notice from Hprs Co. [Harpers Company]

Sunday, March 13, 1864.

Clear and strong wind from West, Detail went on Picket, Sam Ullery went home on furlough, I sent letter and $20.00 by him for Amy, Another lonesome Sabbath, Our new Chaplain preached for us to day, After preaching I took a walk down the Rail Road, Evening intended to go to preaching but set talking till it was too late,

Monday, March 14, 1864.

Partly cloudy & cold — Day I spent in idleness in Camp. Evening I was at prayer meeting. Irwin of Co C died,

Tuesday, March 15, 1864.

Cloudy cold and some snow flying about noon. Forenoon I went to Wagon Train to paint but my partner not being there I did work, Afternoon was dull & I felt quite lonesome, Was going to write a letter but could not collect my thoughts so postponed it,

Wednesday, March 16, 1864.

Cloudy cold & stormy — Gen French & Staff reviewed 3rd Corps, I was not out on Review, Afternoon I wrote a letter to Joel & [unclear: Mat], Evening spent in tent, On account of the Review, boys must again stay over their time on Picket, Uncle Abe orders another draft of 200,000 men, Bully for Old Abe,

Thursday, March 17, 1864.

AM partly cloudy cold PM clear & pleasant, I went down to the Train to paint, but did not do any thing, Wrote a letter to Mr VanCleaf, Boys came in from Picket, Nate Teeter of 1st Ohio Cavalry married to May Jones.

FRIDAY, MARCH 18, 1864.

Clear and pleasant, Painted one Wagon, Recieved letters from Amy & Lavenia, Amy expressed $6.50 to me two weeks ago, Recieved orders at 5 PM to be ready to march with 3 days rations immediately. Companies formed stacked arms & awaited orders. Troops ordered to quarters at 8 P.M. What the scare was I don't know, Got six Photographs,

SATURDAY, MARCH 19, 1864.

Clear pleasant, We painted three Wagons, Recieved Certificate from Probate Judge, Had intended to go to meeting but was otherwise engaged so did not go, Cannonading heard to the South of here,

SUNDAY, MARCH 20, 1864.

Clear and cool. Evening cold windy, Wrote a letter to Amy. Was at prayer meeting in the evening. Was glad I was there, At first I did not feel like going, but went after all. Jasper Jones of 1st Ohio Cavalry married Lib Jay, W.A. Hart of 13th Iowa married to A Miss Moore,

MONDAY, MARCH 21, 1864.

AM cloudy, P.M. clear, Col Kiefer reviewed our brigade, I was out on the review, the first time I have been in ranks for over two months, Evening I spent at Co Hd Qurs in conversation, Lieut Gross promoted Captain of Co. E,

TUESDAY, MARCH 22, 1864.

Cold cloudy until 4 PM then began to snow & blow, In Camp all day and did not do anything — I sent in a furlough for approval.

WEDNESDAY, MARCH 23, 1864.

4 inches snow fell last night, Day clear and snow melted, Ike & Dan went on Picket, I began a letter for Troy Times but did not finish it. I am anxious to hear from my furlough, Sometimes I feel confident of success, then again think it will be disapproved. Gen Grant was to arrive & take command of the Army.

THURSDAY, MARCH 24, 1864.

Clear pleasant and snow melted fast, Lieut Gen Grant passed through on special train to Culpepper. We were formed in line to salute him as he passed but did not get out in time. This has been a very lonesome day. Order read transferring our Division to 6th Corps.

FRIDAY, MARCH 25, 1864.

Cloudy, and a little snow fell, 4 P.M. Soon turned into rain and is raining yet at this writing 9 PM. This has been a very lonesome day to me, the evening passed off more pleasantly as I recieved three letters & had them to read, One from Amy, one from Joel & one from J.K.F. Amy recieved letter and money I sent with Sam Ullery.

SATURDAY, MARCH 26, 1864.

Clear and pleasant, I recieved a furlough for 15 days. I did not expect it and would not believe at first that it was so,

SUNDAY, MARCH 27, 1864.

Clear pleasant, Left Camp at 8 o'clock A.M. took cars at Brandy at 9 arrived in Alexandria 2 P.M. Stopped there half an hour, took boat to Washington arrived there half past 3, went to 244 Pa [Pennsylvania] Avenue got transportation home, Homeward bound! Came to Baltimore too late for train so had to lay over night,

MONDAY, MARCH 28, 1864.

Left Baltimore 9 AM, Harrisburg 2 PM, arrived at Pittsburg after midnight. Passed through dear old Juniata Co [County] and could hardly pass without stopping,

TUESDAY, MARCH 29, 1864.

Cloudy rained, Left Pittsburg at 1 AM Steubenville 6 AM, Columbus 2 PM and arrived home at 5 P.M. Home again I can hardly realise it,

WEDNESDAY, MARCH 30, 1864.

Cloudy damp. At home all day, Evening I went up town and seen several of my acquaintances. O what a satisfaction it is to enjoy one day of quiet at home & away from the everlasting rattle of drums & braying of mules.

THURSDAY, MARCH 31, 1864.

Cloudy, cool, At home forenoon, Afternoon Amy & I went to Mothers and at 5 PM went to Gettysburg in the train, Met Dave Shellenberger in town,

FRIDAY, APRIL 1, 1864.

8 AM Am on the Greenville Creek bridge now writing this, Returned home from Gettysburg in a caboose, Mrs Ullery and Mrs Samon spent the evening with us,

SATURDAY, APRIL 2, 1864.

Cloudy, Started to go to Piqua, but met Kate & family at the depot so did not go to Piqua, All went to Newton in the evening,

SUNDAY, APRIL 3, 1864.

Clear AM, PM it clouded over, Spent the day in Newton, Met many of my old acquaintances and had a pleasant time,

MONDAY, APRIL 4, 1864.

Cloudy rainy, Came up from Newton about noon. PM [unclear: _oted], Kate and her family took 5 PM train for home, Recieved letter from Capt

TUESDAY, APRIL 5, 1864.

Cloudy drizzly, I was in Piqua for trousers & c, Seen Chaplain Harvey, Sent my furlough to Capt to get my transportation to Washington,

WEDNESDAY, APRIL 6, 1864.

Cloudy damp, Was at home all day, Spent evening at Capt Ullery's

THURSDAY, APRIL 7, 1864.

Cloudy forenoon, PM it cleared off, I went to Piqua in the train had negative taken at Gales for Photos. Am to have 9. Paid for them, Evening had company,

FRIDAY, APRIL 8, 1864.

Cloudy and rained hard in the evening, I was at home all day,

SATURDAY, APRIL 9, 1864.

Cloudy cool & hailed a little. At home all day, Evening Amy and I were at Martins and Holsingers,

SUNDAY, APRIL 10, 1864.

Cloudy cool, Amy & I started to Newton, Met Joel at the Toll gate & came back with them & spent the day at home, Evening were at Mothers and Capt Ullerys,

MONDAY, APRIL 11, 1864.

Forenoon clear pleasant, PM was cloudy, Started for the Army at 11 o'clock A.M. A sad parting with wife, mother & my sisters, May God grant I may live to return, Passed through Columbus 3 PM and arrived at Bellaire 10 PM, too late for train so had to lay over,

TUESDAY, APRIL 12, 1864.

A.M. Cloudy, At Bellaire waiting for train to go to Washington D.C. Crossed Ohio River 10 A.M. took a walk to nail factory, 12 M took train for Washington Eat supper at Grafton, All passed off fine to day,

WEDNESDAY, APRIL 13, 1864.

Cloudy, Arrived at Harpers Ferry at day light, part of bridge being washed away train could not cross, passengers crossed River on foot bridge took cars on opposite side & arrived at Relay House 11 AM lay there till 4 PM then took train for Washington arrived there 6 PM, lodged at Soldiers rest, Evening took a walk up town,

THURSDAY, APRIL 14, 1864.

Cloudy, Left Washington AM, Went to Alexandria on Ferry boat, got package at express office $6.50, When cars came no room for more passengers so a number of us went on freight, Engine gave out. Sent back to Alxa [Alexandria] for one. Arrives 4 PM, Start for Culpepper arrive there 10 PM staid all night in town,

FRIDAY, APRIL 15, 1864.

Cloudy, Daylight started for Camp, Found it 2 miles NE of Culpepper, Boys out on Picket, Reported to Col. he sent me to my Co to report for duty. Recieved letters from Amy, M.D.M. "Grimes" VanCleaf, & D. Strayer. Sent letters to Kate Amy Hettie & "Grimes"

SATURDAY, APRIL 16, 1864.

Rained all day, Were to be reviewed but the rain postponed it, Boys came in off Picket, Sent letter to D Strayer. Serg't Josh Deeter recieved Commission for 2nd Lieutenant, David Martin & WM Locke of Co G recieved Lieuts Commiss, J S Deeter sick,

SUNDAY, APRIL 17, 1864.

Cloudy cool, J S Deeter went to hospital, Joshua Furnas a new recruit joined Co., J Babylen returned from Washington Hospital, I was rather lonesome to day, Wrote letters to Amy & JKF, Sent to NY for Photos,

MONDAY, APRIL 18, 1864.

Clear and pleasant, Gen Grant reviewed the 6th Corps near Brandy Station. We had to march about four miles to place of review and then pass in review which was a tiresome tramp. Coming back to Camp I took my time and came in half an hour after the Reg't, Lieutenant Miller resigned

TUESDAY, APRIL 19, 1864.

Clear pleasant, All quiet, I was on guard last night & to day, M Holliday & Sweringer of 4th Ohio were here to see Ike Landis & I,

WEDNESDAY, APRIL 20, 1864.

Cloudy cool, Col Keifer inspected the Reg't, Dan Long sent to Alexandria sick, Josh S Deeter mustered in as 2nd Lieutenant, Wrote and sent letter to Amy, Eight of the band were assigned to Co G,

THURSDAY, APRIL 21, 1864.

Forenoon cloudy, PM was clear, Had drill to day Co AM & PM battallion, Sent letter to Capt, Recieved letter from "Grimes." I feel quite well, but dread the coming march. All is quiet now but it only is the calm before the storm,

FRIDAY, APRIL 22, 1864.

AM clear & very pleasant, PM it clouded over, Practised target shooting AM, PM had battallion drill. Lieut Gross promoted to Capt Co E, Locke also to Co E. I felt quite well to day, Mails from here North reported to be suspended, hope it is not so, J W Teeter bent or broke my pen and is to keep it & pay me $2.75 for it.

SATURDAY, APRIL 23, 1864.

Clear and pleasant, Strong wind from South, All is activity in Camp to day getting ready for action. Recent indications show that we will not stay here two days longer, I pray that we may be successful when we do move, Recieved letter from Amy and answered it immediately & sent photos of generals. J W Teeter paid for pen, J Holsinger owes 60 for photo's, Lute Cooper joined Co.,

SUNDAY, APRIL 24, 1864.

AM clear & very pleasant, PM it clouded over and began to rain 9 P.M. All very quiet & no sign of a move, I attended preaching in the forenoon, Afternoon took a walk out and set under a tree & read the bible, Went to bed early,

MONDAY, APRIL 25, 1864.

Heavy rains last night. Forenoon part clear. PM cloudy again. All quiet to day, Sent letter to Joel,

TUESDAY, APRIL 26, 1864.

Clear, strong wind from North, Commenced making out Pay Rolls, Evening I was to prayer meeting and was surprised to see so many there. Sent letter to Anthonys,

WEDNESDAY, APRIL 27, 1864.

AM very pleasant. PM cloudy & rained a little, Was helping at Pay Rolls, Wrote and sent a letter to Amy, Evening I was at prayer meeting,

THURSDAY, APRIL 28, 1864.

Clear & cool, Strong wind from North. I was not on drill, All quiet in front. Our Chaplain resigned on account of, he says, his wife being sick, but no doubt it is he himself that is sick of the service,

FRIDAY, APRIL 29, 1864.

Clear pleasant, Helped at Pay Rolls, Had Brig [Brigade] drill, but I was not out, I was much disapointed because I recieved no letter from Amy, Recieved letters from W.A. Hart, Aaron Stanfield fell on drill & sprained his ankle,

SATURDAY, APRIL 30, 1864.

Partly cloudy & sprinkled a little P.M. We mustered for two months pay. Part of 5th Corps moved up. Burnside between Mannasses & Rappahannack Station, Our mail failed to come, I was on Camp guard last night, Wrote letter to W.A. Hart, also wrote a letter to Amy in the evening, H Stanfield & the other sick sent to the rear,

SUNDAY, MAY 1, 1864.

Partly cloudy, but very pleasant, We went on Picket ~~North~~ West of Culpepper, All was quiet during the day. I felt quite well, Wrote part of a letter to Amy. Near the part where we are can be seen a sample of the rights the Southerners are getting for commencing this war, its a family once well off, but now beggars,

MONDAY, MAY 2, 1864.

Cloudy and rained in the evening. On Picket, all quiet — Recieved letters from Kate & Capt,

TUESDAY, MAY 3, 1864.

Partly cloudy, cool, Was Picket, All quiet until 5 P.M. when the officer of the day came around & gave us orders to leave picket line as soon as dark & return to Camp & prepare to move to morrow morning at 4 AM, Arrived in Camp 10 P.M. drew 3 days rations, went to bed to sleep a few hours before morning —

WEDNESDAY, MAY 4, 1864.

Clear warm, Revielle was beat at half past two we jumped up got a few bites to eat, fell in, went to brigade Hd Qurs, moved from there at daylight, Crossed the Rapidan at Germanier ford about 5 PM & camped on the South bank, The other corps & two divisions of 6th Corps moved on, No enemy found to day, Had a hard march to day,

325

Thursday, May 5, 1864.

Had a good nights rest — ~~Started~~ Resumed the march but did not get far until we were ordered back returned to where we bivouacked lay there an hour Gen Grant passed us — Resumed march again, turned to left of road lay till one P.M. then took plank road, marched to O C pike were then ordered back two miles to the other divisions soon got in engagement, had a severe fight after dark — Co G Lost 15 killed & wounded — I was hit but not seriously injured

Friday, May 6, 1864.

Clear warm – Fighting began at daylight, Drove the Rebs into their works, I was too lame to take a part in the engagement, Considerable fighting on center AM, we hold our own, I was in the rear till 4 PM when my leg was so far recovered from the bruise that I joined the Reg't, found the boys entrenching, At sunset the Rebs outflanked us with an overwhelming force. The 122nd NY in our front and the — — of 1st Div broke creating a panic in the second line of battle & the whole Corps retreated to inner line, Serg't Ullery missing

Saturday, May 7, 1864.

Clear warm, Our Corps took position in the center to day, our lines were contracted some, The Rebs attacked our left center & were repulsed with fearful slaughter, 8 PM we left our lines & moved South East to get a new position near Spottsylvania C.H. [Court House] Marched all night, ~~Passed Chancellorsville &~~ Tonight we march slowly & halt every few minutes — at every halt I lay down & soon am asleep — I am so weary —

SUNDAY, MAY 8, 1864.

Passed Chancellorsville 8 A.M, halted 2 miles East to get coffee, after breakfast moved a mile further & halted an hour, ordered forward to reinforce 5th Corps which had found the enemy in a strong position about 3 miles from Spottsylvania, 5th Corps had a severe fight with Ewell in the evening, drove the Rebs. After dark we were moved South into woods & drew rations.

MONDAY, MAY 9, 1864.

Clear warm, Built a long line of breastworks — All quiet until about sunset when the Rebs threw some shells but did no hurt, Sharpshooters wounded several of 6th Md [Maryland] Everything goes well so far, Gen Sedgewick mortally wounded by a Rebel! Sharpshooter, last night when we were drawing rations the Reb pickets called out Come here you get you good rations —

TUESDAY, MAY 10, 1864.

Clear & very warm. A battery took position by our Div and opened on the Rebs but they replied very feebly. Very heavy cannonading on our right, also heavy musketry — 2000 prisoners taken, Rec'd the glorious news that Butler defeated the Rebs at Petersburg, Sherman done it to them at Dalton & they are in full retreat, Bully, Black Dan fortified with knapsacks behind a stump, set up a pan then got behind and called to Sharpshooters now hit that & sure one pretty near hit it. Dan lit out —

WEDNESDAY, MAY 11, 1864.

Remained in breastworks all day. Artillery played on the Rebs all day, Rebs did not reply, 3rd Div moved to left in the evening, and occupied other entrenchments. Began to rain about sun set —

THURSDAY, MAY 12, 1864.

Rained all day & was very unpleasant, Rebs opened on us early with artillery but did little damage, Fighting began on the left at 8 AM, our troops charged on the Rebs works Captured them & 8,000 prisoners & 17 pieces artillery, loss heavy in killed & wounded on both sides. 3rd Div moved to the left half a mile & relieved 2nd Div. 126th Ohio was detached from brigade & put in with 1st Div at the "Slaughter pen." 110th lost 1 killed & ten or 12 wounded

FRIDAY, MAY 13, 1864.

Rained considerable, Our Division was moved to the left to Captured Rebel works, lay there till 3 PM then moved back to where we were last night, I seen the most sickening sight at Rebel works ever I beheld Rebel dead laying three or four deep, Sent letters to Amy Kate Joel & D Strayer This is the first opportunity we had to write since leaving Camp — the letters will relieve many anxious hearts

SATURDAY, MAY 14, 1864.

Cloudy & rained, We moved at 3 AM toward Spotsylvania C.H. Arrived at Fredericksburg & Richmond Pike 10 AM, lay there till 4 PM then moved S.E. to a brook [inserted: Po River] lay there till sunset then forded it & took positions on the hill, The Rebs fled as we approached, Some slight skirmishing along our lines to day. 110th went on Skirmish line, To day we made the big charge through the Po River & up the hill through pines & brush, built works,

SUNDAY, MAY 15, 1864.

Cloudy cool, All very quiet to day, Came in from Picket, 6th Corps had orders to advance in the evening but it was countermanded again Had a very uncomfortable night on picket as our clothes were wet from wading the Po and the weather cloudy & damp —

MONDAY, MAY 16, 1864.

Cloudy All quiet, except a little cannonading near the Pike. Recieved our mail, Recieved letters from Amy Joel, J.K.F. J Stahl,

TUESDAY, MAY 17, 1864.

Cloudy cool, All quiet until near sun set when there was some cannonading on the left, At dark 6th Corps was ordered to march, Marched [unclear: North], Wrote 4 letters to day, Amy, Hettie, J.K.F. & J Stahl &

WEDNESDAY, MAY 18, 1864.

Cloudy but warm, 6th Corps marched all last night & arrived on the right of our line at "S — r [Slaughter] pen" at sunrise, went to reinforce our troops, the Rebs made an attack & were repulsed, At noon we returned to left of line & bivouacked where we were yesterday,

THURSDAY, MAY 19, 1864.

Partly cloudy & warm, Marched at daylight, Advanced our line about a mile and a half & built a new line of rifle pits. All quiet in front of 6th Corps, Rebels made an attack near Pike but were repulsed with loss of 300 prisoners & many killed,

Friday, May 20, 1864.

Clear pleasant, our brigade moved a little to the right, This is the first day since we crossed the Rapidan that there has been no cannonading — There was but little skirmish firing. Sent letters to Amy and Kate,

Saturday, May 21, 1864.

Cloudy & a little rain P.M. About half of 2nd brigade was throwing up a new line of breastworks, The whole Army began to move at 6 PM toward Guinea Station on Fredericsburg and Richmond R.R, The Rebs made a feint in our front about sun down and a brisk skirmish took place, Our brigade followed the Column at 9 PM, Rebels shelled our train but did no damage, our brigade was the last to leave the Rebs front,

Sunday, May 22, 1864.

Cloudy warm with a little rain, The Army moving toward Noels Station near the North Ann, Halted at Guinea Station about 3 hours, Bivouacked for the night about 4 miles west of Guinea Station, Passed through some good country with fine farms & residences,

Monday, May 23, 1864.

Clear & quite warm, The Column moved from where we bivouacked about 8 A.M. Our brigade was left as rear guard & did not move until 11 A.M. Overtook Column 2 P.M. drew rations & moved on, the Column reach River, we bivouacked near Applewood about 12 PM. 5 Corps had a severe engagement at the North Ann about sun set, Rebels defeated with heavy loss,

TUESDAY, MAY 24, 1864.

Clear and quite warm. The Column moved from where we bivouacked at 8 AM our brigade was left as rear guard & did not move till 11 A.M, Overtook the Column 2 miles from drew rations & moved to Applewood where we bivouacked at midnight, the Column moved on to the North Ann, 5th Corps had a severe engagement with the enemy at the River, Our side victorious & the Rebs roused Our brigade moved toward the river 2 miles & lay there all day, Evening had orders to be across the river but the order was countermanded — Sent letter to Amy — Heavy cannonading toward Hanover Junction — About 400 Reb prisoners sent to Port Royal —

WEDNESDAY, MAY 25, 1864.

Warm and cloudy with a light thunder shower in the evening. Our brigade moved to woods near North Ann, lay there till 5 PM then crossed the river on Pontoons & took position in breastworks Troops moving [illegible] left, No fighting to day, A little skirmishing, I wrote two letters

THURSDAY, MAY 26, 1864.

Day broke cloudy & soon the rain began to pour & continued till 10 A.M. Our brigade moved out to Noels Station on Va [Virginia] Central RR at 10 A.M. halted a mile South of Noels and were ordered back to rifle pits, 110th went on Picket. Army recrossed North Ann and moved toward Hanovertown on the Pamunky, All quiet except a little cannonading South of Station. This is the third time our brigade was left the last to leave the Rebs front —

FRIDAY, MAY 27, 1864.

Cloudy warm, We pickets left Noels Station at 1 AM moved down the River & crossed on a bridge & marched several miles halted for breakfast, moved on again to Ruther Glen & drew 2 days rations, then moved South East toward Hanoverton, Bivouacked at dark in a field. This has been a hard days march, Overtook our Corps at sun set,

SATURDAY, MAY 28, 1864.

Cloudy warm, Column moved at 6 A.M. and crossed Pamunky River on Pontoons about noon at Nelsons ferry, moved South a mile and a half and formed line of battle, 3rd Div on left of Corps. Entrenched after dark, Rebs threw a few shells, To day we had halted on the north bank of the Pamunky & thought we had time to make coffee but before it come to boil "fall in" "fall in" was the word & we had to go.

SUNDAY, MAY 29, 1864.

Morning quite cool pleasant, We lay quiet near Nelsons ferry where we entrenched last night, 1st Division moved toward Hanover in the afternoon, No fighting to day, This was a very lonesome day to me, Out of rations & no prospect of Supply train coming up to night,

MONDAY, MAY 30, 1864.

Clear and quite warm, 6th Corps moved at day light toward Hanover C.H. [Court House] arrived near the C.H. about 9 A.M, and lay there till noon when we moved South East 3 miles & formed in line of battle in front of the enemy whose rifle pits we could see, heard the Rebs bands play & locomotive whistle, Some brisk skir [skirmishing] took place on left of our Corps — Were out of rations & anxiously looked for the supply train but it did not come —

TUESDAY, MAY 31, 1864.

Clear and very warm, All quiet except little skirmishing until 8 AM when cannonading opened on the right of 2nd Corps. About noon the enemy was driven from their first line of rifle pits & we occupied them, the enemy attempted to drive us back but was not successful, We began to throw up earth works at sunset, & worked till midnight — Recieved our mail, I recieved 2 letters from Amy & gold pen from Mortons. Sent letters to Amy & Mr. VanCleaf,

WEDNESDAY, JUNE 1, 1864.

Clear and very warm, 6th Corps moved from right of line to Cool [Cold] Harbor arriving there about 11 A.M. & entrenched, 10th Corps joined 6th, Evening charged the Rebs out of their works and took about 600 prisoners. Levi Childers wounded in heel. It was encouraging to see the Rebs skedaddle — they left, arms blankets, haversacks with corn bread & tobacco, & c in their works —

THURSDAY, JUNE 2, 1864.

Warm & part of day cloudy, with a little rain. No advance, but brisk skirmishing all day. B. Flummer wounded in thigh, balance of Reg't came from the right where it was on picket and joined us & we were relieved from front line & went to the rear —

FRIDAY, JUNE 3, 1864.

AM cloudy & a little rain, PM clear, Our entire line advanced to within 200 yards of Rebs works, but the right & left of line not coming up the charge ordered was not made, We entrenched under a galling fire, Job Pearson of Co G was killed dead, Jerry Teeter wounded, Hard fighting all day all a long the line, Capt Snodgrass who was acting major was drunk & run the left of

110th 100 yds ahead of the rest of the line & there we lay four hours when we got orders to fall back —

SATURDAY, JUNE 4, 1864.

Clear A.M, PM it clouded over & rained a little, 110th was relieved from front line last night & moved inside the works, Heavy cannonading on right after dark, Brisk skirmishing all day, Sent letters to Kate Amy & A Morton with Pen to be exchanged, I was quite unwell,

SUNDAY, JUNE 5, 1864.

Clear and warm, Brisk skirmishing all day, After dark 1st Div made a charge on Rebs but was repulsed. Recd letters from D Strayer, Joel, J.K. Fretz. Sent letters to D. Strayer, W Hart & Kate,

MONDAY, JUNE 6, 1864.

Clear and quite warm. Brisk skirmishing along the lines. Had a truce this PM for an hour and we met the Rebs half way & exchanged papers, I was almost up to their works, Joe Gill returned to Co., Recieved letters from Hettie & Amy, Sent letters to Hettie & Amy,

TUESDAY, JUNE 7, 1864.

Clear warm, Skirmishing began early ~~until~~ & continued until 6 PM when another truce was had & firing in our front ceased for the day, Heavy cannonading on right & left, 110th was relieved from front line, Sent letter to Troy Times, As tobacco vender was driving along rather near the front he was shot dead — the boys helped themselves to his stock of tobacco —

WEDNESDAY, JUNE 8, 1864.

Partly cloudy but warm, Skirmishing continues, Rebs sent a few shell over us. We are slowly digging up to the Rebs, Sent letter to J.K.F. & recieved one from Kate,

THURSDAY, JUNE 9, 1864.

Cloudy warm, Detail of 110th went on skirmish, All very quiet to day, only a few cannon shots fired. Clay Walker & H. Stanfield returned to Co., Sent letters to Kate, G. Shoemaker & Amy. I was quite unwell,

FRIDAY, JUNE 10, 1864.

Clear warm, But little skirmishing, Some cannonading, 3rd Div was relieved to go to left and relieve Div of 2nd Corps, Did not move till after midnight, Caissons and limber chests are kept under bomb proofs, and musicians and rear bummers have their gopher holes

SATURDAY, JUNE 11, 1864.

Partly cloudy, warm, 3rd Div moved a mile to left, 110th went on the front line, Some slight skirmishing, Sent letter to J Holterman, Loaned H Shell 25 cts,

SUNDAY, JUNE 12, 1864.

Clear and quite warm, 110th on skirmish line, All quiet except a few cannon shots, Recieved letter from Amy & sent one to her, also one to D.R.L 8th O.V.C, At 8 PM Army fell back from Rebs front, we remained on Picket, Army began to move toward the James River,

MONDAY, JUNE 13, 1864.

AM clear warm, PM cloudy, We fell back at 3 AM from Rebs front without being discovered & followed the Column toward Jones Bridge on the Chickahominy & crossed at 9 PM moved a mile South & bivouacked. All very quiet. We had a hard march and the Column was much scattered, A staff officer was hurrying us up, but it was of no avail, the boys were too tired —

TUESDAY, JUNE 14, 1864.

Clear warm, Column moved from Chickahominy toward Charles City CH [Court House] at 6 AM and arrived near there at 1 PM and bivouacked, All quiet not a gun heard, What a relief it is to be out of hearing cannons booming, Passed some good farms, Corn looks promising, This afternoon we lay about a mile from Wilcox's landing on the James —

WEDNESDAY, JUNE 15, 1864.

Clear and warm, 6th Corps remained where it bivouacked yesterday. Trains crossing river, Sent letters to Amy & M.D. Myers, All quiet to day,

THURSDAY, JUNE 16, 1864.

Clear and quite warm, Moved at 7 AM half a mile toward the James and entrenched, 6 PM 6th Corps moved to Wilcoxs landing & embarked on Transports & went up the River to Point of Rocks where we landed & bivouacked, Heavy Cannonading S.W.

FRIDAY, JUNE 17, 1864.

Clear and very warm 3rd Div moved at 3 AM from Point of Rocks & reinforced 10th Corps at Bermuda Hundreds, All quiet except a little skirmishing, Sent letters to Amy & Kate — At dark we move a little to left and rear and bivouacked for the night.

336

SATURDAY, JUNE 18, 1864.

Partly cloudy & very warm, 3rd Div had formed at 3 AM to make a charge, but the order was countermanded & we moved back, Heavy cannonading at Petersburg, Recieved letters from Joel, Kate & VanCleafs, At sunset 3rd Division moved to right near the river & lay in breast works —

SUNDAY, JUNE 19, 1864.

Clear and warmer, All quiet, 10th Corps relieved 3rd Div and we moved toward Petersburg crossing the Appomattox on Pontoons, Recieved letters from Amy, Sent letters to Amy, Kate, and Joel, Division arrived in front of Petersburg at 11 PM — I was so tired that I bivouacked with a number of others before we got there —

MONDAY, JUNE 20, 1864.

Morning cloudy, Day clear and warm, I fell out of ranks last night & slept till this morning & then came up, 3rd Div is now 2 miles South of Petersburg, Rebs threw a few shells, Sent letters to Amy & Troy Times, Recieved letter from J.K.F, About 75 substitutes came to Regt, 11 came to Co G.

TUESDAY, JUNE 21, 1864.

Clear and warm, Remained near Petersburg until 5 PM then moved to extreme left of line & fortified No engagement to day, Sent letters to J.K.F, D VanCleaf & Pen to Morton,

WEDNESDAY, JUNE 22, 1864.

Clear and very warm, Advanced half a mile at 9 AM and a slight skirmish took place, 5 PM fell back to old position & at dark advanced a mile again without any serious opposition, W Ketchman was wounded to day on the skirmish line,

THURSDAY, JUNE 23, 1864.

Cloudy and extremely hot, Lay all day where we halted last night Evening entrenched, Rebs made an attempt to flank us on our left but were foiled, After dark we fell back to old line, Calvary tore up some of the RR, Recieved letter from Genet, Our line now is half a mile SW of the Jerusalem plank road — near the Williams House —

FRIDAY, JUNE 24, 1864.

Clear and hot sultry, Were ordered to advance but order was countermanded, 110th moved a short distance to left & built entrenchments, Some cannonading near Petersburg, If ever there were glad boys it was the boys of the 6th Corps to day when the order, "No advance for the present," came

SATURDAY, JUNE 25, 1864.

Clear and very warm, We cleaned up, All quiet in our front, Some cannonading at Petersburg, Recieved letters from Kate & Jacob Stahl, Sent letters to Kate & Genet. Orders from Corps Hd Qurs to clean up camp ground & dig wells as the Corps is to occupy its present position for some time —

SUNDAY, JUNE 26, 1864.

Clear and extremely warm. Evening there was some appearance of rain but it did not come, Heavy cannonading all night at Petersburg & continued today, 110th went on Picket, Recieved letters from Amy, Sent letters to Amy & Lizzie, Commenced making out Pay Rolls,

MONDAY, JUNE 27, 1864.

Reg't on Picket I did not go. Worked on Pay Rolls — The usual cannonading at Petersburg —

TUESDAY, JUNE 28, 1864.

Clear warm. Cannonading heard South of here — All quiet in our front,

WEDNESDAY, JUNE 29, 1864.

Clear and very warm — Arose early struck tents policed & formed in line ~~While~~ & stood there while Gens Wright & Ricketts passed along the line, after that we pitched tents in regular order, at 2 PM got orders to march & moved at 3 PM toward Reams Station on Weldon RR where we arrived 10 PM & bivouacked —

THURSDAY, JUNE 30, 1864.

Clear & very warm — Were tearing up the RR at Reams Station All quiet — 5 PM we moved toward our old position. Moved slowly & reached Plank Road about 11 PM & bivouacked there —

FRIDAY, JULY 1, 1864.

Clear and extremely warm, I drew the rations & almost suffocated. Recieved 60 drafted men to the Reg't, 2 to Co G Lay at Plank Road until sun set then moved a short distance South & bivouacked for the night, Cannonading heard at Petersburg —

SATURDAY, JULY 2, 1864.

Clear warm — Corps moved back to its old position this AM. It was a hard & hot march. I almost suffocated with heat and dust — All quiet except the usual firing at Petersburg —

SUNDAY, JULY 3, 1864.

Clear warm — In camp & lonesome, All quiet except plenty rumors that a general advance is to be made to morrow, I wrote several letters —

MONDAY, JULY 4, 1864.

Clear warm — Nothing unusual to note — I wrote a letter to the Troy Times —

TUESDAY, JULY 5, 1864.

Clear & warm — All quiet,

WEDNESDAY, JULY 6, 1864.

Clear and very warm — Recieved orders at 3 AM to move immediately. We packed up & marched at Sunrise toward City Point arrived there at 12 M and lay there till 4 PM when we embarked on boats for Baltimore — Anchored about 4 miles below Wilcox's landing at dark, Its delightful riding on the James of a pleasant Summer evening. Report says 3rd Division goes to Harpers Ferry —

THURSDAY, JULY 7, 1864.

Clear forenoon, PM cloudy & a shower. I never suffered so much of heat as to day on deck of boats. Got under way at day light, passed one boat on Sand bar, touched at Ft Monroe at 9 AM, Had a pleasant evening ride on the bay, Wrote letters to Amy, Kate, and Elias —

FRIDAY, JULY 8, 1864.

Clear and warm, Arrived at Baltimore at 2 AM anchored till daylight then landed and immediately took cars for Monaccacy where we arrived at 5 PM & unloaded, formed near the Rail Road & got supper then made our beds & went to sleep. Had a pleasant ride to day. The Stars & Stripes were floating from nearly every house along our route, and the Ladies threw kisses at the boys & cheered them on,

SATURDAY, JULY 9, 1864.

Clear and quite warm — 1st Brig returned from Frederick last night, We arose with the sun drank our coffee after that drew 3 days rations. At 9 AM reports came the enemy was advancing from Frederick, 3rd Div was formed in line of battle on the hill near the river on the E side — Skirmishing began at 10. Soon after 12 M a heavy force of Rebs attacked our left, they were held at bay, till 4 PM when they came in too heavy force & we were driven back and almost surrounded, 300 of 3rd Div captured, Myself among the numbers, I was captured near Baltimore pike by 21 N.C. After I was captured I helped carry our wounded off —

SUNDAY, JULY 10, 1864.

Clear warm — Slept sound last night & never thought I was a prisoner until this morning when I awoke & found guards around — After sunrise I was taken over to mill where I was surprised to meet about 400 fellow prisoners. J Teeter and 4 others of Co G among them. 34 of 110th are among them — Rebs are moving toward Washington, We prisoners moved from Monacacy at 8 A.M. and passed through Urbana Frostburg & Hyattstown & halted after dark 23 miles from Washington — A very hard march to day — I left a note in Urbana for Amy informing her of my fate, The guards treat us well so far — but the idea of being a prisoner is not pleasant and I wish I was with the Reg't again. No parole, no exchange so the prospect for a long imprisonment is good — I will try to bear it as well as I am able, May God grant that soon we may all be at liberty again —

MONDAY, JULY 11, 1864.

Warm clear — Moved early from our bivouack and passed through Rockville at 11 AM and arrived near Tennallytown D.C. about 5 PM — Skirmishing going on in front of fortifications, Several large shells thrown from forts passed over us — Prisoners camped in an orchard — A very hard march to day — Rebs took the boots of some of the boys feet — also took all watches.

TUESDAY, JULY 12, 1864.

Clear and very warm. We lay near Tennallytown until 6 PM then marched toward Rockville. Some skirmishing in front of defenses, Early fell back at dark & retreated toward Whites ford on the Potomac — A few more prisoners brought in — Roser escaped — Provost Marshall very anxious to exchange Confed Money for Greenbacks — his excuse for this is that he wants to send the Greenbacks to a prisoner in Ft. Deleware —

WEDNESDAY, JULY 13, 1864.

Clear and very warm — Marched all last night and passed through Rockville at daylight and moved toward Edwards ferry — halted at noon at [blank] Creek, and drew a pint of flour to each man and remained there till sunset then moved toward the Potomac — the Reb Army moving same way — Marched 20 miles —

THURSDAY, JULY 14, 1864.

Clear and very warm — We marched all night, passed through Poolesville at 3 A.M. and reached Potomac at sunrise, forded it and moved South to a big Spring near Leesburg where we stopped for the night — Another squad of Yankees brought in — Some cannonading heard East of us — Marched 24 miles One pint of flour and half a pound of beef for each were our rations to day —

FRIDAY, JULY 15, 1864.

Clear warm, Prisoners lay near Leesburg, Cannonading at the Potomac — Rebs and Yanks busy trading — Drew the usual quantity of flour & meat — Our forces engaged in the fight at Monaccacy on Saturday last, were the 110 & 4 Cos of 122 & the 126th Ohio 138 Pa 87 Pa 9th N.Y.H.A. [New York Heavy Artillery] 106 & 151 NY 10 Vt 14 NJ and one Reg 100 day men & about a brigade of Md Home guards in all about 4000 men against not less then 30000 of the enemy under Gen Early —

SATURDAY, JULY 16, 1864.

Clear and very warm — Marched at 1 AM toward Upperville, passed through Leesburg at day break — Cannonading heard at Potomac Passed Frostville & Union — Arrived at Upperville at 5 PM and bivouacked for the night, but at 9 PM cannonading was heard in our rear so we were aroused and march through Ashbys Gap toward Winchester. March 28 miles. No rations — No rations to day —

SUNDAY, JULY 17, 1864.

Clear warm — Marched all night, forded Shenandoah at 1 AM, arrived at Millwood at 4 AM and halted for the day. Marched 10 — Paid $ 8.00 in Greenbacks for a small shoulder. Drew a pint of corn meal to a man for our rations to day —

MONDAY, JULY 18, 1864.

Clear warm, Prisoner marched from Millwood to Winchester, halted there an hour then moved to Kemtown where stopped for the night — Drew 1 pt flour — To day I seen one of the boys take a piece of bread out of a dogs mouth & eat it —

TUESDAY, JULY 19, 1864.

Clear warm. Prisoners lay at Kemtown — We are beginning to feel the effects of short rations. The Provost Marshal permitted us to get green apples to eat so we have something to knaw [gnaw] at. One pint of flour & half a pound beef were our rations to day — Fletcher paid $2.50 in Greenbacks for a loaf of bread — I sold my gold pen holder for $5.00 Confed to buy bread with

WEDNESDAY, JULY 20, 1864.

Clear warm AM. PM a heavy shower — Marched from Kemtown at 3 AM & passed thro Newtown, Middletown & Strasburg and halted at Fishers Hill at 3 PM, Rebs sending their wounded up the Valley — No rations to day so we go hungry — I had the pleasure of a bath in Hazel River —

THURSDAY, JULY 21, 1864.

Cloudy but pleasant — Lay at Fishers Hill near Strasburg — 85 more prisoners brought in some of whom were robbed even of their trousers — Rebs trains moving South — Union forces reported at Middletown — I was quite out of patience to day because we got no rations, are half starved — The guards went out & foraged flour and baked it & sold the cakes to us at $1.00 each —

FRIDAY, JULY 22, 1864.

Clear pleasant, Marched from Strasburg at 5 AM passed through Woodstock & Edinburg and reached Mt. Jackson at 5 PM and bivouacked for the night, We drew half a pint unbolted flour and half a pound of beef to a man — Starvation rations — I had almost resolved to attempt to escape to night but was too tired to try it. Hospitals are full of wounded —

SATURDAY, JULY 23, 1864.

Very cool night — Day quite warm — clear — Marched from Mt. Jackson at 5 AM passed through New Market 9 AM, arrived at Big Springs at 2 and rested two hours, then moved on to within 3 miles of Harrisonburgh and halted for the night — one pt of flour & half a lbs of beef. I never was so hungry in my life — $1.00 for a cake of bread of one pound of flour —

SUNDAY, JULY 24, 1864.

AM clear, PM cloudy and began to rain at dark — Moved from 2 miles of Harrisonburgh , passed thro Mt Crawford 10 AM and halted at the river 3 hours drew rations and at 3 moved on and at 7 PM passed through Mt. Sidney and bivouacked half a mile South — Passed a number of Dunkards who I suppose were going to Church — Oh how I wished I could go with them —

MONDAY, JULY 25, 1864.

Heavy rain last night and we got a good wetting — PM was clear — Marched at day break and reached Staunton at 9 AM passed through town and halted in a field to wait for transportation, Paid $3.00 for a pie — cheese $6.00 flour $200.00 pr barrel — At 2 PM took cars for Charlottesville where we arrived at 6 PM got off cars and & bivouacked — Charlottesville is a Hospital of Reb wounded – Apples $1.00 a dozen — Gingercakes sell at $3.00 a dozen — Ice cream $5.00 pr dish — Rebs after Greenbacks keen —

TUESDAY, JULY 26, 1864.

Clear warm. Drew 4 ounces of bread and 2 oz of meat for each man — Took cars at daylight for Lynchburg arrived there 2 PM were march through town and quartered in an old tobacco house — The town is highly perfumed with tobacco — all if can afford — In a Southern Prison! ugh —

Wednesday, July 27, 1864.

Clear warm — The first day in a Southern Military Prison passed very lonesome — Rebs took or wanted to take all our blankets, tents, and knapsacks, but as soon as the boys seen what was up they cut & tore all into pieces — I sold mine — so they did not get many, 730 men crowded on 3 floors. Rebs offer $3.50 of their money for $1.00 in Greenbacks – I paid $1.00 for half a lb of corn bread — Pies $2.00 a piece —

Thursday, July 28, 1864.

Partly cloudy, warm — 600 Prisoners took cars for Danville. 4 PM arrived at Junction and changed cars & moved on toward Danville, Country we passed through is hilly & wooded — soil of poor quality — Farmville is a fine town but full of Hospitals — Eggs 50 cts apiece $5.00 in Confed for $1.00 in Greenbacks —

Friday, July 29, 1864.

Clear warm — Arrived at Danville this morning at 4. Soon as day we got off cars & were marched to an old tobacco house known as Prison No 1 & quartered therein — Got 1 lb corn bread 2 ounces bacon and a pint of rice soup as our days rations. I never was so hungry as to day — Water out of Dan River is what we have to drink — also use it to cook —

Saturday, July 30, 1864.

AM clear & warm — PM cloudy. Well here we are in Prison crowded together so we hardly have room to turn — Wrote letter to Amy —

SUNDAY, JULY 31, 1864.

Cloudy warm — The first Sabbath in Prison a lonesome day it has been — Wrote and sent letters to Hettie & Kate — All the talk is of Parol and exchange — Nothing for breakfast this morning —

MONDAY, AUGUST 1, 1864.

Clear warm. A lonesome day — I began to read the testament with the intention of reading it through — Our rations are 1 lb corn bread made out of chop — 2 ounces old rank bacon 1 pt rice soup — this for one day —

TUESDAY, AUGUST 2, 1864.

Partly cloudy with a little rain, 400 Prisoners from Petersburg arrived — among them 60 niggers, Brigadier Bartly and 40 officers — officers say they were marched through Petersburg in the same ranks with the negroes — Guards shot a man in No 3 for looking out of window —

WEDNESDAY, AUGUST 3, 1864.

Clear warm, I almost had the blues today —

THURSDAY, AUGUST 4, 1864.

Clear warm — 3rd Div officers arrived from Lynchburg and they and the Petersburg officers left for South Carolina — A lonesome day —

FRIDAY, AUGUST 5, 1864.

Clear warm — Not so lonesome to day — Spent day reading & discussing scriptures — Reb papers say their Cavalry burnt Chambersburg Pa.

SATURDAY, AUGUST 6, 1864.

Partly cloudy with a thunder shower — Scrubbed Prison floors and it is more pleasant now —

SUNDAY, AUGUST 7, 1864.

Cloudy with a shower Oh what a lonesome Sabbath in Prison. Nothing for pastime but plenty of rumors of xchange or parol — Several Reb officers in to see us, I feel grateful to God for his goodness to me in giving health — May He grant we soon may out of Prison

MONDAY, AUGUST 8, 1864.

Showery warm — About 25 of us were permitted to go to the river & bathe. Oh how good I felt after taking a good wash – Danville Prices. Onions $4.00 pr Doz — Apples $4.00 pr Doz, Eggs $6.00 pr Doz Butter $10.00 pr lb — Common Soap $6, Molasses $50 pr gallon —

TUESDAY, AUGUST 9, 1864.

Cloudy warm — I did not feel well — To day is the first time since in Prison my appetite has been satisfied. I spent the day reading & talking — A man shot in No 2 — Ripe Peaches at $3.00 a Doz —

WEDNESDAY, AUGUST 10, 1864.

Clear and very warm — A very quiet day in Prison — not even a rumor of xchange or parol —

THURSDAY, AUGUST 11, 1864.

Clear warm — I was well & in good spirits — A late despatch by "tatlers line" says all prisoners are to be paroled immediately and sent to their respective states until xchanged —

FRIDAY, AUGUST 12, 1864.

Cloudy & rained. I felt quite well and have a faint hope of being exchanged soon. Through Reb papers we learn that Ft. Powell was blown up by the Rebs and Ft. Gaines surrendered on the 9th at Mobile —

SATURDAY, AUGUST 13, 1864.

Clear warm — This has been a boisterous day in Prison had two fist fights, 100 Prisoners from Army of Potomac arrived — five officers sent off. Beef brine soup to day. Oh what a beautiful evening — How I would love to take a stroll out in the fields.

SUNDAY, AUGUST 14, 1864.

Very warm & cloudy — I was not well and very lonesome — Eggeman taken to Hospital — Get mess pork now and bean soup. Our bread is corn chop mixed with water and half baked —

MONDAY, AUGUST 15, 1864.

Clear warm — I was not well — Papers say 450 sick & wounded were sent for exchange. We have just discovered that the beans we get are full of rat dung — Oh shame on the <u>Confederacy</u> —

TUESDAY, AUGUST 16, 1864.

Rained hard last night and to day. Dan river is rising — Our drinking & cooking water out of the Dan is no cleaner nor better than if it was taken out of a mud puddle in the road, We got a drink of spring water — I feel pretty well again — But Oh how lonesome in this Prison where we do not hear what is going on outside — have not seen a paper for a month —

WEDNESDAY, AUGUST 17, 1864.

Cloudy with heavy thunder showers — I was carrying water for our squad, and was so provoked at the guards for not letting us get spring water after the officer had promised it that I am sorry I used profane language — May God speed the day when we may again be in the free and happy North —

THURSDAY, AUGUST 18, 1864.

Cloudy warm. I was quite unwell and had the "blues." Rebs took our haversacks & canteens & the few shelter tents we had yet — Some of the boys think it is a sign of exchange, but I believe they took them because they need them to fit out a squad of conscripts who are about to be sent to the front — One of the guards mistaking a towel for a yank trying to escape out of window fired, no one hurt, one died on 1st floor —

FRIDAY, AUGUST 19, 1864.

Clear warm — I was sick and could not rest at all — Confound the boys — they are for ever talking about good things to eat — it makes ones mouth water — with no hope of getting anything but corn bread & <u>rat</u> soup —

SATURDAY, AUGUST 20, 1864.

Cloudy and cool. I am still unwell and wish more then ever to be put out of this loathesome Prison — For what crime are we here? none, only for defending the glorious "Stars and Stripes," Burnside had a fight at Deep Bottom

SUNDAY, AUGUST 21, 1864.

Warm cloudy with a fine shower — I arose early this morning and almost my first thoughts were of home & the happy scenes transpiring there to day — Richmond Enquirer of yesterday says Grant now holds the Weldon RR two miles from Petersburg —

Monday, August 22, 1864.

Cloudy with a shower — I felt pretty well — Played checkers. In a fracas on 3rd floor one man bit anothers ear off —

Tuesday, August 23, 1864.

Clear and warm — To day I picked quite a number of rat "berries" out my soup. Oh shame on the Government this feeds prisoners such stuff — I enjoyed myself reading the scriptures — Dreamed I was at home last night — in a [illegible] or dream My letters written here on 31st recieved at home

Wednesday, August 24, 1864.

Clear until 4 PM then clouded over — I was quite well and enjoyed myself reading the testament — Rumors that Peace propositions are afoot — Negro prisoners taken away to be returned to their former owners —

Thursday, August 25, 1864.

Cloudy and warm — A very quiet and lonesome day — I felt quite well — Battle at Reams Station —

Friday, August 26, 1864.

Cloudy warm — Another lonesome day — Latest report says we will surely be xchanged soon —

Saturday, August 27, 1864.

Rained hard last night. Day clear — I was well and spent the day reading scriptures & playing checkers — Our soup to day was made of Rat fruit and one rat — Our degenerate Yankee cooks steal the best of our meat & trade or give it away — Often see ham at the Cook house, but none of it ever comes to us.

SUNDAY, AUGUST 28, 1864.

Clear warm — the last night was cool. To day has been a hopeful day for us — the Richmond papers say that their government is ready to exchange prisoners man for man and officer, so we hope soon to be out of this detestable place — Was well and spent day reading — No Rats in our soup to day —

MONDAY, AUGUST 29, 1864.

Clear and warm — I was quite well and felt hopeful — the names of the sick and wounded were taken for exchange — 3rd Div 6th Corps had a fight near Charlestown Va,

TUESDAY, AUGUST 30, 1864.

Clear warm. 80 sick and wounded out No 1 and about 100 others taken away for xchange — McCallum, Griffith, Wages of 110th went — Rebs searched us for Greenbacks & found only <u>one</u> <u>Dollar</u> *in No 1 A big thing — Vile business for the Chivalry to go around feeling mens pockets —*

WEDNESDAY, AUGUST 31, 1864.

Clear warm — I was well and finished reading the testament. All quiet. Prisoners are in good spirits and hope soon to be under the Stars and Stripes — P Gen McClellan and Pendleton nominated at Chicago for President & Vice —

THURSDAY, SEPTEMBER 1, 1864.

Quite cool last night — Day clear warm — I carried water for our squad — Nothing new to day — No Rats in our soup to day —

FRIDAY, SEPTEMBER 2, 1864.

Clear cool — I arose early and the first news I heard was that a general exchange of prisoners was agreed on, but alas the papers soon contradicted this good news — Atlanta Ga captured — by Sherman —

SATURDAY, SEPTEMBER 3, 1864.

Cloudy cool & heavy rain — Had a mite of fresh beef for dinner — Corn bread! corn bread! and nothing but corn bread to eat! The prisoners begin to look lean and haggard — the effects of the small rations —

SUNDAY, SEPTEMBER 4, 1864.

Cloudy cool — To day as I heard the church going bell I felt a strong desire to attend, but the barred doors and the Sentinels bayonets said you cant go — I spent the day rather careless, playing checkers. Gen Morgan the raider killed & his staff captured.

MONDAY, SEPTEMBER 5, 1864.

Heavy rain in the morning — Day cloudy — Reb took the number of our Reg'ts and the date when our time of enlistment expires. Half rations of meat — Report that Atlanta has fallen into Gen Shermans hands —

TUESDAY, SEPTEMBER 6, 1864.

Cool cloudy — I was well & in good spirits — We got no meat to day — Our rations to day were 1 lb corn bread and 1 pint rice soup —

WEDNESDAY, SEPTEMBER 7, 1864.

Quite cool last night & to day — No meat to day — and no prospect of any. Reb Soldiers say they must eat what the niggers wont eat — Rat soup to day — Here is the recipe for the above soup — Take muddy, sand & filthy river water — put in wormy beans and "rat berries" boil till half done then throw a little straw and ashes — no salt and its ready for Yankee prisoners

THURSDAY, SEPTEMBER 8, 1864.

Cool cloudy — I was well but almost had the blues — We had fresh beef today and good rice soup —

FRIDAY, SEPTEMBER 9, 1864.

Clear pleasant — I was well, but a good deal out of humor, Why I hardly knew, unless its because there's no prospect of getting out of Prison —

SATURDAY, SEPTEMBER 10, 1864.

Clear pleasant I was well and in good spirits — I begin to long to hear from home —

SUNDAY, SEPTEMBER 11, 1864.

What a lovely morning this is — How I would love to take a stroll out in the fields & enjoy the fresh breeze — No meat to day

MONDAY, SEPTEMBER 12, 1864.

Clear pleasant — I was quite sick about noon but feel better this evening — No meat to day, but a new kind of soup — looks like corn meal soup

TUESDAY, SEPTEMBER 13, 1864.

Night cool, Day clear pleasant — Was well — Rebs are busy fortifying Danville —

WEDNESDAY, SEPTEMBER 14, 1864.

Clear warm — Night was cool — Butlers letter on the xchange question was handed to us by the Major — No meat yet — Chop bread & rat beans —

THURSDAY, SEPTEMBER 15, 1864.

Clear warm — I wrote a letter to Amy telling her to send me a blanket & other clothing — Meat came again — about 2 oz of beef for each man —

FRIDAY, SEPTEMBER 16, 1864.

Clear warm — I was well and spent the day playing checkers — Nothing new — Our meat to day was rank bacon —

SATURDAY, SEPTEMBER 17, 1864.

Pleasant and clear — I was well — Began chess playing — Small [unclear: shaved] me the 6th time — No meat to day nor much rat soup — Oh that I could spend the evening at home —

SUNDAY, SEPTEMBER 18, 1864.

Rainy unpleasant — I was well and played chess — Several letters came for prisoners but none for me — A mite of beef to day — Old Dave on guard in the yard — he's a jolly old fellow. When he sees any of their officers come he hollers out to the boys to go up stairs and then an under tone says I don't care a — — whether you go or not —

Monday, September 19, 1864.

Clear pleasant — I was well & carried water to scrub the floor — No meat to day — Boys are cleaning the beans of rat fruit — Boys are cooking mush out of their bread and making coffee with the crust — Gen Fremont withdraws his name as a candidate for President, Lt J S Deeter mortally wounded at Battle of Winchester, H Shertzer killed, I W Furnas was also killed —

Tuesday, September 20, 1864.

Cloudy cool. I was well and spent day playing checkers & chess — Rebel General [blank] here inspecting Prisons — He inquired of a Yank whether we got enough to eat — Yank answered no not by a — sight — The Gen said that their own men must eat corn bread, and meat they cant get — He also says the nigger is not in the way of xchange — We had an ounce of meat to day —

Wednesday, September 21, 1864.

Cloudy and began to rain, This morning I had to go begging for breakfast and had rather poor success — Was well & spent the day the day playing chess — No meat to day — To day the Reb authorities insulted every Union Soldier in this house by asking us to enlist in their service, and just think they offer good rations and pay in gold or the equivelant in C S bonds, thus tops the climax —

Thursday, September 22, 1864.

Rained last night — To day was cool — I spent day playing chess — Another new wrinkle to day — the Confeds want men to dig coal for them so they can put their men in the Army — Price of Pepper in Danville $1.00 pr oz — No meat to day — 6th Corps & Gen Sheridan routed Early at Fisher's Hill near Strasburg — Gold down to 200 and still going down — Lt J S Deeter died of wound recd 19th [illegible]

356

FRIDAY, SEPTEMBER 23, 1864.

Rained AM, PM cloudy cool — A dull lonesome day — Report says that Early has been defeated near Strasburg and returned to New Market — No meat — Living on chop bread & water begins to weaken us — and some are hardly able to crawl up stairs — The cravings of a hungry stomach are almost unendurable — It is worse than a disease — Boys made a discovery and make coffee of the crust of corn bread —

SATURDAY, SEPTEMBER 24, 1864.

Cloudy rainy — 125 Prisoners transferred out No 6 to No 1 — I was hungrier to day than for a month past, and almost concluded to go out & work to get more to eat — I was well and played chess — No meat to day — Some cabbage leaves cooked without salt — 16 men to our squad — Oh how I would love to spend the eve at home —

SUNDAY, SEPTEMBER 25, 1864.

Last night was cold & it was an easy matter to keep cool without a blanket — Day cool — Clear — I was well and quite lonesome — Hard tack come again — We got six hard tack of Uncle Sams which were sent here by him as xtra rations for us and the Rebs are giving to us as regular issue. A hand bill put up in Prison offering us work on the <u>defenses</u> — it calls all lazy who wont work on them — Some 400 prisoners brought — No meat —

MONDAY, SEPTEMBER 26, 1864.

Clear cool — I never was so hungry in my life as to day — We got seven crackers and half a pint rice soup as our rations — No meat at all — I was much mortified at seeing some of the boys volunteer to day to work on the "Defenses," but the guards did call for them, and I think the boys wont go after taking a second sober thought though starvation will drive a man to do what he abhers [abhors] — Work on fortifications for our enemies! God save us from such a disgrace — J Dunning — H Reese — J Green — W Fletcher — D Nyswonger of 110th and E Fullwiler of 6th Cav offered to work — Report is that Grant has captured 25000 prisoners at Petersburg — Sheridan in Staunton — Early retreating —

TUESDAY, SEPTEMBER 27, 1864.

Very cool last night. Day clear pleasant — I was well and in better spirits than yesterday — Corn bread has come again but meat is still <u>non</u> <u>est</u> [non <u>existent</u>]. Two of 2nd Mass Cav had a fisticuff — Heard something like cannonading in the direction of Richmond — Hope its Sheridan on a Raid —

WEDNESDAY, SEPTEMBER 28, 1864.

Cloudy cool — I was not well — We had a new kind of bread, if bread it can be called — Made of Rye, wheat & corn meal without any leaven or salt. The <u>Confeds</u> have made a raise of some beef & we got a mite for supper but no soup —

THURSDAY, SEPTEMBER 29, 1864.

Cloudy but very pleasant — I felt better & was in better spirits than for a week previous — Reason had enough to eat — Such as it was — A mite of beef corn bread & bean soup —

FRIDAY, SEPTEMBER 30, 1864.

Rained last night & this forenoon — PM cool but pleasant — I was not well but still able for my rations — The Prisoners had a very unpleasant time last night — the fresh beef acting as a purgative and only six prisoners were permitted to be out at a time, so some were obligated to commit nuisances in the Prison — The

Sentinel on Post 19 says alls [blank] — Report that Sheridan has burnt Staunton in retaliation for Chambersburg — I had the pleasure of reading a stray No of Harpers Magazine — Seventeen days in September we got no meat —

SATURDAY, OCTOBER 1, 1864.

This has been a cloudy, drizzly and chilly day — it reminds that tho summer is ended, the Fall is at hand & soon the dreary Winter will be here — Must we shiver & freeze here this Winter. I pray not — I could not help thinking to day, while I was reading an old number of Harper what a pleasure it would be to set in a cozy room & have something good to read — Report is that Grant is within 2 miles of Richmond. Hope it is so — We had old bacon to day — also rice soup — Poleman of the 87th Pa died at the Hospital —

SUNDAY, OCTOBER 2, 1864.

AM cloudy PM clear and very pleasant — Oh how delightful it would be to be out and take a sniff of fresh air — I was well & spent the greater part of day reading — the Ladies of Danville sent us copies of the Southern Churchman and Central Presbyterian both secest [sects] religious papers — Had bacon for dinner the beans in our soup were few and far between — thus boys stole all while shelling them — In my imagination I this evening am at home among or with loved ones tho I can not speak with them — I see them seated in their pleasant rooms chatting — Would that I could be with them in reality — Another handbill put up asking us to enlist in the Reb army — I pulled the bill off —

Monday, October 3, 1864.

Cloudy rainy unpleasant — I had sick headache — Three of the prisoners went to work on defenses and two of them enlisted in old Jeffs [Jefferson Davis] service — Another ounce of bacon strong enough to make a pig squeal — Report is Petersburg is taken — Ten Confed dollars are offered for <u>one</u> Greenback — "Big Yankee" is putting <u>wooden glass</u> in the Windows,

Tuesday, October 4, 1864.

AM cloudy, PM clear warm — I was well & played chess — Some of Prisoners tried to cut out last night but were discovered before getting out, No meat — The River is very muddy and consequently we have to drink sand — Report that we go to Georgia next week

Wednesday, October 5, 1864.

Clear warm — Report that we go to NC next week — I was well & felt in better humor than for sometime — Cause I got some salt — No meat to day — The Union prisoners die at the Hospital at the rate of two or three a day —

Thursday, October 6, 1864.

~~Ra~~ Cloudy drizzly — I was well tho' had symtoms of the "blues" Yesterdays paper says that 10,000 prisoners (sick) are to be exchanged — No meat to day — plenty of rice & sand — A fracas on 2nd floor — Jeff [Jefferson] Davis was in Danville last night & made a speech in which he promised the people peace in 30 days — Had what was intended for wheat bread, but was sour dough —

FRIDAY, OCTOBER 7, 1864.

Clear warm — So warm that we sleep in drawers and shirt without any covering — I was well & enjoyed myself better than for a week past — We had fresh beef — Another fracas — The River is falling & water is not so muddy & sandy — Report that Gen Early is trying to effect a special exchange for the prisoner captured in the Valley — A prisoner who had escaped from Cars brought in —

SATURDAY, OCTOBER 8, 1864.

Cloudy and raw day — the bleak, chilly wind reminds us that the Summer is ended and drear Winter is at hand — the prospect of staying in prison all Winter is anything but pleasant — I was well & carried water — no meat — tomatoes in our soup — Over three Months since I heard from home — Saturday evenings my thoughts will always fly homeward —

SUNDAY, OCTOBER 9, 1864.

Clear and almost cold — last night was cold & we prisoners had a very uncomfortable night of it — What will we do to keep from freezing two Months hence when stern Winter will be at hand — Oh that we may be out of prison before the bitter cold commences — Without sufficient clothing and without blankets some will certainly freeze — To day I was not well — have a severe cold — I can't help thinking of the happy scenes now transpiring in the free & happy North — there the families are gathered around the fireside or are at church and know little how we are suffering in Southern prisons — The prospect of another cold night is not very cheering — I am thankful to God for His goodness to me in giving me good health in this lonesome prison — How I would love to spend the evening at home —

Monday, October 10, 1864.

Heavy frost this morning — Day clear cool — Last night made the prisoners pace back and forth in the room and some were chilled so they could hardly walk when they got up — I had the sick head ache last night & to day and felt quite miserable — The boys had a long talk about things good to eat & each was telling what his favorite dish was — for my part I would take any common dish just so there was plenty of it. We got a mite of beef but no soup — if it was not for the hope of better times coming I would almost feel like giving up in despair, but I still look and hope for the good time coming when I can have plenty to eat and be at liberty to go where and when I please & no bayonets to prevent me — About 75 Yankees who were working on Rebs fortifications broke through the guards and escaped — Great excitement in town in consequence — See the Reb soldiers collected in groups & no doubt discussing the bold Yankee trick — Gold 190

Tuesday, October 11, 1864.

Moderated last night so I slept comfortable — To day was clear pleasant — one of those mellow lovely autumn days. How delightful it would be to be out & enjoy a stroll in the fields — Oh how I long to be <u>free</u> once more — this imprisonment will teach us to appreciate the many blessings we have heretofore enjoyed almost without a thought of thankfulness to the Giver of all good gifts — Nothing heard from the escaped Yankees — Citizens after them with <u>blood</u> <u>hounds</u> — Report says that 6 Rebs were killed yesterday in the affray — Rummel & Pritchard went out to cook — Names of sick taken for exchange — I wrote a short letter to send along for Amy — To day the freemen of Pa & Ohio were asserting their rights at the ballot box but we could not be with them — The sick from Hospital taken to Richmond for exchange

— One of them died at depot before he got on train — his corpse was brought back to No 1 prison — far away from home he has breathed his last — perhaps his parents, sisters or brothers will never know his fate — Such is life — No meat — few beans —

WEDNESDAY, OCTOBER 12, 1864.

Cool last & to day — Clear — I spent day playing checkers — Dave, Big Yankee and one other of the cooks went on special exchange last night — Happy is the man who is on the way to the North away from loathesome Prisons — My thoughts involuntary run to the coming Winter. What suffering there will be in these Prisons among those unfortunate soldiers — Oh that some means may be devised for us to get out of this — Would that we had the faith as of old that we could pray the Prisons doors open — Six dollars Confederate money offered for one green back — $1.00 for a shave & $1.50 c for hair cut & shampoon in Danville Twelve of the escaped Yankees brought in — A Regiment of new issue Reb soldiers passed through town — they cheered lustily, but their tune will be changed before many a day — No meat to day — Gravel soup —

THURSDAY, OCTOBER 13, 1864.

Clear and quite cool — I was well & spent the day playing chess & checkers — We had about 3 oz of beef to a man — No soup — The names of some more sick taken and were to be sent away in the evening but for some cause they were not taken — No further news from the escaped Yankees — The Rebs dont want any more Yankees to work on their defenses — Whites supplies cut off because he refuses to carry water —

FRIDAY, OCTOBER 14, 1864.

*Quite cool last night, boys had to pace the floor to keep warm —
Day was clear & cool — I was well but almost had the "blues"
I felt so lonesome — Report that our forces have cut the Rail
Road between Danville and Richmond & for that cause the sick
were not taken last night — The horrors of prison life are just
beginning to felt & seen — men looking like skeletons & not
able to move and must lay in their filth just for want of help &
attendance — About 30 sick out No 1 taken away — Some half
a dozen well men with them — I sent letter by one for Amy &
requested several to write — Since writing the above five or six
of the run-away Yankees were brought in —*

SATURDAY, OCTOBER 15, 1864.

*Cold last night and the boys had to walk considerable to keep
warm — To day was pleasant — 18 of the boys taken to the
hospital — I was well & spent day playing checkers — Evening I
felt a little sad to think of my situation in this loathesome prison
— Oh how I would love to spend the evening at home or even
just inside our lines in Camp or on the field with the boys in their
sports — I wish the day may not be far in the future when we
will be out of prison and be where there is plenty — where I will
not be obliged to go to the waste barrel as I did to day & pick out
refuse bread — I have nothing on hands for breakfast to morrow
and must go a begging — No meat —*

SUNDAY, OCTOBER 16, 1864.

*Clear cool — Nothing new to day except eight more were taken
to the Hospital. I was quite sick with fever in the afternoon and
Oh how I missed some one to sympathise with me and attend to
my wants — In our situation, we learn to appreciate the many
blessings we used to enjoy — & No meat*

MONDAY, OCTOBER 17, 1864.

Clear pleasant — The Prisoners in No 6 attempted to escape last night but failed as the alarm was given by the Sentinel when they had bucked — for this misdemeanor they had their corn bread & swill stopped for to day — I was better to day but still am quite unwell am taking quinine — Small & 8 others gone to Hospital — Report is that Old Jeff [Jefferson Davis] has come down on the nigger exchange & has agreed to give up all now in their hands — Doubtful — No meat — Since writing the above two of the prisoners in No 6 informed on the leaders in the attempt to escape and they get their corn bread — the two informants were brought to No 1 for safety —

TUESDAY, OCTOBER 18, 1864.

Clear cool — Last night was cold sleeping — I felt pretty well to day — Prisoners in No 2 moved to No 6 and those in No 6 move to Saulsbury, N.C. Several Reb officers in Prison to see us — Put a stove on each floor — this looks as if the Rebs were not going to let us freeze all at once — No meat —

WEDNESDAY, OCTOBER 19, 1864.

Pretty cold last night and tramp! tramp! was the music by the boys pacing back & forth to keep warm — Day was clear pleasant — I was well & played some checkers — Old Dave came on guard in the Hall again — he says he has been in the guard house but he lived better than any of their d — n officers he's a Yank sure — We had about 4 ozs of good beef — I devoured mine in a short time & wished for more — Report recieved that Pennsylvania has gone democratic 7000 This evening the boys are again talking about good things to eat — If I had what Amy throws in the waste barrel I would be glad — I know I would have some good bread at least & some meat too — Battle of Cedar Creek Va Rebels defeated Lt. Simes & J Holsinger Wounded

THURSDAY, OCTOBER 20, 1864.

Cloudy cold & unpleasant — I had a chill again and felt quite sick in the after part of day — Between 200 and 300 officers brought from Saulsbury & put in No 2 — No meat & few beans —

FRIDAY, OCTOBER 21, 1864.

Clear cool — Last night was cold & many of the boys suffered much — Serg't Finley and another of the 2nd Mass Cav made their escape last night — I was not well — had fever — <u>Half</u> a mite of beef — Two others had escaped this evening through the roof of the Privy but were discovered before they got away — they were then brought in and bucked for the night —

SATURDAY, OCTOBER 22, 1864.

Cloudy cold — Evening clear — ~~I was~~ We got some coal to put fire in our stove — Another half a mite of meat & cabbage soup — I am better today — It would be pleasant to spend the evening at home — among loved ones, and have a good substantial supper such as I know I would get if I was there — If it was not for the consoling hope of a good time coming I would give up in despair — Sometimes when I look back upon the scenes of the past five Months I shudder to think of the awful Slaughter of humans — and why? — because a few hot headed leaders could no longer rule they began this war & now the blood be upon their hands, & not ours —

SUNDAY, OCTOBER 23, 1864.

Last night was cold & much shivering was the consequence, We had fire in the stove but it done our end of the house no good — I had a miserable time of it — Day was clear pleasant, I was pretty well — Very lonesome Sabbath — We got no meat and very few beans — A fisticuff in 106th NY — result two slightly bloody noses and two very tired boys — I imagine this evening I can see at many a Northern home a scene something as follow — the family seated around the table on which sets a clean bright lamp and every member has a book paper or something else to spend the evening pleasant with — Some grow tired & drop the book — the good woman goes & brings a waiter well filled with pies, cakes & c and a basket full of apples is also brought and thus the evening is spent while we are — doing what? freezing in a lousy dirty Southern prison — Not very pleasant to contemplate, but wait boys there's a good time coming for us if we ever get out of this detestable place —

MONDAY, OCTOBER 24, 1864.

Partly cloudy and cool — I was well and carried water for our squad — Green and Kane had a skirmish — no bones broke — I also was in a great passion because Fulwiler said that any man in this prison would do as the cooks do — Steal our meat & sell it — I spoke my mind free & didn't care who it hit — I know there are <u>some</u> honest men among us yet — We had a small ration of beef — We would get more if the cooks were honest and there were not so many "bummers" out, I had a dream last night which was almost provoking. I dreamt I was at home and had chicken pot pie for dinner & also plenty of custards and further that my Sisters each had promised me a chicken pie as soon as I came to see them. When I awoke here I was in prison yet and nothing but dry corn bread for breakfast.

TUESDAY, OCTOBER 25, 1864.

Not so cold last night, Day was one of those mellow and beautiful October days that any one loves to spend out in the field — in gathering the rich fruit, nuts & c and Oh how I would love to be out doing farm work — but here how long? Oh long must so many of us languish?, I was not well this afternoon & expect to spend a restless night, We had no meat to day but got more beans than usual — Sweet potatoes sell at $3.00 per Doz — We have several exciting rumors but of course they are unfounded — Very little news comes by "Tatlers line" now, the reason is the boys have been decieved so often that they dont take stock in what come by that lying line — by "Tatlers."

WEDNESDAY, OCTOBER 26, 1864.

Cloudy cold — I was not well — had chills — We hear that the elections in Indiana Ohio & Pa have gone Union — We got about a gill of cane molasses for each man — No meat — Why not record some of my dreams? Last night I was at home as usual in my dreams and had plenty to eat and had plenty of "Greenbacks" in my purse, but behold when I awoke here I was in Prison with not even corn bread for breakfast & "nary" Greenback in my purse — that was rather a damper on my sweet dreams — but I hope ere long to realise what I dream of now —

THURSDAY, OCTOBER 27, 1864.

Cloudy and rainy — I felt pretty well to day & spent the day patching an old blanket I traded for — Jerry & I have two blankets now so we can keep comfortable as long as it dont get too cold — I got an old blanket, a pair of old shoes & ten dollars for my old boots — Sweet potatoes sell at $1.00 a piece — We hear for the third or fourth time that Gen Early has been completely cleaned out. hope it is true at last — We got another half a mite of fresh beef —

FRIDAY, OCTOBER 28, 1864.

Rained hard last night, To day was pleasant & clear — I felt pretty well — Another dream last night of home and plenty good things to eat — I paid $1.00 for six small apples — they first I bought since we are here — Old Jeff [Jefferson Davis] has certainly made a raise somewhere for we again got half a mite of fresh beef — if it was not for the thieving cooks and house Sergeant we would get considerable more, but as it is they steal about one half the beef brought here for us — We got half a loaf wheat or what they call wheat bread here, Three months to day since we entered this Prison —

SATURDAY, OCTOBER 29, 1864.

Clear cool — I was not well had a touch of the ague — We got no meat but have the promise of some tomorrow — Larue called Reese a liar and recieved several hard knocks on his "blinkers" for it — so hard that he measured his length on the floor twice — Well this Saturday again and as usual on this day my thoughts fly homeward & to what is going on there. I know if I was there I would have a good supper & all I could eat — I got up this morning without a morsel for break fast & had to wait until we drew corn bricks before eating — About 300 prisoners brought from Lynchburg — 100 of them were put in No 1 — half of them look like real Rebs — having traded all their clothes to the Rebs for theirs —

SUNDAY, OCTOBER 30, 1864.

Clear and a very pleasant Fall day — a day I would love to ramble over the fields in search of chestnuts, apples & c. I am not well to day, but I would feel happy still if I was not surrounded by the prison Walls — If in after years I may read these lines it will remind me of a period in my life when I was deprived of all that is dear to ones heart it only learns me to appreciate the thousands of blessings I used to enjoy almost thankless — hereafter I shall if I get out again, enjoy life all the better for this confinement — Another fisticuff fight — Got another mite of meat — Just at dark there was another knock down in 2nd Mass —

Monday, October 31, 1864.

Clear cool — A Rebel Sergeant was in our Prison trying to get recruits for the Rebel Army — the boys laughed him to shame — if a Rebel can be ashamed. he says they pay $16.00 pr months and butter is $8.00 pr lb & other things in proportion — I asked him a man with a family was going to live with this pay & necessaries of life at such prices. he replied that cared nothing about the families — its Soldiers they are after — it shows how hard they are up — I felt pretty well only I still have pains in my legs — Old Dave one of the Reb guards rode on a rail up & down before the guard at guard mount this morning, because he left his post & went in the cook house — Jerry removed as CS and Miller of 34th O.V. [Ohio Volunteers] put in his place — Got meat 11 days in this Month — Weighing in the aggregate about 22 ounces — No wonder we are getting slim —

Tuesday, November 1, 1864.

~~Clear and a very~~ Clear and very pleasant for November — I felt pretty well and in good spirits — Old Collins of the Regulars enlisted in old Jeffs [Jefferson Davis] Service — Sweet potatoes are $35.00 pr bushel — Salt $2.00 pr lb & Apples $4.00 a doz — I eat $2.00 worth of apples to day — Last night one of the guards went strike a prisoner with his gun and it went off frightning both much — No meat, but had beef head soup —

WEDNESDAY, NOVEMBER 2, 1864.

Rained and the most unpleasant day of the fall — it was quite chilly in Prison — I was well only the pains in my legs — We got a pretty good ration of beef, but no soup or beans — For some purpose the names of the Prisoners were enrolled — A Reb Sergeant was in Prison trying to buy a pair of Suspenders of the Prisoners for one of the Reb Generals — they must be hard up indeed when they go to Prisoners of war to get such articles —

THURSDAY, NOVEMBER 3, 1864.

Cloudy, drizzly, and unpleasant — I was well, but chilly for want of clothes — Two prisoners who were left behind on the way to N.C. last night from Richmond like fools walked into town to day & reported themselves and were lodged in No 1. well to day brought something new in the ration line — it is Cod fish or Haddocks — We got one to each man. Got no meat, but beef head soup — tongues, chops, brains & c in fact the whole head boilt up together — It is getting very chilly and the boys are beginning to suffer for want of clothing, Oh for an exchange soon — it makes one shudder to think of the coming cold — May God protect us from freezing — Oh how delightful it would be to spend the evening around the fireside reading the papers or some interesting book —

FRIDAY, NOVEMBER 4, 1864.

The sun showed his cheerful countenance at different times during the day & it was not so dreary as yesterday — I was sick last night, feel better to day — Every day the desire for domestic life again grows stronger — and I do long for to hear the grating of the plane & saw & the rattle of the farm wagon — the lowing of the cattle as they are driven from the pasture to the barn — All this would be cheering indeed could we enjoy it as we used to

*do in times of peace. We had a small piece of beef, but no beans
— Bread rations are getting smaller & we in consequence more
hungry — I had not half enough for supper so I go hungry to bed
and hungry rise, Which will certainly diminish my body in size
— Jerry traded his bread off for meat — he dont think of what I
and Fletcher done on the way down here —*

SATURDAY, NOVEMBER 5, 1864.

*Clear cold. I was quite sick last night — To day I felt better but
still not well — About 75 officers arrived and were put in No
2 — We got Cod fish or Haddock again, but no meat — Bread
is getting very scarce in consequence of the loaves being made
smaller — Not a crumb of bread is wasted now — No meat —*

SUNDAY, NOVEMBER 6, 1864.

*Morning cold — Day clear and pleasant — I felt pretty well until
evening then pains in my bones began — To day I spent altogether in idlness. I did not spend it in as good manner as I should,
though I am not aware that I done any great wrong — Sunday
evening and in prison, How cheerless — How are matters at
home? — Codfish to day and only one spoonful of beans —*

MONDAY, NOVEMBER 7, 1864.

*Rained last night — Day was cloudy — I felt pretty well only
had not half enough to eat — I go supperless to bed — I at least
had the pleasure of dreaming last night of being where there is
plenty — Oh that the time of our deliverance may soon come —
We had fish again but only half as much as the first time — Got
two spoonsful of beans to day — if this aint Starvation I know
not what it is —*

TUESDAY, NOVEMBER 8, 1864.

Cloudy foggy & warm — I was pretty well — To day has been a great day in the North — the people to day decided at the ballot box who shall be their ruler for the next four years — The prisoner had no voice in the election and I for my part care not whether Lincoln or McClellan is elected its all the same to us — the prisoners held an election just to see how the boys would vote — No 1 gave Lincoln 20 majority — No 4 gave Mac [McClellan] 100 majority I would have loved to have been at home to day at the Election, but alas here I am a prisoner and no prospect of soon getting out.

WEDNESDAY, NOVEMBER 9, 1864.

Partly cloudy, warm — I was well, but had the "blues" to think that we must lay here in prison & suffer & starve and hardly know why or what for — Oh that our government may see to have us released — I heard a man say to day with tears in his eyes that he served his [blank] years faithfully & now when he should be at home with his he must lay here & freeze & starve — We got good wheat bread to day but it was so little that I eat all mine at once so I go supperless to bed — No fish or meat to day — Several raids on haversacks last night — Jerry lost all his fish — one the Sentinels in a crazy fit last night shot at one the prisoners, missed then struck him with the muzzle of his gun, let it fall & run into the hall calling turn out the guards vote for president in all prisons stands one maj [majority] for Lin [Lincoln]

THURSDAY, NOVEMBER 10, 1864.

Clear pleasant, I was well, but very hungry Dreamed twice last night that I was at home — Got beef but no <u>slop</u> — One of the 10th Vt died yesterday — A Rebel agent was in trying to Mechanics of all kinds — Wants them all Germans — I believe the Rebs want to get the foreigners out & then coax them into their Army

373

FRIDAY, NOVEMBER 11, 1864.

Clear cool but pleasant, I was well and had about half enough to eat — No meat, but more beans than usual — Great excitement in Prison about an exchange — report says we are to be sent to Savannah for exchange, bogus of course — We hear that Lincoln has been re-elected — Hood says rumor is across the Tennessee — Dunning was in luck this evening and got a loaf of bread and gave me a slice so I felt pretty well after eating it — Jerry traded his bread off again — I have a notion to tell him what I think of him for acting so niggardly & uncharitable —

SATURDAY, NOVEMBER 12, 1864.

Cloudy AM and rained in the afternoon until 3 and then cleared off cool — I was well & went sleep in better spirits than for a week reason why — Rummel sent me in a pound loaf of corn bread and I eat my fill it. The exchange rumor is still current — Report is that there are a large number of letters here for us. Our names Co and Reg'ts were taken for some purpose — Yesterdays Examiner says Lincoln has carried all the states except NJ & Mo — "Tight fist" took it very hard when I told him what I think of him — No meat

SUNDAY, NOVEMBER 13, 1864.

Partly cloudy & snow flakes flying — cold — I was well and for once had enough to eat — Read two chapters in testament — Some of the boys got letters, but mine has not come up — hope it may come to morrow — exchange still all the excitement — Irish potatoes sell in Danville at $1.00 p qtt and Liquor $3.00 a drink — Selling liquor, tobacco, segars and pipes is the entire business of Danville —

Monday, November 14, 1864.

Last night was cold & ice froze — To day was clear cold — I was not well — had severe head ache — Exchange is about played out —

Tuesday, November 15, 1864.

Cold cloudy — I was well and had enough to eat for once such as it was — We got about two ounces of good beef — The cooks & "bummers" still take more than twice the number of men should have — Report is that Old Abe has called for 500,000 more — hope he will draft them forthwith — Some more letters come in — "General Exchange" is dead for want of believers — the boys will certainly learn not to believe these prison reports. McClellan carries only NJ KY & Mo

Wednesday, November 16, 1864.

Partly cloudy cold — I was well & carried Water. I was very glad to recieve four letters to day though they were on the road near three months — Recieved one from Kate, one from Hettie and two from Amy — three of dated August 23rd and one Sept 25 — all well then its cheering to hear from home — No meat to day, but got a head soup. My first letters written from here on the 31st July were mailed at Old Point Comfort August 18th and recieved at home 22nd of August —

Thursday, November 17, 1864.

Clear and not so cold as yesterday — I was well and hungry as a wolf — I sent a letter to Amy — Letter came for D J Martin — We got a half mite of beef, but no beans — Someone has made another raid in Jerrys haversack — Hood (Rebel) is marching with his Army into Tennessee and Sherman (Union) is marching toward Savannah & Charleston — Beauregard is moving toward Memphis —

Friday, November 18, 1864.

AM clear — PM cloudy — I was well and in better spirits — Sent letters to Kate & to Co G 110th — No meat but head soup & beans — Nothing unusual to note —

Saturday, November 19, 1864.

Cloudy and rained and the most unpleasant day this fall — was well and felt in good hopes of an exchange soon — We got beef but no beans — Gold in New York 220

Sunday, November 20, 1864.

Cloudy, drizzly & very unpleasant — I was well and had almost enough to eat such as it was — but I felt very lonely in this dreary unpleasant prison, give a man all the comforts in the world and deprive him of his liberty & what is he? — a poor miserable being. Oh may Heaven grant that the time may soon come when we can again enjoy liberty — Oh how I would to drop in unannounced at home this evening — it would be the greatest pleasure I could ask — Meat & cabbage water —

Monday, November 21, 1864.

Rained & was foggy — Another exchange to go off immediately — am well & just have finished my evening "skirmish" & have killed many of the "gray backs"— How comfortable one will feel when once he will get clean clothes on and rid of these everlasting pests, The prisoners look like skeletons — the effects short rations — We got molasses, and head soup — No meat — Gold in New York 216 Was up to 227 in the AM —

TUESDAY, NOVEMBER 22, 1864.

Cold cloudy — I was well only have pains in my legs again — Sent letter to D Strayer and wrote one to Hettie — No meat but a small mess of head soup or "head cheese" as the boys call it — it is made by or of beef heads boiled altogether — teeth, eyes, dirt, and beans & sandy River water —

WEDNESDAY, NOVEMBER 23, 1864.

Clear and very cold — Last night the boys suffered much with cold — I slept pretty comfortable under one old quilt — To day I was cold all day — and I was hungry too — We got a little beef but no beans — every crumb of corn bread is eat up and not a bit wasted — Sent letter to Hettie — ~~Gold~~

THURSDAY, NOVEMBER 24, 1864.

Clear and quite cold — Last night was a cold night on us poor prisoners who have to lay here without blankets & almost without clothes — Kane returned from the Hospital — I felt angry to day to see how the Cooks and "bummer" (men who are out on parol) cut into our meat — We dont get half that we would if we had honest cooks — Got beans & meat — Thanksgiving in the North — Army of Potomac was to have 50000 turkeys & 50000 barrels apples for dinner to day — Wish I could be there —

FRIDAY, NOVEMBER 25, 1864.

AM clear cold — PM it moderated and clouded over — I was well but hungry as a bear — We got a half a pound of wheat bread and I eat all mine for breakfast — Got a small ration of beef & beans — Peace rumors are afloat again — 30 Prisoners died in hospital yesterday — Again I had to look on in anger at the Cooks and paroled bummers stealing our meat — they are meaner than the Rebs —

Saturday, November 26, 1864.

Last night was cold — To day was not so cold as yesterday & it clouded in the afternoon and the sky has a snowish look — We got no meat today and only one spoonful of beans for each man so we go quite hungry to bed — Report says that our Cavalry are in Lynchburg Well this is Saturday again the eve when my thoughts always will turn homeward to its loved ones — how are they and what are they doing — I imagine I can see them seated around the table engaged at their evening meal — Oh how I would love to be with them — May God grant that I may once again enjoy the happiness of meeting loved ones —

Sunday, November 27, 1864.

Moderate cloudy & sprinkled a little — I was carrying water for the squad — & for once beat the cooks in getting soup — the cooks still steal our meat — We got meat but no beans — Eleven prisoners buried to day & five more dead — thus they are exchanged

Monday, November 28, 1864.

Clear pleasant — I was well but went to bed hungry as a wolf — the bread I get dont make a meal for me — Another exchange excitement — We got meat but no beans — the Cooks stole more meat to day than ever — one of them sent in about five pounds to one man —

Tuesday, November 29, 1864.

Clear and the pleasantest day we had for several weeks — I was well but still hungry — eat all my bread for breakfast — We got beans and meat — also got pretty good wheat bread — The cooks did not steal as much meat as usual —

WEDNESDAY, NOVEMBER 30, 1864.

Clear warm — the warmest weather ever I experienced — feel comfortable in shirt sleeves — I felt very well only the craving for something more to eat is almost enough to sicken one — I have very pleasant dreams of home last night and some not so pleasant of other things Dave one of the Reb guards standing on a barrel and has a ball and chain to his leg for getting drunk — Beans but no meat 11 days no meat — 4 days Codfish — 1 day molasses 3 days wheat bread —

THURSDAY, DECEMBER 1, 1864.

Clear and very pleasant — We got meat but no beans —

FRIDAY, DECEMBER 2, 1864.

Cloudy & drizzly, but warm — I was well and not so hungry as for some days — I was very glad to get a letter from Amy — dated Oct 9th She had not sent box yet — Josh Deeter & H Shetters are both dead — S Stahl drafted Sent letters to Amy and Isaac Furnas —

SATURDAY, DECEMBER 3, 1864.

Cloudy but not cold — I was not well, but still able to eat my rations & looked for more — We got wheat bread but it was coarse & rough — No meat and only two spoonfuls of beans — The boys cook beef eyes and Wind pipes to eat —

SUNDAY, DECEMBER 4, 1864.

Clear and pleasant — I was not well and took quinine — We got Meat but no beans — On account of not being well I had enough with my rations. This evening my thoughts take their flight homeward & I imagine I can see Amy & Jennie seated around the table each with a book or something else to interest them — How I would love to drop in unexpected and surprise them — How long Oh how shall be confined here yet — God grant that some way may be made for us to be released —

MONDAY, DECEMBER 5, 1864.

Cloudy & cold — I felt pretty well & not so hungry as usual — Had wheat bread No meat & only spoonsful beans — Boys cooked another mess of wind pipes & eyes — A Reg't of New guards come in — the old guards go to the front — hope some of them will get their heads cracked —

TUESDAY, DECEMBER 6, 1864.

Last night was cold — Day clear clear and very pleasant — Washed our floor to day — Last night I was sick, to day felt better — Dont feel much hungry to night — 15 prisoners came in from Lynchburg — We got head meat and 3 spoonsful beans

WEDNESDAY, DECEMBER 7, 1864.

Rained last night AM cloudy — PM was clear warm — I was well — Got meat — no beans — 300 prisoners from Tennessee arrived

THURSDAY, DECEMBER 8, 1864.

Clear cold — I was hardly able to eat my corn bread — Five months to day since I am prisoner Got one big spoonful of beans, & meat — Sent letter to Joel —

FRIDAY, DECEMBER 9, 1864.

Cloudy and snowed so the ground is covered — Cold — 58 prisoners from E Tenn come into No 1 — Our Cavalry on a Raid 25 miles from here — I had a chill last night to day feel better — Had wheat bread bean — No meat — Bangle of 106th NY died last night of dyptheria

SATURDAY, DECEMBER 10, 1864.

About 3 inches of snow fell last — Day cold & cloudy — Parker of 2nd Mass Cav died very suddenly last night We got meat — No beans —

SUNDAY, DECEMBER 11, 1864.

Cloudy until eve then cleared off — Cold, tho' snow melted — I felt pretty well and not much hungry — tho' we got no meat & only one spoonful of beans — Have abstract in Danville paper of Lincolns message nothing special in it — Debt of U.S. 1 800 000 000

MONDAY, DECEMBER 12, 1864.

Last night was very cold & we shivered much — to day was not much warmer — We got beef & beans —

TUESDAY, DECEMBER 13, 1864.

Cloudy and cold — Last night was a very cold night on the prisoners — I was not well but able for all I got to eat, We got a little <u>head</u> <u>meat</u> & beans —

WEDNESDAY, DECEMBER 14, 1864.

Clear and pleasant. We got a mite of beef but no beans — Our bread is growing less by degrees — We get for a days ration a piece about 3 in Wide 2 thick and 7 long — it is made out Corn Chop — The Col gave a shirt pr shoes & blanket to one of the prisoners

THURSDAY, DECEMBER 15, 1864.

Cold cloudy — I rested better last night than for a week previous, I dreamed I was at home and had plenty to eat — We got cabbage soup and a little <u>shank</u> <u>head</u> & liver as meat —

Friday, December 16, 1864.

Cloudy warm — I had the "blues" to day — My hope of an exchange this Winter is about gone — We got shank & shin meat, no beans —

Saturday, December 17, 1864.

AM Cloudy — PM clear and warm so warm that it was comfortable with prison Windows open — We learn Sherman is all right at Ft McCallister on the ~~Savannah~~ Oguchee 6 miles from Osawba Sound — Meat & beef broth — J W Teeter gone to Hospital,

Sunday, December 18, 1864.

Cloudy & colder — A lonesome day to me — Well we had a new dish to day — it was potatoes about 2 ounces to a man — The boys got a lot of stale beef heads and cooked them — Got no meat or soup —

Monday, December 19, 1864.

Cloudy but not cold — We got potatoes and a little beef — Also good wheat bread —

Tuesday, December 20, 1864.

Cloudy & colder — I am getting very hungry again — am reading "Uncle Toms Cabin" We got potatoes, no meat — Once more the exchange excitement is up —

Wednesday, December 21, 1864.

Rained hard last night — Day cloudy unpleasant — J W Teeter died at the Hospital last night — So gather the rich & poor — Potatoes — No meat — Craig of Co F 110th and several others escaped last night through roof of <u>telegraph</u> office —

Thursday, December 22, 1864.

Turned cold last night & was quite cold to day — I was well & hungry as a wolf — eat all my bread for breakfast — Head meat and potatoes — One of hundred day men turned traitor & reported to the Col where the prisoners got out —

Friday, December 23, 1864.

Clear and cold — Prisoners had to shiver last night — Got small ration <u>small</u> potatoes, No meat — Rebs after Yankees to fiddle for them at a ball to night —

Saturday, December 24, 1864.

Clear cold — I was well & carried Water — I had not half enough to eat — our rations are getting less every day — To day we got a small piece of corn bread and three small potatoes — No meat —

Sunday, December 25, 1864.

Cloudy cold — A hard day on the Prisoners — Oh what a horrible Christmas for us — 3/4 lb wheat bread and 1½ ounces salt beef is all we got to eat to day — I had for breakfast dry bread — for dinner a little bread & beef — supper <u>nothing</u> — Cooks & bummers stole about one fourth of our meat to day —

Monday, December 26, 1864.

Rained last night — Day cloudy & not cold — I am not well — have sore throat — Starvation begins to look us in the face — To day we had nothing to eat but our usual ration corn bread and two of our government crackers — No meat — No soup — Sent letters to Amy and J K Teeter —

TUESDAY, DECEMBER 27, 1864.

Cloudy moderate — My throat is better and I am hungry as a Wolf — Our rations for to day were a small piece of burnt corn bread and a pint of cabbage water — that is water in which cabbage had been cooked and the bummers eat it — No meat — Hear that Savannah is <u>ours</u> — Rebs reported evacuating Richmond.

WEDNESDAY, DECEMBER 28 THROUGH SATURDAY, DECEMBER 31, 1864.
[PAGES MISSING FROM DIARY]

SUNDAY, JANUARY 1, 1865.

Cold clear — Oh what a miserable N [New] Year day — In prison half naked, nearly froze and lousy — Horrible! God grant that this soon may be bettered — Beans — No meat — No meat

MONDAY, JANUARY 2, 1865.

Clear cold — Yesterday & today I was quite sick — Oh horrible that a man must suffer here so — Got wheat bread — No meat —

TUESDAY, JANUARY 3, 1865.

Cold cloudy and a skift of snow fell — I feel better to day tho' still unwell — Corn bread & beans. No meat — Two spoons full beans —

WEDNESDAY, JANUARY 4, 1865.

Clear & not so cold — I am still on the sick list — Rations are, sour wheat bread and beans — No meat — Oh this horrible prison life! When will it have an end, it is almost a living death Men are freezing and starving —

Thursday, January 5, 1865.

AM clear and pleasant — PM partly cloudy & cold — I am yet sick — Oh what a great blessing good health is. How we should prize it & feel thankful to God when He gives us good health — Our rations of bread are near a third larger and report says are to continue so — Wheat to day — Two spoonsful of beans. No meat —

Friday, January 6, 1865.

Cloudy rainy & very unpleasant — I feel pretty well to day and thank God for it. Corn bread about one fourth larger than usual — One spoonful of beans. No meat —

Saturday, January 7, 1865.

Rained heavy last night — To day was clear and pleasant — I was well & had enough to eat of corn bread — No meat — Cabbage water. Here is Saturday again and still in Prison. Gloomy indeed —

Sunday, January 8, 1865.

Partly cloudy & cold. I feel pretty well & had a plenty of corn mush cabbage water. No meat How I would love to drop in this evening at home and surprise them. & then after that have a good supper. Hope on

Monday, January 9, 1865.

Cold cloudy — I was pretty well & had almost enough to eat — We got wheat bread a small ration of fresh beef — No beans.

Tuesday, January 10, 1865.

Began to rain last night & rained hard all day — Dan river rising rapidly — Thundered and lightened this forenoon — Corn bread and two spoonsful of beans — No meat —

WEDNESDAY, JANUARY 11, 1865.

Clear cool — Dan River over its banks — & we have to use the thick muddy water for cooking and drinking — Got sour wheat bread & one spoonful of beans — No meat — I am well this evening & not hungry — reason I got a loaf of bread from outside —

THURSDAY, JANUARY 12, 1865.

Clear cool — I feel pretty well and not so hungry as usual — Got wheat bread and two spoonsful of beans — No meat —

FRIDAY, JANUARY 13, 1865.

AM clear. PM cloudy — I felt quite unwell — To day we had nothing to eat but dry wheat bread — No beans. No meat — Boys carry water from River barefooted through cold mud —

SATURDAY, JANUARY 14, 1865.

Clear cool — I was not well, but able to eat all I got — Got wheat bread — loaves small as formerly and a small mite of beef — Bummers stole half our meat.

SUNDAY, JANUARY 15, 1865.

Clear cool — I was well but lonesome — Reb Preacher was here and preached a short sermon and distributed tracts — Nothing to eat but dry corn bread — No meat — Six prisoners escaped

MONDAY, JANUARY 16, 1865.

Clear and pleasant — Had plenty of corn bread, but that was all — No meat — We hear Sherman has taken Charleston — Seven prisoners escaped Ben Blackburn Co B died

TUESDAY, JANUARY 17, 1865.

Cold cloudy — Was well & had my fill of corn bread, Three of escaped prisoners brought back

WEDNESDAY, JANUARY 18, 1865.

Clear, pleasant — Had beef — No beans — I carried water for squad — Had a good soup of shin bone — Reb preacher here —

THURSDAY, JANUARY 19, 1865.

Cloudy cold — I was well & not hungry — Got corn meal gruel. No meat —

FRIDAY, JANUARY 20, 1865.

Cloudy cold — I was well and had my fill of mutton head soup — Williams saved me two sheep heads — bully for him Got beef. No soup

SATURDAY, JANUARY 21, 1865.

Rained all day and froze as it fell — I had a mess of mutton brains for breakfast — Got corn meal gruel — No meat nor soup

SUNDAY, JANUARY 22, 1865.

Cloudy rainy — We had nothing to eat but corn bread — No meat. No beans — Small returned from Hospital —

MONDAY, JANUARY 23, 1865.

Cloudy cold — I was out to work at a Warehouse Got bacon & corn bread for dinner — In prison had corn meal gruel — No meat in prison

TUESDAY, JANUARY 24, 1865.

Clear cold — I was out working at Warehouse, but done very little on account of being too weak after seven Months imprisonment — Got bacon out — No meat, nor beans in prison —

WEDNESDAY, JANUARY 25, 1865.

Clear and quite cold — I carried water for squad — No meat — nor nothing else but corn bread — Minister preached to us again

THURSDAY, JANUARY 26, 1865.

AM clear & very cold. PM cloudy — I carried water — Beans for dinner — No meat —

FRIDAY, JANUARY 27, 1865.

AM clear and very cold. PM cloudy & cold. I carried water — No beans No meat — All the talk is about peace — God grant it may soon come.

SATURDAY, JANUARY 28, 1865.

Clear and very cold — Dan River almost frozen over — I carried water — Got beans — No meat

SUNDAY, JANUARY 29, 1865.

Clear and very cold — I carried water — No beans. No meat — No nothing —

MONDAY, JANUARY 30, 1865.

Clear cold — Got beans — No meat — Two Reb Citizens here wanting to buy Greenbacks offern [offering] $10.00 Confed for $1.00 US

TUESDAY, JANUARY 31, 1865.

Clear and moderated — I was not well — Got beans No meat —

WEDNESDAY, FEBRUARY 1, 1865.

Clear pleasant — I felt better — Nothing to eat but dry corn bread — No meat — Reb Minister here and preached rather an interesting sermon —

Thursday, February 2, 1865.

Partly cloudy but sun shone enough for the ground hog to see his shadow so according to old wonderous sayings we will have cold for 6 weeks yet — Corn meal gruel — No meat — Men are dying by inches —

Friday, February 3, 1865.

Cloudy drizzly — Nothing to eat but dry corn bread & a little gruel — Oh how long will or must this starvation continue No meat —

Saturday, February 4, 1865.

Clear and spring like. I was quite sick and almost wished myself dead just to be out of this horrible prison — Bread and gruel — No meat — Seward reported to be in Richmond on a peace mission.

Sunday, February 5, 1865.

Partly cloudy cold — I feel better to day, but something serious is the matter with my lungs and this confinement is making it worse — Nothing to eat but dry corn bread — No beans No meat — Starvation —

Monday, February 6, 1865.

AM Clear pleasant — PM partly cloudy & colder, Nothing but corn bread — No meat — No beans — Snow & sleet

Tuesday, February 7, 1865.

Snowed & sleeted and was very unpleasant — 3 inches snow fell — Corn bread & nothing else to eat, No meat — The prisoners are getting so weak from starvation that they can hardly crawl up stairs — 22 days since we had a morsel of meat

WEDNESDAY, FEBRUARY 8, 1865.

AM clear, PM cloudy and cold — Nothing to eat but corn bread — No meat — No beans — Factory burnt last night

THURSDAY, FEBRUARY 9, 1865.

Cloudy cold and very winterish — Corn bread, No meat — Large store in town burnt last night —

FRIDAY, FEBRUARY 10, 1865.

Clear and rather pleasant but still the snow is not all gone — We had a few small potatoes — about two to a man — I got a lot of frozen ones and had a good mess — No meat. Clothing came for prisoners — Bread is less again —

SATURDAY, FEBRUARY 11, 1865.

Clear and thawing — I carried water — Three of our officers in to see us — Boxes and some letters came for prisoners — also some Northern papers – old. No meat — Reb Soldiers say they don't get enough to eat

SUNDAY, FEBRUARY 12, 1865.

Clear and cold — as cold we have yet had this Winter, I enjoyed myself reading Northern papers, though old they are very interesting — No 4 & 6 getting their new "duds" — Nothing to eat but corn bread — No meat — Reb guards beg bread of prisoners —

MONDAY, FEBRUARY 13, 1865.

Clear and quite cold — I think coldest day we had so far — 12 Bakers ordered to Richmond A new exchange report — Nothing to eat but corn bread. No meat ~~12 Bak~~ Guards beg bread & I still get no meat so they dont fare better than we —

TUESDAY, FEBRUARY 14, 1865.

AM clear cold — PM cloudy & moderating I was well and took a wash — Bread larger again No meat, No bean No nothing — Clothing being distributed to No 4

WEDNESDAY, FEBRUARY 15, 1865.

Cloudy drizzly & cold — I was well & had enough of corn bread to eat, but that was all — No meat — nor beans — Clothing being issued to No 1 — Order recieved for all prisoners here to go for exchange on Friday & Saturday — Good!

THURSDAY, FEBRUARY 16, 1865.

Cloudy, but not so cold as yesterday — I was not well — Fletcher gone to Hospital — More clothing issued and I am astonished to see some of the boys sell theirs to the Rebels, Blankets for $30.00, Trousers $35, Shirts $20

FRIDAY, FEBRUARY 17, 1865.

Cloudy rainy — Balance of clothing issued to prisoners — Reb officers in buying blankets of boys — Respectable business for Reb officers to be trading the boys out of their blankets — Meat seems plenty now at $12 pr lb — 1000 prisoners were to go for exchange but transportation failed so were put in prison again — 10 o'clock PM 1000 prisoners go & our floor with them Hurrah. No meat —

SATURDAY, FEBRUARY 18, 1865.

Clear, pleasant. Last night at 12 we bid adieu to Danville & its Prison & took train for Richmond where arrived at 2 PM and were marched to Libby where we went to sleep without any rations — I am surprised find Libby so clean as it is — rather cleaner than Danville No 1 — Apples sell for $1.00 each, buiskets $1.00 *each and thats all that is to sell in the city — Rebs just from Mt Lookout ~~fat~~ look fat & hearty while we look like skeletons — <u>No Rations</u> to day*

SUNDAY, FEBRUARY 19, 1865.

Clear pleasant — I spent the day in Libby Prison and Oh what a dismal place it is with its grated windows & barred doors one gets not even a smell of fresh air — Our names were taken for parol — Got corn bread, molasses & rice — No meat —

MONDAY, FEBRUARY 20, 1865.

Clear and cool. I was well & spent the day in "Libby" very hungry owing to small rations — We got half a lb corn bread 2 ounces salt horse & a little rice — We were parolled at 5 PM, not to take up arms again until regularly exchanged — We are to go North in the morning & then for something to eat, Thank God — Got meat —

TUESDAY, FEBRUARY 21, 1865.

Clear cool — Left Libby Prison at 7 AM took boat for down River & met our flag of truce at 10 AM marched across to Aikens landing & took our flag of truce boat for Annapolis. We got soft bread & pork —

WEDNESDAY, FEBRUARY 22, 1865.

AM clear, PM cloudy Arrived at Annapolis Md at 9 AM landed and were marched to college Green baracks where we got clean clothes & something to eat — Mustered for ration money. How good one feels to have clean clothes on once again —

THURSDAY, FEBRUARY 23, 1865.

Cloudy, drizzly and muddy — Spent day in College Green barracks — Got our pay for rations,

FRIDAY, FEBRUARY 24, 1865.

AM cloudy — PM clear — Was in Annapolis & had my fill of oysters & ham & eggs.

SATURDAY, FEBRUARY 25, 1865.

Cloudy rainy — Western prisoners took cars for Columbus —

SUNDAY, FEBRUARY 26, 1865.

Cloudy Cool — Arrived at Martinsburg at daylight & stopped to await the repairing of a bridge — Lay at Martinsburg all day — I was quite sick —

MONDAY, FEBRUARY 27, 1865.

Cloudy — We remained all day at Martinsburg the bridges not being yet rebuilt. I am still sick

TUESDAY, FEBRUARY 28, 1865.

Cloudy cold — Left Martinsburg at 5 AM & arrived at Cumberland at 6 PM

WEDNESDAY, MARCH 1, 1865.

Clear pleasant — Arrived at Oakland at day light & remained till noon then left & passed Grafton at dark —

THURSDAY, MARCH 2 AND FRIDAY, MARCH 3, 1865.
[NO ENTRIES FOR EITHER DATE]

SATURDAY, MARCH 4, 1865.

Cloudy & a little snow — Arrived at Todd Barracks at 2 AM one week from Annapolis & Ohio men mustered for pay immediately. I got no sleep — In Todd Barracks, met J Holsinger he told me much that was interesting about Co G, I Furnas, H Shertzer, L

Butt were killed. L Childers died of wound, Another time disap-
pointed. I expected to be at home to night but we were not paid
— so here I am in the old barracks —

MEMORANDA.

Jan 4th
H Stanfield is in debt
to me for 2 paper pkg   60
J Kenny 1 pkg   30
April 23   *J Holsinger is*
in debt to me for Photo's   60
~~May 31st~~   ~~*H Barnhart*~~
~~*Dr To Money loaned X*~~   ~~15~~
May 22nd   *W Harry Serg't*
Major   *Dr*
To Sword $ 2.00
June 7   *J Holsinger to [unclear]*   25
~~*" 14*   *H Barnhart*~~   ~~10~~
~~*" 16*   "   "*~~   ~~5~~
~~*" 20*   *J Holsinger*~~   ~~*pays*~~   ~~15~~
~~*J W Teeter*~~   ~~*Dr*~~
~~*To Expenses incurred on the march to Prison*~~   ~~*$ 3.00*~~

MEMORANDA.

	Miles
Distance marched 1864.	
From Culpepper to Wilderness	15
" Wilderness to Spotsylvania	14
Spottsylvania to N Ann	20
North Ann to Hanover	22
Hanover to [blank]	6
Hanover to Cool [Cold] Har [Harbor]	12
Cl Harbor to James	40
Jas [James] to Petersburg	10
To left of line	8
T [To] Reams Station & back	15
To City Pt	12
	174
Monocacy to Baltimore	60

CASH ACCOUNT. JANUARY.

		Received.	Paid.
1	Sundries		2.00
31	Months pay	13.00	

CASH ACCOUNT. FEBRUARY.

		Received.	Paid.
4	Sundries		2.00
29	Months pay & c [et cetera]	17.00	
31	Jan 1865		
	Feb 1865		
22	Commutation	56.75	

CASH ACCOUNT. MARCH.

		Received.	Paid.
1	Pie		.25
4	Butter		.25
"	Sundries		.75
8	Postage		.15
"	Harpers Weekly		2.80
"	Co. Memorials		2.00
"	"		.50
9	Oysters & c		1.00
"	Postage Stamps		1.20
	Butter		.35
10	Shaving & hair cut		.50
"	Express		.35
11	Sundries		.40
13	Cheese & c		.30
16	Butter & c		.60
18	6 Photographs		3.00
"	Sundries		.20
25	Butter & c		1.00
30	For Home	13.00	11.30
			26.90

CASH ACCOUNT. APRIL.

		Received.	Paid.
1	Expenses on Car		3.00
4	Pair Pants		5.00
11	Fore to Reg't		12.68
"	Expenses on Way		3.50
14	Express		1.00
"	Cash	6.00	
17	Photo's of Gen [General]		1.00

24	Daily papers		.15
25	Pen	2.75	
28	Daily Papers	.10 [deleted]	.10
30	Months Pay	13.00	
		21.75	26.43

CASH ACCOUNT. MAY.

		Received.	Paid.
18	Gold Pen		2.50
"	Note Paper		2.00
20	Beef		.25
24	"		.25
31	"		.20
"	Spoon		.10
"	Sugar		.20
"	Paper Sold	1.50	
"	Months wages	18.00	18.00
		19.50	5.50

CASH ACCOUNT. JUNE.

		Received.	Paid.
1	Tobacco Sold	2.00	
4	Sugar & c		.30
"	Postage stamps		.30
9	" "		.25
10	Tribune		.35
14	Liver		.10
"	Stamps		.25
15	Ham		.40
"	Sugar		.15
30	"		.30
"	Wages	18.00	
		20.00	2.40

CASH ACCOUNT. JULY.

		Received.	Paid.
17	Pen Holder	2.00	
18	Gun blanket	3.00	
25	Shelter tent	1.00	
18 to 25	Eatables		6.00
31	Months Pay	18.00	
		24.00	6.00

CASH ACCOUNT. AUGUST.

		Received.	Paid.
31	Months pay	18.00	

CASH ACCOUNT. SEPTEMBER.

Received.	Paid.
18.00	

CASH ACCOUNT. OCTOBER.

Received.	Paid.
18.00	

CASH ACCOUNT. NOVEMBER.

Received.	Paid.
18.00	

CASH ACCOUNT. DECEMBER.

Received.	Paid.
18.00	

SUMMARY OF CASH ACCOUNT.

	Received.	Paid.
Jan.	13.00	2.00
Feb.	17.00	2.00
Mar.	13.00	26.90
Apr.	21.75	26.43
May	19.50	5.50
June	20.00	2.40
July	24.00	6.00
Aug.	18.00	
Sept.	18.00	
Oct.	18	
Nov.	18	
Dec.	18	
	*217.75	71.23

*[*miscalculated, should be $ 218.25]*

MEMORANDA.

Dollars. Cts.

	Dollars	Cts
My clothing bill from the time we left Winchester to March 31st / 64 is	37	16

Prisoners marched	Miles
From Monacacy [Monocacy] to Tennallytown	35
" Tennallytown to Leesburg	40
Leesburg to Upperville	28
Upperville to Millwood	10
Millwood to Winchester	10
Winchester to Staunton	92
	215

BACK COVER

David Longenecker
Co G 110th Ohio Vols.
2nd Brig 3rd Div 6th Corps
Army Potomac
May 21st, 1864.
Line of battle near
Spotsylvania C.H. [Court House] Va

This book is a dramatization based on the Civil War. At times, names and descriptions of actual people and locations have been changed or fictionalized to protect the innocent. Events and other information portrayed in this book are based on descriptions obtained from various sources, including but not limited to various media, records, history, and the personal diary of a soldier of the Civil War era with firsthand knowledge of such events or information. Certain events are interpretive as a result of being drawn from different sources with different versions of the events. No individual portrayed in this book is now alive since the period of this book will be 150 years ago.

NOTES

NOTES

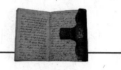

NOTES